C000139519

Antonina Irena Brzozowska was born, grew up and was educated in the north-east of England. A former teacher, she has a deep love of the magical Hawaiian Islands, its friendly people and interesting culture and traditions. Being of Polish extraction, her interests extend to Polish traditions and culture; extending further to the wonderful, scenic country of Canada with its interesting history and warm people. These special experiences have influenced her writing.

To Hella (Wijatyk); thank you for being my sister and friend.

To the lovely people of the Hawaiian Islands; thank you for the precious memories.

Antonina Irena Brzozowska

LOKEMELE'S QUEST

AUSTIN MACAULEY PUBLISHERS™
LONDON • CAMBRIDGE • NEW YORK • SHARJAH

Copyright © Antonina Irena Brzozowska 2023

The right of Antonina Irena Brzozowska to be identified as author of this work has been asserted by the author in accordance with sections 77 and 78 of the Copyright, Designs and Patents Act 1988.

All rights reserved. No part of this publication may be reproduced, stored in a retrieval system, or transmitted in any form or by any means, electronic, mechanical, photocopying, recording, or otherwise, without the prior permission of the publishers.

Any person who commits any unauthorised act in relation to this publication may be liable to criminal prosecution and civil claims for damages.

This is a work of fiction. Names, characters, businesses, places, events, locales, and incidents are either the products of the author's imagination or used in a fictitious manner. Any resemblance to actual persons, living or dead, or actual events is purely coincidental.

A CIP catalogue record for this title is available from the British Library.

ISBN 9781528915359 (Paperback)
ISBN 9781528915366 (ePub e-book)

www.austinmacauley.com

First Published 2023
Austin Macauley Publishers Ltd®
1 Canada Square
Canary Wharf
London
E14 5AA

Part One
Lokemele

Chapter One
Kauai, Hawaii, USA

Cool, lazy waves washed over the white sands. Rosemary felt their cool touch rippling over and in-between her toes and feet, which were aimlessly wandering with no sense of direction, as she placed one sodden foot in front of the other, the wet hem of her Indian print skirt twisting around her bare ankles, her eyes looking out into the distant horizon where they feasted on the fiery, spectacular sunset. She felt nothing her heart heavy, like her wet feet, kept going, beating, walking, beating as she wished her pained heart would stop and her inner misery to end.

Abruptly, she turned away and sauntered towards the soft lilting sounds of Hawaiian guitars, quickly rushed past happy-go-lucky holidaymakers, through the marble floored foyer, with its sumptuous displays of tropical foliage and exotic colourful blooms, up the stairs and into her room where she locked the door and swiftly delved into her treasured stash. Bringing out a bottle of Mai Tai, she hastily unscrewed the top, poured out a generous measure and began to relax in its comfortable release. But, it wasn't enough. Glass after glass followed until its effect, and the soft lulling tropical music outside her window, eased her into a restless sleep.

Disturbed, fragmented images floated in and out of her fitful dreams. In one broken fragment, he was by her side; in another he was with her rival, until shards of early morning light started to break through the gently swaying palms and into her room. Her eyes flickered, opened and stared at the silhouetted leaves splintered with shafts of light, daring to gently touch her window and entice her out of her nightmare, her head banging like the onslaught of frenzied native drums and her heart heavy… always heavy.

Her tired eyes strayed to the empty bottles strewn around the room and closed again. This was no way to exist, she told herself. And yet, it was her only way;

for, she did not have the mental strength to free herself of her misery and even this idyllic, heavenly place on the planet failed to release her from the bondage of torturous nightmares. Laboriously rising from her bed, she placed one wobbly foot in front of the other and slowly strode to the bamboo framed mirror, inwardly flinching at the pale, thin face and the stark eyes staring back at her; her long, limp blonde hair dangling untidily around her shoulders and white T-shirt stained with last night's Mai Tai.

She closed her eyes tightly against the disturbing image, the urge for more alcohol overtaking her rapidly. Quickly, she rummaged in bags, in the night table cabinet, everywhere she thought she may have stashed a bottle and, at last, retrieved half a bottle of white stuff with a foreign label she was unable to recognise, exhaled a loud sigh of relief and slugged a generous measure. Taking two painkillers for her throbbing head she had a quick shower, put on a clean pair of denim shorts and a pink T-shirt, tied her hair up in a chignon, stuffed her treasure into her beach bag together with a best seller which, so far, had not been opened, slipped into her flip-flops and swiftly walked out of the compounds of the hotel and towards the sanctuary of a deserted beach.

The gentle lapping of the early morning waves against the silky sand and the soft, murmuring swaying of long, luscious palm leaves did nothing to quell her torturous soul. She knew there was only one medicine. Walking along the quiet, deserted beach she looked out into the distant horizon. She had hoped to find her answer in this paradise; an end to her nightmares. Instead they continued on and on, like the ancient waves continually replacing themselves, yet constant, monotonous... never ending; on and on they came and went... ebbed and flowed... on and on...

Finding herself a secluded spot by a pink flowering hibiscus shrub she sat down and retrieved her treasure. She spotted the solitary figure from afar and took another gulp of her potent liquid. Oh God, I hope he just passes by and doesn't embark on some trivial holiday talk. She hoped against hope as she took another swill and, thinking she had better look occupied in a different way, hid her bottle into the depths of her beach bag, retrieved her best seller, opened it and glued her eyes fixedly on the text, she had no intention of reading. The ominous figure was drawing nearer and nearer. Now she could see his bright blue Hawaiian printed shirt and his black shorts as her eyes involuntarily rose to his plump, short body, his dark face and generous crop of ruffled black hair and rested on his twinkling, dark eyes. Swiftly, she directed them back on to the text below.

"Aloha."

Just go away, she silently urged, and leave me alone. "Aloha," she begrudgingly muttered without raising her eyes. Please, please, please just go away, she secretly pleaded.

"You… British… on holiday?"

Immediately, she recognised his accent to be native and, not to appear offensive, she reluctantly raised her eyes and saw only warmth. She smiled. "Yes, I am from England."

"On holiday or are you here on business?"

"Holiday." She dropped her eyes to her book, hoping he would take the hint, and was relieved when he did.

"Hope you enjoy our beautiful Island of Kauai, Ma'am."

She heard the echo of his voice as her eyes followed his slow retreating figure. Her impatient fingers delved into her bag and retrieved the bottle.

Chapter Two

Day after day, her routine continued. Alone with her bottle for company, she existed in paradise not feeling the sunshine against her skin; not feeling the touch of waves on her feet; not hearing the gentle sounds of swishing palms or soft guitars; not hearing the call of tropical birds; only feeling her deep inner pain. For, how could he, after one year of marriage, just walk out on her and take up with her best friend, Claire? How could they have both betrayed her in this callous way? She had loved Tim since she was seventeen and at sixth form. They had grown into adults together, listened to the same type of music, gyrated at discos and shared secrets, problems, dreams and ambitions; planned a life together and now… She dug her hand into her beach bag, brought out and looked longingly at the only friend she had, and closed her eyes.

"That is not the answer, my friend."

Abruptly, her eyes snapped open, as inwardly she raged at the impolite intrusion into her solitude. Opening her mouth to allow a barrage of discourteous words to spew out, it remained open unable to utter a single word. Blatantly she took a generous swill of her potent liquid, hoping this obnoxious man would disappear. Her disappointed, exhausted eyes followed him as he slumped down on to the soft white sand, his broad back settled comfortably against the rough rings of an aged palm tree.

"My name is Keoki."

She rose. "I must go." She pinned on a forced smile.

"Please stay a while longer."

Something in his eyes, as she looked down at him, made her reluctantly sit back down, bring her knees up to her chin and stare out into the undulating ocean wishing she was thousands of kilometres away, back home where she could drink in peace to her hearts content.

"And, what is your name, Ma'am?"

She felt his curious, dark eyes on her; studying, observing, assessing her as she secretly cursed him for this silent, forthright examination. Starkly staring into the vast blueness beyond she said softly, "Rosemary; my name is Rosemary."

"A beautiful name fit for a beautiful lady." He smiled while she ardently wished he'd cut out the crap, say what he had to say and go. "So, why are you so sad, Rosemary?"

"Who said I was sad?" She replied, her voice monotone; not daring to turn and look at this strange man, lest he should catch a glimpse of the truth. "And anyway," she droned on, "what business is it of yours?"

For long minutes, they sat in silence with only the sound of the waves around them. "I know sadness when I see it," he said almost in a whisper.

She turned and something in his eyes told her he was stating the truth.

"Do you want to talk about it?"

She looked at him as one would look at a distasteful worm, rose and snapped. "No, I don't want to talk about it; for all I know, you could be a serial killer or worse, a womaniser." She heard the echo of his hearty laughter as she stomped off along the beach, wondering what kind of maniac he really was.

He sat still, his shrewd eyes watching her disappear out of sight, his ears attune to the sound of the comforting sound of the ocean, which had been his constant and faithful friend throughout his forty-one years on this planet. *Yes, she was a sad and broken woman.* His eyes stared out into the far distance.

Keoki drifted in and out of Rosemary's mind, infuriating and calming her in equal proportions, making her question, wonder and want to know more about him. She took a gulp of her precious liquid. *Who was this curious busybody and why did he want to know so much about her? Perhaps he was a lunatic, after all.*

She saw him again, a couple of days later, as she walked along the beach feeling the worse for wear and didn't know whether to run, stay or ignore. She walked towards him and watched his smile broaden. For the first time in months, she smiled a little. "I am sorry, K-K…"

"Keoki."

"Keoki; I was so very rude to you the other day."

He looked her in the eyes. "What is a little rudeness? Life is too short to dwell on things that have passed us by. Let's sit, Rosemary."

Curiosity got the better of her again and she couldn't help but ask, "Why do you walk alone on the beach, Keoki?"

He turned his calm eyes on her. "Why does anyone walk on the beach alone, Rosemary?"

"Please call me Rose."

"Okay Rose; I walk on the beach alone each morning to meditate."

A religious freak! She silently exclaimed. *That's all I need.* "To meditate?"

"To meditate; yes, I like to focus my thoughts."

"On what?" She turned to face him taking in his plump, dark, friendly face and waited for his answer.

"I like to meditate on a different theme each day."

"And today?"

"Today, I meditate about you."

"Me?"

"You; why you look so sad; why you are so unhappy in a tropical paradise."

Her eyes focussed on him and abruptly she looked away into nothingness. "I don't know," she lied.

He saw beneath the lie. "Then to live, you must find the problem, tackle it and learn to be happy again. As they say, life is too short." He rose, turned and said softly, "I wish you well, Rose," and left her with her thoughts and the bottle in her beach bag.

Taking her treasure out, she unscrewed the metal top and took a gulp, her eyes staring out into the blue vastness. Her pain eased; but it was still there. *How could Tim and Claire have done this to her? What had she done to have deserved such cruelty; such betrayal from the two closest people she had in the world?* She took another gulp. They did not go away; their images becoming larger and clearer as she took another gulp and then another, as she stared into the emptiness of oblivion with Keoki's words echoing loudly in her head... *to live you must find the problem, tackle it and learn to be happy again... A tall order,* she mused; *a very tall order.*

She lay on her bed, the soft lilt of Hawaiian guitars drifting to her ears through the open window, intermingled with laughter and talk. *Oh, what she would do to be out there, a carefree holidaymaker; to laugh, enjoy, savour and embrace life and not to throw it carelessly away; or, wish it to end and with it the misery of existence.* Keoki drifted into her mind... *such kind, knowing eyes. Who was this mysterious man? Where did he live? Did he have a family and children? What kind of job did he have? Whatever he had or did,* she told herself, *he had an air of calmness about him she craved for herself.*

Grabbing her bottle, she stared at the brown liquid inside. *What did it give her? Nothing,* she answered her own question, *but a sore head and more questions.* She placed the bottle back on to her bedside table and walked out of the hotel and on to the beach. The warm sand got in-between the straps of her sandals and her toes. Taking her sandals off she walked barefooted along the ocean edge, her heart slicing in two as she caught sight of a loving couple walking hand in hand, giggling, kissing now and then, totally oblivious to her presence. Her mind drifted…

Chapter Three

It was the long, hot summer of 1976. Elton John and Kiki Dee had hit the number one spot with a quirky song, hosepipes were banned and sixth form was forgotten, at least for six glorious weeks.

He strode into the cafe where she worked as a Saturday girl, ordered a coffee and set her heart on fire. But then, any guy giving her a second glance produced the same effect. Rosemary Longsdale was a pretty girl with long, blonde hair. She was a bit on the podgy side, her confidence resting with her academic abilities and dreams of, one day, becoming a teacher; confidence with boys was lacking and so she didn't bother with them, except when they paid her some attention. As far as she was concerned, there was time for that kind of *nonsense* when she arrived at teachers training college. *She looked at him and smiled back.*

Later, as she poured out the coffees and teas for customers, she threw him a cursory glance. He wasn't looking her way and, more to the point, seemed totally oblivious to her presence. Her eyes were drawn to him. There was something she liked about him; though, she couldn't quite pin it down to one thing. Half an hour later she watched him sweep past her without paying her the slightest bit of attention. Her fast beating heart deflating rapidly she shot into the kitchen, cracked an egg and watched it spread on the hot oil.

"For you."

Rosemary looked down at the folded paper and raised her quizzical eyes to a pair of kind eyes and a conspiratorial smile. "What is it, Joy?" She asked her middle-aged colleague.

Joy's smile widened as her eyes dropped to the note in Rosemary's hand. "And he left you a tip, my dear."

The young girl's eyes widened, her heart resuming its fast beat as if it was about to explode, as with impatient fingers she unfolded the note and read.

Your smile makes me want to dance.
Speaking of which, meet me at the Coffee Pot. Next Saturday. 8.00pm.
Bring a friend.
Tim.

She read and reread the note a hundred times; his fair hair, slim face and shining eyes etched firmly in her memory by day and invading her erratic dreams by night. Who was this guy? What made him take any notice of her? Was he teasing her; or, was this for real? Was he at college, working, unemployed? What did he want from her friendship; sex? Her mind was bombarded with hordes of intelligent and not so intelligent, questions and, added to these questions, were more questions. Should she accept his invitation? Who would she take with her? What would she wear? What would she say? How should she act? "Oh God," she sighed as it all went round and round in her confused head.
"Rose!"
She snapped out of her reverie, her nostrils breathing in the pungent smell of burnt toast.

"Rosemary... Rose... Is that him?"
She felt the sharp tugs on her sleeve, as her eyes followed Claire's finger in Tim's direction.
"Yes... yes, I think so." She peered past the young revellers gyrating to the latest sounds, her eyes resting on Tim. "Yes, it's Tim."
"Let's go."
Rosemary managed to grab Claire's arm as she began her urgent advance. "Where are you going?"
"We are going to inform him that you are here."
"No, I don't think so."
"Come on." Claire grabbed Rosemary's reluctant hand and dragged her towards the small group of young males.
What she saw is what she got; a young, friendly guy, well-mannered who liked a joke, a beer, a dance and a laugh. Rosemary liked what she saw. Tim seemed everything she could ever wish for in a boyfriend. He was caring, kind, considerate, honest; or, so it seemed, and Rosemary was the happiest girl alive. Everything was going well; though, there was one dark shadow on the horizon; her dream of becoming a teacher. Would Tim wait? Would he get bored of

waiting? Would he find someone else? He assured her he would wait. She trusted him and he did not let her down. On the eve of her graduation, he asked her to be his wife and the next day, she walked on to the stage to receive her degree from the Vice Chancellor of the university, with all her dreams coming to fruition.

Their engagement party was a quiet affair, exclusive to close family and friends. It was a happy occasion; though, the exchange of furtive looks between Tim and Claire made Rosemary freeze to the bone.

Firmly she forced her doubts, fears and any reservations, regarding her imminent marriage to Tim, to the back of her mind. She was imagining things and, even if they had exchanged looks, they didn't mean anything, she told herself fervently. It was all in her head.

They married and Claire played the role of chief bridesmaid to perfection, pleasing Rosemary outwardly and Tim secretly; though, both Tim and Claire knew their fling was just that, a pleasant distraction which meant nothing at all.

They honeymooned in Hawaii and built dreams, hopes and aspirations out of sand and into sand they disintegrated leaving Rosemary, a year later, with a broken heart, fragmented dreams and a bottle as her only friend...

Kauai

Sharply she snapped out of her dismal reverie, her eyes looking out on to the vast ocean and wished she had the courage to walk and never stop walking. Instead, she sat a little away from the water's edge, drew her knees up to her chin and luxuriated in the warm breeze that swept off the mighty Pacific, watching the surf roll in, feeling a comforting rush of cool water splashing her bare toes. She sat for minutes... hours looking out into the timeless waves, which had rolled on and on for thousands... millions of years and wondered who it was that had first set foot on this exotic paradise. Looking out into the dusky sky she saw tiny diamond pinpricks in its soft, dark velvetiness. She had heard that the first pioneers had ventured forth on their perilous journey with only the canoes they had made and the stars above as their guides. Oh, how she wished she had been the first lonely intruder; or, even a modern day Crusoe with only the sun, the trade winds and the ocean as her companions; no liars or cheats; no betrayers only nature as her friend; always reliable and true.

She stared out into the invincible waves performing their ritualistic nightly metamorphosis, as they transformed into a rolling carpet of sinister darkness, gloom and despondency, her wayward mind drifting to her betrayers. "How could they?" She yelled at the top of her voice. "How could they?"

"A message for you, Miss Longsdale."

She took the envelope from the concierge, climbed the stairs, slumped on to her bed and fell into a deep sleep.

Chapter Four

She opened her eyes to a sunny, bright room and a deep, uncomfortable craving for alcohol; any type of alcohol so long as it took the edge off the urge. Rummaging in her beach bag she retrieved a half filled bottle of some kind of liquor she could not identify and, unscrewing the metal top, she longingly brought it up to her parched and needy lips. Catching sight of the forgotten envelope on her bedside table, she lowered the bottle as curiosity got the better of her and, raising the envelope closer to her eyes, she scrutinised her hand written name, roughly ripped the seal open and extracted a hand-written note.

Aloha,
My wife, Luana, my children and I warmly invite you to our humble home
for a traditional Hawaiian meal.
Please meet me on the beach, by the pink hibiscus tomorrow evening at
seven o'clock.

Keoki

She stared unblinkingly at the neatly written invitation, her eyes inadvertently straying to the bottle on the bedside table and back to the invitation; her guts ripped in two one part craving for the contents of the bottle, the other seeing kind Keoki and his warm, dark, all-knowing eyes as her will wrestled with them both giving her no peace.

She grabbed the bottle and hastily shoved it into the back of her night table for another time. This time Keoki had won; for, there was something… something she did not know what, about him that intrigued her and she wanted to know more about him. But, more to the point, she did not want to disappoint him. Why? She did not know why.

She wandered along the beach, went in and out of shops, lay on her bed, reread Keoki's message and all the while her guts, head and heart craved for a drink; just one gulp, one swallow, one drop. The bottle remained firmly closed and her guts continued gnawing for something she would not allow herself to have. The day was long, hot and torturous.

This is not paradise, she told herself. *This is hell* and she grabbed the bottle from the depths of her night table, only to put it back again, unopened, her guts gnawing mercilessly as the hands of the clock, like the natives, moved calmly, never hurriedly along, because on these ancient islands time was real; but, of no real importance.

She started to get ready at five o'clock, merely for something to do to take her mind off alcohol. Her mind remained firmly on the alcohol, knowing it was within her reach. *In seconds, the potent liquid could be sliding down her throat making everything all right. She had only to reach out for it, open the metal top and...*

Dressed in a long, flowing, tropically printed sundress with a white plumeria behind her right ear and her small, white clutch bag tightly grasped in her hand, she walked towards the hibiscus shrub and immediately spotted the lone figure.

He smiled broadly, carefully placing a lei of wonderfully scented plumerias around her neck. "Aloha." He said softly as he kissed her on the cheek and, as she inhaled deeply the intoxicating jasmine-like smell, she thought she was in heaven.

Reality hitting her as the sound of the waves lured her to the present, her eyes searched the deserted beach. "Your wife, Keoki, is she not here?"

"She is at home, preparing things for us all."

"But why, Keoki; why put yourselves out for me? You don't know me. I don't know you. You..."

"Sh." He took her hand into his own and linked it around his plump arm. "You ask too many questions, wahine. In Hawaii, we take it easy; hang loose." He extended his chubby thumb and small finger whilst curling his three middle fingers before casting Rosemary a grave look. "You promise me, Rose, this evening you go with the flow; yes?"

A smile burst on to her lips, her eyes emitting a sparkle that had, for a long time, been missing from her life. "Okay, Keoki; tonight I hang loose."

They walked along the beach in silence, with only the sound of the endless rolling waves as their sole companions. As their feet left the soft, white, powdery sand the haunting echo of the hypnotic waves grew fainter and fainter and eventually became a distant echo. On and on, they walked in silence, the trade winds sweeping over the ocean and kissing their skins with their soft caress, as they approached an ancient winding path fringed by lush tropical foliage and walked beneath its cool, whispering canopy.

"How refreshing." Rosemary smiled feeling as if she was in a blissful heaven. "Keoki, your island is truly beautiful."

"It is indeed heaven." He confirmed, making her instantly wish she was a native of the island.

Her eyes diverted to a group of bare chested men sitting on stumps of gnarled tree trunks, chanting an old Hawaiian mele, whilst splitting coconut husks on sharp spikes which had been secured into the ground. Her inquisitive nature propelled her to ask, "What are they doing, Keoki?"

After waving and cheerfully greeting his friends, Keoki turned his brown, chubby face to Rosemary. "A coconut is a very precious item in Polynesia. Nothing is ever wasted. Of course, the oil is extensively used for medicinal purposes; the fibre of its husks is eventually used for items such as mats, doormats and brushes; the coconut shell powder is used for incense sticks; the flesh of the coconut may be dried and used in baking or eaten fresh; the liquid may be used for a variety of drinks and, of course, the leaves are used for thatching and the wood of the palm tree may be used to make furniture."

"A versatile crop."

"Versatile indeed. Ah... we have arrived."

The sweet aroma of traditional Hawaiian cooking reached Rosemary long before she spotted Keoki's humble dwelling and, for the first time since she started her vacation ten days ago, she felt ravenous her eyes straying to the podgy, short figure attired in a brightly coloured Mother Hubbard walking briskly down the uneven, stone steps on to the equally uneven path below, her chubby arms extended in a welcome, her smile wide and her small, brown eyes glistening with warmth. "Aloha. Welcome Lokemele." A colourful lei was gently placed around Rosemary's neck, as her bewildered eyes turned to Keoki.

"Your name in Hawaiian is Lokemele and this is Luana, my wife."

Rosemary smiled back feeling the tight embrace of Luana's welcome.

"Come... come," urged Keoki.

Rosemary followed her hosts on to the veranda, suffused with the sweet pungent fragrance of colourful tropical blooms weaving around the wooden balustrades. Swiftly Luana disappeared, reappearing minutes later with three large Mai Tais, as Keoki's cautious eyes followed Rosemary's eager hand as she reached for the tall, dew-bejewelled glass. He had completely forgotten to warn his wife about his suspicions concerning his friend's possible problem with alcohol.

Rosemary's eyes switched to his concerned eyes. "It's all right, Keoki; truly, I'll be fine."

He trusted her; for good or bad, he trusted everyone. It was in his nature. He smiled. "Aloha."

They clinked glasses as Luana disappeared once more into the bowels of her small kitchen. Rosemary turned to her friend. "It is very peaceful here, Keoki."

"Yes, here we have peace and joy in our hearts."

She looked around the simple structure constructed of locally grown materials and surveyed the lush foliage around, her eyes setting on Keoki's calm eyes wondering. *How can he be so happy with so little?* Her short moments of silent pondering stopped, when her eyes caught sight of two small children timidly approaching Keoki's side.

"Ah my children; my treasure." He smiled broadly, grabbing them both into his tight embrace and placing them on to his chubby knees. "Akamu and Liliana, say Aloha to our special guest."

"Aloha." They simultaneously enthused, their shyness waning as they smiled showing gaps in their milk teeth as, clumsily, they placed their frangipani leis around Rosemary's neck.

"Aloha." Rosemary smiled, her heart clenching at a stabbing thought of what she could have had with Tim.

Tucking into their platefuls of kālua pork and rice, five pairs of eyes shot to the source of a cheerful greeting at the open door.

"Aloha!" The intruder called out happily.

Immediately Luana rose, excused herself from the table and rushed to greet her unexpected visitor. "This is a fine surprise!" she exclaimed enthusiastically. "What brings you here?" She hugged and kissed the welcome gate-crasher, as he placed a colourful lei around her chubby neck and two excited children laughed and squealed at the sight of their guest. *For this,* they both thought, *was happiness indeed.*

"Uncle Kai... Uncle Kai..." They cried excitedly as they hugged him tightly.

"Luana's younger brother." Keoki informed Rosemary and turned his serious eyes on her. "Beware, he likes the ladies." He left her seated alone as he went to greet his brother-in-law; unintentionally leaving her to feel like a first class intruder at their family gathering. This feeling was short-lived as, in seconds, all were seated back at the table, an extra plateful of pork and rice set on the table and Kai's eyes firmly fixed on Rosemary, his broad smile revealing white, even teeth set against his golden bronzed complexion, making her inwardly shrivel beneath her calm exterior; for, she had met his type before and she knew the warning signs. She did not like what she saw; an over confident, self-assured, handsome guy *who clearly,* she assessed, *craved to be the centre of attention.* For, while she was certainly not overlooked by her hosts, who couldn't be more hospitable if they tried, *Kai,* she thought, *liked the sound of his own voice; though his smile,* she mused, *had the potentiality of mending a broken heart. But, at what cost? She better stay clear,* she determined. *And she would; for, what possible future connection could she possibly have with him?*

He turned his dark, smouldering eyes on her making her feel vulnerable and uneasy. "So Rosemary… Lokemele, you are from England. Wow… that's a long way away. Are you here on vacation?"

Yes, I'm here because of a broken heart, if you must know. She wanted to scream and instead replied, "Yes; I go back in three days." She looked down at the bowl of passion fruit and fresh pineapple in front of her and wished his eyes would not scrutinise her; for, she felt them boring into her very heart and soul.

"In three days! Then we must show you the island."

"I have seen it, thank you."

"Ah but not all of it; I shall be your guide, Lokemele."

Rosemary's eyes darted to Keoki for help and assistance; but, he had left the table and was in the process of preparing coffee. Her eyes involuntarily switched back to Kai.

"You will allow me to be your personal Hawaiian guide?" He queried cautiously, already knowing her answer.

Silently she nodded her head and immediately regretted her silent gesture of consent. *This,* she glumly thought, *does not bode well.*

Chapter Five

Fragmented dreams of deserted beaches, luaus, Keoki and Luana's simple home, dewy bottles of Mai Tai and Kai's handsome, smiling face haunted her restless night as she tossed and turned, swept her lightweight duvet off the bed and dragged it back on; got up, lay down, closed her eyes, opened them while all the time wishing she could turn back the clock and her agreement to a date with Kai. Why? She did not know. She mused in the semi darkness. *He had been polite, attentive, interested in what she had to say and yet... There was something... something about him she could not quite put her finger on. Yes, he did like the sound of his own voice; or, was that simply genuine natural exuberance on his part? For, while he talked, everyone was captured with what he had to say, including herself. Clearly he was adored by the children and loved by Luana; but, there was an element of caution in Keoki's words and it was those words which gnawed at her the most... he likes the ladies... he likes the ladies...* Tim crashed mercilessly into her whirling head and, with him, the sudden, strong urge for a drink. Frantically she withdrew her bottle from the depths of her night table, thrust it back into its secret hiding place, briskly strode to the shower cubicle and turned the knob to full throttle, where she stood naked under the powerful, fast flowing cascade of hot water as she allowed it to wash away her thoughts, ideas, dreams, fears, ambitions, betrayal, deceit, lies and dark secrets; to wash away her identity; to wash her clean of the past and leave the debris of her broken heart behind. A few minutes later she stepped out the cubicle feeling totally refreshed and ready to give life another go.

The light taps on her door, followed by a hearty, "Aloha!" alerted her to the fact that her Hawaiian escort had arrived. Quickly she took a glance in the full-length cheval mirror and as she looked back at her pale yellow sundress, white sandals, beach bag and wide brimmed straw hat she gave herself a smile of approval. Her heart racing erratically, she opened the door to a cheerful Hawaiian with a flashing smile and twinkling dark eyes, dressed in a Hawaiian print shirt, denim shorts and flip-flops. "Stunning; you look absolutely stunning, Lokemele." His smile widened as he unashamedly planted a kiss on both sides of her cheeks and a frangipani lei around her neck. "Aloha," he said softly making her guts writhe and wrench, as she silently cursed herself for allowing this *Casanova* anywhere near her. Taking in her serious, tight-lipped face he said, "You know, Lokemele, here in Hawaii visitors are not allowed to frown." His eyes locked with her eyes.

"I was not aware I was frowning."

"Or snapping; that most certainly is not allowed under any circumstances."

She withdrew into herself and wondered *what on earth had possessed her to agree to a date.*

"Or regret coming on a date; that is most definitely a no-no." He read her innermost thoughts like a book, as a silent war raged in her head; *for, it was not too late to change her mind and call the whole thing off.*

"Hey, come on; life is too short, Lokemele."

And she remembered Keoki's words... *life is too short... he likes the ladies...* Unlocking her eyes from his hypnotic glare, she grabbed a bottle of ice cold water from the fridge, locked the door behind her silently asking herself, *What have I got to lose?*

Involuntarily her eyes widened as they walked out of the hotel compound towards a red open-topped convertible, which only confirmed what type of guy he was: showy, pretentious and status conscious; the complete opposite to herself and when she caught his eye, it told her he was waiting for her approval. She gave not the slightest hint of approval, silently wishing she had never clapped eyes on him; or his flashy motor.

"You like?" He gave her a sideway flash of his dazzling smile which was completely lost on her stern set, grim façade as her eyes stared ahead seeing nothing in particular. He allowed her secret reverie. He had met her type before; *A tough nut to crack but not impossible,* he smiled to himself and revved up the engine.

The car sped past idyllic desolate beaches and winding narrow roads bordered on both sides by lush blooming foliage of hibiscus, cascading blooms of the rainbow shower tree; yellow, pink and red frangipani and ginger. Rosemary gave a deep sigh as she caught the soft and peachy fragrance of a cluster of red and yellow blooms. "Frangipani." Kai informed her as he stopped the engine and, abruptly jumped out of his seat. Her wary eyes followed him as he plucked out a white bloom, with a yellow centre, and attached it above her left ear giving her a peck on the cheek, making her quiver inwardly as she stared straight ahead. "In Hawaii, a flower on the right side indicates a wahine is available; on the left, she is taken."

She looked at him and smiled. "I am not taken."

"For today you are." He smiled making her blood boil as he, once more, revved up the engine and sped along the hairpin bends.

"Where are we going?"

"You'll see."

What had possessed her to accept this date from hell with this overbearing, pompous guy? She asked herself for the umpteenth time, glancing at her watch and craving a very potent drink. She closed her eyes in an attempt to dissipate her growing urge, her ears attune to the sound of soft guitars on the radio, thinking of the large Mai Tai she was going to have when they stopped for refreshments.

Kai was in it for the long game. He liked Rosemary. *Quite an unassuming, pretty and intelligent female,* he thought. *Yes, his kind of wahine.* But, he was in no rush to make his move; after all, he was a Hawaiian born and bred and in Hawaii one never rushed, even when one's pants were on fire.

She woke with a jerk unaware of her surroundings; for, the soft music had taken over her senses and had lulled her into sleep. Slowly, it all came back to her... *Kai... red convertible... on the road to...* "Where are we?"

He rushed to her side of the car, helped her out and led her in the footsteps of some excited tourists. "Have you ever been to the Grand Canyon on the mainland?"

She shook her bewildered head as she walked on.

"Well, this is our version, Waimea Canyon. People know it as the Great Canyon of the Pacific. It is about three thousand and six hundred feet deep and about ten miles long and one mile wide."

"What did you say it was called?"

"Waimea."

"What is so special about it?"

"You'll see."

She turned her eyes to him. "You like keeping people in suspense, don't you?"

"Oh yes," he smiled, "I do."

They walked on. He grabbed her hand to slow her down and steady her.

She stepped to the edge of the rail, her stunned eyes wide as they soaked in the vast panorama views of deep valley gorges and jagged crags, the emblazoned interior landforms of shimmering red, green, brown, orange and gold; the spectacular vistas that seemed to go on and on for endless kilometres. Suddenly, an overwhelming urge to jump overtook her; to jump into their depths and forget forever the memory of Tim. Staring into the hypnotic redness, the greenness and deep orange shades she felt them all closing in on her, covering her, comforting her, taking her for their own. "It's beautiful," she whispered as she stood transfixed.

He broke the spell; abruptly forcing her to snap out of her tantalising reverie. "Waimea is the Hawaiian word for reddish water and this, in turn, is linked to the erosion of this spectacular canyons red soil."

"My, you are a mine of information, Kai." She said with a touch of irritation lacing her voice.

"Yes I am, aren't I?" He stared into the raw natural beauty of the abyss, as he had done so many times before, with so many different wahines.

As they left the stunning view and made their way to the car, Rosemary cast her escort a surreptitious look inadvertently catching his eye. Their eyes locked. Abruptly she looked away; but, not before she saw something she had also seen in Keoki's eyes; a kindness and inexplicable calm; eyes that knew and felt more than mouths could ever say and, as she eased herself into the soft, pliable leather upholstery of the car, she felt a calmness overtaking her body. *Perhaps,* she mused, *he wasn't that bad after all; perhaps, she could give him a chance.* "Where are we going now, Kai?" she asked.

"You'll see."

They both smiled.

They walked along the deserted beach, two virtual strangers with Keoki as their link and two very different pasts haunting them; for, in the midst of paradise, two hearts were tortured. Rosemary bore a heavy heart of deceit and betrayal; Kai's heart was full of regret; for, while he had lived a blissful and carefree life in beautiful, serene Kauai, he was aware how many lives he had ruined; how many beautiful wahines he had bedded purely for his own pleasure, with no intention of honouring any brief relationship. One thing, however, clawed more painfully at his heart, he desperately yearned for a son. Surreptitiously he threw Rosemary a look. *A pretty wahine… yes; marriage material, no. She could never adapt to the true Hawaiian lifestyle; sleeping partner? He was working on it.*

Unfolding a blanket they sat facing the rolling ocean as Rosemary watched, with idle curiosity, as Kai brought out, from the depths of his wicker basket, a veritable feast of Hawaiian delights. "Wow!" she exclaimed.

"A little taste of Hawaii," he winked.

They exchanged smiles and tucked into the mouth-watering portions of chicken katsu, macaroni salad and rice. "It's what you call a plate lunch," he said.

She picked up a piece of chicken katsu and, before placing it into her ravenous mouth, asked, "And, I suppose you are going to tell me what a plate lunch is?"

He looked at her in mock offense.

"Go on," she laughed, "I know you're dying to tell me."

"Well they kind of originated in the sugar and pineapple plantations, way back in the eighteen eighties. The workers would bring their lunch in containers called bento boxes. Anyway, these boxes would contain leftovers like meat and fish from the previous evening. Rice would be added to make these meals more filling. In time, carts and trucks came to the plantations and the employees would buy cheap plates of food. Later, macaroni salad was added to the meal and that, my lovely Lokemele, is how plate lunches came into being."

She studied his face his shiny eyes and black hair, ruffled by the trade winds coming off the ocean, and his lips. She looked away. "Thank you," she said.

They ate and looked out into the vast waters, keeping the conversation on a trivial basis, neither wanting to delve into the past; neither thinking it was necessary to do so, when they both knew they were immersed in a brief liaison without any substantial roots.

As they walked along the lapping shore words escaped her mouth, as her eyes stared out into the rolling waves. "Why did you ask me out today, Kai?"

They walked on as his frantic mind searched for a suitable answer, while his guilt ridden conscience silently screamed, *To have an easy lay.* "Because I liked what I saw," he said truthfully adding, "I felt I could show you the true Kauai."

"You have."

"Not yet, I haven't."

"There's more?"

He winked making her heart jump.

In the open-topped convertible, they sat in the balmy silence surrounded by their own thoughts. "It's going to be a fantastic sunset." Kai announced.

"Sunsets in Hawaii; they are what my friends dream of seeing." Rosemary mused aloud.

"They are beautiful; just like you, Lokemele."

Like a jagged knife on ice his innocent words ripped through her heart; for they were words Tim had once said to her and, cruelly, she snapped. "Do all men read the same book on romantic phraseology?"

"Oh wow!" He looked aghast and hurt. "Did I hit a nerve?"

She closed her eyes tightly, silently condemning her spontaneous outburst. "I am sorry, Kai; I didn't mean…"

"You have been hurt in the past; yes?"

She looked out on to the small boats sailing into shore and wished she was on board one of the vessels. "I don't want to talk about it." She mumbled.

Once again they lapsed into silence as small groups of people, lovers and loners gathered and gazed at the silent sun as it began its ancient nightly farewell ritual.

"Come on," enthused Kai jumping out of the car and grabbing her by the hand, forcing her to run down the embankment and on to the silky, smooth white sand, as the lazy waves broke apathetically on the shore and touched their bare feet. The majestic sun sank into the ocean, splaying rays of glorious, colourful light over the tropical sea as it said farewell to the island and she felt his strong arms around her waist, his warm lips covering her mouth as she yielded to them and, like the sun, sank deeper and deeper into depths she didn't know. And, as he withdrew his lips from her mouth she opened her eyes. "I must go." She tore herself away from his comforting embrace, turned her back on the sinking sun and ran to the sanctuary of the car.

"I am sorry, Lokemele." She heard him say softly.

"Just take me back to the hotel, Kai." She snapped feeling an uncomfortable, inexplicable rage surging through every vein in her fast pulsating body; threatening, like the volcanoes of Hawaii, to erupt.

She tossed and turned throughout the night. Tormented fragments of dreams haunted her mind; broken images of Tim… Claire… Kai mingling and intermingling, until they were one huge mass of whirling confusion and distortion. Springing out of bed she stood on her balcony and looked out into the silhouetted, gently stirring palm leaves. *Two days to go and she would be on her*

30

way home. Her heart tugged. *Where would she find peace, if not here?* In the far distance she could see the white surf rolling wave upon wave... wave upon wave... never ending... wave upon wave... upon wave... upon wave... She could hear the subdued roar of the waves renewing themselves, constantly and always a source of wonder. They did not stand still. They did not allow themselves to be forced into a rut. They did not immerse themselves in self-pity. No matter what nature threw at them: storms, winds, tsunamis, sun, drought they were constantly on the move, determined, rolling on and on... on and on... on and on... She snapped her eyes shut and, still, she could hear them. Her eyes drifted to the night table. *In there was her medicine; in there her remedy... life... death...* She turned her eyes away. Quickly she changed into her jeans and kimono style jacket and walked out on to the dark beach. A couple was walking along the shore, hand in hand; a solitary man was quietly strumming his guitar and another propped against the bark of an aged palm, looking the worse for wear. She sat a little across the way, propped against a bark and watched the drunk. *It was,* she thought, *a rare sight on this tropical island and, yet, here he was a broken man with broken dreams.* Her eyes glued on him she watched him bring the bottle up to his crooked mouth, down the last precious drops and fall into an uneasy sleep and in that quiet moment, as the ocean rolled on and on, she felt an inexplicable urge. Turning her eyes away she rose and ran back to her hotel room, withdrew her hidden treasure and poured the contents down the sink, the last gurgles of alcohol echoing loudly in her ears.

Chapter Six

Her heart stopped and restarted beating wildly as she heard the tap on the door. Throwing a sundress into her suitcase she opened the door, her heart deflating; for, her unexpected visitor was not who she had expected. Her mouth broke out into a smile. "Keoki… come in, come in." She extended the door allowing her friend, and his family, inside.

"Aloha!" In turn they greeted her with Hawaiian enthusiasm; each placing a colourful lei around her neck.

"We have come to say a fond farewell to you our dear friend, Lokemele." Keoki smiled warmly, his brood following suit, as Rosemary's heart tore into shreds; for here, she knew, was true friendship; the memory of which she would always carry in her heart.

After spending some time together in the hotel garden, Akamu and Liliana handed her a small gift bag. Tears glistened in Rosemary's eyes as she retrieved a heart shaped jewellery box, made out of small seashells. "You will forever be in our hearts, Lokemele." Luana kissed and hugged Rosemary.

"And you all in mine," said Rosemary her words quivering with emotion as she swallowed a hard lump in her throat; knowing she would miss these natives dearly.

She watched them go and Keoki retrace his steps. Taking both her hands in his he said softly, "Lokemele; remember, life is too short. Be happy. Aloha." He gave her another tight hug. She watched him grow smaller and smaller as, in the distance, he re-joined his happy and carefree family, leaving her to feel like the loneliest woman on the planet.

Her mind turned towards home, work and the day to day living in a country where sunshine was never taken for granted. She would miss Kauai; for, here, she had found some of the peace she had been searching for.

She bumped into him as she turned the corner, on her way to the grocery store. Her heart froze. "Kai!"

"Aloha, Lokemele; I was looking for you."

She stared wide-eyed at his soft, brown, twinkling eyes and felt herself drowning in their luxurious depths. "You've found me." She heard herself say, her voice sounding like an echo in her head. Silently she reprimanded herself for her cool aloofness and forced a smile. "What brings you here?"

"A luau; I am inviting you to a traditional Hawaiian luau."

"I have to pack." She said as Keoki's words, like a raging tsunami, crashed into her head... *He is a ladies' man...* She turned to go and felt his hand on her arm.

"But not tonight," his soft voice said, "not tonight."

"No not tonight."

Their eyes locked.

"Then, will you do me the great honour of allowing me to escort you to the luau?"

"Why not; I'd love to." She heard the echo of her own words as she threw Keoki's cautious advice to the wind.

"Seven o'clock pick up. Aloha!"

His cheerful voice rang in her ears, as she watched his printed shirt disappear amongst a group of holidaymakers; leaving her to ponder on her all too eager acceptance of his invitation; her incapability in declining his offer. *There was,* she mused, *something irresistible about Kai; something unfathomable and mysterious that captured and intrigued her and, for better or worse,* she decided, *she wanted to know more about him.*

At seven o'clock precisely he pipped his car horn and, in seconds, his appreciative eyes scanned the length of Rosemary's body. "Ah... the hibiscus is on the wrong side, Lokemele." He adjusted her flower, pecked her on the cheek and revved up the engine, while she wondered what she was letting herself in for.

The sound of slack key guitars and ukuleles, telling stories of long ago, greeted them as they wandered through the luscious gardens and, soon, they were caught up in the spirit of aloha. They sat amidst an array of pink and yellow plumeria; the nearness of his body close to her making her feel weak and helpless. About to rise and go she abandoned her *get up and go* as he enthused, "You know, Lokemele, here on these islands we have luaus for all kinds of events such as graduations, birthdays and even weddings. Before eighteen nineteen the men sat separately from the women folk and children. It was our King

33

Kamehameha the second that thought it would be a good idea to eat with females and children and it was, during these huge feasts, that the name luau began to float around. King Kamehameha the Third, it has been reported, in eighteen forty-seven was host to a luau which apparently boasted of one thousand, over three thousand fish, two hundred and seventy-one hogs and two thousand, two hundred and forty-five coconuts. Let's hope our luau doesn't disappoint."

"I am sure it won't disappoint anyone, Kai." She dared to look at him and wished she hadn't, as his smouldering eyes set her senses into orbit.

The haunting sound of a conch shell alerted them to the fact the kãlua pig was ready to be unearthed and, thankful for a merciful interruption, Rosemary heaved an inward sigh of relief as they followed a group of people to the pit. She watched carefully as the layers of leaves and cloth were taken away and the cooked pig exposed. They followed the throng of happy natives and holidaymakers to the large barn, where an abundance of Hawaiian fare was placed on long makeshift tables.

"It smells and looks delicious!" Rosemary exclaimed, unable to keep her hungry eyes off the enticing, mouth-watering culinary delights.

"Wait until you taste." Kai winked, hoping she would catch the hidden meaning of his words.

She did and it made her quiver inside.

They feasted on the star of the show, the kãlua pig; allowing themselves to sample and enjoy the lomi salmon, lau lau, aki poke, sweet potatoes and steamed rice with boiled cabbage. "Now taste a little of this and tell me what you think."

Rosemary turned to a forkful of grey matter which, so far, she had stubbornly and emphatically resisted.

"It's poi," enthused Kai.

"I don't thi—"

"You must," he interrupted her objections. "When visiting the islands, it is a rule; one must try poi. It is an important part of the Hawaiian diet."

Tasting the grey, mushy substance for the first time, she couldn't fathom out what all the fuss was about; to her it tasted a little like potato.

"You like?" He raised a quizzical eyebrow, his fork ready and poised to gather another helping.

"I'd eat it if there was nothing else to eat on the island."

They burst into laughter. He rose and, to save her from further torture, stated still chuckling, "I'll get us both a Mai Tai."

About to object, she let it go. *After all,* she surmised, *what harm could one innocent drink cause?*

She stared at the dewy glass long and hard, tasting its potent golden-brown liquid before it touched her lips; already feeling its warmth in her body.

"Aloha."

"Aloha."

They touched glasses and Rosemary tilted the liquid into her eager mouth, secretly welcoming it as one would welcome an old friend and, when Kai grabbed her hand and gently squeezed it, she wanted more... much more.

After savouring a generous slice of traditional Hawaiian Haupia, served with freshly ground coffee, they enjoyed another glass of Mai Tai as they sat on a bench outside. "Drink up," he encouraged. "I want to show you something."

Feeling warm, calm and happy she allowed him to take her hand and lead her out of the compounds of the luau. "Where are we going?"

"You'll see," he winked.

"What about your car?"

"Too many Mai Tais; it will be safe here. I'll pick it up in the morning."

Obediently she went with him along tropical lanes of lush foliage and up narrow paths, the rolling ocean pounding beneath them. Up and up they went until, finally, they turned a sharp corner.

"My home," he announced proudly.

She stood and stared at the palatial structure, her mouth opening and shutting unable to utter a single coherent word.

"You like?"

She nodded her head silently; lest her mouth betray her undiluted shock.

Holding her hand, he took her inside. She heard the sound of her clicking heels on the highly polished wooden floor, mingling with the sound of distant pounding waves far below. She was sure the erratic beating of her heart out-ruled all other sounds; for, she certainly had not been expecting what she now saw before her. Her astounded eyes darted around taking in the spaciousness and airiness and everything Hawaiian; the furniture made from bamboo, the paintings depicting Hawaiian history; colourful blooms of plumeria, hibiscus and expensive orchids set against luscious foliage and set in huge crystal vases; tastefully placed tropical fruits of pineapple, passion fruits and kiwis and wooden carvings of ancient Hawaiian gods; her ears attune to the sound of soft traditional guitars and ukuleles, emitting from a very expensive looking music centre.

Finally, she found her voice, her eyes resting on her host. "Wow! This is truly magnificent, Kai."

"Yes, I am very proud of my home." He smiled.

Who wouldn't be? She asked herself and wondered, *How on earth he had come to possess such wealth and luxury.*

"May I offer you a Mai Tai; or, perhaps something else?" He volunteered.

"A Mai Tai will do." She said without analysing the situation, as she continued to revel on the beauty her eyes feasted upon. *To live here,* she mused, *would be heaven.* "And you haven't got a wife?" The words escaped her mouth before she could stop them and immediately she cursed herself profusely for her overwhelming and damning stupidity, as she felt the colour rise to her cheeks. Abruptly she turned away and walked over to the wall-to-wall windows; lest he should see her deep humiliation.

He saw and said nothing. He'd been asked the same question many times before and he always gave the same, silent answer; making his female interrogators secretly ponder. He joined her at the glass sliding door, which led out on to the vast balcony bordering the entire side of his house, which looked down on to the far away ocean. Taking her glass from her hand he said softly, "Let's meet the sunset, Lokemele."

Her pounding heart was in her throat. Never before had she seen such a spectacular panorama and she feasted her eyes and senses on what she was privileged to see. Below them swished the long leaves of palms, stirred by the soft touch of the trade winds and, further below, she looked out on to the soft canopy of luscious foliage of intermingled dark and light shades of green, interspersed with patches of vivid colour, leading to the mighty ocean and the distant horizon meeting its old friend. She felt his strong, masculine presence behind her; felt his strong arms envelope her body as they both stood silent and still, like two Hawaiian gods. She yearned to reach out her hand and stop the descending sun; for, she did not want the day to end; she did not want to say *goodbye* to the island; she did not want to go home; for, to go home she would have to face reality and to break the magical spell.

"What are you thinking about, Lokemele?" Kai asked softly.

"Sh."

Body against body they stood and watched the glorious sun sink majestically into its watery bed. He turned, took her in his arms and kissed her long and hard on the mouth and, just as the ocean had claimed its prize, he claimed Rosemary's body, soul and heart.

They lay naked body against naked body, intertwined, as the early morning sun greeted them through the open glass door.

"Aloha," he said softly.

"Aloha," she whispered revelling in what had been, what still was and what would always be entwined in her memory.

Kai took her to the airport, pressed into her hand a sealed envelope, kissed her and was gone.

As the plane took off she turned her head back and saw the twinkling lights of Kauai grow smaller and fainter, as the plane soared higher and higher and disappeared into the clouds. Opening the envelope, she withdrew the small card depicting a Hawaiian sunset and read silently:

Aloha,
Your memory, Lokemele, will always be in my heart.
Kai x

A solitary tear dropped on to his name, making it instantly smudge into a grey blob, as her lips broke out into a smile. *He had set her free from Tim and, for that, she would be eternally grateful.* "Aloha," she said softly.

Chapter Seven

In a stark delivery room, surrounded by sterile hospital paraphernalia and serious looking staff, Rosemary gave birth to a baby boy. Instantly, after birth, he was whipped away leaving her with an aftermath of physical and emotional pain. "Where is my baby?" Her feeble voice cried, barely audible above the medics' low voices.

The midwife rushed to her bed and, taking Rosemary's hand into her own said softly, "Your baby's heart is a little irregular. The doc…"

Ice sliced through Rosemary's fast beating heart. "But…"

"Now try and get some rest, Miss Longsdale."

Rosemary obediently closed her eyes, her body craving sleep and sleep came, bringing with it a set of repetitive nightmares where she plunged into a journey of no return and, when she awoke, she plunged deeper into its inescapable reality.

Months ago, the stark realisation that she was pregnant shook her to the core; it had been the last thing on earth she had been expecting and she neither wanted the baby; nor, did she yearn to be a mother. Her instant reaction to the shocking news was to have a termination; forget all about the unfortunate matter and to learn from her mistake. A fleeting passing thought about Kai, one day as she was sitting alone in the classroom marking books, stopped her in her tracks and forced her to rethink the whole situation. *Could,* she asked herself, *the baby be an eternal link with her beloved Kauai; or,* she frowned, an involuntary crease forming on her forehead, *Was it a way of, somehow, punishing Tim?*

During the course of her pregnancy, she had regretted her final decision many times, seriously considering giving the baby up for adoption, when termination was no longer a feasible option; but, for reasons unknown to herself, she turned her back on these thoughts and now, she lay on her hospital bed, totally regretting the path she had chosen; knowing she was completely on her own; for, she had no family to speak of to call on for support and all her friends had their own families, husbands and partners. She was on her own, in a world where her child would never know the identity of his father. She closed her eyes tight wishing the nightmares to overtake her senses; for, they were more bearable than reality.

Kauai

Thousands of kilometres away, when Rosemary was giving birth to his son, Kai was marrying his childhood sweetheart, the wahine who had stood by him and forgiven him for his indiscretions.

He had thought about Rosemary many times; for, although she was another woman in his long list of women he had bedded, somehow, she was different compared to the others. And, as he stood by his fiancée, making his marital vows, Rosemary flashed through his mind making him stammer.

"Kai?"

He heard the soft voice of the woman standing beside him and as her anxious eyes looked into his rich, brown eyes he felt himself drowning in his own self-deceit.

"Kai?"

He forced a smile on to his lips trying to reassure his fiancée and, above all, himself.

England

The soft thud on the carpet made her eyes dart to the door. Another *bill,* she sighed wearily ignoring its presence, the baby's cries alerting her to the fact it was feeding time. Striding to the cot, her eyes caught sight of the colourful postage stamps on the envelope, her heart leaping to the highest heavens when she recognised them to be American; her heart immediately deflating when she identified the sender. After seeing to the needs of her son, she grabbed the envelope, tore it open, sat down and read aloud: "Aloha my dear, Lokemele. Luana, Akamu and Liliana send you their love and their Aloha smiles." She smiled as she read on and imagined *the warm, white sands of Kauai, the pounding surf and the warm trade winds coming off the ocean, skimming the palms that fringed the beach. She could almost feel the sun on her arms, the stray bit of driftwood lodging between her toes as she walked on the silky sand...* Her heart turned to ice as her eyes stared starkly at the next words... *Kai has married his sweetheart... Kai... married... sweetheart...* The words swam before her eyes in a vivid, crazy dance whirling and swirling... *married... Kai...*

sweetheart... Kai... sweetheart... married... Whichever way they danced they amounted to the same thing. Kai had married his sweetheart. She got up and slumped back down on to the kitchen chair and squeezed her eyes tightly conscious only of her fast, pounding heart; left to rot in her well of emotions, like the driftwood on the deserted beaches; useless, unwanted, dead and forgotten.

For long moments she sat with the tear stained letter in her hands, her mind in another land where dreams did come true for other people. Slowly, her betrayed heart resumed its natural beat, her eyes stuck on the blurred words, she could barely make out through the veil of bitter tears. *How could he?* She asked herself over and over again. *How could he? But, he could,* she told herself, *just like Tim and Claire; they had betrayed her too,* she concluded, *because she was a pushover; someone to be used, abused and tossed away.* Abruptly she stood ramrod straight and, roughly brushing away her tears with a swipe of her hand; she strode to the cradle and gently took out her sleeping baby, sat down and rocked him in her arms. "My son," she whispered into his soft, dark hair, "I will teach you how to respect all women, men, yourself and the beautiful world we live in," and, made a firm resolve to forget all things Hawaiian.

Chapter Eight

Being a single parent was not easy; teaching full time was hard and exhausting; *but nothing,* she told herself firmly, *that couldn't be done.* And so she took on board all the challenges life threw at her with determined zest and vigour, allowing nothing to get in the way of moulding her son into an educated, caring, honest, patient, kind and charitable man and, to establish this, she dug deep into her own experiences, successes and mistakes to find the right formula. Despite her firm resolve to forget all things Hawaiian, and much to her annoyance, her mind often drifted to the islands, and to one island in particular; Kauai where she had found Keoki, Luana and a glimpse of peace, love, security, kindness and the pure simplicity of life and her heart and soul yearned for the soothing tranquillity of Kauai. When she closed her eyes tight, she could feel... *the soft silkiness of the warm, soothing sand, the coolness of the waves splashing her bare toes, the warmth of the sun on her skin;* she could hear the... *soft swishing of the palms and the lulling, comforting sound of Hawaiian guitars and, as she gently swayed to their hypnotic rhythm in Kai's strong arms...* her eyes snapped open and strayed to the sleeping baby in the cot, Kai's son; the son he knew nothing about. She closed her eyes her heart, wrapped in a heavy blanket of guilt, clenching mercilessly. *For, didn't Kai have the right to know about the existence of his son?* Her eyes snapped open wide. "No!" She stated out loud. "He has no right." But, deep within the bowels of her conscience, she was fighting a raging, silent war.

Chapter Nine
Kauai

Kai had found his love. She had always been there waiting for him to sow his wild oats and to, finally, return to her heart, body and soul. Her patience and unwavering faith proved fruitful; for, not only did Kai wed her, he denounced any future involvement with any other woman and he stuck stoically to his promise. He loved his childhood sweetheart with all of his heart and vowed to honour and to protect her until death parted them.

The news Leialoha, his wife, was pregnant made Kai the happiest man on the island and everyone he came into contact with felt uplifted in the shadow of his overwhelming joy. Keoki and Luana awaited the happy arrival with eagerness. They had both been pleasantly surprised by the way Kai had ceased his roaming ways and settled down to married life with Leialoha; for, they held the young woman in high esteem, had watched her mature into a graceful wahine and inwardly flinched at the way Kai had openly flirted with a host of other women, praying fervently for the day he would finally grow up. Their prayers were answered; however, Keoki's heart gnawed with a secret dread; for, he had often wondered what had become of Rosemary, especially as all correspondence from England had ceased and all of his and Luana's recent letters returned. Secretly, he blamed Kai.

Since her departure Rosemary had fleetingly flitted in and out of Kai's mind; but, within each passing day her image became fainter; the memory of their brief union becoming more fragile until, one day, it disappeared into the sands of time where it lay dormant.

On the nineteenth of December on a beautiful sunny morning, as the sound of Mele Kalikimaka was drifting through an open window, Leialoha gave birth to a baby girl and, as Kai held his daughter in his strong arms, he vowed to be the best father ever, as he successfully hid his disappointment of being denied a son. They were now a family unit. *And no one,* he determined, *would ever be allowed to cast a shadow over their happiness.* Little did he know the gods had already cast their die and the fate of the happy family was sealed.

Chapter Ten

At the age of ten, Hanale was a strikingly handsome boy inheriting his mother's quiet nature, polite manners and academic prowess and his father's golden complexion, brown eyes and dark, curly hair. Girls were automatically drawn to his friendly, polite nature and his good looks. His male friends enjoyed his happy-go-lucky personality and his athletic ability made him a firm favourite for sporting teams. He was a popular boy, a competent pupil and his prospects were good.

Rosemary was proud of her son; for, despite having no father figure around he was a well-balanced lad and seemed to lack nothing; the credit lay entirely with her. Often, under trying circumstances, she was both an exemplary mother and *father* to her one and only child, often denying herself the pleasure of socialising, holidays, friendships; denying her own career rise for the sake of her son's well-being.

One friend never gave up on trying to lure her out into the social world. "Oh go on, just one drink. Surely you can make an exception on my birthday… please…"

Rosemary sighed heavily. "Okay," she said resignedly.

"What!" exclaimed Susan. "You've actually agreed; am I hearing things?"

"No, you are not hearing things, Susan." Rosemary smiled. "Actually Hanale is having a sleepover at his friend's; so, yeah, why not?"

"Why not, indeed; I can't believe this." Susan enthused.

"Well, as they say, everything happens to those who wait long enough."

"You won't regret this. I'll ring you later about the details."

Regret was already seeping into Rosemary's veins, making her question why she had agreed to her friend's request, when she didn't have one decent thing to wear on a night out.

The second she walked into the throbbing pub, she yearned to run out. *It was,* she concluded, *too crowded, too smoky and far too loud. Why, you couldn't even hear yourself think. No, it was not for her. She would,* she decided, *have a quick drink and make her excuses.*

Two hours later, she was in the midst of the crowd. No excuses had been made as she savoured one drink after another, completely captured by the joviality of the atmosphere round her. Everything was new and yet she felt quite at home; for, she had regularly frequented pubs in her late teens; but, there was still an unfamiliar incongruity to it all as her eyes took in the latest fashion wear, hairstyles and make-up and her ears listened to an occasional chat-up line while her mouth swallowed the disappearing orange liquid in her glass.

"It's about time you had something stronger, Rose."

Rosemary's eyes lingered on the alluring liquid in the hypnotic glass; her mind closed to a thousand nightmares, she had buried deep down in the recesses of her mind years ago.

"Rose."

Her eyes flickered open to the tantalising liquid inviting her to take a sip, as her fingers reached out and curled themselves around the clear, thin stem of the smooth glass. Slowly she brought it up to her lips and opened her mouth. She lowered the glass. "I prefer pineapple juice." She smiled reminiscently, her thoughts flashing back to the pineapple plantation she had once visited.

In the corner of the crowded bar room, a well-dressed man, in his early sixties, liked what he saw and, as Rosemary looked abruptly away from the searing temptation burning in her glass, her eyes clashed with the clear, blue, inquisitive eyes of Alan Tompkinson. Abruptly she looked away; for, she did not like what she saw; *a self-assured man full of male ego and selfish optimism.* She had been severely burned before and knew well that a lingering look could be fatal. Swallowing her pineapple juice, she grabbed her coat and bag and jumped to her feet. She froze at the light touch of his fingers on her arm and cringed inwardly at the sound of the soft silkiness in his voice.

"May I introduce myself? I am Alan… Alan Tompkinson."

Her eyes rose to his and momentarily locked. Sharply she pulled herself together and rose saying, "I am sorry, Mister…"

"Tompkinson." He prompted. "May I buy you and your friend a drink?"

"Oh, yes please," enthused Susan, as she grabbed Rosemary by the sleeve bringing her back down.

Begrudgingly Rosemary sat and closed her eyes, as she struggled to contain her rising anger as, with a fleeting glance, he assessed her discomfort and, for a few brief seconds, regretted his advances.

"Lighten up, Rose." Susan chuckled, whispering in Rosemary's ear. "I think he fancies you."

Rosemary cast daggers at her old friend, silently wishing she would shut up and grow up, as she inwardly prepared herself for half an hour of torture before making her escape.

An hour later she was no longer attempting to escape and, sipping a fresh pineapple juice, found herself interested in this stranger she had just met. But, although she found it surprisingly easy to relax in his company, the red flag was up and, at the end of the evening she declined his offer of the three of them meeting up again.

Swiftly she erased Alan out of her mind. He had been a fleeting distraction; *but, like all men,* she concluded, *she was better off without him; for, all men in her past had brought her heartache, misery, lies, betrayal and deceit.* Once again she redirected all her attention on to her son.

The knock on the door, the following weekend, brought a bewildered looking Hanale to the kitchen. "There's a stranger at the door, Mum, and he's asking for you," he announced.

Her eyes rose to a lean face and still, blue eyes; rising further to a head of silver-grey hair swept neatly to one side, her eyes involuntarily resting on a smiling mouth, as boiling anger surged through every vein in her body; her accusing mind throwing an array of silent curses at Susan for her betrayal, as her eyes finally bore into the gentle eyes of Alan Tompkinson and she silently asked, *How could he just land on my doorstep without an invitation? What kind of bad mannered human is this?* Unblinkingly she stared at and through him, wishing to God he'd just go away and leave her in peace. Begrudgingly she gave him a hint of a smile.

His smile widened; her fear tightened. "Your friend, Susan, thought you wouldn't mind if I took the liberty of taking her advice and called on you. I hope you don't mind, Rosemary."

I do mind! I do mind! I do mind! She wanted to scream from the rooftop. *How dare you just come here and expect…*

He watched her lips form again into a trace of a smile, her eyes serious and unwavering. *Just like Mona Lisa herself,* he thought, *secretive, alluring, mystical; no great beauty but exuding a seductive attraction it was impossible to ignore.* Her light cough broke the spell and he was reminded of the purpose of his visit. "Rosemary," he said with a hint of caution in his voice, "I thought you might like to accompany me on a date." His warm smile broadened sending unwarranted shivers up and down her spine, as she tried desperately to claim back control of her whirling thoughts.

She smiled making his heart jump. In seconds, his heart deflated as he heard her damning words. "I am sorry, Mister Tompkinson…"

"Alan," he interrupted.

"Alan… but I am not interested in any date."

"But…"

"But, no." She attempted to close the door.

"But… why?"

"No reason. I am sorry for your wasted journey and time."

He stared at her retreating body through the closed glass door as a heavy veil of regret began to take over his senses. *This is a nice lady,* he thought, *and it would have been an honour to have been her friend.* He turned and walked briskly in the opposite direction.

Rosemary resumed washing the dishes, Alan's gentle image haunting her senses. *Why on earth couldn't she have given this man a chance?* She asked herself. But, she knew why. Vigorously she dried the pots and firmly resolved to cast Alan Tompkinson out of her mind.

Chapter Eleven

An invisible knife plunged into Rosemary's heart writhing and twisting, leaving her feeling deeply hurt, bitter and betrayed as she clutched tightly the telephone wire, released the tension before snaking it round and round her fingers until they became entrapped; a twinge of relief giving her a touch of respite, knowing Susan could not witness her unwarranted bitterness and jealousy, surging through every throbbing vein in her body. She coughed in an attempt to bring a level of control into her voice. "That's... that's wonderful news, Susan. I hope you shall be very happy." She forced her strangled words out of her arid mouth, aware her last sentence sounded so utterly false.

"You... you don't mind?" Susan questioned cautiously. "After all, it was you he really wanted to go out with."

"Of course I don't mind." Lied Rosemary as bitter regret gnawed through her. And yet, if Alan had asked her out a second time she knew, without a doubt, her answer would be the same. *And so,* she wondered, *why the duplicity; Why the insane, raging jealousy? What the hell was wrong with her?*

From the side-line, Rosemary watched as Susan and Alan's relationship blossomed and, as Susan grew more and more in love with Alan, his feelings towards her never grew and consequently, the more he saw of Susan, the more he craved for Rosemary. What it was that pulled him towards Rosemary he did not know. She was, he admitted, pleasing to the eye in appearance but, he thought, a cautious woman with a faraway look in her eyes, which made him think she was haunted by some sort of memory. *Maybe,* he mused, *it was something to do with her son.*

Rosemary gave all men a swerve. According to her own philosophy, after her experiences with Tim and Kai, they weren't worth the effort. Yet, Kai often haunted her thoughts; for, in a sense, he had set her free from Tim and yet she felt restrained; bound in invisible chains she could not escape from; though, where she would escape she did not know. Alan crashed into her mind. *Maybe he could have been her escape* – Her thoughts often drifted to the Hawaiian Islands where, for a brief time, she had found peace and tranquillity. Perhaps her answer lay in the mystical Isles. She closed her eyes and… *felt the soft sand creep delicately in-between her toes, the trade winds lightly caressing her skin as she strode leisurely along the white beach; the coconut palms swaying lazily above their carpet of warm sand as the waves fell in subtle folds splashing over her feet; her eyes hypnotised by the tireless, tranquil sea. In Kauai she could find peace once more; or… not.* She swiftly concluded as an image of Kai's smiling face gate-crashed her peaceful reverie and Keoki's words echoed loudly in her consciousness… *To live, you must find the problem, tackle it and learn to be happy again…* She thought she'd found the problem and, more to the point, tackled it in the form of freeing herself sexually with Kai and erasing Tim from her mind. *But,* she concluded grimly, as she stared out of the kitchen window on to the skeletal branches of the apple trees, *Tim was still there; not prominent but still there and his memory haunted her and prevented her from being herself and trusting another human; from loving; from being truly free.* Thoughts of Kauai became more vivid and frequent and with these thoughts came a deep yearning to escape to a faraway island where no one knew her; where she could not be hurt. *If only she could afford to escape. Maybe… one day,* she mused.

New Year was fast approaching and, with its imminent arrival, an unexpected invitation came thudding through the letter box. Immediately it caught Rosemary's attention. The invitation trembled in her hands as her disbelieving eyes lingered on the words.

Chapter Twelve

New Year's Eve party.
Why not let bygones be bygones?
It would be great to see you again…

Her incredulous eyes glared at the sender's name, as her heart tried laboriously to restart its normal beat, her guts writhed; her senses reeled mercilessly. Reaching out she grabbed a nearby chair and slumped down, the invitation still visibly shaking in her hand. Slowly her misty eyes reread the words, a thousand questions whirling around in her buzzing head, as a thousand twisted scenarios gnawed at her confused mind, her eyes dropping once more to the sender's name, evoking a multitude of emotions as the pain of Tim's betrayal, his lies and unfulfilled promises and his deceit seared every throbbing vein, making her close her eyes against it all. She squeezed them tightly, ever more tightly, so that she could drown in the blackness. When, finally, some semblance of reasonable thinking began to emerge, she asked herself over and over again… *Why… Why… Why?*

The night was long and fitful as she tossed and turned; rose, reread the invitation a number of times, crept back into her bed and willed sleep to take her for its own. By dawn, she had made her decision.

Chapter Thirteen

With heavy trepidation beating in her racing heart, Rosemary walked down the long, straight road wondering what had possessed her to accept the invitation. The answer hit her with alarming clarity; curiosity, revenge and determination. Curiosity in why her former husband should suddenly request her presence; revenge in showing him that, despite his abandonment of her, she was still standing without him; determination in demanding his attention into acknowledging her as a survivor. As her feet came closer to the house, her whole body yearned to turn and flee the scene. She walked on doggedly, through the gate and stood ramrod straight at the door, her heart beating like a frantic Hawaiian drum, her eyes peeled on the closed door. *There was still time to…*

"Rosemary!"

His familiar voice reverberated loudly booming in her head, her feet standing firm, yet feeling like two wobbly pieces of jelly as a thousand butterflies performed crazy, erratic dances in her tight stomach; her will to be stoical quickly crumbling away. Slowly her eyes rose, her mouth opened to dry words; inside, her guts quivered and trembled as he brought her to himself and gave her a tight hug and it felt so… so…

He pulled her gently away and scanned her pale face, her hair pulled into a tight chignon, her black satin knee length dress doing justice to her shapely figure. "You look wonderful, Rosemary; truly wonderful." He smiled appreciatively.

She stood like a statue taking in the man who had once been her friend, her lover, her husband, her… betrayer wondering again what had possessed her to accept his invitation. She remembered, pinned on a false smile and said softly, "Thank you." Her inquisitive eyes strayed beyond him and into the throng of partying revellers.

"She's gone, Rosemary."

"Who?" Her eyes darted back to him.

"Claire, the two timing bitch; I threw her out."

A cynical smile slid on to Rosemary's mouth. *So that was it; he's got his comeuppance and now he wants me back. If he thinks...* A sudden idea crashed into her mind and he watched her brow furrow.

"What is it, Rose?"

His mere voice made bile rise to her throat. *But, if her plan was to work...* Her cynical smile turned to one of reassurance. "You'll survive, Tim; you always do. Anyway," she enthused excitedly, and somewhat uncharacteristically. "Lead me to the party."

She felt out of her depth, like the proverbial fish out of water; but, for her plan to work, she had to play the role perfectly. Suddenly she had an overwhelming craving for revenge; not simply to show him she had survived his betrayal but a deeper, more sinister revenge which involved payback.

The party was in full swing and soon she was in the throng of it all talking to complete strangers, dancing, enjoying the party food; aware that one pair of eyes was secretly following her every move. Her eyes strayed to the motley array of bottles which made up the makeshift bar and, after a long spell of total abstinence, her body craved for the one thing she knew could ruin her as it once almost ruined her before. Still, she looked and craved; needed, wanted and yearned.

"Why don't you have one?"

Her eyes glued on the potent liquid in the glass rose to Tim's glittering eyes. Without further hesitation she took the glass from his hand and downed the liquid in one gulp; the strong potency of the clear substance bringing a sudden warm glow to her whole body which, in turn, made her feel more relaxed. "I'll have another." She held out her empty glass and wondered why she had denied herself this pleasure for so long for its effect seemed to make everything all right. Tim was instantly forgiven for all his past misdeeds and, as she watched him approach her with a refilled glass, she felt a flutter of excitement surge through her. They danced, drank, ate and laughed. They did not delve into the past; both fearing and avoiding the onslaught of the other.

"Why did you accept the invitation, Rosemary?"

She raised her wavering eyes to his still, questioning eyes. "Oh, I don't know, Tim; curiosity, I guess."

"Well, you know what happened to the cat?"

"Yes, I know." She smiled grimly and turned to walk away into the blur of happy revellers.

He held her tightly as they relaxed into a smooch and, for a few brief seconds, she allowed her body to yield to his; to feel again his taut body against her; to allow herself to dream once more; *for,* she mused, *it had not all been bad. They had enjoyed some good times; some very good times before... before...* She pulled herself away as Claire's image crashed into her head and the full force of their lies and betrayal loomed to the forefront of her mind and then she remembered why she had accepted his, out of the blue, invitation. "I have missed you, Tim," she said softly as she looked deep into his deceiving eyes. "I have missed you so very much."

"And I have missed you, my darling." He kissed her forehead and brought her closer to himself while, inside, her guts twisted and writhed into a hateful tight knot.

"Let's go somewhere private, Tim; where we can talk."

He led her out of the bustling, noisy room and up the familiar stairs and, as she followed meekly, her heart thundered, her guts wrenched; her dry throat yearning to throw up a mouthful of vomit that wasn't there.

The door closed behind them and they were alone in the room she had known so well; the room where they had made love and promises; the room in which he had betrayed her trust by bringing into their bed her best friend, Claire; the room where their marriage was sealed and broken.

"Oh, how I have dreamed of this moment." He said softly kissing her forehead, cheeks; his lips sliding down to her waiting mouth, his impatient fingers unclasping her bra as he brought down his hungry mouth to her erect nipples and sucked.

She felt his hardness as he lay on top of her and, as he wriggled out of his trousers she wriggled from beneath his weight and standing half naked asked, "Do you want me, Tim?"

"Yes... yes..." He reached out for her hand which she swiftly withdrew from his grasp.

"Then beg; yearn and beg, Tim for that is your lot in life." Swiftly she threw on her dress, stuffed her bra into her clutch bag and smiled victoriously at the half naked bundle on the bed. "Yearn for me, Tim, like I once yearned for you."

He heard the door bang behind her.

She walked through the happy crowd counting down the old year, "… eight, seven, six, five, four, three, two, one; Happy New Year!"

And as she walked back down the long, straight road she raised her eyes to the colourful sky as gold, red, green and silver stars splayed the velvet sky followed by an array of multi-coloured zigzags, jagged lines and shooting stars. "Happy New Year, Tim," she said aloud, smirking, as she added a vigorous spring to her steps.

And, for the first time in a long, long while she felt in control.

Chapter Fourteen

They found her in a crumpled heap on the living room floor, empty bottles strewn around her, the remnants of what looked like a shepherd's pie half on and half smudged into the carpet of the cluttered floor, dirty mugs on the coffee table and visible signs of vomit staining the sofa, the carpet and the black satin dress she was wearing.

Susan's eyes darted to a shocked Alan. "See to Hanale and make pots of black coffee," she ordered.

Obediently he employed the young boy into making the coffee while he wandered back into the living room, wondering what had propelled Rosemary to sink so low. *Granted,* he told himself, *he didn't really know her well; but this...*

In the days following, Susan took charge of Hanale and Rosemary, moving into their home and tending to their every need. She had always found Hanale an easy boy to get on with and enjoyed his sunny disposition, his laid back manner and caring attitude. However, it was all uphill with Rosemary; for, with her friend, she was up against a silent wall. Rosemary's mouth remained firmly clamped, refusing to share her reasons for her binge, no matter how hard Susan tried and what means she employed.

It was agreed that when Susan went back to work and Hanale back to school, Alan was to take care of Rosemary; for, Susan was adamant that her friend was not to be trusted to be left alone. According to Susan, Rosemary had far too much to lose if she ever fell so disgracefully again.

Rosemary lived in her own world, begrudging Susan's interference and Alan's presence. She knew she didn't have a say in the matter; so, decided against any verbal oppositions to their plans, existing in her own world of silence and bitter regret, at having succumbed to her first alcoholic drink after years of abstinence and she placed the blame, as always, at Tim's door. *He,* she told herself, *was solely to blame; for, without his treachery, she would never have taken to the bottle, years ago, in the first place.* A wicked smile flickered on her lips, when memories of her abandoning him in his moments of need flashed through her mind. Instantaneously her smile died, as her need for alcohol surged through every pulsating vein in her craving body. She cast her cold eyes on the man she barely knew; the man who could have been her boyfriend and her security; the man who was holding her a silent captive, a prisoner in her own home, feeling a surging hatred which seethed and bubbled away in her guts for this man sitting next to her; her jailer. She caught his eye and his smile and looked abruptly away.

He sensed she was a troubled soul. He also knew it was not his business to intrude into private, sensitive matters and so he tried to engage her in mundane, trivial matters; respected her silence and waited patiently for things to change and, one day, they did.

"I need a drink; an alcoholic drink, Alan." She had begged him for the hundredth time and, for the hundredth time, he had denied her request. He had seen it all before; his former wife had died, due to alcoholic poisoning after years of abuse. "Please Alan."

"What drink would Madam care to have?"

Her eyes lit up; already she could taste the soothing, potent liquid. "A Mai Tai."

"And where does such a drink hail from?" He asked interestingly; for, being a non-drinker himself, he had never heard of such an alcoholic beverage.

"Hawaii."

And there began his first lesson on the Islands of Hawaii, which was to change both their lives for ever.

Chapter Fifteen

Day after day Alan took care of Rosemary and, gradually, she began to eat more, became livelier and started to relate to Alan, who was an avid listener, about all she knew about the Hawaiian Islands. He was fascinated with her enchanting accounts. "I can picture you there, Alan," she smiled.

"I'd like to go there one day; perhaps, you will be my escort." He chuckled lightly as sporadic flashes of Kai guiding her around the Island of Kauai flashed through Rosemary's mind. He cut into her meandering thoughts. "In the meantime, when you have fully recovered, why don't you, Hanale, Susan and I hold our own Hawaiian evening? We could invite our friends and Hanale could bring along his classmates. Don't you think it would be fun, Rosemary?"

"Lokemele; my Hawaiian name is Lokemele and, yes, I think it would be great fun." She stated excitedly, her eyes sparkling she began making plans in her head. "We could have our own luau, a Hawaiian feast, with traditional island food and music. Oh, that would be so much fun, Alan." And, without thinking, she planted a kiss on his cheek; her smile immediately dying a death as she realised what she had unwittingly done, as her shining eyes stared into his blue, steady eyes.

"Has anyone ever told you, Lokemele; you look absolutely beautiful when you smile?" He pulled her gently towards himself and kissed her softly on the mouth, sending immediate tiny electric tingles rushing up and down her spine. He pulled away leaving her wanting more. "I am sorry, I shouldn't have done that." He said, a flash of Susan's image hurtling into his mind.

But, Rosemary was not sorry. She wanted more, much more, and was left with a hollow, sinking feeling she knew only too well.

Susan felt the idea of a Hawaiian evening was fantastic and all of them set to work on creating the perfect Hawaiian success.

But, neither Rosemary, nor Alan, forgot their brief kiss and it created a guilty hole in their respective consciousness; for, Alan had never in his life so much as thought of deceiving a woman and Rosemary felt she had accused Tim for no apparent reason; *for, wasn't she now acting in exactly the same way? Wasn't she guilty of betraying the trust of a true friend?*

Rosemary's house was decorated in the style of a traditional Hawaiian home, with subtle differences in the form of artificial tropical foliage hanging from the ceiling and along the walls and banister; huge vases of fake hibiscus and plumeria were placed tastefully around and colourful leis, painstakingly made, were ready to be bestowed around the necks of their guests. Traditional Hawaiian music played softly in the background and a long makeshift table, set out on trestles, was heavy laden with Hawaiian delights. The guests arrived and the party started.

Rosemary's heart thudded at the sight of Alan; for, he had awakened in her something she could not explain and, as he bestowed a lei of artificial frangipani around her neck and she felt his soft lips against her cheek, she feared her legs would give way. *But was this feeling love, lust or just simply a yearning for something that she could not have?* She could not answer her own question.

"Aloha Lokemele." His soft words of greeting made her heart melt, as she forced her eyes to avoid his for fear of what she may see there, turning her gaze to Susan, her eyes skimming over her tropical green printed dress and rose up to her dark hair sleek and straight, noticing that pinned behind her left ear was a white plumeria. *Yes she is taken,* Rosemary concluded glumly, *by a lovely, gentle man. S*he felt her own heart break.

The venture was a roaring success, with everyone throwing themselves into the leisurely gaiety and spirit of an Hawaiian evening. From the side-line, Hanale noticed that his mother seemed totally at ease in her Hawaiian surroundings; little did he know that while he was watching her she was thinking of his father, an invisible knife searing through her already broken heart and ripping it in shreds.

Hanale knew very little of his father's identity; for, there was little Rosemary could tell her son about him. He knew, of course, that he was Hawaiian, born and bred; well off and a happy natured man who, apparently, had a fling with his mum. Although he treated his father's identity with respect, he did not crave to seek him out. He was content knowing that he had a father, somewhere in Hawaii, and that he was a good man. What he couldn't have he didn't miss.

Rosemary was secretly thankful her son did not yearn to search for his father; for, she herself, preferred no contact, especially now that he was married; though, from time to time, he slipped into her mind and suffused her with a warm glow.

Hawaii resided in her heart and soul and, whenever she craved for peace, she escaped to its distant shores in her dreams and in her thoughts; but, had she the finances available…

He saw her weaving her way to the makeshift bar, engaging a friend in conversation; her hand reaching out for a tall glass filled with a potent, golden-brown substance and was at her side in an instant.

"Take this one instead, Lokemele."

"Oh Alena." She used his Hawaiian name as she stared at an identical looking glass in Alan's hand.

"A non-alcoholic Mai Tai." He smiled congenially and watched her smooth brow furrow.

"But…"

"No buts, Lokemele."

His stubbornly fixed smile told her she was not going to win the argument. With a good measure of inward fury rampaging through her body, she took the non-alcoholic drink from him, placed down her own and forced a smile on her face. "You're probably right," she said begrudgingly.

"I know I am right." He stated determinedly as he touched her wrist reassuringly. "I know I am right, Lokemele," he repeated softly as their eyes locked and Susan came rushing towards them.

From the corner of the room where Rosemary stood, engaged in casual conversation with Hanale and his mates, she saw them dancing to a slow Hawaiian lilt, her eyes riveted to the two lovers as they swayed together in close proximity; Susan's hands possessively around Alan's neck, his hands tightly around her waist as together they moved in unison, oblivious to all around while Rosemary's heart tore into tattered threads as raw loss overtook her senses; loss for Tim; loss for Kai; loss for the future she could have had and was now claimed by her best friend. *What an utter fool she had been,* she scolded herself severely as she shook her head from side to side, unconsciously biting her lower lip a*nd for what… to prove a point; to be alone; to wallow in self-pity; to drink?* She turned away, unable to force herself to look at happiness she could not have; the urge to have a proper drink rising within her cajoling, enticing, tempting, begging her to have a sip, just one little sip, just to ease the pain a little. *Who was he to tell her she couldn't have a drink? It was her Hawaiian party, her house, her booze.* She cast a surreptitious eye at Susan and Alan, wrapped closely in each other's embrace, a hard lump rising to her parched throat and, before she could stop them, her feet made a beeline to the bar. Swiftly she downed the contents of one Mai Tai and grabbed another to savour. *Alan would never know,* she smiled wickedly, *alcoholic and non-alcoholic Mai Tais looked the same.*

He knew instantly. He knew the tell-tale signs: the loosened tongue, the high-pitched laughter and tactile touches; he'd seen it all before. He kept his mouth closed and his eyes opened.

Susan liked what she saw; for too long, she thought, *Rosemary had been pent up, like a coiled spring; a closed book no one was allowed to open, read and enjoy. This talkative, giggling, amusing friend she liked very much. She could see them both clubbing in the near future.*

Hanale kept a secretive eye on his mother and his friend's attention away from her. He had seen this side of her behaviour before. He didn't like it; didn't want it and wondered what on earth he could do about it. He watched intently as his mother brought the glass up to her lips, took a generous gulp and placed her free hand tenderly on Alan's arm; he also witnessed the way Susan's eyes followed her friend's every move.

Kitchen duties were abandoned by the hostess and, reluctantly, taken over by Susan who made sure there was a constant supply of freshly made Caesar salad, shoyu chicken and rice, salmon, bread rolls, slices of fresh pineapple and other tropical fruit and Haupia, while Rosemary replaced one Mai Tai with another, not caring about her hostess duties, her appearance as a respectable teacher, her role of an exemplary mother; caring only about her next drink as she crashed into revellers and tables, knocked down drinks, laughed at nothing in particular and talked gibberish. Guests took note. Some left prematurely; others stayed to gloat. Susan and Alan took care of her when all had finally disappeared. Hanale disappeared into his room and wished he knew his father.

Chapter Sixteen

She woke up with an excruciating headache, a bowl full of vomit and no memory of what had happened; her blotched, heavy eyes strayed to stark eyes staring back at her.

"We have to talk." The stern voice stated.

Her eyes closed, her mouth followed suit and remained firmly clamped, as she portrayed the image of a stubborn, spoilt child whilst laying on her bed of self-imposed pain, wanting only to take her last breath and expire into a world of peace, where no one would nag at her.

"Rosemary, we have to talk."

The cold, unyielding, authoritative words boomed loudly in her throbbing head and in the heavy silence she opened her bloodshot eyes and stared into the depths of Alan's eyes, where she saw nothing but her own misery.

"Welcome back to our world, Rosemary."

Her exhausted eyes flickered and closed.

"We have to talk."

"I don't have to do anything." She muttered, wishing to God he'd go away and leave her in peace. "Where's Hanale?"

"Gone."

Laboriously her eyes opened and, with a struggle, she managed to prop herself against her pillow trying desperately to focus. "Gone where?"

"For now, he is staying at Susan's parental home. He is refusing to see you in this state, Rosemary."

She heard his stark words; none sunk into her consciousness; none made any sense. She was conscious only of her guts as they twisted mercilessly and her pounding head as her senses reeled. She lowered her heavy head on her pillow and closed her eyes.

"Oh, no you don't." Alan grabbed both her arms and shook her gently forcing her red, heavy eyes to open. "You have to face up to your problem, Rosemary."

These words, somehow, managed to penetrate deep into her consciousness and intermingled with similar words spoken to her, a long time ago, on a distant island… *To live, you must find the problem, tackle it and learn to be happy again… Dear, dear Keoki…* For a few brief seconds her mind relaxed in a tranquil paradise. "You do know you have a problem don't you, Rosemary?" Her eyes and mind remained firmly closed; for, as far as she was concerned, she had solved her problem when she had served Tim his portion of sweet revenge. "I think," Alan said his words soft and cautious, "that you need professional help, Rosemary."

"And I think you should leave me in peace." She snapped her icy eyes swiftly darting to him. "After all, who do you think you are, Alan; you barely know me."

"I am your friend, Rosemary."

She heard the door click softly behind him and imagined his feet retreating away from her and towards Susan, his love, Closing her eyes tightly she allowed his words to freely hammer in her tortured, tired head *I think that you need professional help… I am your friend… friend…friend; a friend but never a lover*, she concluded miserably, *someone who belongs to another belongs to another… belongs to another* His haunting words threw her into an uneasy sleep, where an assortment of distorted images intermingled and wove together forming a picture of utter chaos, where nothing made any sense as… *faces loomed large and faded, only to loom again in an array of distorted mouths, crudely displaying blackened and missing teeth, snapping and growling like dogs on a vicious mission snarling… howling… biting her as they desperately tried to claw at her heart and to viciously rip it apart…* She woke with a start, grabbing a nearby glass and gulping down the cool water, yearning for alcohol, any type would do: vodka, brandy, whisky, beer cider… meths… Roughly throwing the duvet off her bed she placed one wobbly foot on to the carpet then, cautiously, placed down her other foot. Slowly she stood up, her trembling fingers holding on to the night table for support, as the room spun and whirled around her; the solid oak wardrobe and her dressing table merging into the magnolia painted walls with their lopsided, blurry pictures and distorted lampshades all whirling round and round; spinning, tossing, turning, going round and round like an out of control roundabout. Summoning up her inner strength she placed one wobbly foot in front of the other; for, she was sure there was a bottle of some sort of alcohol hidden in the depths of the kitchen cupboard. Her leg gave way and she felt herself falling… falling… like a crumpled, wasted autumnal leaf and then she felt nothing.

Finally, when she opened her eyes she snarled bitterly, "Oh, it's you."

"It's me." Alan smiled. "Your friend."

The following days were torturous for all concerned. Susan and Alan took turns in caring for their reluctant patient. When Susan went to work, Alan stayed with Rosemary until Susan relieved him in the evenings and stayed the nights, caring for her friend's every need. Hanale remained in the care of Susan's parents, where he found firm friends who, in their turn, willingly took on the role of surrogate grandparents.

Rosemary was aware of everything that was going on; flatly refusing to acknowledge anything.

Alan knew the score. He had lived through similar scenes with his wife until her premature death. He knew it was a waiting game. He also knew the victim could lose her life in the process of playing this dangerous and unpredictable game. He was well aware this was a very delicate situation, in which the victim had to acknowledge the problem before any real progress was made. And so, like the gods of Ancient Greece, he played with the toss of the dice and waited for what fate would bring.

Slowly Rosemary began to eat, to gain strength and to start thinking her chaotic, whirling thoughts laboriously beginning to form a logical picture; a picture she didn't want, or felt ready to assess. On reflection, she secretly conceded she had a problem but what it was she did not know; neither did she want to know… not yet.

She began to skirt around trivial subjects; what kind of supper Alan was preparing, the programmes they would watch on the television, the novel Alan was currently reading. Nothing else mattered and nothing alluding to her alcoholism was mentioned. Everything seemed to be on an even keel until one afternoon Alan tentatively referred a name he had heard repetitively, whilst Rosemary was in the midst of sleep. "Who is Keoki, Rosemary?" He cautiously asked, watching her intently as her eyes immediately lit up and his heart deflated. "Is he a former boyfriend?" Involuntarily the words escaped his lips as he silently cursed himself for his spontaneous uncharacteristic stupidity. He continued to observe her as her eyes shone and sparkled, feeling the hard lump rise to his throat as he heard her light chuckle and anxiously waited for her answer which hung in suspense.

"Keoki Keoki." Her lips formed into a wide, beaming smile. "Keoki is a very special man, Alan."

He continued to watch her feeling his heart dying inside; his eyes did not waver. *So, that was her problem.* He assumed sadly. *That is the root of her sadness; this Keoki fellow.* He let it be, not daring to delve further for fear of what she may reveal.

Chapter Seventeen

But, the name haunted Alan. *Keoki... Keoki... who was this despicable man who had caused such sadness in Rosemary's life? Where did he live? What had he done?* And the more he thought about him, the more questions bombarded his bemused mind and the more urgent the need to find out more. Tentatively he mentioned Keoki's name in casual conversation and, in return, received a distant longing look he did not comprehend.

The mention of Keoki's name was like a soothing balm to Rosemary's tortured soul, automatically enveloping her with a luxurious blanket of security; for, his name conjured up blissful memories of peaceful deserted beaches, the timeless ocean and a deep longing for something she could not have. And, when an envelope, addressed in Keoki's handwriting, dropped through the letter box her heart leaped for joy. Hurriedly she ripped the envelope open, hastily withdrew the flimsy paper inside and with her eager eyes read the contents.

Aloha, my dearest Lokemele.
Greetings from sunny Kauai.
Luna and the children send you sweet Alohas and keep asking when you are going to grace us with a visit. Though we are happy you have resumed communication once more, we are saddened that you keep fobbing us off with umpteen excuses and now we are going to take no more. We insist you come and stay with us on our beautiful island...

Already she was there in spirit feeling... *the comforting trade winds caress her skin, her ears attune to the rolling waves, her toes feeling the warm grit of the soothing sand...* She forced her eyes back to the paper she was holding and read the devastating news... "Alan!" She exclaimed as she heard the click of the door, silently cursing her intruder for his untimely visit as she hastily shoved Keoki's letter into the depths of her pocket; her grim, sad eyes and pale face betraying her secret feelings of inexplicable loss as she forced a reluctant smile on to her drawn face.

"What is it, Rosemary; you look like you have seen a ghost?"

"It's nothing." Abruptly she rose and walked over to the window, where he could read nothing from her facial visage. "Actually, it's just a letter from Keoki. It's… it's nothing."

His eyes dropped to the floor, unable to look at the woman he loved from afar. *So, they were still corresponding… there is something there. She still has hope.* And with that silent statement he set his own fate, while she stared out the window and saw only… *Kai's beloved wife dead in a fatal car crash; a grieving Kai and their only child, Ocean Tia, without a mother and an inconsolable father.*

The following days were a blur to Rosemary. Restarting work after a month of sick leave she saw less and less of Alan and Susan and thought more and more of Kai and his daughter, Ocean Tia; though she had never met her. Spontaneously, and at the most inconvenient of times, they crashed into her mind when she was in the midst of delivering a lesson, in the middle of an engaging soap, during a staff meeting, at the till in the supermarket. She saw a… *a dishevelled Kai walking the lonely beaches… a young girl staring across an endless ocean, wishing it would bring back her mother… a tearful Luana and a consoling Keoki and still the glorious sun of Kauai which never failed to rise; still the waves rolled on and on without a care in the world; still, without success, the soft trade winds tried to soothe their broken hearts…* as she felt her own heart breaking into fragments for them all; her fractured heart yearning to be there; to comfort them in their time of need, just as they had once comforted her. Spontaneously she grabbed her coat, caught the bus into town, determinedly strode into the travel agency, sat down and waited to be seen. And as her heart raced, her toes tapped nervously on the hard floor and black doubts crept stealthily into her racing mind as Kai's smiling face crashed into her consciousness. *Only now,* she thought glumly, *he would not be smiling; he would no longer be his cheerful, happy-go-lucky Hawaiian self. He would be a broken, grieving man.* She picked up her bag and walked out the door into the cool, fresh air glad that she was in England; glad that she was away from the sinister sunshine of Kauai which promised endless, sunny days and instead brought heartache and grief; glad that she was walking down long, drab streets and not on soft, white sand which promised so much false comfort; glad that her ears were attune to horns peeping and cars driving swiftly past and not hearing the soft Hawaiian guitars lulling her into a false sense of security where, in fact, she told herself, *there was none; for nothing,* she glumly concluded, *stays sunny forever. After the sunshine comes the rain and it lashes down in torrents.*

Kauai

After the traditional Hawaiian ritualistic internment, Ocean Tia stood silently by her motionless father. Two heartbroken victims displaying a scene of honourable decorum as they graciously accepted colourful leis and comforting hugs and kisses from sympathising mourners. One victim stood determined to rise above the grief; a symbol of pride to the memory of Leialoha; the other already sinking into a private deep pit of silent despair.

Luana watched her younger sibling withdrawing deeper and deeper into his own shell and was becoming increasingly worried. No longer did Kai spontaneously arrive on her doorstep with leis and a cheery smile; they hadn't seen, or heard from him, in weeks. He had refused all forms of communication. Luana let it be. He was grieving. He needed time.

Ocean Tia witnessed her father's rapid decline from a jovial, energetic, enthusiastic and ambitious father to a silent, brooding, apathetic man; not wanting to talk, eat or engage in work; wishing only to join his Leialoha. She attempted, on several occasions, to engage her father in trivial conversation, cooked sumptuous meals, encouraged him to take walks along the beach; her attempts were unsuccessful. He closed the blinds of his bedroom windows and stayed enclosed in his silent tomb, with only his memories as his companions. To his relief Ocean Tia went back to boarding school and he was left in peace.

England

Some weeks later a foreign stamped letter came through Rosemary's letter box. With a hundred and one tasks to do that morning, she hastily shoved it into the depths of her bed table drawer and completely forgot about it.

Chapter Eighteen

The news shook her to the very core of her being. With trembling fingers, she dialled a short number, placed the receiver back on to its cradle and picked it up again.

Click.

"Hello."

"A. Alan."

"Yes. Is that you, Rosemary?"

"Can... can you come over?"

Instantly, on hearing Rosemary's troubled voice he detected something was wrong. "I'll be there."

She heard the click of his receiver and slowly placed hers down, her eyes roaming around the room before resting on her bedside table, her feet swiftly followed her eyes and her fingers her feet, as she hastily retrieved the only medicine, she knew, would soothe her breaking heart. The gentle knock on the door alerted her numbed senses.

"Rosemary." The soft voice was balm to her aching heart. Immediately his eyes darted to the bottle, his heart soaring with relief as he saw the bottle was unopened. Without thinking he grabbed her trembling body into his strong arms and kissed her forehead, her cheeks; her mouth and, in her grief, she responded. He pulled himself away sensing something was not right, as her hungry mouth yearned to be possessed. "What is it, Rosemary?"

"Please." She pressed her mouth to his, as she tried to shut him up and force him to continue.

Instead, he took both her arms and led her downstairs to the sofa and, looking into her glassy eyes asked, "What on earth is it, Rosemary; tell me, please?" For long moments they sat in silence her mouth tightly clamped, her thoughts thousands of kilometres away, while he waited patiently. "Rosemary." He finally encouraged softly. "Please tell me."

She opened her mouth and tried to forcibly exterminate her bone dry words, threw the telegram at him, sat down and diverted her eyes to the enticing golden liquid inside the unopened bottle.

He read each word slowly as they weaved into a scenario. *So, this was what it was all about; Keoki. And now… he was no more.* His heart danced; his soul leaped; his senses reeled with untold happiness. *For the chain that was keeping Rosemary a prisoner was broken. She was free.* His eyes flitted to the woman he secretly loved and immediately his heart stopped dancing; his soul came crashing back down to Earth; his senses numbed as he realised this was no time for rejoicing; for, the deep sadness haunting Rosemary's eyes told him this was going to be a long haul and her spontaneous stab at intimacy a few minutes ago was only her outpouring of grief. He broke the heavy silence with his kind words. "I am proud of you, Rosemary; you didn't touch a drop of alcohol." He glanced at her pale, stern face and his heart ached for her.

"Keoki is dead." She stated in a monotone voice, her eyes glued to the bottle.

"Yes, he is dead." Alan reverberated as a heavy surge of guilt, for the sense of relief he couldn't help but selfishly feel, overtook his consciousness.

"Keoki is dead." She repeated over and over again to the forbidden liquid in the sealed bottle. "Keoki is dead."

"Yes, he is dead, Rosemary." Alan rose and took the bottle off the coffee table.

"Don't you dare," she hissed. "Put it back."

One look at her determined face told him she meant what she said and, obediently, he placed the bottle back on to the table, wondering how the whole scenario would end; *for,* he glumly thought, *it did not bode well.*

Two figures sat in stoic silence, wrapped up in their own misery, as the clock ticked on timelessly. The shrill ringing of the phone alerted them to the present time; five minutes later Alan announced, "Susan has asked me to stay the night here; she's caught up in some kind of emergency at work. Is that all right with you, Rosemary?" She nodded her head silently and they reverted back to their silent musing.

As twilight covered them with its light blanket and they sat in the gathering gloom, the coolness in the air alerted them to the fact that they had been sitting there for ages and had not eaten. As Alan prepared a light meal, Rosemary… *walked along a beach in Kauai and as she took another gulp… she heard his soft words, 'That is not the answer, my friend.'* Abruptly, she opened her eyes, *inwardly raging against the impolite intrusion of her solitude. She opened her mouth to find she could utter no words. Blatantly and unashamedly she took another swill of her potent liquid, hoping this obnoxious stranger would disappear. Her exhausted eyes followed him as he slumped down on to the soft white sand, his broad back leaning against the bark of an aged palm...*

"My name is Keoki." She said aloud, her eager fingers reaching out for the unopened bottle on the coffee table and felt a strong hand covering her hand, like a warm protective glove.

"That is not the answer." Alan said softly. But it was not Alan's voice she heard but Keoki's and, slowly, she released her grip on the cool glass, which had promised so much.

They both forced a cheese and pickle sandwich, with a side plate of salad, down their throats and drank their tea. Looking at her intently he said, "I think you should fly over for the funeral, Rosemary."

Her shocked eyes darted to him.

"Yes, I think you should go; it will, I feel, bring you closure."

"Have you gone mad, Alan?" She stated as a bout of sudden involuntary laughter escaped her mouth, her incredulous eyes staring at him.

"No, I think it is an opportunity for you to say your goodbye properly."

Undiluted rage bubbled and surged furiously through every throbbing vein in Rosemary's tensed body. "But, I don't want to say goodbye." She yelled at the top of her voice.

And there, he dismally concluded, *was her problem. Rosemary Longsdale couldn't; or, wouldn't, let go of the past and, until she did, there would be no hope of her ever finding peace.* "I think you should." He dared to say.

"And how do you think I am going to finance the trip; with coffee beans?"

"I shall finance it for you." He said softly.

Incredulously she stared at him, and through him, seeing nothing but a mass of chaotic absurdity in his ludicrous suggestion.

"Think about it." And with these words he walked out the room and embarked on contemplating his own thoughts in the sanctuary of the spare room.

She took his advice and thought about it... all night long. By morning her mind was made up.

Chapter Nineteen
Kauai

The journey was long and tiresome; from Heathrow taking the long flight to Los Angeles and from there a six hour flight to Kauai. She had ample time to reflect, take stock and prepare herself for what was to come. She was relieved that Hanale had declined Alan's financial offer of accompanying her.

As the plane made a smooth landing, Rosemary looked out on a sunny day and a shimmering stretch of tarmac as she watched the airport staff, in their Hawaiian attire, going about their business. Already she could feel the friendliness and calm exuding from the island. *But this time,* she sorrowfully concluded, *it was going to be so very different.* Her only hope was to be strong enough to survive the onslaught of impending grief. *More importantly, did she have the strength, and courage, to stand face to face with Kai and deny him the privilege of knowing that he had a son?*

She espied Luana and her children from afar and her heart shattered into a thousand tiny fragments. *What would she say to them? What could she do to ease the heart-breaking grief of these gentle people?*

They hugged her tightly, as if not wanting to let her go, and she instantly felt their overwhelming pain, as they placed their frangipani leis around her neck while around them people greeted each other with smiles, laughter and cheerful talk. *Why are you all so damned happy?* She admonished them silently. *Don't you know that Keoki is dead?* Casting them secret cursed looks, she buried her tearful face in Luana's tight embrace.

They rode back to Luana's house in silence. No words were needed. Everything that needed to be said was silently spoken. As Rosemary surveyed the beautiful flowering trees and blossoming foliage, she silently cursed them for thriving so healthily when Keoki was dead and cold.

As Rosemary watched Luana bustling around the kitchen, preparing the evening repast, she said softly, "Thank you for allowing me to stay in your lovely home, Luana."

"It is a great pleasure." Luana smiled warmly; though, Rosemary knew this woman's heart was in shreds. "It is what Keoki would have wanted."

"What happened?" Rosemary asked tentatively.

Luana wiped her hands on her apron and sat down opposite Rosemary. "It was sudden, Lokemele; a heart attack." *At least,* thought Rosemary, *this good man was spared the pain of prolonged suffering.*

They sat on the veranda with the sound of the distant waves as their companions. "If only he'd taken the doctor's advice," said Luana softly and regretfully, as she looked out into the far away distant vastness of the mighty ocean far below.

"What do you mean?" Rosemary's inquisitive eyes flitted to her friend.

"Well, the doctor kept warning him about his heart; he ordered Keoki to go on a diet and to participate in some form of exercise."

"I didn't know he had a health problem," stated Rosemary.

"And Keoki acted as if he didn't have one. His motto was: *Life is too short to worry*, and so he carried on without a care in the world; happy and content in his self-imposed denial that anything was wrong and now he finds himself at Saint Peter's gate."

Rosemary smiled. *Yes,* she mused, *that was the nature of Keoki and he certainly lived and died with that motto in mind.* "Do you think he would have done anything different if he knew how it was going to end, Luana?"

"Do you?"

Both women shook their heads and smiled whimsically.

"Oh, I have got something for you, Lokemele."

Rosemary's eyes shot to Luana, as her plump body rose from the rattan rocker and retreated into the gloomy interior of the house, leaving Rosemary with thoughts of Keoki. Minutes later, Luana returned with an envelope in her hand. "For you, Lokemele from Keoki You are not to read this until you are on the plane, on your way back to England."

Carefully, as if it was a rare jewel to be treasured forever, Rosemary took the envelope and scrutinised the array of yellow hibiscuses depicted cheerfully on one side; for, whatever was inside the envelope, she knew, would be sound advice; the last piece of advice Keoki would give her. She closed her eyes tightly. *It was going to be a long, torturous day tomorrow.*

The first ray of sunlight burst into her bedroom as Rosemary woke up with a start. *Where was she? What was she doing here? Was this a dream?* Slowly it all came back to her. *She was on the Island of Kauai in Luana and Keoki's house and this bright, sunny morning was heralding the day of her dear friend's funeral.* Her guts and mouth craved for an alcoholic drink to numb the gnawing pain; to erase the senses; to allow her to function. The envelope with its bright yellow splayed flowers caught her eye. *Today was Keoki's day; a day to honour and pay her respects to him; a day to remember; a day to treasure forever.*

After taking a refreshing shower she took out her outfit and lay if carefully on the bed. *It was going to be hot,* she mused glumly; *but, still, needs must.* The gentle knock made her eyes flit to the door.

Luana stood at the doorway with a tray of fresh blueberry muffins, slices of fresh pineapple, a fresh pot of coffee and a small vase displaying colourful tropical blooms. "Aloha." She smiled; her smile dying as her eyes rested on the outfit on the bed.

"Is it not suitable?" Rosemary stared with horror at Luana's shocked eyes. She was not prepared for what followed as Luana placed the laden tray on the bedside table, slumped down on the bed and broke into a burst of heart wrenching, uncontrollable sobs, making Rosemary wish she could be swallowed up instantly by a huge black hole.

She stood transfixed by Luana's sudden display of grief and not knowing whether to wrap her arms around the heaving woman, say something or run she stood staring and as she stared she was thrown into further chaotic bemusement, as a bout of hilarious laughter suddenly replaced the heart-breaking sobs. For long moments, one woman stood still as a rod; the other trembled and raked with uncontrollable laughter. Abruptly, the laughter stopped and Luana wrapped her podgy arms around her much confused friend. "My dear, Lokemele; Keoki would rise up and run away from his own casket, if he thought you were contemplating on wearing that outfit."

Rosemary felt deeply hurt, and secretly offended; for, she had spent her own small fortune, and painstaking time, choosing the outfit. "What do you mean?" She cast her serious, questioning eyes on Luana, who was still trying desperately to stifle her escaping laughter.

"Keoki would only allow casual, colourful, cheerful style of attire at his funeral; lots of colourful leis, the sound of soft Hawaiian guitars and lots of laughter and good cheer."

"What!" exclaimed Rosemary unable to believe what she was hearing.

"Keoki would insist on a Hawaiian party; a proper Hawaiian luau. He never wrote his wishes down, that was not his style; but, he did mention it once. No, there's got to be fun, colour and happiness at Keoki's farewell get-together. Incidentally, Lokemele, don't ever call it a funeral. I am sure that at the mere sound of that word he would rise up and die again."

Rosemary cast a forlorn look at her splayed out funeral attire. "Then what am I to wear?"

"Exactly what you are standing in; or, something similar; anything that is casual and, of course, a smile is mandatory."

Rosemary was totally bemused. *But then,* she concluded, *Keoki was Keoki.* Comprehension seeped in.

A couple of hours later standing in a pink Hawaiian print dress, a white frangipani lei around her neck and white sandals and beach bag she felt she was going to a beach party rather than a funeral; though, her heart wrenched mercilessly at the thought of going to Keoki's funeral to party; for, all she wanted to do was wear black, cry buckets and say a quiet prayer for her dear friend. The sight of Akamu and Liliana, almost grown up; laughing and chatting heartily in the garden made her instantly reverse her thinking. *Yes, this was a special time to celebrate Keoki's life; for, he indeed was a good man.*

One underlying gnawing thought, which had been her constant companion since stepping on the plane at Heathrow, tortured her mercilessly; Kai.

Chapter Twenty

Her heart clamped tightly like a vice, as the tropical leafed casket was lowered into the cold Hawaiian earth; the painful regret at not visiting him, when she had the money and the chance, gnawing at every fibre of her unforgiving body. With a heavy heart she turned away from Keoki and followed his family, friends and neighbours to his former home where an informal lavish banquet, in the form of a luau, was prepared; soft guitars playing an old traditional Hawaiian mele. Rosemary saw the dark, long haired girl, attired in a light blue hibiscus printed dress, from afar and wondered who this girl was, standing alone and apart, staring at Keoki's smiling portrait, perched on a bamboo glass topped table, surrounded by opulent colourful blooms and luscious foliage, in a corner of the garden. She had not seen this young girl at the requiem service. *Then again,* she thought, *she wasn't really looking, being wrapped up in her own silent grief with the unnerving thought she may bump into Kai at any given moment.* He was, she was relieved, nowhere in sight. *Probably,* she wrongly concluded, *he was too busy and wrapped up in his own busy life to pay his brother-in-law his last respects.* She jumped as she felt a presence at her side. To her relief it was Luana. "Who is that girl?" Rosemary asked directing her attention once more to the lone figure.

"Oh, that's our lovely Ocean Tia, Kai's daughter; my niece."

Instantly Rosemary felt her heart turn into a block of ice, as the evocative name reverberated in her head, like the distant waves below. Swallowing hard the lump in her throat she managed to say, "A beautiful name for a beautiful girl."

"Yes, yes," agreed Luana.

"Kai..." The strangled name in her throat managed to exhume itself from Rosemary's parched mouth.

"Let's not talk about him." Luana linked her arm through Rosemary's arm. "Come, let us reminisce over some photographs of Keoki taken in much happier times." Together they made their way to a large display board, bordered on all sides with a rich display of colourful hibiscuses, plumerias and frangipanis; interwoven with lush, green foliage on which numerous photographs were displayed. Rosemary looked intently at the images of a smiling Keoki with his family, her eyes switching to a particular image where he was balancing on a surfboard and another in which he was swimming leisurely in the ocean; her eyes flitted and stayed on the photograph of him in the midst of a beach walk, her mind wondering why Luana had abruptly switched the conversation away from Kai. Curiosity got the better of her; an onslaught of questions bombarding her head. *Why wasn't he at the funeral? Why was Ocean Tia alone? Why did Luana not wish to discuss her brother?* A sudden, inexplicable urge to see him overtook her and, turning away from Luana, she took tentative steps towards the young girl.

"Please don't." Luana was instantly at Rosemary's side. "Ocean Tia needs time."

"Time for what?"

"Time to adjust; to find herself; to find her father."

Rosemary's brow visibly furrowed into creases. "Where is he?"

"Nobody knows."

Chapter Twenty-One

Rosemary needed time alone to think; to remember; to reminisce and to forget. Alone on the beach she wandered, as she had done many years before, looking out on to the expansive ocean. *Where does it end?* She asked herself. *Other islands... other lives... loves lost and found... loves never to be rekindled, lost in the mists of time. But Keoki,* she mused, *would never be forgotten. He had too much life and hope; too many dreams for his memory ever to be extinguished.* Her mind drifted to the first time she ever set eyes on her beloved friend... So many years ago, it seemed like yesterday when... *She spotted the solitary figure from afar and took another gulp of the potent liquid. Oh God, I hope he just passes by and doesn't embark on some trivial holiday talk, she hoped against hope, taking another swill and thinking she had better look occupied in a different way, hid her bottle and retrieved her best-seller; opening it and gluing her eyes fixedly to the text she had no intention of reading... The ominous figure was drawing nearer and nearer. Now she could see his bright blue Hawaiian printed shirt, his black shorts as her eyes involuntarily rose to his plump, short body, his dark face and generous crop of ruffled black hair and rested on his twinkling dark eyes. Swiftly she diverted them back to the text below... "Aloha." She replied begrudgingly... Just go away, she silently urged, and leave me alone...* She opened her eyes to the reality of it all. *And now,* she thought, *he has gone away forever.* Her eyes swam around the deserted beach. "Where are you, Keoki?" She asked aloud, half expecting him to reply. "Where are you?" She repeated. Her question was answered; for, she felt his presence all around her in the blue sky and the roaring waves; in the brilliance of the majestic sun and the hypnotic beauty of tropical blooms; alive in the luscious foliage around and in the soft breeze of the romantic trade winds; in every kind word and gesture; in every smile and tear. He was everywhere and in everything and everyone; always and forever.

With a renewed spring in her step, she was about to turn and make her way out of the boundary of the beach, when she spotted Ocean Tia scanning the beach and looking far out into the ocean. Cautiously she took steps towards the young girl, who was totally oblivious to the older woman's presence; lost in her search for something she could not find. Tentatively Rosemary took further steps towards Ocean Tia, mysteriously drawn to her and feeling something was troubling this lone figure who was Kai's daughter and Hanale's half-sister. The Hawaiian girl turned and gasped. "Oh, Aloha." She smiled displaying rows of perfectly formed, pristine, white teeth.

Rosemary smiled back. "You are Ocean Tia; yes?"

"Yes, yes." She nodded as she twisted a thin stem of a pink hibiscus in her long golden-brown fingers, her warm brown eyes on the stranger before her. "I am sorry; do I know you?"

"Yes… no… not really. You were at Keoki's funeral; I saw you standing by his portrait."

The girl smiled reminiscently. "Yes, my dear beloved Uncle Keoki; how I shall miss him."

How we shall all miss him, Rosemary was about to say; deciding not to utter the words, lest they sound too familiar and forward.

Ocean Tia silently scrutinised Rosemary with her dark, mysterious eyes. "You are from…"

"England." Rosemary prompted.

"Ah… England." The girl looked far away into the vastness of the ocean, from where her name came. "How I long to go there one day. I have heard so much about London, the Houses of Parliament, the Tower of London, Big Ben." She fell silent, lost in her own daydream.

"And, one day, I am sure you will visit my country."

The girl's smile widened. "Maybe," she whispered.

They stood in awkward silence, staring out into the shimmering blueness beyond; two strangers with Kai and Hanale as their bond.

Rosemary's heart wrenched mercilessly longing to tell Ocean Tia about Hanale; *for,* she concluded, *she had a right to know.* Instead, she said softly, "Ocean Tia; what a beautiful name."

"Yes, yes, it is. My mother wanted me to have an evocative name, which induced strong images and feelings. She loved the lure of the mighty ocean; she was always entranced by its spell and Tia comes from a Greek name meaning goddess, apparently Tia was my father's addition."

The two names combined, thought Rosemary, *conjured up a strong romantic image.* "Your parents certainly gave you a name full of meaning." She smiled.

They continued to stare into the desolate ocean and, except for the constant roaring of wave upon wave, they stood in silence. Eventually Ocean Tia softly said, "I often come here to think about my mother. She… she was killed in a car crash." The girl's eyes looked into the far away distance, her following words making Rosemary's heart stop. "Now, I come here to look for my father."

A multitude of questions urged to escape; to ask, to probe and to seek answers. Rosemary clamped her lips tight, biting her lower lip to prevent desperate words from seeping out. But, she needed to know. And now the girl had proceeded to walk on. The moment was lost. And soon she would be going back to England, thousands of kilometres away across the world, to a different continent. *She might as well live on the moon.* Rosemary dismally concluded. *For the chances of ever seeing Ocean Tia again were very remote.* And so she let the words fall out of her mouth. "What happened to your father, Ocean Tia?"

For long moments, no answer was given, as they walked along the beach in silence, with only the background sound of the hypnotic waves, and some birds screeching away in the distance, then Ocean Tia spoke softly. "He is grieving for my mother." Swiftly she turned away from the waves, smiled sweetly and said, "It was lovely to meet you. Aloha." She turned her sad face away from Rosemary and left the older woman to continue with her solitary walk, a thousand resurrected thoughts whirling around in her head.

Looking out at the blue undulating blanket of water rolling on and on, Rosemary came to a decision. She would have to find out everything she could about Kai, before it was too late; for, one day, his son, Hanale, would need to know.

Chapter Twenty-Two

She had three full days to find out all that she needed to know and then she would leave the Island of Kauai forever and, with it, the secrets of the past; secrets her son, Hanale, had a right to know for they concerned his father and were a link to his identity. *But,* she mused, *Luana seemed tight-lipped, unresponsive to reveal anything about Kai* making Rosemary feel there was something disturbing in the mystery of it all. She clung tight to this notion, intending to find out the truth. Her chance came sooner than she had expected. She had not prepared herself adequately for the bitterness of the truth.

Slipping into her flip-flops Rosemary espied Luana walking out the lounge, with a large vase of drooping tropical blooms, and she ceased her opportunity. "I have been talking to Ocean Tia on the beach," she said casually as her eyes intently scrutinised Luana's reaction; seeing her flinch as she placed the vase on a nearby cupboard, her back turned to Rosemary. The stony silence told her she had hit a raw nerve; her need to know more propelled her to stretch her curious tentacles further. "She says she is searching for her father."

The oppressive silence charged the room with a heavy blanket of mystery and suspense, which seemed to overpower the two women, suffocating them with anxiety and uncertainty. "Luana."

"I heard you, Lokemele."

"Can you tell me anything about Ocean Tia's father?" Rosemary stared unblinkingly at the hunched back while the podgy fingers, she could not see, were picking nervously at drooping blooms and dead foliage.

"What business is it of yours, Lokemele?"

The abrupt tone inwardly shook Rosemary; she ploughed on undeterred. "I knew Kai."

"You slept with him. You did not know him."

Luana's harsh words stung. Laboriously Rosemary gathered a defensive string of words and formulated them into a sentence. "No, I didn't know him,

Luana; but, I had feelings for him; I still care for him." *Damn it, you stupid woman; I have had his son!* She desperately wanted to scream. Instead, she clamped her lips tightly and waited, with bated breath, for Luana's response.

"Better you don't care." Luana stated coldly taking herself, and her vase with the dying foliage and blooms, into the inner sanctuary of the kitchen and leaving Rosemary more bemused than ever.

Her chance came again, when Akamu and Liliana had gone out for the evening to a friend's birthday luau and the two women sat on the veranda, watching the sun set at the end of a glorious day. "Kai is a beach bum." Luana stated starkly into the still, dusky evening air. Her unvarnished words shocked Rosemary to the very core of her being, her eyes shooting to the older woman, who seemed to be staring straight into the dark pit of oblivion, from which she dug out more scathing words to add to her hoard of verbal ammunition. "He is a good-for-nothing bum, who not only is ruining his own life but the life of his one and only child too."

Rosemary couldn't believe what she was hearing. Suddenly she felt the distant ocean and the changing sky closing in on her, suffocating her; killing her with their calm, tropical beauty as she felt herself floating uncontrollably; lost somewhere in a parallel universe, where everything was out of kilter and she was whirling, twirling and spinning out of control. She blinked hard and blinked harder, as she turned her bemused eyes to the woman sitting next to her; the woman who was, in fact, Hanale's auntie. "What do you mean, Luana?" She asked, feeling as if her voice did not belong to her; or, she to it.

Raw, undiluted silence reigned with only the distant echo of the waves accompanying their distorted thoughts. Finally, Luana broke the ice and, staring directly ahead as if into a different world, she said, "Kai, as you know, lost his sweetheart, the only woman he really ever loved." She turned her sad eyes to Rosemary, who stared directly ahead, feeling a sharp blade slice through her heart. Plunging the knife deeper into Rosemary's heart Luana continued, "Despite having countless relationships with numerous amounts of women, Leialoha was the only woman Kai really cherished and loved. And, when she was taken by the good Lord, he fell into a deep pit of misery and despair from which he has not climbed out. He has lost everything his money, his business, his contacts, his home and cars and other possessions as well as his friends; but, most of all, he has lost his self-respect. He has become a liar, a cheat, a thief and a drunkard; but most of all, what really hurts, is that he has abandoned his one and only child, Ocean Tia, who now resides with her maternal grandparents. She combs the local beaches every day for any sign of her father; she will never give up."

Like the blade, Luana's words thrust deeply into Rosemary's heart; each word piercing deeper and deeper; each word more probing and more damaging to her image of Kai the handsome, extroverted, cheerful Hawaiian who seemed to have had it all.

Luana cut through Rosemary's thoughts adding, "Nobody knows where my brother is; nobody cares except, that is, for Ocean Tia. She cares. She searches in every nook and cranny. She goes home to her maternal grandparents and comes back the next day to resume her search."

"I thought she resided at the boarding school."

Luana emitted a scathing laugh. "With what to finance that kind of education, Hawaii's finest coffee beans?"

"Where did all his money go?"

"Alcohol… Oh, I don't know where the rest has gone." She shook her head despondently; an afterthought prompting her to switch her eyes to Rosemary, regret lacing her exhausted eyes. "I am sorry, Lokemele; I did not want to mention alcohol. I know you had some problems with…"

"Keoki told you?" Rosemary interrupted.

"There were no secrets between us."

"No." Rosemary smiled sadly. "But still, Kai had you and Keoki to turn to."

Luana did not reply and silence reigned once more, leaving Rosemary to feel there was more and it was painful. She probed further. "Did he not come to you?" Witnessing a veil of tears shroud Luana's eyes she quickly added, "I am sorry."

"He robbed us. He took all of Keoki's money, which wasn't much, and since then we have not seen him. He did not even bother to turn up for Keoki's farewell luau; that hurts."

"Perhaps he didn't know about Keoki's passing."

"He knew." Luana's glassy eyes stared out into the distance, where the golden sun flamed as it majestically bowed into the depths of the ocean, making the distant water around a liquid gold. They sat in still, tropical silence; both wrapped up in their dismal thoughts which, somehow, mismatched the night's beauty. Luana felt Keoki's comforting presence and her pain was eased; Rosemary felt nothing but a lonely, empty void enveloping her; feeling that the island she loved had lost its warmth, serenity and beauty and had become cold, troubled, empty and cruel. She yearned to be on the plane going home, away from this so-called tropical paradise, which now seemed to represent death, betrayal and a world she no longer wished to inhabit.

She tossed and turned. Fragments of images crashed in and out of her fitful sleep. Images of Keoki were replaced by images of Kai which, in an instant, became Keoki once more. One moment they were both alive healthy and smiling; in the next fragment they were in the gutter dishevelled and stone dead. She woke up with a jump not knowing where she was. The gentle rustling and tapping of the palm leaves against her window alerted her to her geographical position and, with it, came dark thoughts of Kai… *wandering along the desolate beach; dirty, dishevelled; a bum. And… Ocean Tia searching… always searching; never giving up… searching…* And with these images came a stark and brutal realisation. She had to do something… before it was too late.

Chapter Twenty-Three

Rosemary had no time to lose; two days in which to do something. She racked her empty brain, whilst picking unenthusiastically at her light breakfast of tropical fruits. Nothing came to mind. Quickly scribing a note to Luana she grabbed her beach bag, slipped on her flip-flops and walked down the narrow, tropical bordered bendy lanes to the beach. How brilliant, virginal and unspoilt it looked. Ocean Tia came crashing into her mind.

She had to find her, to find out more about her and time was of the essence. Scouring the deserted beach she turned to go when, in the distance, she espied a lonely figure. Her heart leaped. It was Ocean Tia. *But, how would she approach her? What would she say to her that would not sadden her further?* She knew she had to tread very carefully.

Ocean Tia's warm smile melted and pained Rosemary's heart.

"Any sign of your father?" asked Rosemary.

The young girl's eyes strayed out on to the far horizon and Rosemary knew her answer. As they walked together, the cool water lapping over their feet, they engaged in casual conversation and, as the talk turned to England, a sudden and persistent idea haunted Rosemary's mind, causing spontaneous words to spew out of her mouth. "Would you like an English pen pal, Ocean Tia; I know someone who, I think, would jump at the chance?" The moment the words escaped she regretted her impulsiveness, wishing she could turn back the clock. The look in the young girl's eyes told her she could do no such thing; for, they shone out in excitement; an exuberance; a new hope to cling to. There was no going back.

"Who?"

"Oh, just someone I know," replied Rosemary wondering what on earth Hanale was going to make of all this.

It was settled. Addresses were exchanged and, before they parted, Rosemary touched lightly the soft, golden skin of Ocean Tia's arm. "You will let me know if you ever find your father?"

"Of course." Ocean Tia smiled warmly. They hugged and the young girl ran along the beach with an added spring in her youthful steps.

Rosemary walked off in the opposite direction, feeling as if she had just stirred a hornet of angry wasps.

Chapter Twenty-Four
England

Alone and stern-faced he stood at the arrivals area. The sight of Rosemary stirred his heart and he forced a smile, making Rosemary's smile vanish instantly sensing something was not quite right.

"Is Hanale okay?" She asked nervously as they hugged.

"It's Susan." Alan grabbed hold of Rosemary's suitcase to avert his troubled face. "She knows I funded your trip and she's adding six and six and getting sixty-six. She's got it into her head that we are betraying her; that we are…"

Rosemary didn't hear the rest as one word hammered loudly in her head; the word which was so familiar to her; the word she had accused Tim and Claire of doing and now it was being used unfairly against her.

"I hope you put Susan straight, Alan." She stated as the car sped along the motorway. His silence unnerved her and her eyes darted to him. "Please tell me you did put her straight, Alan." She was met with more silence as her heart raced, like the expensive car she was sitting in. "Alan!" Her heart now thumped mercilessly as his lips remained firmly compressed. *Oh God,* she thought, *what Hell have I come home to?* She stared ahead seeing yet another friendship in tatters.

The news of his mother, hooking him up with a girl thousands of kilometres away, drove a wedge between mother and son. Hanale told his mother, in no uncertain terms, that he wanted nothing to do with this… this Ocean Tia; least of all write to her. "What kind of name is Ocean Tia anyway?" he smirked.

The name of your half-sister, Rosemary wanted to shout back at him; instead, her lips remained clamped.

She ploughed through the following days, being out of sync with her son and having gained a silent enemy out of her friend, who refused to speak or see Rosemary who, in turn, drew on her memories of Kauai as her only source of comfort, from which she derived an inner, inexplicable hope. The thought of Ocean Tia made her hope real; for, she was the link between the past and present; Kauai and England; Kai and Hanale; the past and the future and, like the great expanse of water she was named after, she represented renewed life.

One evening in October, as the nights were fast drawing in, Rosemary closed the curtains and relaxed to a CD of soft, tropical music, taking her back to the island she always regarded as her second home. Her eyes rose to Hanale as he walked in from football practise, slumped down on the sofa and, in a monotone voice, asked, "Did you see my father in Kauai?"

She had been expecting a question regarding Kai for many years and, yet, it shook her to the very core; for, although she had rehearsed a thousand times what she would say, she now found herself devoid of all words; let alone the one needed to answer her son's straightforward question; her eyes staring starkly at… *a dishevelled, filthy figure walking the lonely beach* and a sharp iced blade thrust deeper and deeper into her thudding heart.

"Mum… Mum; are you all right?" Hanale stared at his mother's ashen face, her eyes stark and wide and staring straight ahead. "Mum!"

She turned and faced her son.

"Did you see my father?" All of a sudden the urge to know his father's whereabouts was of paramount importance, as he began to wonder why his mother wouldn't; or, couldn't answer a simple question and then came his answer.

"No." Rosemary stated wanting to scream, *But I saw his daughter, your half-sister,* her eyes staring directly at her son; but, thousands of kilometres away, her heart torn in shreds.

The youngster shook his head in mild despair, rose and ran up the stairs for a shower.

But, her own stark, unspoken words whirled round and round in Rosemary's head… *I saw his daughter… I saw his daughter…* and she knew the day was fast approaching, when she would have to tell Hanale everything.

The back burner of her mind was full of things simmering away, threatening to boil over if she didn't start attending to them soon. But, before she could put a lid on her problems a distraction came to her door.

Chapter Twenty-Five

The banging on the door was ferocious and was followed by another round of equally demanding thuds. Before she opened the door, Rosemary knew exactly who she was to encounter, bracing herself for the onslaught.

"What the hell do you think you are playing at, Rosemary Longsdale?"

As Rosemary stared back at the angry eyes, the red face and twisted mouth she knew she was in for a hard time and she was not to be disappointed in her premonition. "Come in, Susan."

Susan crashed her way in, almost knocking her friend down in the process, and propped her back against the sink cupboard, her arms akimbo. "What on earth do you think you are playing at?" She repeated icily. And, before Rosemary had time to figure out a line of defence, she added, "If you think you can drive a wedge between my man and me, you can think again." She wagged her stubby finger in front of Rosemary's nose. "I shall never—NEVER! allow you to steal my man away from me."

Rosemary side-stepped her friend, as a surge of uncontrollable laughter spewed out of her mouth in fitful bursts. "Steal, steal your man! Have you gone stark raving mad, Susan?"

"He funded your trip. What favour did you bestow on him in return, Rosemary?" Susan asked coldly, her icy eyes steadily fixed on her friend. "I am not stupid. I know how much a trip to Hawaii can set you back."

With great determination, Rosemary managed to still her laughter and said in a steady voice, "Then you will also know, if you cared to research deeper, that I promised to pay Alan back every single penny."

Suddenly Susan felt a fool, her eyes dropping to the tiled floor as she admitted quietly, "No; I didn't know that."

"Well, before jumping to ludicrous conclusions in the future, Susan; I suggest you get to grips with the facts. Do you want a coffee?" She turned and grabbed the kettle.

But, as they drank their coffees, in a rare subdued atmosphere, Susan dropped another bombshell, as she stared into the depths of her black liquid. "I have seen the way Alan looks at you, Rosemary."

Rosemary brought her coffee cup up to her lips and took a lingering sip. *Yes, she had seen the way he looked at her too.* But; even more worrying, she knew she also felt something for the man she had once rejected.

Chapter Twenty-Six

Hanale stared at the envelope, with its foreign stamps, addressed to him and his young heart turned into a lump of stone, as he shook his head in bitter incredulity at his own mother's audacity. He had thought that one day, in his own time and in his own way, in the distant future, he might search for his father; never expecting this delicate issue to be thrust upon him without prior consultation. After long, torturous, indecisive minutes he ran down the stairs, the burning envelope in his hand, as a hoard of accusing words swam round and round in his head and his pained heart beat with betrayal. Abruptly he stopped, his angry eyes focussed on his tearful mother and his heart melted. Reluctantly he stuffed the sealed envelope into his jeans pocket, his mouth abandoning his rehearsed words of bitter accusation and hastily formulating a string of sympathetic words. "Mum, what's the matter?" He looked at her bent head, heard her muffled snuffles and stared at the woman he owed everything to. "Mum." Slowly she raised her glassy eyes to him and dropped them, overtaken by a fresh bout of tears. "Mum, what's the matter?" He sat down on the opposite chair and his heart broke. *How could he have secretly cursed this woman he dearly loved?* He asked himself and, at that moment, he decided he would not break his mother's heart further by mentioning the letter. It would be his secret.

Her tears turned into heart wrenching sobs and he left her to grieve alone for Keoki; to grieve secretly for Kai, her son's father who had given him life and now was destroying his own life. *Where was this all going to end?* She sobbed, her fingers touching the crumpled envelope in her apron pocket. Bringing it out, her blurry eyes tried to focus on the neatly addressed envelope. *Ocean Tia,* she mused, *their only hope.* A silent tear dropped on to the envelope and immediately created a greyish-black smudge, making her hand-written name illegible. Gradually her sobs subsided and, brushing away the residue of tears from her face, she roughly tore open the envelope and read:

Aloha. It was a true blessing to have found you on the beach, Lokemele; for, now I feel I have a friend I can share my feelings with, even though we are thousands of kilometres apart... I thought I saw a glimpse of my father yesterday; but, by the time I had a chance to catch up with the lonely figure, he had disappeared. Where? I do not know. I shall keep searching. An old lady told me she had seen him at the local church. He is not a church goer; but, I shall scour all the local churches just in case... We are having wall-to-wall sunshine; but, in my heart I feel only a numbness I cannot describe... An icy blade thrust into Rosemary's heart as she read on. *I have sent your son, Hanale, a letter of introduction. Perhaps we could be friends. Please keep in touch, Lokemele. Aloha.* Rosemary reread Ocean Tia's letter, folded it up and placed it back into the envelope. *It's strange,* she thought. *Hanale has not mentioned any letter. Perhaps it hasn't arrived yet.*

Dormant thoughts which had slept soundly in the depths of Hanale's heart began, like a grumbling volcano, to wake and stir. Questions his young heart had buried deep bubbled to the surface and he found himself thinking more and more about his father. His haunting image was like a chameleon, changing constantly according to Hanale's mood. One day he was a cheerful, happy-go-lucky Hawaiian riding the majestic surf; the next he was a seriously minded academic who would accept no nonsense from anyone; another time he would be a gentle, softly-spoken, sunny smiled man. But always the image was of a good, caring man. So, the seed was planted and it began to grow slowly and consistently and with each passing day Hanale wondered more and more, asking himself more and more questions which he couldn't possibly answer, knowing the knowledge lay with his mother. She could tell him more, he was sure, but not at the present time. She was grieving and needed time, not pressure, to grieve in peace.

Rosemary felt she was at a crossroads, aware that in the centre of the crossroads lay the future of the lives of two people. *That,* she told herself, *was not in the lap of the gods; it was in her own hands.* She was facing a stark choice; to run away from Kai forever and deny her son the privilege and right of knowing his biological father; or, she could embrace life with all its warts and blemishes and turn them into a thing of beauty. Whichever road she took she knew, without a doubt, it would be a long and challenging road full of doubts, obstacles, fears and possible regret.

Chapter Twenty-Seven

As she opened the door a smile spread on the faces of two dear friends; their recent confrontation over Alan forgotten. Minutes later Rosemary felt her heart turn to stone as Susan's words rushed out.

"So, anyway, we have set a date and, it goes without saying, you shall be my chief bridesmaid. You will, won't you, Rose?" She didn't wait for her friend's answer as she rambled on excitedly, "You and I are both too long in the tooth for frills and flounces; so, you can choose your own frock, as long as it doesn't outshine mine, of course. I don't want Alan regretting it isn't you he is marrying. Say something, Rosemary... Congratulations maybe." She prompted giggling softly. "Anyway, girl, get something special we can drink out of your cupboard."

"You know I don't drink alcohol." Rosemary muttered almost inaudibly, as she tried desperately to summon up a grain of happiness for her friend; feeling instead a growing inexplicable loneliness, as if something very precious was slipping away.

"Surely one won't harm," piped Susan her eyes silently challenging her friend.

Rosemary's heart raced; in seconds her impatient fingers were delving into a cupboard and, from its inner depths, she withdrew a small bottle of brandy and, pouring out a generous amount into two glasses, sat and stared at the entrancing liquid.

"Cheers!" Enthused Susan bringing her glass up to her lips, her eyes intently focussed on her friend.

"Cheers." Rosemary raised her glass, caught her friend's eyes and slowly lowered the glass. What she had seen in her friend's eyes chilled her to the bone, froze her heart and awakened all her senses.

"Come on, Rose; aren't you going to drink to my future with Alan?"

Rosemary's eyes flitted back to Susan's eyes and in them she saw deceit, envy and malice. In that instant, she recognised Susan for who she was a cunning, conniving foe who wanted to destroy her life in a secret revenge. "I am sorry; no." Rosemary stated, hoping her so-called friend did not detect the involuntary venom which had slid slyly into her voice. She rose and swiftly poured the golden liquid down the sink, still longing for its comfort.

Half an hour later Susan was gone, leaving Rosemary with a multitude of uncomfortable questions and yearning for the one thing, she knew, she could not allow herself to have; for, one drop could send her off the precipitous cliff.

Throughout the long evening her mind was bombarded with thoughts of Hanale, Kai, Ocean Tia, Luana and interwoven with torrid thoughts of Susan. Finally, a picture began to emerge. *Ocean Tia was the key and she needed her. To be of use to anyone she herself would have to be sober; to remain sober, she had to get to the bottom of Susan's devious intentions.*

Standing outside the door her heart raced wildly. As it opened she was standing face to face with the man Susan was planning to marry.

Chapter Twenty-Eight

His puzzled eyes softened and he smiled warmly. "Rosemary; how nice to see you. Come in... come in," he gestured with his hand.

She followed him through the airy, spacious hallway into a large lounge, fully aware she was trespassing on Susan's territory; feeling she had no right to be there with the man who was soon to marry her best friend. Nervously her eyes darted around. He sensed her apprehension. "Susan is not here, Rosemary."

Heaving a heavy sigh of relief she refused his offer of a coffee and plunged into the deep. "Susan came round, Alan. She told me about your engagement, asked me to be her chief bridesmaid and tried to persuade me to drink alcohol." She could feel his inner wrath, though his warm eyes remained steadily fixed on her.

"You didn't..."

"I swilled it down the sink." She interjected, feeling his gentle hand on her arm and the surge of tiny electrical sparks moving up her arm, as a flutter of crazy butterflies performed a merry dance in the pit of her stomach. She dropped her eyes to the plush cream carpet where it was safe to stare.

"I am so very proud of you, Rosemary. What you did, I know, would not have been easy."

She digested his comment choosing not to honour it with a reply; instead she dared to raise her eyes to his stating firmly, "I don't know what Susan is playing at, Alan; but..."

"I know exactly what she is playing at, Rose. She has not forgiven me for financing your trip to Hawaii. She thinks you are a threat. She wants you out of the way."

"By sending me on the road of no-return?"

"By any which way she can." He retorted bluntly.

"And you want to marry a woman with such a jealous mind?" Instantly she regretted the words which had escaped her mouth. The words he said shook her to the very core of her being, making her whole body freeze like some sort of solidified statue. *No; I don't want to marry Susan.* His stark words echoed loudly in her head; she turned her eyes away from him. "I've got to go, Alan." She grabbed the door handle and felt his hand on her hand like a protective glove; felt her entire body go from ice into meltdown. Harshly thrusting his hand away, she opened the door and ran out on to the drive and the sanctuary of her car. Staring starkly ahead she switched on the ignition and accelerated out the drive. She paid no heed to the car approaching the drive from the opposite direction.

Susan's heart raced wildly as her car headed towards the entrance of the door. Her worst fear had been realised.

Chapter Twenty-Nine

Rosemary felt as if her whole life was falling apart. Keoki was gone; her so-called best friend was not to be trusted; Kai and his daughter tortured her thoughts and her son had become withdrawn and moody for no apparent reason. *And, as for Alan...* She felt herself falling deeper and deeper into a dark and dismal mire and knew, if she was not careful, she was in danger of drowning. *And that,* she thought sadly, *would be very much to Susan's satisfaction. They had been good friends; but now a deeper, darker, more sinister side of Susan was emerging; a side which was volatile and dangerous; a side she did not want to know* as she asked herself the same questions over and over again. *Why did Susan want her to start drinking; what could she possibly gain from her downfall?* The reality became stark and real. Susan was no friend. *As for Alan, he had made his proverbial bed; or had he?* She asked herself as his stark words crashed into her head... *No; I don't want to marry Susan.* Mercilessly they haunted her throughout the ensuing days, mingled with more pressing issues rising to the forefront.

Hanale began to drop a few casual enquiries about Kauai and one specific question which cut Rosemary's heart in two. They had been sitting together watching some dull soap on the television when, out of the blue, sprang Hanale's words. "Do you know whereabouts my father is in Kauai, Mum?" His words were innocent but were laden with meaning. And, as she struggled in vain to find the appropriate words, he made matters worse by involuntarily throwing guilt, remorse and a sense of betrayal at his mother's door. Her eyes stared starkly at the moving screen, full of images she did not register, and silently shook her head from side to side. His next words made her racing heart stop. "I have a letter from Dad." Two pairs of eyes stared at the screen as a heavy, stifling silence covered them like a death shroud.

Nervously Hanale dug his fingers into his jeans pocket, dug out a crumpled envelope and placed it on his mother's lap and waited for a response, feeling his guts wrench ferociously, while her head whirled with one nagging conflicting thought... *How on earth could Hanale have received a letter from his father when, apparently, Kai's only interest was inducing his own premature death?* Slowly her eyes dropped to the sealed envelope on her lap and her heart skipped a beat, as a huge wave of blessed relief washed over her tortured soul and a smile danced on her lips. "Son, this letter is from your Hawaiian pen-pal." She stated as, in that instant, he felt his whole world come crashing down and around him; his eyes still glued to the moving screen, the images he saw seemed to be the only real things; everything else seemed unreal, detached, belonging to a different world, a world he did not want to be a part of; for, since the envelope had dropped through the letter box, his casual attitude towards his unknown father had changed into a secret hope and now this hope was dying before it ever began to truly thrive. "It's from Ocean Tia." Rosemary looked at her son's sad eyes. Silently he rose and strode out of the room leaving his mother with her thoughts and a raw realisation that her son's attitude towards his father was changing; his disappointment was evident. She closed her eyes tightly musing dismally... *If only he knew the full story that his father, who was once a charming, upstanding islander of Kauai was now a beach bum and that the girl who had written to him was his half-sister and that his mother had always harboured secret feelings for this man she could never have...* She shook her head. *It didn't bear thinking about.*

Chapter Thirty

In the throes of grave suspicions, Susan steam-rolled into preparing her engagement party; she was certainly not going to allow the likes of Rosemary Longsdale to get in her way. She planned to marry Alan whether he wanted to or not.

Alan had a different plan. He was going to let Susan down gently, then make a cautious move on the woman he truly loved.

Rosemary had no plans at all. What fleeting feelings she had for Alan, she firmly locked away in the back of her mind; never, as far as she was concerned, to be resurrected. Susan was going to marry her man and that was the end of the story.

Susan had lots of doubts and suspicions niggling away in her overactive mind and they all involved Rosemary. Her latest and most worrying thought was that she had seen, with her own jealous eyes, Rosemary driving away from Alan's house and, to add fuel to her envious fire, Alan did not mention a word about her visit. She decided to keep silent on the matter; the last thing she wanted was a full-blown confrontation which could, she concluded, result in a broken engagement.

Rosemary dreaded the party, conjuring up umpteen different excuses; knowing they all sounded futile for a *no-show* at the party would throw up instant suspicion. She was thankful Hanale was invited and surprised when he accepted; so, armed with a secret plan of an early exit, she made her way to the posh hotel, her heart racing as the lively music and hearty laughter drifted out the opened windows, dreading the moment she'd come face to face with her secret nemesis and her man.

She spotted him at an open doorway; Alan relaxed, laughing and chatting with friends; his fiancée glued to his side, like a limpet, showing off her man, her ring and their unity to the whole world. Pinning on her best smile Rosemary strode purposefully on, her heart freezing momentarily as she caught Alan's warm smile and Susan's firmer grip on her man and her fixed smile, as dangerous as venom. "Rosemary… Hanale, how wonderful to see you," she gushed.

Rosemary's heart tugged, her smile also fixed as she hugged Susan.

The evening was long and torturous as Rosemary engaged herself in the art of laborious mingling, with people she barely knew and most she didn't know at all; secretly disappointed that Hanale had left her side to socialise with some friends. Excuses to leave early were unsuccessful. Making the most of a bad situation, she found some acquaintances and began dancing to the latest beat.

Two pairs of eyes were watching her; uncharacteristically jealous, possessive eyes scrutinising her every move, wishing the woman dancing was the woman standing by his side.

Despite her inner reservations, Rosemary found she was enjoying herself. *The food and music were good, the company surprisingly pleasant and even Hanale,* she thought, *was having a good time with his mates. And why not? He would experience sadness soon enough.* She did not see something slip into her pineapple juice; she did not taste the alien substance as she gulped the liquid down; she only knew she was feeling happy and relaxed; the first time she had felt so good since… since… she didn't know when. And, after a second, third and fourth drink, she felt she wanted to party all night and forget about Alan, Susan, Keoki, Kai, Luana, Tim, Claire and Ocean Tia and, yes, to forget about her only son and to dance… dance… dance until dawn; to feel like a teenager without any cares, any worries, any responsibilities, any past; just to be herself young, carefree, happy and free.

Alan's attention was drawn towards this lively, atypically gregarious woman; as an uneasy feeling stirred in the pit of his stomach, while a devious smile spread on his fiancée's lips; for, her plan was maturing into fruition, as Rosemary gyrated wildly in front of her revengeful eyes; joyous laughter emitting from her happy mouth, as she took another gulp of her juice spiked with straight vodka.

Susan turned her victorious eyes to her fiancé. "I think my chief bridesmaid is looking too much the worse for wear." She giggled as Alan's concerned eyes looked on, a deepening suspicion lacing his thoughts.

Rosemary was totally oblivious to everybody's thoughts and oblivious to her son's worried, surreptitious glances as alcohol began to take hold of all her senses. She had not felt so happy, so free in years and she wanted more of this magic; much more.

Susan was only too happy to oblige her friend. Alan was not. Young Hanale's secret fears were growing by the second. Then, all hell let loose as a laughing Rosemary came crashing down on to a table, laden with an assortment of multi-coloured drinks. Hands came quickly to her aid and amongst them was one caring, helpful pair of hands.

The party carried on. Susan's private vendetta came swiftly to an end; her evil plan crashing in and around her as she begrudgingly watched Alan abandon her and run to Rosemary's side. A hard, sickly lump rose to Susan's throat, as her eyes enviously lingered on her fiancé, as he gently helped Rosemary to the sanctuary of another room. *Her plan had worked,* she smiled wryly; *but, at what cost?* Her heart thumped mercilessly as her eyes darted to Hanale. He had seen his mother's despicable behaviour, of that she was certain; but, from where she was standing, he seemed to be more concerned than disgusted. *Her plan had back-fired,* she concluded miserably. *And now, all she could do was to look on and wait for the fall-out, which was sure to come.*

And it did.

Chapter Thirty-One

An hour after her suitcase was unceremoniously dumped outside Alan's door, Susan posted two envelopes one addressed to Rosemary; the other to Hanale and smirked deviously.

Alan had no regrets. Secretly he had been intending to disengage himself from his insincere fiancée; for, without sincerity and trust, he knew, the relationship was doomed. As he watched her walking down the drive to her car, turning back to take a last glimpse of what she had lost, he heaved a heavy sigh of relief as he said aloud to her disappearing figure, "You, my dear, would have indeed been a heavy yoke around my neck." His thoughts drifted to Rosemary. What had happened to her on the night of the party was not of her own making, of that he was certain; equally determined was he to help Rosemary every step of the way.

Rosemary stared starkly at the envelope in her hand, immediately recognising the identity of the sender as heavy dread descended over her. Tearing open the envelope, she withdrew the contents and read silently, *Dear Rosemary (Actually forget the 'dear;' for you are no longer dear to me.) I hope you are happy, now that you have snatched the only person who meant anything to me. You; who droned on and on about your own poor, pitiful broken heart, blaming Tim and Claire for your own damned inadequacies. If you ask me, Tim had a bloody lucky escape. You, Rosemary, are a deceitful, cunning, fucking bitch that ruins lives; then tramples over the remnants giving no second thought. Well, I hope you drink yourself to death and, after a torturous death, may you burn throughout eternity in the deepest depths of hells alcohol fumed fire.* The letter was not signed. There was no need for a signature. Rosemary reread the words, her glassy eyes fixed on the last few words as the mist lifted. *So that was Susan's intention all along; to induce her into an eternal, drunken sleep where she would be out of the way and no longer a threat. And, all for nothing,* she smiled faintly, *for now Susan has nothing and she could have had it all.*

Hanale read the contents of his letter, squeezed it into a tight ball and threw it disdainfully into the waste paper basket. The sudden knock on the door brought him swiftly to it and a fear into Rosemary's fast beating heart. She was in no mood for a confrontation with Susan.

Alan's soft words brought a calming effect to her soul, mingled with a surge of anxiety, which quivered wretchedly deep in her guts; for, this was the man who had, inadvertently, caused one woman much misery and another a secret yearning desire. Her eyes lingered on the two male figures; then followed one disappearing up the stairs. "Alan," she managed to say softly.

He sat down beside her and, without preamble, related the facts and announced his love for her, while she listened attentively like a child listening to a spell bounding story, her mouth firmly clamped against all comments, her eyes riveted to the pale carpet below, lest she should catch something in Alan's eyes; her fingers tightly clenched, lest he should reach out for them and she feel his comforting warmth. They sat side by side as he told her everything; she a solid statue as both secretly yearned for the others embrace. Finally he rose and left her in peace to contemplate his honest words, feelings and hopes. Instead she felt empty and void of all feelings as she stared blankly into space, Susan's written words gate-crashing her mind… *you are no longer dear to me… you have snatched the only person who meant anything to me… You, Rosemary, are a deceitful, cunning, fucking bitch who ruins lives; then tramples over the remnants… I hope you drink yourself to death…* The suggestion was tempting and the more she thought about it, the more tempting it became. The temptation disappeared when Hanale reappeared, unceremoniously snatched the letter away from his mother's hands and stated starkly, "She's nothing but a fucking bitch herself."

Rosemary's shocked eyes darted to Hanale. She had never heard him swear and abhorred his filthy words. About to reprimand him severely, she decided to let it go this time. *He had,* she dismally concluded, *enough to contend with at the present time without a full-scale argument about swearing.*

The following days were lived out without incident. Only, one day, Rosemary knew Alan would be back. Having bared his heart and soul he would want her answer and she had to be ready with the right one.

Chapter Thirty-Two

A second letter, addressed to Hanale from Kauai, dropped through the letter box and his heart fell. *This girl, Ocean Tia, whoever she was, was not going to give up,* he mused, *and, for some mysterious reason, his mother found comfort in her friendship.* Reluctantly he picked up the envelope, surveyed the neatly written address, admired the colourful postage stamps and, in the solace of his room, tore the seal as curiosity got the better of him. *For,* he concluded, *she was certainly persistent, if nothing else.* He admired people with guts and determination. He read the casually written letter with a measure of disinterest, his eyes abruptly stopping at one sentence… *and, so you see, I am searching for my father and one day, I know in my heart of hearts, I shall find him…* He felt a sudden empathy with this stranger from thousands of kilometres away. *For wasn't he without a father too? Didn't he secretly think that, one day, he would find his father?* He reread the letter slowly from start to finish. *Maybe,* he thought, *this island girl and he had something in common.* In that moment in time, he decided to write back to her and, in turn, letters from Kauai became a regular, and welcome, feature on the carpet under the letter box.

Rosemary was delighted that her son had established contact with Ocean Tia; however, her delight mingled with a niggling, haunting thought. *Sooner, rather than later, she would have to inform the pen-pals what relation they were to each other and, in so doing, would release the whole truth about Kai to her son.*

Alan distracted her immediate attention. He called on her, as promised, after giving her a month to contemplate. Although she was ready with her answer, she did not want to think of the consequences; for, without a doubt, they would bring loneliness.

They sat in silence, as the cool evening dusk gathered around them like a heavy mantle. Finally Alan turned towards the woman he wanted a future with. "Well, Rosemary, would you like to put me out of my misery?"

Dismally she reflected on his sad choice of words and with subdued eyes and a low, regretful voice gave him his long awaited answer. In the gloom, she could feel his heart clench; she could feel her own heart breaking. Her final sentence gave him a tiny glimmer of hope. "This is not the right time, Alan. You need to lick your wounds and heal; me, well, I have to sort things out in my head before I can move on. Maybe in the future…"

These optimistic words rang in his ears as he walked to the door and out of her life… for the time being.

Chapter Thirty-Three

Loneliness shrouded Rosemary. It became her constant, reliable companion and she became adept at conforming to its will. Hanale spent increasingly more time at school clubs and apart from her job she had no other form of socialising; neither did she want it preferring her own, solitary company to sharing her life, and feelings, with others. After Tim, Claire and Susan her trust in people had faded to nothing and, so, she lived in her self-imposed solitary confinement and there she felt comfortable and at ease, knowing she would not be hurt.

Hanale had found a new and engaging interest. Ocean Tia proved to be an interesting character and her tales of Kauai were always a source of wonder to the young man. He began to feel a bond with the far away island and, with the bond, grew a yearning to know more about the land of his conception. Their letters became more detailed and, already, Hanale was beginning to feel he knew something of the girl behind the mystery. Still, she intrigued him.

Rosemary heeded the warning signals and knew she had to say something to her son. Still, she delayed the dastardly role she had to perform; the role of informer; the giver of truth; the breaker of idealistic romantic images, which had started to form in the impressionable head of her innocent son.

Sadness, like a canopy, hung over Hanale's head; sadness for Ocean Tia's seemingly futile search for her father, mingling and intermingling with his own feeling of loss of never having known his own father. He placed the blame firmly at fates door. He had often seen the sadness in his mother's eyes, knowing it was deep and too far rooted for him to blame her in any way.

During this unsettling time a worrying letter from Luana reached Rosemary. With excited fingers, she tore open the envelope her eyes, some seconds later, veiling with tears as she read... *And so my dear, Lokemele, you see, as Ocean Tia's current academic year is drawing to an end, Kai's dream of sending his only child to university ends with it. Ocean Tia now needs to find a job...* A hard lump rose to Rosemary's throat; for, she felt for Ocean Tia as if she were her own daughter. Secretly she admonished Kai for his recklessness, wishing she could finance the young woman's education; knowing this was a futile dream and, while she pondered over the impossible, a wayward thought hurtled into her mind and, like a seed, it grew and matured into an idea; for, it dawned on her that there was a way out; there was hope for Ocean Tia's academic future; but, it meant going cap in hand to Alan's door.

Chapter Thirty-Four

He opened the door and felt all his Christmases rush in on him. Never had he expected to see Rosemary at his door. "Rosemary!" he exclaimed. "Come in… come in."

With heavy trepidation in her fast beating heart, she took cautious steps inside; feeling the ghost of Susan's presence as if she was haunting the place. She sat bolt upright in a comfortable armchair feeling anything but comfortable, knowing Alan had jumped to the wrong conclusion. *For,* she thought, *how could he possibly know she had come to his home on a begging mission?*

"Coffee?" He asked raising a quizzical eyebrow.

Shaking her head, she focussed her serious eyes on him and began her nervous plea and his soaring heart began to sink.

He listened to her every word, took it all in and said nothing, making her wish she had not acted so impulsively. She rose to go. "Wait; stay."

There was hope. She sat back down and waited for his demands. There were none. "There may be a way." He stated in his steady, calm voice. "Leave it with me, Rosemary." She rose once more and he let her go. *She was not ready.*

She walked down the road with hope beating in her heart; for, somewhere deep inside, she knew, Alan would not fail her.

Chapter Thirty-Five
Kauai

Early one sunny morning Ocean Tia received her letter of hope and she dared to dream further, as she continued her lonely search for her father. So far he had been elusive. She had heard various reports of sightings on this or that beach; but, when she hastened to them, they were desolate. Still she searched.

Kai was a shadow of his former self. Now he was a dirty, dishevelled beach bum, who used to pity such characters. He shunned any contact with human beings, lived on scraps of raw fish, fresh coconut, pineapple, other tropical fruits and anything he could find, after dark, in garbage containers. His mind was very much alive and well and, although he cast a lone, pitiful figure he never felt lonely; the memory of his late wife accompanying him day and night; memories interspersed with rare sightings of his beloved daughter, Ocean Tia. On these occasions, his senses briefly sobered up; for, he knew exactly what he had done, and was doing, and his heart broke in two. Still, he walked on; sometimes wondering what had happened to his lovely home; sometimes wondering how Keoki and Luana were getting on; missing their children, Akamu and Liliana, and always wondering about the well-being of Ocean Tia; for, he had never stopped loving her. On occasion, for he had all the time in the world, he reflected and brooded on the memory of his many conquests and, sometimes, he would smile. One conquest held a special memory; a lady from England by the name of Rosemary Longsdale; his Lokemele. A sad smile now haunted his lips, his heart laden, his bare feet making imprints in the sand, as they walked along the edge of the beach, where the sea touched the sand; his tired eyes staring out into the far horizon.

England

Rosemary stared out on to her *horizon* of hope, tinged with a streak of trepidation for fear of what Alan would want in return for his generous gift. She cast a surreptitious eye on her son, who was popping a spoonful of cereal into his mouth, whilst taking a last look at his homework. *Had she done the right thing in getting involved with Ocean Tia?*

The next evening brought Alan to their door. Yes, he was in a position to help; but, he thought, it would be better for the young lady to be educated in England, where they would be in a position to get to know her better and to provide her with any further help needed. "After all," he smiled, "hadn't she expressed a wish to get to know this country?" He left mother and son with their thoughts, dreams, hopes and dread and Ocean Tia's future hanging in the balance.

Chapter Thirty-Six
Kauai

Ocean Tia tore open the envelope with zest and sat down on the silky, white sand; her slender back propped against the bark of an aged palm tree, as she put her head into her hands and sobbed. This was not what she had hoped.

Wiping the salty tears from her eyes, she looked out on to the shimmering ocean. *How could she possibly agree to their proposal and leave her beloved, serene Kauai? How could she abandon her father in his hour of need? And, yet, if she stayed, what kind of future lay ahead?* Her watery eyes continued to stare out into the far, far blurry distance. *Somewhere, across the vast ocean, was a foreign land with English people and their English ways; a land that was offering her a future; but... but... to leave this haven, this paradise...* She felt a deep, sharp, iced blade thrusting into her young heart. Abruptly she rose and walked away from the ocean and all it represented.

A silhouette of a shadow flashed across her eyes. Blinking hard she looked intensely into the copse of palms and saw nothing but bendy trunks and, beyond them, the quiet road separating the beach from an assortment of low structured buildings. *And yet,* her alert mind told her, *there was someone there. She had felt a presence in her bones.*

He watched her from his secret hiding place, as he had watched her many times before; daring to come a little nearer each day to catch a glimpse of his beloved daughter.

On reaching her grandparent's home, Ocean Tia ran swiftly to her room, took out her plumeria embellished stationary and wrote two letters; one addressed to Lokemele in England; the other to her father, somewhere on the Island of Kauai.

England

In England, a young man stared out the classroom window brooding; the possibility of his pen-pal's refusal to leave Kauai gnawing at his heart.

Chapter Thirty-Seven

Excitement surged through the veins of three people, as they waited at the arrivals gate of the busy airport. A fourth person adjusted the white plumeria above her right ear, thrust a comb through her long silky hair and smoothed straight her tropical printed dress, before stepping into the aisle of the plane.

Ocean Tia's heart raced wildly; her footsteps were slow and calm as she walked elegantly and serenely into the interior of the busy airport, causing men of all ages to stop and look and their wives, or partners, to cast the cause of their lust a disparaging eye; secretly envying her innocent, exotic beauty. Ocean Tia's dark, mysterious eyes flitted around the vast array of rushing people; her ears bombarded with alien sounds coming from every direction. Already she missed the soft, lilting sounds of Kauai; the thundering waves with their white surf, the swishing sound of palm leaves stirred softly by the touch of the trade winds; the warm, silent sun on her face and arms and, above all, the calm and serenity of Kauai.

Hanale moved from foot to foot, his excitement growing with every passing second; his eyes peering this way and that, in search of an exotic creature resembling the one he held an image of in his trembling fingers. He spotted her from afar; for, there could only be one Ocean Tia. He waved furiously, trying to catch her eye.

It was Lokemele she recognised and it was to her she bestowed her first lei hugging and kissing her; for, she felt Lokemele was her saviour. Hugging Alan she turned her exotic eyes to Hanale and her heart tugged. "Aloha Hanale," she smiled.

His heart felt full to bursting as he stared at the beauty before him. "A... Aloha," he stammered, his hypnotised eyes staring unblinkingly at the beautiful girl before him. *She was,* he kept telling himself, *just a teenager like himself; but, she had a confidence, a grace, a poise and maturity far above any teenage girl he knew.* His smile died on his lips, his guts wrenched as a dread filled his soul. *What would she want with the likes of me?* His eyes dropped to his feet.

Alan was quick to notice the despondency in the young lad's face and leaped to the rescue. "Let's get you home, Ocean Tia," he enthused reaching out for her suitcase.

The drive home was experienced in four different ways. Rosemary was fully aware the time was drawing near for the whole truth to be revealed, her guts gnawing with an inner dread; Alan was feeling a great sense of satisfaction at being able to help and, therefore, to ease Rosemary's burden; Hanale was secretly experiencing the first pangs of love, *or, was it infatuation?* He asked himself; Ocean Tia marvelled at the striking contrast between her own island and the flat plains of Lincolnshire and, already, she was feeling a deep loneliness in the depths of her soul.

The ensuing days brought a stark revelation to Ocean Tia. Everything, and everyone, was a sharp contrast to the happy-go-lucky, laid back, easy ways of Kauai and its islanders. *In England,* she thought, *everything seemed to be happening at an alarming pace, whether it was the quick routine of breakfast time, the rushing around doing daily chores in the house, the fast moving traffic outside, even the images on the television screen seemed to be moving at an exhilarating rate*; though, she knew, her last assumption was most certainly her mind playing a game with her. *The food was worlds apart too,* she concluded. *Gone was the immediate freshness; no fish on her plate now, had been plucked out of the ocean half an hour ago; no coconut opened which had recently fallen on to the white sands; no fresh slices of pineapple, sprinkled with a pinch of salt for added flavour.* Instead, she was grateful for a glass of pineapple juice straight out of a carton and cereal for breakfast. No one seemed to stroll about casually, she noticed; in fact, people used their cars to get to the corner shop and that she couldn't fathom out at all. Conversation seemed to be rushed, jumping from one topic to another, without really finishing the latter. Uncharacteristically, and secretly, she picked holes in everything because everything was so alien to her. She felt like the proverbial fish out of water. She yearned for the soothing trade winds to ease her pain in her homesick heart; the glorious rays of the sun to kiss her soft skin; the sound of the thundering waves to wash over her loneliness as she yearned for home.

Hanale, Rosemary and Alan did everything in their power to make Ocean Tia's first few days welcoming and homely. They took her to the cinema, went for walks in the countryside, attended church services, invited friends to come round and she enjoyed everything they had planned for her; but, still, she yearned.

Hanale saw the sadness in Ocean Tia's eyes and one day he announced, "Ocean Tia, put your glad rags on tonight; I'm taking you out. Have you ever been to a disco?" He didn't wait for an answer; instead he turned his attention to his mum. "I'm taking Ocean Tia out this evening; is that okay?"

His rhetorical question cut deep into Rosemary's consciousness as warning lights flashed. Before she could stop herself, she said softly, "Okay." Instantly she regretted deeply her spontaneous answer. *But,* she told herself when she had calmed down, *to have opposed would, at once, have aroused suspicion and this was not the time. Tomorrow,* she told herself sternly, *we shall sit down and I shall tell them both what they need to know before… it is too late.*

Chapter Thirty-Eight

The music pounded and invaded their ears long before they arrived at the venue and, as they walked through the grubby paint-peeling doors of the youth club, Hanale felt like the luckiest and proudest young guy in the world, with the most beautiful young woman by his side. His ego soared as his eyes saw the looks he and Ocean Tia were given, intermingled with admiring and envious looks; others thrown with the venom of poison-tipped daggers. Hanale savoured each one; Ocean Tia was oblivious to them all, totally blaze about her beauty; for, she attached no relevance to outward appearance only to beauty within, where she attached much importance. Kindness, honesty, sincerity, respect and serenity were the precious jewels she strived to achieve and to find in others.

They sat by themselves in a corner, her inquisitive eyes on the styles of dress and wondering how any girl could wear her top so revealingly low; or, skirt so suggestively high. Hanale's eyes rested on Ocean Tia; for, the more time he spent with her, the more he felt himself falling under the spell of this mysterious island girl.

"Hi Hanale Who is this gorgeous beauty?" grinned Si, an old friend, seating himself down next to Ocean Tia and offering her his hand. "Simon... Simon Teal."

"Aloha Simon," smiled Ocean Tia, sending the young man into orbit and Hanale in a fuming inward rage, especially as his mate seemed to have settled down as a permanent fixture for the evening and Ocean Tia didn't seem to mind his presence at all.

After a few smuggled in alcoholic drinks, of which Ocean Tia abstained, Hanale's fuming temper rose to fever pitch, his guts twisting mercilessly, as Si rose, extended his hand to his new friend and asked her if she would care to dance and when Ocean Tia accepted, Hanale felt his whole world come crumbling down on him.

He watched beneath hooded eyes as his best friend and Ocean Tia danced; oblivious to her natural body rhythm; oblivious to the smiles she threw his way; only conscious of his friend dancing with Ocean Tia; his girl. A surge of uncharacteristic hatred swept over him. Abruptly he rose, pushed his way through the smooching teenagers, grabbed Ocean Tia by the hand and dragged her unceremoniously off the crowded dance floor. "We're going home, Ocean," he snapped.

Like a meek lamb she followed him, her young heart thumping hard, her calm equilibrium ruffled for the first time in her life and, for the first time in her life, she felt angry and hurt as they walked home in complete silence, submerged in their own bitter thoughts.

At the gate, he stopped abruptly, turned her body to face him and said, "I am sorry, Ocean; but, in my country, it is not customary for a guy to take his mate's girl away from him."

To his utter astonishment she emitted a stifled giggle and he could see her dark eyes sparkle, as he tried desperately to control his rising temper at her sheer flippancy. "In Kauai," she smiled sweetly, "we have no such rules."

"But we are not in Kauai, are we?" He heard the anger in his own voice and silently cursed himself for his childish outburst.

"No, we are not in Kauai." She replied softly, a trace of sadness lacing her words.

Without thinking he took her in his arms and kissed her; the first girl he had ever truly kissed in his life.

A curtain above twitched and a heavy foreboding sank into the very depths of Rosemary's heart, rapidly turning into despair.

Chapter Thirty-Nine

Rosemary's tired eyes flitted from Hanale to Ocean Tia and rested on her son, as she desperately tried to focus on her well-rehearsed words, which had been whirling around her head throughout the long and torturous night. The air in the room was thick and heavy, covering the threesome with a thick veil of suspense, as the minutes ticked on monotonously. Finally, she opened her mouth. "Hanale; Ocean Tia, what I have to say to you is of the greatest importance and will affect you both as long as you both draw breath."

Two pairs of young, inquisitive eyes shot to Rosemary where thy lingered in silent expectation.

Taking a deep breath, her serious eyes firmly fixed on her son, Rosemary continued. "There is no easy way to tell you this, Hanale, than to tell you straight. You father, Kai, is Ocean Tia's father too." Her eyes dropped to the table, unable to witness the shock and horror of the revelation in her son's eyes and in the eyes of Ocean Tia. Their raw pain surged through her own pained heart; their hurt invading her mind, soul and heart and saturating theirs; her betrayal like a jagged sword thrusting through them all and leaving them in emotional tatters. Feeling like an unwanted intruder Rosemary rose, freezing instantly as she felt the warmth of Ocean Tia's hand on her own. Slowly she sat back down her eyes unable to look at her; unable to look at her son as the heavy weight of betrayal threatened to suffocate her lying and deceiving body; to obliterate the blot; the deceiver. "Please tell us about it, Lokemele." Ocean Tia encouraged softly.

From the depths of her own despair, Rosemary heard the echo of Ocean Tia's softly spoken request, as an urge to yell at her for her lack of anger bubbled furiously within her threatening to boil over. Surreptitiously her eyes flitted to her son's bowed head and she wondered what he must be thinking in his dark, silent reverie. Slowly she turned her eyes on the young woman. "There is nothing much to tell. I was in a bad place after a betrayal. I thought I could find peace in Kauai. Your father was there. We had a fling and Hanale was conceived. We carried on with our separate lives." Her eyes dropped from Ocean Tia's still, fathomless eyes to her untouched cup of coffee and felt herself drowning in its black, cold liquid.

"And did you find peace?" Ocean Tia enquired.

"Yes, yes, I found peace and much, much more than peace." Rosemary's eyes flitted to Hanale who was still unresponsive.

"Well then, that's all that matters, isn't it, Hanale?" Ocean Tia's hand switched to Hanale. He abruptly shrugged it away, not bearing to feel her soft touch against his skin. "You need time, Hanale." She said softly. "Come, Lokemele, let us give him time."

And like a child following its mother, Rosemary followed Ocean Tia out into the brightness of the garden.

Hanale's mind was in turmoil; his heart full of hatred for his mother and the girl he had hoped would be his girlfriend and now, to his utter disgust, he had found she was his half-sister. The need to find his father had rapidly dissipated; no longer did he want to create a bond with a man, he was told, was now apparently a beach bum, somewhere on the tropical Island of Kauai. The island itself he likened to Hell; for, although it had seemingly brought his mother some sort of peace, he felt, it brought him nothing but disappointment. Ocean Tia he ignored at all costs, staying out longer after sporting sessions, shunning her when at home; locking himself in his room and making her feel as if she had brought untold misery into the house and its occupants.

She yearned to go back home, to be with her own people; for, no matter what crises they experienced, they stuck together like glue. But going home, she quickly realised, was no option. Her life and future were here, at least for the next few months.

The greatest sorrow pierced Rosemary's heart; knowing that she had inflicted this pain on her son and Ocean Tia and she carried this sorrow deep within her heart.

Alan saw, and felt, the pain of the three most cherished beings to him. He became a regular visitor to the house and, in time, Rosemary began to slowly open to him, unable to contain the sorrow solely in her own heart. "You have to give them time." He urged.

"Time! Time! Time! I'm sick of the word *time*, Alan." Rosemary fumed. "Ocean Tia is always referring to this so-called *time* and now you." Her eyes full of hurt, anger and confusion met his calm eyes, as he leaned across the kitchen table and took her clenched hands into his own.

"She's right. You cannot force these things, Rosemary. You need time to allow them to sink in and mature. Hanale and Ocean Tia need to adapt to the news and think about it; they need time to reflect, after all, how would you react if you were in their shoes?"

Hot blood boiled, bubbled, boiled and bubbled. *Why,* she asked herself, *does he always seem so damned sensible?* She raised her eyes to his and slowly withdrew her hands. "I have to wash the dishes."

He let her go, silently resolving to try and make her see things from the victims viewpoints.

All three felt more at ease when Alan was present. Ocean Tia thought he was a very understanding, patient man; more like a Hawaiian than an Englishman. Hanale looked on him as a respectable, honest person; a man to be trusted. Rosemary felt safe and secure in his presence.

Alan had a fond regard for the three people under his secret, protective umbrella. Hanale, he thought, was a very fine young man, who needed to find his roots. Ocean Tia was a young woman he admired; for, she seemed to have an aura of serenity and wisdom which surpassed her tender years. Rosemary he wished, one day, to make his wife.

Chapter Forty
Kauai

In the shadows, she thought, she saw a silhouette of a figure huddled against some tangled foliage at the bottom of the garden; however, when Luana crept stealthily around the periphery of the garden, there was no trace of any human. She shook her head from side to side. She was sure she saw someone.

He saw her and his heart clenched tightly; for, apart from Ocean Tia, Luana and her family were the only blood relatives he had left on the island and Kai missed them dreadfully. He withdrew from the tangled heap, of what was a ready-made bonfire, and peered around the silhouetted, ghostly shapes inhabiting the garden; his eyes darting from shadowed palms, to bushes, to clusters of low hanging blooms; their mournful shapes and shadows set beneath a majestic moon, accompanied by a myriad of twinkling diamonds piercing the soft velvet sky. Stealthily he crept along the edge of the lawn lest he be spotted, stopping abruptly at any slight sound. Slowly… slowly he crept, like a cat burglar on a secret mission; his secret mission far more important than to steal a rare precious jewel; it was one of survival.

He watched as the kitchen light went out and, a few minutes later, saw the subdued bedroom light and, after a few more minutes, the building stood in blackness; still, like the grave. Slowly, continually looking this way and that, he crept along; the sound of night birds willing him along, until he reached the veranda. In, he crept, silently thanking Luana for never locking the door. Into the kitchen he sneaked, his grubby hands cautiously opening the fridge. Quickly, like a flash, he grabbed whatever he could and ran out the house, out the garden and down the bendy lane; his feet not stopping their ceaseless running until they reached the beach. Now looking subdued and sinister, the moon cast its disapproving look on him; silently condemning him for breaking the eighth commandment. *But,* he told himself, *he had stolen so many times before; what would one more act of theft matter?* Only this time his devious act started to niggle his conscience; it began to feel more like a sin than an act of survival; this time he had stolen from the mouths of his kin; this time the food and drink he stole were hard to digest, as the grave moon and silent stars admonished him. Taking another swill of Mai Tai, he closed his eyes against the silent accusations bombarding his head, his eyes staring out into the blackness as the rolling waves thundered.

Without seeing him face to face, Luana knew the identity of her midnight visitor and felt her heart tug.

Kai's expeditions became a secret nightly ritual and Luana made sure the fridge and the cupboards were well stocked with her brother's favourite fare and always kept herself well out of the way. Like all true Hawaiians, she thought, time and patience were of the essence. All would come into fruition when the good Lord willed it to be.

Kai's life became a little easier, knowing that his search for food was no longer an issue. Secretly, he felt, Luana knew everything; however, his mind, heart and soul were not ready to face full-blown reality.

England

A smiling Ocean Tia presented Rosemary with a piece of paper and said, "The best news ever my dear, Lokemele."

Rosemary immediately read the contents of the letter aloud and smiled too; looking across to Hanale, who abruptly rose and stormed out of the house.

In the cold north-easterly wind of an autumnal day, he ferociously kicked the multi-coloured red, purple and golden-brown leaves as he briskly strode down the long road. Where he was going he did not know, neither did he care; his only concern was to get as far away from his mother and so-called half-sister, as fast as his legs would carry him. The echo of his father's name thundered persistently in his head; the image of a dishevelled, dirty tramp loomed largely in his eyes; the thought of such a despicable character in his life making his whole body cringe. On and on, he walked trying desperately to dispel the nightmarish image; but, with each step the image became larger, closer, more real; *for, this tramp was a part of his life and he was a part of him; always to be united, no matter what the circumstances or the distance apart; for, they had the same family bloodline running through their veins, which only a blood transfusion would dilute and even then…*

Ocean Tia was in a blissful bubble. Her father was alive and surviving and she knew, in her heart of hearts, Luana would make sure her brother would not go without. And with that knowledge in her heart, the young woman was able to hope.

Rosemary too thanked all the gods for this news.

Alan was secretly weaving his own intricate plan, in which Rosemary and Kai played the prominent roles.

Chapter Forty-One

Alan Shaw was a man of integrity; kind, patient, understanding; a man to be trusted. From the age of fourteen, he had a paper round, did all the menial jobs for his elderly neighbours, who yearned to give him more than a few pennies he took from them. He had left school to work in a local grocery shop; a job his parents, teachers and friends thought was beneath his intellectual prowess. He proved them all wrong. Securing a loan, when the owner of the shop retired, he bought the shop and made it into a roaring success, with all kinds of interesting initiatives; bought another shop and then another until he owned a string of shops. Always fair and just to his employees, they worked hard for him and, as a consequence, they all enjoyed the fruits of his success. Now he was retired, his shops run by an army of faithful, loyal managers; a man of means with a big heart, many good friends and a great deal of common sense. And when an idea brewed in his head, all stood back and waited; for, they knew it was going to be good.

Alan thought his plan was good; but, challenging. Time was needed for it to simmer and bubble; everything had to be seasoned at just the right time for it to mature and blossom and, at present, he wasn't quite sure Rosemary was ready to take up the gauntlet. He put a lid on it, watched the proceedings carefully and waited.

As they were having supper one evening he probed gently. "Have you heard anything from Kauai, Ocean?" He felt Hanale stir uneasily, avoided his eyes and switched his whole attention on the young woman sitting opposite him.

She smiled. "Luana's food is disappearing on a nightly basis. Father is alive."

He returned her smile. "Good... good." He nodded exchanging smiles with Rosemary. Her eyes switched to Hanale and followed him as he silently withdrew himself from the table and disappeared up the stairs. Watching, Alan made a mental note to have a man-to-man talk with the troubled teenager; but, not before having an honest word with Rosemary.

The opportunity came that very evening, when Ocean Tia spent the night at a girl friend's house and Hanale an evening out with his mates. Whilst enjoying a cup of freshly ground coffee, and a slice of home-made Haupia cake Alan cautiously asked, "The taste of coconut is so indicative of a tropical island; does it remind you of Kauai, Rose?"

He watched as a smile rose to her lips. "Yes… yes." She took a small bite, savoured it and said, as her eyes stared into the far away distance, "Haupia is traditionally served at luaus; it is a traditional Hawaiian cake. Yes, I do enjoy making it, as it always brings back to me lovely memories of my time out there."

"Would you like to go back there one day?"

"I often go there in my dreams." Her smile became wistful, as did her eyes. In a heartbeat, the dreamlike mist disappeared, as it occurred to her that Alan might be pumping her for ideas for a secret, surprise get away. Rising, she hastily gathered the plates and rushed to the sink.

The moment had gone. *He would,* he reluctantly decided, *leave his tentative enquiries for another day.*

Rosemary's thoughts often drifted to Kauai; more prominently she wondered about Kai; where he was, what he was doing and how he was managing to survive. Her worries had eased; secure in the knowledge that Luana was secretly looking after her brother.

Kauai

Kai's erratic, chaotic and aimless thoughts were slowly formulating into coherent snippets of thought; laboriously he began to think not just about mere survival; not just about the loss of his beloved wife; but about what he had; a daughter and a sister who cared for him deeply.

As he tucked into some bread and goats cheese, washed down with a modicum of Mai Tai, for now he had tried to control his intake of alcohol, his mind wandered to thoughts of Ocean Tia, bringing with them disturbing and haunting thoughts. *He had not seen her for days… weeks. Had she abandoned him? Had something happened to her?* Another thought crashed into his head… He would have to find out and Luana had the key.

His reserve kept him captive. To boldly arrive at Luana's door, bearing his heart and soul, his misdeeds and his dishonesty was a gruelling thought, which whirled viciously in his head. *And yet, if he didn't face up to Luana, and more importantly to himself, the fate of his daughter would never be known,* he dismally concluded.

Luana hoped against hope that Kai would, one day, just simply come to her door and they would talk. While she was hoping, an idea sprang into her head.

That evening, when all the house and grounds were in darkness, Kai headed for Luana's fridge. His eyes dropped to a silhouetted shape of a high-backed rattan chair, standing directly in front of the door of the fridge and, as he extended his hand to move the chair, he touched something soft. His fingers grabbed the article and shook it into shape. It was a shirt. Underneath he found a pair of shorts, underpants and a pair of flip-flops. A smile spread on his lips as he took the clothes, and the prepared food, and made for the quiet, desolate beach. There he sat at the base of an aged palm, put his head into his hands and sobbed; his whole body heaving as the mighty waves pounded in the dark distance. When his eyes and heart could cry no more, he ate his feast, had a drop of Mai Tai and looked out into the darkness, where he saw a tiny spark of light. He blinked and it was gone. But it had been there and that tiny spark of hope ignited his will to start to live.

Chapter Forty-Two

It was a slow, laborious process. Each night Kai continued to take the food, leave his dirty clothes on the chair and pick up a set of freshly laundered attire. He noticed in the pocket of his shorts there was a couple of dollars, enough to buy himself a drink. With that thought in mind, he started to plan. His plan was simple. He would have a vigorous swim in the ocean, put on his fresh clothes, eat his breakfast and then would come his challenge. However, with the challenge came doubts and the simple task of entering a coffee shop and ordering a coffee became his Mount Everest. And, the more he thought about the peak, the more daunting the prospect became, until he abandoned the challenge altogether.

But the thought reappeared and loomed. Day after day he took up the gauntlet and laid it back down again until, one day, he stated firmly to himself, "No challenge; no food tonight." His resolve firmly planted and sealed in his head, he set off.

The sweat poured in droplets down his face, his tightly clenched fists felt clammy, his fast beating heart pounded mercilessly, as one foot after another brought him out of the sanctuary of the desolate beach and on to the pavement; the living world. His wary eyes darted this way and that, his ears waiting for someone to call him a tramp, a vagrant, a beach bum, a good-for-nothing imbecile; waiting for scathing, condemning looks and stares; waiting for pointing, accusing fingers. His anxious wait did not bear fruit, as his astounded eyes watched strangers pass by, some greeting him with a smile, others with a friendly, "Aloha." With each step, his confidence started to grow. He began to smile back, to nod, to whisper, "Aloha," as he walked on. As his hand reached out for the door he stopped, a sudden thought hitting him like a heavy rock. *What if someone recognised him?* The thought hovered and pounded in his head making his senses reel, making him abruptly turn back.

"Aloha."

His heart stopped.

"K-Kai; is that you?"

He felt he'd died and gone to Hell. Turning he came face to face with an old friend.

"It is you! How are you my dear, dear friend?" The man hugged him tightly and Kai felt like a prisoner in a friendly jail.

Inside the coffee shop Kai sat alone, savouring each drop of his rich, strong coffee his eyes taking everything in, as if he was seeing everything for the first time; for, everything was the same and, yet, everything was different. The aroma of the coffee smelt richer, the Hawaiian print on shirts and dresses were more vivid in colour and design, snippets of conversation drifting to his ears was clearer and the sound of soft Hawaiian guitars was sweeter than he ever remembered. He took a long, luxurious sip a smile dancing on his lips, and dying, as Ocean Tia crashed into his mind. *Somehow, from somewhere, from someone he would have to find out about her,* he silently determined. *She was his life.*

Luana smiled as she washed her brother's clothes. *He was fed and clothed and, somewhere, he was sheltered.* She wondered how he had spent the money, secure in the knowledge that it would not be enough to make him drunk. She made up her mind to trust him with more and so the nightly ritual continued and, with each passing day, Kai became stronger in mind, body and spirit with only one dark thought pervading his inner peace.

The taste of Haupia cake lingered blissfully in his mouth as he walked into a small, quiet church. There he sat and prayed to a God he did not believe in; a God Ocean Tia firmly believed in, and he caught hold and clung on to the tail end of her faith, hoping fervently his prayer would be answered.

His answer came, some days later, in the form of a letter which was pinned on to a freshly laundered shirt. By the light of the majestic moon, and its faithful army of stars, he nervously tore open the envelope and read aloud, "Aloha Kai. I thank the good Lord that you are alive." His heart died as he read, "By now you have probably heard that Keoki has slipped into eternal peace." He lowered the paper feeling it bend in the light breeze, as he looked out into the rolling mass of sea. After long minutes, he read, "Ocean Tia is fine. She is studying in England." His sad heart leaped and, in that instant, he felt his soul recharged with a new energy, which kick started his will not only to survive; but, to live a purposeful life. His heart and soul dancing, his eyes strayed back to the vast rolling ocean and there he saw, felt, heard, smelt and tasted hope.

Intermingled thoughts of Keoki, Ocean Tia, Luana and her children and his late wife, Leialoha, wove in and out of each other, like an ever changing tapestry lulling him into a peaceful and restful slumber and, in the light of a new dawning day, he felt refreshed and ready to face what challenges he had to conquer.

With a new zest for life and with the money Luana left him, the next day he bought a coffee and, instead of Haupia cake, he bought a small writing pad and pencil. That night, as he gratefully took his provisions, he left Luana a note and a spray of freshly picked plumeria.

Chapter Forty-Three

Ocean Tia had settled into the English way of life, although she still yearned for her homeland. She was a popular sixth former and had acquired many friends of both sexes. She was different; an exotic, natural beauty who, with her dark, alluring looks; helpful and cheerful attitude and serene, unassuming manner drew people towards her, and some away; for, there were always enemies lurking in the background; the latter, she ignored. *Life,* so her Uncle Keoki used to say, *was too short to waste on such foolishness.* One such enemy was within her camp, living in the same house, sharing the same father.

Hanale's hatred for his half-sister grew daily. She felt it; Rosemary and Alan witnessed it in Hanale's behaviour and he was well aware of his uncontrollable, negative feelings towards her. To ignore her at sixth form was not hard; to ignore her at home was a different matter altogether. His brusque, sharp, unfriendly attitude towards her caused her to spend many an evening in tears and a rift in the Longsdale household. Alan took Hanale aside one evening and cut straight to the point. "I think you may be jealous, Hanale." He stated looking straight into the teenager's wavering eyes, giving him no scope to escape. Hanale's eyes dropped to the floor, while his whole body writhed with undiluted hatred for the man standing in front of him; the man who dared to confront him so starkly; who had dared to pierce his heart with the truth as he stood motionless, unable to accept or deny the damning statement. "There is no need to be envious; Rosemary has plenty of love for all."

From somewhere in the depths of his soul, words spewed out; but, they were not the words he wished to utter. "She betrayed me. My mum betrayed me just… just like she betrayed your fiancée."

Alan took a sharp intake of breath. He had not been expecting these words. He swerved the sway of conversation. "How did she betray you, Hanale?" Deep down he knew the answer and, knowing the answer, he knew that only Rosemary and Kai could adequately explain their actions to their son. Without waiting for

Hanale's answer he continued. "Your mother loves you very much, Hanale. She gave up many opportunities to have you; to rear you as a single parent and, believe me, in those days it was not an easy thing to do."

"She could have told me about Ocean Tia being my half-sister, Alan." Hanale looked the older man straight in the eyes and there he found his silent answer. *She couldn't. The pain of it all was far too deep rooted and, like the Hawaiians, she needed... time.*

The next few weeks brought a veil of peace over the household. While there were no obvious signs of bonhomie between Hanale and Ocean Tia, neither was there a full-scale war. A silent truce ensued in which both teenagers had time to think, assess and plan. And, it was in this interlude, that Alan carefully put the final touches into his plan; waiting patiently for the right moment to spring it on Rosemary. In the meantime, he watched and assessed the situation.

Luana's letters to Rosemary and Ocean Tia brought joy to both women, a smile to Alan's lips and a heavy trepidation into Hanale's heart.

Chapter Forty-Four

He was alive and well and, by all accounts, Kai was on the road to recovery. Rosemary and Ocean Tia's silent prayers had been answered and Hanale's secret nightmare began and, while Rosemary couldn't help but smile; Hanale's heart felt like a block of heavy stone; his thoughts and feelings jumbled together in a confusing, conflicting, tangled mass; for, he wanted nothing to do with his father while, at the same time, he secretly craved to meet him one day. His college work suffered; he found it impossible to concentrate; neglecting his sports training due to lack of energy. He stopped socialising; his friends deserted him. Alone with his thoughts, he felt he had no one he could turn to and, slowly, he turned into an island of his own creation; a dark, brooding island where no sun was allowed to filter through only a mass of dark, threatening clouds. He prevented anyone from entering his private island and soon it shrouded him with a heavy veil of ugly thoughts. He began to miss college; started to make new friends outside of the academic establishment, with boys who were ready and eager to accept him into their gang and he willingly joined.

Rosemary tried, without success, to curb his unruly behaviour. Ocean Tia didn't get off the starting block. In the end, Alan took things into his own hands, before the lad he cared for crossed over the point of no-return.

On one rare occasion, when they were all sat at the supper table together, immersed in their own silent thoughts, Rosemary cautiously stretched her hand across the table and touched her son's hand. "It's nice to have you back at our family table, Hanale," she said softly.

Sharply he withdrew his hand from her touch and threw silent daggers at Alan with his angry eyes. "He's not family," he hissed.

"Hanale! You must apo…"

"Mother…" Hanale turned his scathing eyes on Rosemary his bubbling anger rising to the surface and, like an angry volcano spewing out it's wrath, stated, "You stole your best friend's man after plying yourself with booze, and don't deny it, Auntie Susan wrote and told me all about it; yes, I took her letter out of the bin and read it. You deceived me and her." He pointed a long finger at Ocean Tia, "You denied us the truth and now you want us all to play happy families. Well, you can fucking well think again!"

Bitter boiling anger surged through every vein in Rosemary's fast pulsating veins. "Hanale!" She shouted as she watched him rise and walk away from the table.

"Hanale, perhaps something I am about to suggest might help matters." Something in Alan's calm voice made Hanale turn, sit back down and cast his disparaging eyes on the older man; his puzzled eyes following Alan's hand, as he withdrew something from the inner pocket of his jacket and placed it on the table.

Three pairs of bewildered eyes looked at the article on the table; silence casting its heavy veil over the foursome.

Chapter Forty-Five

Silent, inquisitive eyes looked down on the mysterious white envelope, as one pair of eyes flitted from Rosemary, to Ocean Tia and finally rested on Hanale, "Open it," enthused Alan as Hanale continued to stare at the envelope, as if it was a piece of red-hot coal.

"Open it, Son." Rosemary encouraged moving the envelope towards Hanale, her own curiosity playing havoc with her head as she asked herself, *What on earth could be inside that envelope that could possibly help matters?* And, as her eyes focussed on Hanale he snatched the envelope, roughly tore open the seal and allowed three separate items to drop to the table. "Tickets," was all that he could utter and picking one up, after scrutinising it intently added, "to Kauai."

As Ocean Tia and Hanale slid into thoughts, dreams, doubts, ambitions and fears of their own, Rosemary picked up the tickets. "But where is your ticket, Alan?" She asked as her questioning eyes flitted to him.

His kind eyes met hers. "This is not my story, Rose." He smiled warmly and left the house, leaving them with their conflicting thoughts.

All three tossed and turned throughout the night. Ocean Tia was beside herself with excitement; to be going home to her family; to feel the soft kiss of the Hawaiian sun and the cool silkiness of the waves on her bare feet; to hear the gentle swish of the palm leaves and the soft sounds of Hawaiian guitars and see the beauty of tropical foliage were things she dreamed about. To see her father would be a prayer answered.

Rosemary had a restless night bombarded with conflicting thoughts. The thought of a peaceful, relaxing vacation on the island she loved was marred with the stark reality of the loss of Keoki... *Never would she see him wandering on the beach; never again would she hear his wise words or see his twinkling dark eyes, his cheerful smile; or, feel his optimism oozing out of every pore and then there was... Kai.* Guilty, nagging thoughts pervaded her heart and mind. *Kai had no idea he had a son. Would her betrayal hurl him back into the clutches of alcoholism? Would he ever forgive her?*

Hanale experienced the worst night of his life; his mind fighting a raging war with his heart, in which neither won and so his troubled thoughts continued to fume and fight. One part of him wanted nothing to do with this stranger living thousands of kilometres away, worlds and cultures apart; another part of him wanted to know everything about this stranger who was, apparently, his father. Day after day he fought these gnawing, conflicting thoughts; day after day he thought less of his new friends, the gang he had joined fading into insignificance and, as he was an unimportant member, he wasn't bothered with potential consequences. More and more Kauai, the island on which he was conceived, became an integral part of him.

Kauai

Intermingled happiness and sorrow reigned in Luana's soul at the news of their arrival.

Kai opened the folded piece of paper, which had been placed into the pocket of his laundered shirt; seated comfortably against a smooth bark he read the contents. He reread it three times before looking out into the ocean. "Soon," he said, "my Ocean Tia will be crossing you. Speed her well and bring her home safe."

Chapter Forty-Six

After a long and tiresome journey, filled with a mixture of excitement and trepidation, their plane landed in Kauai. Rosemary and Ocean Tia exchanged smiles. It was balm to their souls to see Kauai's airport staff in their Hawaiian print shirts and their cheerful faces; already they could feel the peace of the island silently invading their souls; the heat, as they walked on confirmed that they had reached *home*.

Hanale felt like a spare part. And, while the two women bombarded him with information about Kauai's traditions, culture and customs he felt more and more like an interloper; an intruder who had wandered into an alien world where he did not belong. Already the sound of soft Hawaiian guitars, the sight of casually attired natives and their laid back attitude were getting on his nerves. The thought of seeing his Hawaiian father, made him yearn to turn back and catch the next plane home where, he felt, he belonged.

Tears streaked down Luana's happy, chubby face, as she waddled hurriedly to welcome her special visitors; her Mother Hubbard clinging stickily to her fat thighs, her two grown-up children beaming with excitement.

A hard lump rose to Rosemary's throat, her heart clenched. There was no Keoki to meet them; but, suddenly feeling a comforting presence she smiled. *He was here, after all.*

While they talked, ate and laughed Hanale sat rigidly and forced himself to smile at all the right times, whilst cursing his decision to come to *this most boring place on earth.*

Stealthily, a figure crept across the garden. This time his mission took on a different role. He was not there to take clothes, food and money. This time his mission was laden with far more importance and would provide Kai with a heart full of joy. Cautiously his eyes peered around the corner, through the subdued lit window he peered, catching a glimpse of a young man he did not know, his eyes switching to Lokemele; his heart froze, restarted, clenched tightly his eyes rested on his daughter. Tears glistened in his happy eyes, as his lips emitted a satisfactory sigh of relief. She was more beautiful than he had remembered her to be and, as his watery eyes lingered on his daughter, a lump rose and lodged in his dry throat. *So many days, weeks, months lost; so many precious moments and, for what?* Unable to look at what he had lost, his eyes turned away and stared into the silhouetted shadows of Luana's garden and, in the tangled dark mass of foliage, he found his answer, crept out of the garden, ran down to the beach and took a generous gulp of golden-brown liquid to soothe his pained heart. Immediately he felt the potent liquids comforting warmth and, bringing the bottle back to his mouth, took another gulp and another. Propping himself against a bark he closed his eyes against the ghostly, dark rolling waves, tipped by incandescent surf, and allowed an uneasy sleep to take over his troubled soul.

She found him during her morning walk; a heap of a man, slumped awkwardly against the bark of a bent palm tree, an empty Mai Tai bottle by his side and she fell down beside him, her eyes brimming over with salty tears, her heart torn in shreds. For this was not how Rosemary had imagined their encounter to be.

Chapter Forty-Seven

Laboriously his tired eyes flickered and opened to three sets of ominous eyes looking down on him, patiently waiting for him to stir from his drunken stupor. A sharp pain shot through his heart and he averted his eyes from the three females, unable to look at them any longer. But, he had registered their concerned eyes and felt their disappointment. He closed his eyes, silently urging them to leave his bedside, feeling deeply his own raw failure.

Luana, Rosemary and Ocean Tia sat wordlessly and unwearyingly, their eyes pinned on the man they loved in differential ways.

Hanale wandered alone on the beach, skimming shells into the roaring ocean and wondering what all the fuss about Kauai was about. *Sure,* he told himself, *it was a tropical paradise; but, so were many other places in the world, he had seen on the television or read about in books and magazines; the natives seemed friendly enough; but, nothing special; the food, so far, was not to his liking and, as for the music...* He wondered where the women had got to; they had made some excuse about going somewhere urgently; but, he hadn't bothered to take it all in and, now, wished he had. As he looked out into the shimmering distance, he wondered what his father would be like. By all accounts, he had had everything, lost everything and now was on the road to recovery, after having had a pretty rough time of it all. He had no sympathy for drunks. He walked determinedly on.

Hour replaced hour and, still, the women continued their vigil as they whispered to each other in low voices. Kai heard their concerned snippets of conversation and kept his eyes firmly closed to them. *Rather this way,* he thought, *than to be confronted with a multitude of questions he was not ready to answer; or, worse, to be openly accused for his actions.* He knew he had gone backwards. He knew he had been on the point of reaching for what was precious, only to lose it again in the bottle. His body craved for more alcohol.

Hours later, when he opened his eyes, there was one figure at his bedside. "Lokemele." He tried to smile his dry, parched mouth preventing him.

"Here, let me." Rosemary helped him to take a sip of cool water from a glass.

"What are you doing here, Lokemele?"

"Sh." She stifled her tears. "Just sleep." And, as if Keoki was prompting her with words she added, "There is time enough for talk."

He closed his eyes and fell into a deep, relaxed sleep while she sat and held his hand; her mind drifting back, rolling back the years… *and as she tucked into her plate of Kalua pork and rice, her eyes turned to the source of the cheerful greeting at the door. "Aloha!"… She didn't like what she saw; an over confident, handsome guy who, clearly,* she had assessed, *craved to be the centre of attention… And, here he is,* she mused sadly, *still the centre of attention.* Deeply she felt a silent wedge between them; a wedge which had been her secret for seventeen years and, now, this secret had to be exposed; for better or worse, she had to set it free. She looked down at his relaxed sleeping face, the dark stubble peeping out of his chin. *He had aged,* she glumly concluded. *But, hadn't they all? A weak man,* she silently surmised, *who had lost all his physical, mental and emotional strength. Would she be able to help him? Would he be strong enough to take the whole, undiluted truth? Would she be strong enough?*

"Lokemele."

Sharply, she withdrew from her solemn reverie, her eyes on her ex-lover. "Kai." She whispered softly, wishing he had delayed the moment of waking up a while longer. Gazing on him she wondered how she would approach the painful subject that had been haunting her for so long. She decided she would remain on safe ground, at least for the time being and said softly, "Ocean Tia will be back shortly, she's just nipped out for a change of clothes for you."

Ocean Tia; her name was like a dose of medicine; instantly he wanted to get up, get washed and prepare himself for his daughter's arrival. Turning back his light cover, he placed one wobbly foot down on to the cool tiled floor, then another and fell into Rosemary's waiting arms.

"You are not strong enough, Kai. You need plenty of rest." Gently she helped him back into his bed.

"I have wasted enough time, Lokemele."

His stark words prompted her to spontaneously say, "We need to talk, Kai." Immediately regretting her hasty words she added, "When you are stronger." She watched, with secret relief, as he closed his tired eyes, a sudden exhaustion taking over his mind and body.

She stayed a while, watching his cover rise and fall in tune with his rhythmic breathing, as she gazed at his serene face caught in the depths of sleep and, with a heavy heart, she rose and left his side. *Let him sleep,* she thought, *for when he wakes they will have a mountain to climb.*

She strode out the cool, air-conditioned interior of the hospital and into the balmy air outside and, within minutes, felt hot, sticky and flustered. Heading straight for the beach to cool off, in the far away distance, she spotted a solitary figure. The ominous figure was drawing nearer and nearer; but, it was not Keoki; it was a younger version of Kai, with the whole world on his shoulders; for, he had since found out where they had all been. "How is he?" His words were cold, detached, indifferent; their iciness burning a hole in Rosemary's heart.

"He is okay." She answered softly her eyes on the smooth, white sand beneath. She stopped walking, took both his arms into her hands and looked into his sad eyes. "Hanale, the time has come when you and Kai need to meet; maybe… in time, to build a father-son relationship."

He looked past her on to the empty stretch of beach ahead. After long seconds he said, "I have decided against seeing him, Mum; I want to go back to England."

She said nothing as they walked silently on; both feeling as if they were drowning in the ocean they were walking along.

Turmoil, raging inner conflict and silent despair tortured Rosemary, haunting her mercilessly day and night, giving her no respite. Sitting in Luana's garden watching Akamu, Liliana and Ocean Tia chatting and sharing a cool juice, she tried to weigh up her own desperate situation. *On the one hand, they could go back to England and allow Kai to live in ignorant bliss; on the other hand, there was his right to know he was a father to a son, whom he had not known about for seventeen years and then, there was Ocean Tia to consider…* And it all became too much, as she felt herself suffocating beneath the scorching heat of her betrayal.

Ocean Tia sat by her father's bed as she and her father were going through the slow, painful process of making amends, restoring broken bonds and building new bridges; but, in restoring one bond, Kai felt he had lost another. Rosemary no longer came to visit and he felt hurt and sad. As Ocean Tia took her father's hand she looked into his eyes and saw his sadness, felt his hurt and knew why. But, she could do nothing. It was not her call to make. His stark question struck her at the very core. "For what reason did Lokemele, and her son, come to Kauai, Ocean?"

She looked deeper into her father's eyes and remembered Alan's words. "It is not my story to tell, Makuakãne."

He sighed inwardly. *So, there was something more.*

That night he stared at the ceiling and found his answer. *Lokemele Longsdale was in love with him and she'd, obviously, come to Kauai to relight the fire that had once, briefly, united them.*

Chapter Forty-Eight

The minds and hearts of two grown-ups and two teenagers were twisted and gnawed with unanswered questions, unsolved quandaries and time was running out. Both Hanale and Rosemary were counting the hours their plane would take off; Ocean Tia and Kai desperately yearned to hold the clock back, as Hawaiian time ticked on leisurely and ignored their silent pleas.

Being ever vigilant, Luana felt the atmosphere in the air. Hanale and Ocean Tia barely acknowledged each other; Lokemele seemed edgy and nervous and Ocean Tia had also become uncharacteristically sullen, her sunny smile had vanished from her lips. Instinctively Luana knew there was a reason for their mood changes and suspected the reason lay with Kai. As with all problems, she knew food was the answer. *A good Hawaiian luau,* she firmly concluded, *never failed to soothe the body, heart, mind and soul; always bringing answers and peace.* And so she set her active mind into planning a luau before Rosemary, Hanale and Ocean Tia flew back to England.

Kai greeted the invitation with great inner excitement. *His first luau since…* he couldn't remember; *a chance,* he thought, *to spend the evening with his daughter and, perhaps, a chance to reacquaint himself properly with Lokemele.*

Rosemary and Hanale dreaded the idea both feeling that, out of sheer politeness to their generous hostess, they had no option but to comply.

Ocean Tia's smile returned. *Maybe,* she dared to dream, *this could mend the rift between herself and her half-brother; perhaps Hanale would, at long last, meet his father and Kai his only son.* Her smile widened.

From the small bedroom window, Rosemary espied Luana and Keoki's old friends coming from all directions; some with laden plates of delicious island food; others with bouquets of colourful flowers or bottles of Mai Tai; all of them with tropical leis and happy smiles. She smiled whimsically wishing, at that instant, that she was one of the happy-go-lucky natives. *Their lives,* she mused, *seemed much simpler and happier.* Oh how, she wished, Keoki would appear from around the corner and give her some of his sound advice. He would know exactly what to do in her predicament. *He would,* she silently concluded, *always lean on the side of truth and honesty, no matter how much it hurt.* She closed her eyes tight, her ears unable to block out the sound of the soft Hawaiian rhythms drifting in her direction and the answer came to her; Keoki's answer.

She felt a presence and knew it was him, as she wished her fast pulsating heart to stop beating and, thereby, prevent her from the painful confrontation that awaited them. It beat faster with no regard for her feelings. "Kai," she whispered hearing the tremor in her own voice.

"So, Lokemele, you left a poor man to die in a hospital bed."

She smiled and felt the tremor in her voice transferring to her lips, "You were hardly going to die."

"From a broken heart, I feel."

"I am so sorry about your wife, Kai."

"I wasn't thinking about Leialoha." He smiled whimsically.

Rosemary dropped her nervous eyes to the floor, not bearing to look at the man she once made love to; the sudden urge to run subsiding as her eyes rose and drifted to their son and, she knew, she had to stay, feel and face the truth. "We have to talk," she said softly.

"I agree." Kai smiled warmly. "Perhaps you would like a drink, Lokemele?"

"I think you and I better stay off the Mai Tai's, Kai."

"I was thinking of pineapple juice on the rocks."

She watched as he strode towards the makeshift bar. *Still a handsome man,* she thought, *though grief, alcohol abuse and life had clearly taken their toll. There were more crow's feet around his eyes, his face was thinner.* Her mind drifted… *as they were sitting amidst an array of pink and yellow plumeria, the nearness of his body close to her making her feel weak and helpless. About to rise and go she abandoned her get up and go as he enthused, "You know, here on the islands, we have luaus for all kinds of events…"* She smiled at the memory of his vivid account of King Kamehameha the Third's lavish luau, her mind still drifting as her words seeped out of her mouth. "How many fishes?"

"|Over three thousand fish, two hundred and seventy-one hogs and two thousand, two hundred and forty-five coconuts." Kai pressed the cool glass of juice into her hand.

"You're still a mine of information, Kai."

"Thankfully," he winked mischievously, "the alcohol has not taken that away from me."

"But it has taken other things away from you, Kai." She raised her eyes to his.

"Yes, yes." He agreed softly. "It has robbed me of many precious things."

But I have brought one precious son back to you. She desperately wanted to yell and clamped her lips tightly. *This was not the place.* From the distance, she saw Luana approaching, her face beaming at the sight of them both together. *The minutes were ticking away,* she concluded. *She needed to act fast, before it was too late.* "Kai, I need to see you alone; tomorrow, at sunset, on the beach." Her heart beat faster as his drowned in a sea of confusion.

The luau did not altogether go to plan; for, it left Ocean Tia and Hanale further estranged; Luana with many unanswered questions; Rosemary with heavy trepidation beating in her heart and Kai thinking there may be a glimmer of hope.

A few holidaymakers and natives had gathered on the beach, as Rosemary's eyes swept out on to the ocean and rose to the changing sky. *Soon,* she concluded, *Kai's life would be changed for ever.*

Kai strode on to the beach that had been his sanctuary and his solace. From afar, he spotted Rosemary and waved. She waved back and felt her heart starting to solidify, like the rehearsed words she had been practising all night. He pecked her on the cheek and they made their way to a suitable vantage point, to say *goodbye* to the retiring sun. They stood side by side and stared at the glorious, round, orange ball as it sank lower and lower to meet its lover, the mighty ocean and, as the sun touched the water, Rosemary knew it was time. She turned her eyes to him. "Kai," she whispered. "Kai…" And he took her in his arms and kissed her long and hard on the mouth.

"Mum!"

Two hearts raced.

"Makuakãne!"

Two hearts died. Rosemary's lips were released. Slowly they both turned to Hanale standing with Ocean Tia.

Four hearts raced. All words dried up as stark eyes stared; son at mother, daughter at father, mother at son, father at daughter; all feeling as if they were standing in some weird twilight zone, as the waves rolled leisurely on.

Time stood still.

The urge to run returned. Rosemary turned her stark eyes on Kai. "This is your son." Her eyes switched to Hanale. "Son, this is your father." She turned and walked away, leaving the silent family members on the sun deserted beach.

Chapter Forty-Nine

Father stared at son; son at father and Ocean Tia's eyes flitted between them both, while all three hearts thundered like the ocean in the background. For long moments, they stood as if super-glued to the cooling sand beneath their feet, their eyes on each other, their ears attune to the sound of the waves, as their thoughts fragmented like the grains of sand. The sun had abandoned them and so had Rosemary; leaving them to make some kind of coherent sense out of the debris of the past. Finally, Ocean Tia broke the spell and said, "Let's hug."

Reluctantly, father and son obliged, each feeling a current of uncertainty flow through their fast pulsating veins. Hanale pulled away and walked off, leaving two pairs of eyes looking after him; a turmoil of mixed emotions fighting a raging war in Kai's questioning eyes; they switched to his daughter. "Is this true, Ocean Tia?"

She nodded silently.

"Hanale is my son."

"Hanale is your son and my half-brother."

His puzzled eyes remained on his daughter. "How long have you known, Ocean?"

"Not long, Makuakãne."

"But long enough to have kept it a secret; to keep the truth away from me."

In the gathering gloom she searched his still, deep eyes for a sign of forgiveness. "I did not want to hurt you with the truth," she said in all honesty.

He dropped his eyes to his toes, half submerged in the white sand below. "You mean, I was not man enough to…"

"You were not strong enough, Makuakãne. I. I didn't want to make it worse for you." She interjected feeling his sadness.

He closed his eyes to her, his conflicting emotions threatening to suffocate his icy soul; the essence of his being. "I wasn't man enough." He repeated as he walked away, leaving her alone on the now deserted beach.

Hanale found his mother alone on the veranda, sitting still and silent on the rattan chair, her eyes staring into the darkness. Feeling a presence she raised her head, feeling a tight band clenching tightly her chest, her mouth firmly clamped. He stood a metre or so away from her, her stillness and silence transferring to him, as he wished he had the courage to hug her tightly and tell her she was forgiven. Instead, he stood still and stared, while she felt a wedge of raw betrayal between herself and her son. She heard his footsteps retreat; listened to each echoing step, as each step became more distant, yet, louder in her ears. *She had betrayed him and now he was walking away from her. What did she think would happen?* She chided herself severely for ever letting her thoughts think otherwise.

The teenager fell on to his bed and closed his eyes. Images of the man on the beach; the man he had been sitting so close to at the luau and, yet, had no inkling of who he was, bombarding his head; images of this man kissing his mother. *They had,* he dismally concluded, *both betrayed him for all of these years.* He wished the hours would go so that he could leave this island and all that it represented. He wished he could forget about Ocean Tia. He wished he could forget about his mother. *But how could he forget,* he concluded miserably, *when they were permanent fixtures in his life?* The gentle knock on the door made his eyes snap open. She came in without being invited and sat on the edge of his bed. He closed his eyes again. "Hanale." He heard the gentle whisper and wished she would disappear into a black hole. "Hanale." He did not stir a muscle, hot fury bubbling through every vein in his young body. She nudged his arm into opening his eyes. "We have to sort this out." Reluctantly he propped himself up against the pillows and glowered at his half-sister, making her shrivel up inside. Despite feeling like an irritable ant she continued on her mission. "Hanale, you are my half-brother; Kai is your father as well as being my father."

Her words made him cringe inwardly, invoking a sudden urge to run down to the ocean; to wash himself clean of Kai, Ocean Tia and his mother. Abruptly rising to his feet he made for the door. Her following words made him halt, the door knob half turned in his hand. "What did you just say?"

She repeated the words he half heard on his rush towards the door. "My heart will break if I never see you again, Hanale, and that's what will happen if you don't acknowledge us. We are a family."

And, for the first time in his life, he felt part of a family.

Chapter Fifty

An overpowering craving to drink; to forget what he did on the beach; what he heard on the beach and to throw himself into the comforting arms of oblivion, where no one could hurt him with mere words, tormented Kai. He stared at the rich, brown liquid in his tall glass and knew it would fulfil his wish of forgetfulness if he succumbed. He didn't feel the presence; but, felt the soft touch of her hand, some seconds later, and her gentle words. "This is not the answer, Kai." His yearning eyes turned away from one love and on to another, as Rosemary sat down beside him and he silently cursed her for her untimely arrival. She turned her face to him and rested her eyes on his sad eyes. "When I was in a very dark place, Keoki once told me, that to live you must find the root of the problem, tackle it and learn to be happy again."

Slowly he raised his sullen eyes to her his words slow, concise and serious. "You betrayed me, Lokemele."

After, what seemed like an eternity of silence, she said in a quiet, steady voice. "Yes, I betrayed you, Kai; I betrayed Hanale and I betrayed myself. That I can never undo and I will have to live with my betrayal for the rest of my life. In my defence, I acted in the best will. I thought I'd never see you again; so, what was the point of bringing you into Hanale's life?"

"The point is, you denied me the role of being a father to my son, Lokemele."

His words cut deep, every word pierced her heart, condemning her for her actions. "Will you ever find it in your heart to forgive me, Kai?" She asked her voice almost a whisper.

"Will you ever be able to forgive yourself, Lokemele?" He rose and left.

She sat and stared at the untouched Mai Tai, her fingers reaching out and feeling the cool dew bejewelled glass and imagined the silkiness of the liquid sliding down her throat, warming and comforting her. Abruptly she withdrew her hand, rose and swiftly left the premises, her head swirling with Kai's condemning question… *Will you ever be able to forgive yourself, Lokemele?…*

Will you ever be able to forgive *yourself, Lokemele?... Will you ever be able to forgive yourself, Lokemele?...* echoing louder and louder until, she thought, she was going out of her mind. And, while Rosemary thought she was going out of her mind, a thought crashed into Ocean Tia's mind, which had the potential of threatening her entire future.

Chapter Fifty-One

Conflicting thoughts wove and interwove in Hanale's head; Ocean Tia was in the centre of them all. Putting an end to his torment he decided on a course of action and, ready to apologise for his behaviour towards her, he went out to seek her out. About to enter the kitchen, he heard voices and pressed his inquisitive ear to the partly opened door.

"No, I won't be going back to England, Auntie Luana. I shall be staying here in Kauai, my home; it is where my family and my heart reside."

"What about your education?" He heard Luana's concerned, serious voice.

"I am not going back, Auntie Luana." Ocean Tia stated determinedly.

Hanale felt as if his whole world was whirling out of control and Ocean Tia was jumping off its crazy roundabout and into safer territory. He turned away, his heart heavy; for, he couldn't imagine life without Ocean Tia. During her time in England she had brought a secret joy, a unique fragrance of her own into his life. *And though he had acted despicably towards her, she was like no other,* he thought. *There was an aura of serenity about her and, in her presence, one couldn't help feeling loved; her kindness, honesty, caring attitude and work ethic were just added bonuses. Life,* he concluded glumly, *would not be the same without her. It would be dull, boring, lacking a unique sparkle and those she would leave behind would, undoubtedly, feel a void in their hearts; but, how to stop her from acting out her decision?* His heart clenched tightly.

Rosemary craved a stiff drink when she was confronted with the news; she sat rigid her eyes focussed directly on Luana, feeling the dull pain clawing at her heart; for, she had grown to love Ocean Tia as if she were her own daughter; but, above all, it was the young woman's education she was worried about. She grabbed her friend's hand. "We have to stop her, Luana."

"She has made up her mind, Lokemele."

"Her mind can be changed."

"I am not convinced it can be changed." Luana's tired eyes wavered on Rosemary as the younger woman rose and grabbed her beach bag. "Where are you going, Lokemele; breakfast is almost ready."

No answer was given.

Rosemary hastened down the narrow, uneven paths, bordered on both sides with colourful blooming flowers; her pace quickened as she jogged down... down... down to the ocean and there she walked along the beach, her eyes fixed on the undulating water, folding and unfolding as it had done unceasingly since the very dawn of creation. And here she found her solace and her answer. For, just like the ocean she was named after, Ocean Tia had to be set free. She could not be restrained, contained, controlled; she was a free spirit belonging to no one.

For a few brief seconds on hearing his daughter's news, Kai was delighted; his short-lived happiness turning to dismay, when he stopped to think about the future consequences of her actions. But, he also knew his child's strong, resolute will and knew he was not strong enough to fight it.

A heavy blanket of stifled emotions overpowered the small group at Lihue Airport. This was not the departure any of them had predicted or wanted. They stood like five strangers not daring to catch each other's eye, in case they revealed something of themselves; each in a world of silent despair, where no one was allowed to enter; all breathing a secret sigh of relief when the flight for Los Angeles was announced.

As the plane soared upwards and away, hopes and dreams were left behind. This time, Rosemary did not look out the small window on to the twinkling evening lights of Kauai, her heart was broken.

Chapter Fifty-Two

She espied Alan amongst the throng in the arrivals area, her heavy heart heaving a sigh of relief and abruptly deflating, as she caught sight of his puzzled eyes looking beyond her and Hanale and her heart boke afresh as it felt his sorrow, his unfulfilled dream. "I am so sorry, Alan."

She broke down in his comforting arms and allowed herself to be hugged tightly as he said softly, "You can tell me all about it later."

Outwardly, life slotted back into a scheduled routine of college, housework, homework, college assignments, work, football practise, cooking and all the usual necessities and distractions of daily life. But, something deep and meaningful; something very precious was missing in Rosemary and Hanale's lives and both knew it was Ocean Tia; for, she was their link with the past and now they seemed to be cruising along without their anchor; both felt unsettled; both felt a deep loss that no one else, and nothing else, could replace.

Alan felt their loss and his own. He observed closely and said nothing; for, like the Hawaiians, he was a great believer of time and patience and so he allowed time to take its natural course and determine their fate.

Hanale tried desperately to fight his inner turmoil by erasing Ocean Tia from his thoughts and focusing on his college work, giving all he got to his sports and going out with his mates. *After all,* he told himself, *she was only his half-sister who he barely knew.* But, still, she kept seeping into his thoughts.

Rosemary welcomed Ocean Tia to infiltrate her mind; but, with these thoughts came a secret despair; for, she knew, things would have been very different had it not have been for the immature, irresponsible kiss she had shared with Kai on the beach and, she knew, she would never forgive herself. She was also aware that her selfish actions went deeper, much further back, when she had embarked on the road of betrayal and deceit.

It was early October and already Christmas cards and decorations were appearing in the shops. Hanale hated this time of year because, it was at this time of year, as a child, he felt the odd one out; the kid without a father; the lad who never had a father on Christmas day; the child who would search all day long and never find a Christmas gift from his dad; the small boy who pretended to be happy playing with his new train set with his mum; the innocent boy who regarded Father Christmas as some sort of mystical, magical father figure, who would visit him secretly once a year, bestow on him lots of presents and vanish again. *Still,* he had concluded, *this magical, mysterious figure was better than no father at all.* Aimlessly he wandered into a small shop, picked up a random box of cards and flicked through the contents, his unenthusiastic eyes scanning the images depicting sweet looking kittens under colourful Christmas trees, cute dogs attired in Santa outfits and magical Christmas scenes, where country cottages and skeletal trees were iced with snow and his mind drifted… *far away, to a distant island where it never snowed… where Ocean Tia had never thrown a snowball or sped down a snow hill on a sleigh… where her father… his father…* A sudden, erratic thought crashed into his mind, extinguishing all other thoughts and, with that flaming thought burning in his brain, he ran all the way home.

Startled eyes stared at the panting, red-faced, excited-eyed teenager as he struggled to catch his breath. "I think we should invite Ocean Tia and her father for Christmas, Mum." His words rushed out of his mouth, like gushing water from a freshly thawed river.

Rosemary sat perfectly still and silent not believing what, she thought, she had just heard, her shocked eyes staring at her son while her heart raced.

Staring back at his mother's obvious incredulity, he repeated his request and vacated the house, the clicking of the door reverberating loudly in Rosemary's ears, as a thousand thoughts whirled about in her head, accompanied by a thousand conflicting scenarios.

Sometime later Alan found her in a daze looking into space and, sitting down beside her, he took her hands into his comforting, warm hands. "What is it, Rosemary?" Without looking at him she repeated Hanale's strange request. He squeezed her hands gently, reassuringly and smiled at her pale face. "I think it's a great idea, Rosemary." He watched the glimmer of a smile dance on her lips and a dancing sparkle slip into her eyes. "I really do, Rosemary; I think it has the potential of tying up a lot of loose ends."

She lifted her eyes to his kind eyes. "Or stir up a hornet's nest."

He rose and filled the kettle with water, his words travelling from the kitchen sink. "You know, Rosemary, you should take heed of your Hawaiian friend's words. Didn't Keoki once say to you that you should find the problem, tackle it and learn to be happy again?"

Alan and Keoki's words intermingled, reverberating loudly in her mind and she nodded her head. "Yes, yes; that's exactly what Keoki said to me."

"Well then; I think you should take notice of Keoki's sound advice, Rose." She caught Alan's sincere smile and the tenderness in his eyes, a sudden frown etching on her forehead which Alan saw and added, "And, don't even think about how you could finance the trip."

Her face turned serious. "You can't, Alan; it is not your problem to…"

"It isn't a problem at all." He smiled genially. "Learn to live a little, like a Hawaiian, Rose."

"How come you know so much about them, Alan?" She smiled back.

"I have engaged in a spot of research regarding the Hawaiians and, anyway, who knows, maybe, one day, I might accompany you to that lovely paradise." Little did he know, this would happen in a way neither of them could ever predict.

"Who knows?" Without thinking she placed her arms around his neck and kissed him on the cheek.

"Don't I get a proper kiss?" He winked mischievously.

She withdrew her hands and smiled softly.

"Then, there is hope," he chuckled.

She secretly hoped so as they clinked coffee mugs. "Aloha," they both enthused.

Preparations were made on both sides of the world as Christmas fast approached. The house was lavishly decorated, home-made Christmas cake and mince pies placed into tins and non-alcoholic beverages stocked away in cupboards. Everything was ready; but, the people concerned. Mixed excitement and trepidation beat in hearts; for, in the hope of fulfilling dreams of unification they knew, that for true unity to occur, they needed to delve into the nitty-gritty; into issues which had long been buried beneath mounds of secrecy; they would need to dig deep into themselves and find their true selves.

Kauai

Heavy trepidation resided in Kai's heart and soul. He felt he had been much too hasty in his acceptance. He did not see light at the end of the proverbial tunnel; he saw only despondency. *What would a trip across the world accomplish, if not more heartache?* He asked himself. To see Rosemary, the woman who had denied him his son, was something he was not sure he could deal with; to be in close proximity of his son, after having been denied so many years of a father-son relationship, he knew, would be extremely difficult. And, yet, he felt a strange pull, a tug of the heart telling him something was missing. He felt it deeply; a hole no one could see and inside the hole something gnawed and twisted giving him no peace.

Ocean Tia was counting the days. Christmas in England was something she had always dreamed about. She smiled wistfully, hoping it would snow.

Luana remained neutral on the subject saying nothing, secretly worrying if her brother was strong enough to take it all in his stride, without reaching for the bottle. *What could she do,* she asked herself, *except wait patiently for what fate would bring?*

Chapter Fifty-Three

The uneasy feeling of déjà vu hit Rosemary, Kai, Hanale and Ocean Tia, momentarily taking them back to different experiences in Kauai. Now, they knew they had to cross an emotional bridge and to safely get to the other side, where they could find happiness; they had to prepare themselves to acknowledge and listen to each other, as well as to their own feelings; to allow anger and frustration to spill whether, in the course of doing so hurt them or not; they had to be ready to accept anything and everything thrown at them and, so, with fast beating hearts, they hugged each other and fervently hoped for the best, while Alan looked on silently and secretly prepared himself to catch the emotional debris which was bound to fall.

Ocean Tia broke the ice and linked her arm with her half-brother. "Hanale, it's so great to see you again. I have missed you so very much."

His heart melted as his watery eyes turned to her. "I have missed you too, Ocean."

They walked on ahead, leaving the grown-ups to fend for themselves; Kai feeling as if he had Mount Everest to climb, the coolness between himself and his son visibly noticeable and deeply felt.

Feeling the sharp, icy tenseness between Rosemary and Kai, Alan took over the reins slipping into casual conversation and gradually they felt the tension ease; but, the reprieve was short-lived when, out of the blue, Alan stated, "Now, the two of you need to talk. You need to sort things out between yourselves, Hanale and Ocean Tia. Remember, you have to tackle the problem to find happiness." And with these haunting words firmly implanted in her head, a fresh dread invaded Rosemary.

With dishes washed and stacked away and Alan away for the evening, they sat at the table with no more excuses to allow their escape. To move on, they all knew that they had to face each other with the truth. Finally, Kai opened his mouth. "Well, this is it, Lokemele." He raised his rich, brown eyes to Rosemary's eyes where they locked.

"It is." Rosemary smiled bleakly deflecting her eyes.

"Do you want Ocean Tia and me to leave, Mum?" Hanale rose from the table.

"No." Rosemary and Kai said in unison and Hanale, reluctantly, sat back down, catching Ocean Tia's reassuring smile, his ears attune to his father's words.

"You know how I feel, Lokemele, about…" Kai switched his eyes to his son, "… about Hanale; the fact I did not…" The words remained stuck in his dry throat.

An invisible, ruthless knife stabbed through Hanale's heart as, into his mind crashed an image of Kai dressed up as Father Christmas, bestowing an abundance of gifts at his bedside and he finished off his father's sentence. "No, you did not know I existed." And, as he said the words a new realisation rammed into his head. *How could he possibly blame this man for not being there, if he didn't know he had a son; how could he blame him for not dressing up in a Father Christmas costume and bringing him gifts, if this man didn't know his little boy was thousands of kilometres away, eagerly awaiting his secret midnight visit?* A new, alien feeling entered Hanale's heart; pity for the man, sitting opposite him, who never knew he had a son; for, at least he himself knew he had a father somewhere in the world. Kai's words crashed into his head.

"Hanale, please do not blame your mother."

Three pairs of eyes shot to Rosemary; but, her eyes had dropped to the bare table, where they became absorbed in the ingrained wood, as she focused on one black spot, wondering how it had got there.

Hate had entered Hanale's young heart; not for the loving, caring mother Rosemary had always been but for her deceit; for, no matter how lengthy or in depth their talk would be, what she did could not be undone. It was there for all eternity and, with her secrecy, came years and years of loss that could never be recaptured. He flinched at the light touch on his arm and heard Ocean Tia's soft words. "Try and think of what you have now, Hanale; of what you can have in the future with your relationship with your father. You have time to spend with each other; to get to know each other." Her hopeful eyes darted to her father and he took the hint.

"Perhaps, Hanale, we could get to know each other; maybe by spending a day together?"

Hanale's eyes flicked to his father and, after heavy seconds of suspended silence said, "Why not?"

Chapter Fifty-Four

The eerie dawn silence, and the empty coffee mugs on the table, told Rosemary that Hanale and Kai were no longer in the house. They had set off on their father-son bonding mission leaving her with warring, conflicting feelings of hope, dread, happiness, sadness, optimism, pessimism and silent despair; these tortured her relentlessly throughout the long day.

She spent the day with an excited, optimistic Ocean Tia as they searched the shops for unique Christmas gifts; went into one boutique after another, in the hope of finding glamorous gowns to wear for the Christmas party, Alan had insisted in throwing and ended up in a stuffy, crowded cafe with armfuls of parcelled up packages and no gowns. Sipping their hot, steaming coffees, Ocean Tia focussed her eyes on Rosemary and said softly, "Thank you, Lokemele."

The older woman raised her questioning eyes. "For what?"

"For giving my father and Hanale a chance."

"Don't thank me, Ocean; it was Alan who was the master planner; he enabled it all. On my own, I could have done nothing."

"He is a good man; yes?"

Rosemary's steady eyes remained on the young woman. "Yes, he is a very good man, Ocean."

"And he loves you."

The hot liquid flew everywhere, scorched Rosemary's fingers and made her splutter. After managing to catch her breath and resume normal breathing, she fixed her eyes firmly on her cup, unable to meet the eyes of her interrogator and stated in as calm a voice as she could muster, "I shall pretend I didn't hear that comment."

"But you know it's true, Lokemele. Alan is a good and honest man; what more could you possibly want?" Ocean Tia's young eyes remained fixed on Rosemary as both women lapsed into silence.

Kai and Hanale barely spoke as they sat side by side in the coach, yet thousands of kilometres apart; each wishing he could turn back the clock, and their agreement, on spending time together; both thinking they had nothing to link them together, apart from the fact they were united by blood.

As Kai looked out the window on to the flat, frosty fields he yearned to be back in Kauai; to be wandering along a deserted beach; to feel the warmth of the Hawaiian sun on his skin; to feel the waves lapping his bare feet and to hear their thundering call. Here, in England, he felt his soul dying a slow death and his heart following suit.

As if reading his thoughts Hanale said softly, "It's different in Kauai, isn't it?"

"It's different." Kai murmured, "Yes, it is very different."

Both lapsed into the depths of grim silence once more; each in their own private world of thoughts.

"We're here!" Someone announced.

Both father and son had been so immersed in their own reveries, neither had noticed their approach towards the magnificent, awe-inspiring bridge. Their eyes shot to the eye-catching engineering structure before them. Kai's eyes widened; never in his whole life had he seen something so breathtakingly ingenious, as his captivated eyes tried to take it all in.

"It's called Humber Bridge. It now supersedes Golden Gate and is the longest, single-span, suspension bridge in the world; though, others are desperately trying to beat our record," stated Hanale.

"Wow! Wow!" Was all Kai could manage to extol out of his mouth, as he continued to listen avidly to his son's low-down of the bridges history.

"And, the Queen came to officially open it in nineteen eighty one."

"The Queen; was that Queen Elizabeth the Second?" Kai asked, his eyes still firmly fixed on the bridge.

"Yes, yes; Queen Elizabeth the Second." Hanale confirmed.

"Wow!" Kai relapsed into silence, only for a spurge of words to escape a few seconds later. "You know, the Hawaiians Islands are steeped in royal history." And, as Kai divulged into Hawaii's link with royalty, and with much detail about King Kamehameha the Great's formation of the Kingdom of Hawaii, his son listened with much interest and wanted to know more and more.

They walked side by side on the windswept bridge; two men; father and son. No longer strangers; more than mere acquaintances; friends. *Yes,* Kai mused, *they were becoming friends and that,* he thought, *was a good foundation on which to build.*

Casual snippets of conversation passed between them; to begin with about the bridge and aspects of its brilliant engineering skills; then they switched to contrasting England and Kauai; slowly personal references came into the equation and, gradually, Kai began to learn a little about his son.

Hanale found out nothing about his father; he seemed to be a closed book and the teenager was not ready to probe deeply. They walked on; friends.

By the end of the day, they had walked over the bridge, shared sandwiches and coffee, learned something of each other's country and began to smile. And, as they walked in through the door, Ocean Tia's heart leaped and Rosemary's heart dared to hope.

Chapter Fifty-Five

Alan was a rare visitor, giving Rosemary and Kai space to work things out for the sake of their son. Rosemary craved to see him and the more he kept away, the stronger her desire to see him became. She missed his calming and stabilising influence, his cheerful smile, his softly spoken voice. Kai was no longer the outgoing, self-assured charmer he was years ago. There was an air of quietness about him; brooding, almost dark and sinister in nature and Rosemary felt uncomfortable under its veil and, so, she made sure she was never alone in a room with Kai; for, she was aware how quickly his mood could change and, with it, her own growing despondency and despair and, ultimately, her craving for the one thing, she knew, she could not have; alcohol. Kai felt her silent withdrawal from him and the more she withdrew, the more he wanted her.

On the evening before Christmas Eve, Ocean Tia suddenly gave a shriek of delight and, uncharacteristically, throwing down her knife and fork with a clash on to her plate, she ran out the door into the cool, white floating whirl of snowflakes. Rosemary, Hanale and Kai followed and watched as she danced around the garden, catching swirling snowflakes and holding them up in her hand, before they disintegrated into nothing, her happy eyes twinkling with amazement at such wonder, her long silky hair delicately decorated with soft flakes, like some unique Hawaiian headdress, as she continued to twirl and whirl in unison with the gently falling snow.

Hypnotised by what she saw, Rosemary forcibly withdrew her eyes from the enchanting vision and focussed them on Kai. In an instant, as if in a trance, she was by his side, her hands wrapped around his waist. As he felt the touch of her hands on his body, he turned and the magical spell was broken.

"I'm sorry... I'm sorry." Rosemary reiterated as she averted her eyes, stepped away from his intoxicating presence and ran, as fast as her feet would carry her, into the sanctuary of her home.

That night Ocean Tia played a starring role in her disjointed nightmare. In one fragment, *she was dancing naked in the garden, while thick snowflakes whirled and twirled around her;* in the next fragment *she sang happily, her lyrics conflicting, "Alan loves you, Lokemele… Kai loves you, Lokemele… Alan loves you, Lokemele…"* She woke up with a start, her heart pulsating rapidly, her mouth as dry as a bone, beads of visible sweat on her forehead and with a craving for something much stronger than water. Her eyes strayed to the luminous green lights on her alarm clock. *Quarter past two.* All was quiet like a tomb. All was still apart from her fast beating heart, which threatened to jump out of her heaving chest. She lay back on her pillow and tried to force sleep to take her for its own. Instead, the same haunting words bombarded her head… *Alan loves you, Lokemele… Kai loves you, Lokemele…* Sitting up she glared into the dark, as Ocean Tia's words continued to echo in her head, now taking a different stance… *Alan is a kind, good, honest man, Lokemele. What more could you want from a man?* And the words involuntarily came out of Rosemary's mouth. "Indeed, what more could I want from a man?"

Chapter Fifty-Six

Rosemary attended church on rare occasions: christenings, weddings, funerals and always Midnight Mass. She was a lapsed Catholic; educated in a Catholic school, had religion thrust upon her and rebelled against it. Midnight Mass was different; it was personal and special to her; it was a time to gather her thoughts together, to make peace with her God and to start anew. But, sitting in-between Alan and Kai, Rosemary was far from gathering her thoughts together, her inner peace ruffled; for, in different ways, she loved both men. Alan was the slow burner, who charged her with common sense and made sure she was thinking straight; he was her anchor. Kai had been her lover, be it only for one glorious night and thousands of kilometres away, on a beautiful tropical island; he had been her temporary port, when her head was in the midst of an emotional storm. She felt the gentle squeeze of Alan's hand and the electrifying presence of Kai's still body so close to her, as she stared ahead at the pink and red poinsettias, adorning the incense scented altar and her mind drifted... *The car sped past idyllic desolate beaches and along winding narrow roads, bordered on both sides by lush foliage displaying blooms of yellow hibiscus and red and white frangipani and above, the cascading rainbow shower tree. She gave a deep sigh as she caught sight of clusters of pink and yellow blooms. "Frangipani." He had informed her. Stopping the engine he abruptly jumped out of his seat. Her wary eyes followed him as he reached out, plucked out a white bloom displaying a yellow centre, attached it to the side of her left ear and gave her a peck on the cheek, making her quiver inwardly as she looked ahead. "In Hawaii a plumeria, or any other flower, worn on the right side indicates a wahine as available; on the left side, she is taken." She looked at him, smiled and informed him she was not taken. "For today, you are taken." He smiled, revved up the engine and sped along the hairpin bends, making her blood bubble with a mixture of excitement and apprehension...* It seemed so long ago. *And yet, she mused, it was just as if it had happened yesterday.* She gazed up at Kai and, feeling her eyes on him, he looked at Rosemary their eyes locking. Instantly they both looked away, as if singed from the contact, their eyes focussing directly on the altar; for, there was the ultimate deterrent, dragging them away from temptation. But, it was too late to stifle what they had both felt in those fleeting seconds.

Christmas Day and Boxing Day passed happily without incident as they expanded their knowledge of each other's Christmas traditions and enjoyed the relaxed atmosphere. Rosemary, Hanale, Ocean Tia and Kai were astounded by Alan's culinary skills; for, in his own modest way, he was a consummate amateur chef; however, his mouth watering fare almost landed Kai at the dentist's door. Being a traditionalist, Alan pulled out all the traditional stops and, as they were tucking into the Christmas pudding, a sudden "Agh... ooh..." alerted their eyes to an alarmed Kai, as he dropped his spoon and brought his hand up to his cheek, while Alan and Rosemary broke out in spontaneous, rapturous laughter, as a bewildered Ocean Tia looked aghast at her pained father. "Ooh..." Kai sprang up, rushed to a nearby mirror and examined, as best he could, the offending article in his mouth; truly mystified at the mysterious cause of his pain, as he took the small, hard object out of his mouth and tried, without success, to identify it.

"Ah... a silver sixpence; one of our Christmas traditions." Alan chuckled softly and all saw the funny side of the incident.

"You know, in Hawaii," said Kai, "we need to import our Christmas trees way before the special day. The trees are transported on a ship, we call, the Christmas tree ship."

"What about Santa, does he wear the traditional red outfit? Did you dress up as Santa for Ocean Tia?" Hanale was intrigued to know; a bitter-sweet wave of regret sweeping simultaneously across his heart and eyes.

Kai laughed lightly. "Santa wears an Aloha suit and, instead of a sleigh and reindeer, he arrives on an outrigger canoe, with an escort of dolphins."

"Wow! I'd love to witness that spectacle," exclaimed the teenager.

"Who knows, maybe one day you will," smiled Ocean Tia.

"I'd like that," said Hanale quietly, as Alan caught the exchanged smiles between Rosemary and Kai.

"Merry Christmas." Alan raised his glass of pure pineapple juice. "May our guests be as happy as we are."

"Mele Kalikimaka." Ocean Tia responded and they all clinked glasses.

"Mele Kalikimaka." Hanale, Rosemary, Alan and Kai enthused happily, as Kai and Hanale exchanged a warm fatherly-son smile.

Chapter Fifty-Seven

It was a happy festive gathering; though a secret seed of uncertainty had taken root and was already taking hold of one person as, for the first time, a gnawing doubt started to niggle. It made him feel uncomfortable and uneasy about his future; but what worried him most was that his doubt was intermingled with an uncharacteristic spurge of envy. He had seen the way Rosemary and Kai exchanged smiles, and he had witnessed the bond between father and son. He had seen with his own eyes, and heard with his own ears, how interested Hanale was becoming with all things Hawaiian and he sensed a drifting away, as if he did not belong in their world. What hurt Alan the most was that he had been the instigator of his own misery; for, had he not financed Ocean Tia's education; had he not encouraged Rosemary to be present at Keoki's funeral; had he not proposed the idea of Kai and his daughter spending Christmas in England, he would still have Rosemary for himself and maybe, one day, would have her as his wife and Hanale as a step-son. Now, he didn't know what was going to happen.

Rosemary detected a sadness in Alan's eyes and put it down to memories of Christmases gone by. She was starting to feel very much alive, with a happiness in her heart and soul she had not experienced before. Now, she had her little family and Alan, her rock. For the first time in her life, she felt truly secure and was looking forward to what the New Year might bring.

Ocean Tia's eyes sparkled with excitement. There were the New Year celebrations to look forward to and the thought of making up a foursome with Hanale, a casual girl friend of his and Simon Teal. She had finally bought a gown and, as she looked at her reflection in the full-length mirror, she smiled. Her choice of a floral print dress made her feel she was not betraying her Hawaiian roots and, as she picked up her white artificial frangipani and pinned it to her right ear, she said to her reflection, "I am not taken… yet."

166

In the next room, Rosemary was making final adjustments to her full-length, midnight-blue, strapless, satin gown. She sighed deeply wondering what the night held in store.

The men folk prepared themselves as men folk invariably do; without fuss; or, seemingly, much thought; but turning out immaculately attired in black suits, except for Kai. His golden tan was highlighted in a white suit and colourful tie; though, if he had his way, he would be wearing a Hawaiian printed shirt and a pair of black shorts. In formal dress, he felt uncomfortable, not himself, and most certainly out of his comfort zone. He exhaled a deep sigh. *He would have to grin and bear it for tonight as he would, somehow, have to bear watching Alan, his host, escort Lokemele throughout the long evening ahead.*

Alan was determined to make this a night to remember; a night to make an imprint on Rosemary's heart before... it was too late.

Both men's eyes rose to Rosemary as she walked down the narrow staircase, which did not do justice to her elegancy. Alan smiled, took her hand and kissed it softly, his lingering eyes not able to leave her face. Kai could only look on a hard, dry lump settling uncomfortably in his throat. He snapped out of his secret daydream, as his eyes fell on the innocent beauty of his daughter; his Hawaiian princess. *Her future yet to be lived,* he concluded, *and it was his duty to direct her back to her Hawaiian roots.* He had not liked what he had seen in England. The girls often seemed rough, using language which shook him to the core; stayed out all night and got up to God knows what and smoked substances he'd rather not know about. *No,* he mused, *this was not the place for Ocean Tia. Like her namesake, she belonged in the calmness and gentleness of Kauai. To uproot her permanently away from the sunshine, the ocean, the soft sands would be like slowly choking her identity out of her. He had to take her back home, before it became too late and she became a clone of the girls he had seen.* "You look beautiful, Ocean." He said softly giving her a kiss on the cheek. "Now, this evening, stay close by Hanale's side; please be careful."

"Aren't I always?"

"Yes... yes." He nodded knowing she was; but, it wasn't Ocean Tia he was worrying about.

Secretly Rosemary watched as Kai let Ocean Tia leave his side, feeling his inner loneliness and anxiety. "Come Alan." She tugged at his arm. "Let's go and cheer Kai up."

Obediently he followed, his happy heart deflating a degree.

The party was in full swing when they arrived at the venue. Four types of musical entertainment was on offer: a classical piano area, where haunting sounds of Chopin drifted through; a Caribbean steel drum area, where Rosemary espied energetic bodies engaging in impressive moves; a small orchestra playing waltzes and tangoes, and the like and a lively, loud, pulsating disco, to which Hanale and Ocean Tia were immediately drawn towards.

Alan felt the pressure on his arm as he was about to head for the classical area and, to his disappointment, was directed, by Rosemary's guidance, towards the steel drums. *The closest thing to Hawaiian music,* she thought, *Kai was going to have.* She had seen the sadness in his eyes and knew the cause of it was loss. On catching Rosemary's smile, Kai tried hard to shirk off his growing dark mood; but, it had lodged deep in the bowels of his heart and, he knew, there was no medication for this type of ailment.

During the course of the evening comfort and ease did not sit well with Alan, Rosemary or Kai. Each portrayed a false, see-through display of happiness; each secretly fighting with their private doubts and anxieties.

The meal they sat down to was sumptuous; though Rosemary had noticed that Kai had barely eaten a morsel. Immediately recognising that he felt out of place, she engaged him in trivial conversation; her heart feeling heavy laden with his loss, intermingled with her own secret loss of losing something she never really had; something she could never stamp her claim on; a brief, passionate love, which had evaporated into the realms of her memory, as soon as it was consummated; cherished always and never to be forgotten. She had locked it away in the vault of her heart and now she was sitting next to the source of that love; the flame and it burned deeply.

His sad eyes rested on his one and only daughter, the blossom of his undying love for Leialoha; his dead wife. Ocean Tia was engaged in happy conversation and laughter with a guy she was sitting next to, making Kai wonder, and question, who it was who was taking the whole of Ocean's attention. *What kind of family did he have? Was he a student? What were his future prospects? Why was Ocean Tia so engrossed with him?* An instant dislike for this potential suitor surged through Kai's veins; *for, be it on a temporary basis, he had already stolen his precious daughter.* Politely excusing himself he rose and left the table; surreptitious eyes following him and Alan watching Rosemary.

She found him in the quietness of the hotel garden; a solitary figure sitting on a bench, while she stood perfectly still wondering what she should do. Following her heart she took cautious steps towards him. "Aloha Kai."

Abruptly he turned and exclaimed, "Lokemele!"

They sat side by side in silence feeling only their own fast beating hearts, their ears attune to the babble of distant voices and laughter drifting from within; two pairs of eyes looking out into the darkness each seeing an opposing vision, as one pair saw hope and the other a dismal future. Spontaneously she took his hand into her own and, feeling its smoothness, thought, *This hand is not used to hard labour.* Quickly she withdrew her hand as she felt his eyes on her and she waded in, before he had chance to announce any further declarations of love. "It is good, Kai, that you and Hanale have a bond. I. I am sorry for everything." She rose and felt the sharp tug of his hand pulling her back down. She sat like a solidified statue, her unblinking eyes fixated on the velvety darkness beyond, her ears hearing the haunting sound of a distant owl and Kai's words. "I am sorry too, Lokemele." She felt the bonds around her heart stiffen as her chest became tighter and tighter. *She had hurt him deeply and they were both paying the price.* Her pain turned to shock as she heard his next words.

"I hurt you, Lokemele." He turned his eyes to her stern face, not daring to face him, and studied the silhouetted outlines of her cheekbones, the soft roundness of her chin, as his mind drifted off to a time long ago... years and decades ago when... *he took her glass away and said softly, "Let's meet the sunset."... Below them gently swished the long leaves of palms, stirred by the softest whisper of the trade winds and further down below, the soft rolling carpet of luscious foliage of varying greens, interspersed with pockets of vivid colour, leading to the sweeping ocean below and the horizon meeting its old-time friend...* And he remembered stating to himself at the time... *If I have a daughter, I shall name her Tia...* It was his wife, Leialoha's idea to precede Tia with the name Ocean. How he wished he could grasp that moment back and to never let it go as his mind drifted once more and... *he was standing behind Lokemele, his strong arms enveloping her body as both stood silent, like ancient Hawaiian gods honouring their sun... They stood together, body against body, watching the majestic sun sink into the waiting ocean. And he turned her to himself and kissed her full on the mouth, long and hard; tongue exploring tongue and, just as the ocean claimed the sun, he claimed Lokemele's body, soul and heart. They lay naked body against naked body, intertwined as the early morning sun greeted them through the open glass door…* And, from that time, she had claimed a tiny part of his heart; but, the remainder of his heart, and his undying love, his wife had claimed for her own. Without thinking he took Rosemary into his arms, his hungry mouth upon hers. She succumbed to her own yielding vulnerability as futile thoughts of resistance washed over her. Abruptly she pulled away. "I can't Kai."

"Why?" His burning question was urgent, his voice husky, as he tried to pull her back.

"I can't." Ruthlessly she shrugged his hands away, turned and ran towards the lively sounds of youth. *Oh Lord, what torturous hell am I in now?* She asked herself, trying to adjust her eyes to the flashing lights and her ears to the relentless boom… boom… boom… of modern rhythms as she concluded, *No one in their right mind would classify this atrocious din as music. No one!*

There amongst the throng of gyrating bodies, flashes of bright lights and the monotonous pulsating rhythm she felt safe; away from Kai; away from Alan; away from her mistakes of the past. Here she could not delve and dig because, here, she could not think; here, she just breathed.

She sat alone amidst a crowd of young revellers who clinked glasses, laughed, joked and lived life; smiling obligingly when they offered her a glass of something, she thought, was very tempting; feeling like an intruder, who had stumbled into a world in which she did not belong. While, in other areas of the vast complex, Alan was wondering where on earth Rosemary had got to and Kai was feeling like the loneliest man in the world.

Chapter Fifty-Eight

Closely clasped in Alan's strong arms, Rosemary's mind drifted back to the scene on the bench and how she had felt when Kai had kissed her. *Was it love?* She asked herself. *No.* She replied emphatically; *infatuation?* No, she didn't think it was that either; *lust?* Forcibly she switched her mind and her full attention on to her dancing partner. She couldn't bear to think what the consequences could be of her truthful answer.

Excitement was in the air as midnight was fast approaching and, with it, the New Year. As Rosemary sat on the balcony, her non-alcoholic cocktail in her hand, her eyes closed to the sound of hypnotic Caribbean rhythms, her mind wandered… *What had the last year brought them? A mixed bag of everything,* she answered her own question. *Great sadness intermingled with great joy… the loss of dear Keoki… the addition of Ocean Tia to their lives… the union between Hanale and his father and now… confusion.*

"What are you thinking?" Alan broke the silence with his soft words. She was relieved he could not read her thoughts, as she took a generous gulp of her cocktail. "Rosemary…"

"Oh nothing… just… well, the passing of another year; it always evokes memories."

"Good memories?" He cocked a quizzical eyebrow.

"Some."

They lapsed into silence once more, Rosemary's mind delving into forbidden thoughts; Alan hoping the secret plan he was weaving would come to successful fruition and, as Rosemary's eyes glazed over in confusion, Alan's mouth broke into a secret smile.

"Ladies and gentlemen, it's time to replenish your glasses."

"Come; let's get nearer to the stage." Alan enthused, taking Rosemary's hand and dispelling her erratic thoughts.

"Ten… nine… eight… seven…," called the Master of Ceremonies as everyone joined in the excitement, "… five… four… three… two… one; Happy New Year!"

"Will you marry me, Rosemary?"

"Yes." She felt her lips reply, as her answer thundered mercilessly in her head and Alan's hands tighten around her waist. As his lips took hers, secretive eyes lingered on the happy couple and a breaking heart started to die, to the sounds of a happy Jamaican tune and the merry laughter of the New Year's party revellers.

Alone, in their own beds, the first night of the New Year provoked a mixture of feelings; hopes, raised dreams, dashed spirits lifted and deflated. Hanale slept like a baby, blissful in a teenager's drunken stupor; Ocean Tia was experiencing the first pangs of real love and couldn't get Simon out of her whirling mind; Alan was sleeping peacefully, with the happy thought of Rosemary accepting his hand in marriage; Rosemary suffered a torturous night tossing and turning, getting up, reading, drinking endless mugs of tea, going back to bed, only to renew her bouts of tossing and turning while conflicting, disturbing thoughts ruled her mind causing her, one minute to silently announce her deep love for Alan; the next to deny love for him as her erratic mind drifted to Kai and so the hours dragged on and her thoughts along with them. Kai was in a dark place; his wife was gone; Lokemele was betrothed to another and the worst, sharp pain was the knowledge that his daughter was drifting silently away from him; for, he had seen the youngsters dance and look at each other and it reminded him of the way he danced with, and looked at, Leialoha. *Time,* he dismally thought, *was a curse and not a healer* and he, momentarily, despised his fellow Hawaiians for having such a sedate, naive view of things. *There was,* he concluded, *nothing for him here. And yet, what was there back for him in Kauai?*

New Year brought with it hope and despair.

Chapter Fifty-Nine

A solitary figure walked away from the small group. He looked back once, smiled and was gone breaking Ocean Tia's young heart; making Alan's heart soar to the highest heavens; Hanale's heart happy and Rosemary's mind with the secure knowledge of a lasting bond between father and son. As she watched Kai's brightly coloured Hawaiian print shirt and black trousers disappear through into departures, she closed her eyes. *It could have been so very different...*

"A penny for them." Alan squeezed her hand.

"For what?" She asked her voice monotone, her eyes stuck to the now empty departures entrance.

"For your thoughts."

She raised her thoughtful eyes to his. "Come on; let's go."

There was a heavy emptiness. Hanale felt it; Ocean Tia felt it; Rosemary felt it. It was a void only Kai could fill; but, he was gone. Alan felt an emptiness too; his was of a different nature and one which only Rosemary could fill; for, despite his initial happiness and inner excitement, he felt she was not entirely his. Partly, he felt, this was due to their not having consummated their relationship and, partly, due to her bereavement over Keoki and now Kai's departure. He began to question the validity of their own relationship and subtly tried, on several occasions, to confront her. He failed miserably in his attempts and decided to let *time* sort everything out.

Rosemary went about her daily routine feeling she was weighed down by a heavy, crushing weight. Now an engaged woman, having solemnly promised herself to Alan a good, caring, responsible, honest, kind man, she knew, her future lay with him; though, her thoughts drifted thousands of kilometres away to Kai, who she could not get out of her head or heart. Wherever she went, whatever she was doing, he would stealthily creep into her consciousness shattering her peace; for, while she was betrothed to Alan, she felt herself inexplicably drawn to Kai; while Alan was waiting patiently for her to join him in his bed, she was dreaming of a wild, passionate night in Kai's inner sanctum. Her conflicting thoughts clashed and fought fiercely, leaving her mind with the residue of their ruthless war; a yearning for something she could not have. The alluring tentacles of alcohols calming balm became a constant gnawing thought, growing more ferocious until she could think of nothing else. She resisted knowing what nightmares, consciously and unconsciously, it would inevitably bring. Finally, unable to contain her inner anguish any longer she brought all her secret thoughts, fears and concerns to the door of the only person she truly trusted; the only person, she felt, knew and had lived through alcohols devastating consequences; the one person, she knew, she could trust with her life.

Chapter Sixty

Intently she listened to every single word, her young eyes still and serious; her young self, knowing what it was like to suffer the effects of someone else's alcoholic abuse, because she had been its unwilling victim. And, as Ocean Tia raised her warm eyes to Rosemary, her reassuring smile soothed the older woman's tortured soul. "I will help you, Lokemele. I will always be there for you; no matter what, I shall always be there."

"Just like the ocean." Rosemary smiled softly adding.

"Yes, just like the ocean." The young woman returned the smile, as she took Rosemary's hands into her own. "This can be our secret, Lokemele."

Rosemary nodded silently; secretly grateful that Ocean Tia had decided to resume her studies in England. Now she had found her anchor; but felt an undercurrent of uneasiness settling into the depths of her soul.

Hanale felt his mother's uneasiness often witnessing a faraway look in her eyes and sensed her mind was somewhere else a long, long way away. He decided to let it be.

Alan's suspicion was growing and, with it, came a heavy veil of blame, a barrel full of rhetorical questions and the regret of a hasty proposal.

While Rosemary, Alan and Kai were drowning in their own self-made wells of misery, Hanale and Ocean Tia were starting to live. According to Hanale, everything was going well and far better than he had ever thought possible. Through frequent letters and regular phone conversations, the bond between himself and his father was growing stronger and so was his growing interest in all things Hawaiian. And, just as Rosemary tried to subdue her inner feelings and forget about Kauai, Hanale brought her back into its tropical grasp, by asking her a multitude of questions, bringing Hawaiian based literature home from the library and splaying it on the kitchen table; he even began to play Hawaiian music, which drifted from his bedroom. And, as much as Rosemary yearned to forget and dispel memories they, involuntarily, crashed into the forefront of her mind making her think and yearn. Ocean Tia added to her torture by simply being Hawaiian.

Simon Teal was taking a keen interest in Ocean Tia and she in him. *It was a good match,* thought Rosemary and wondered if she should relate the news, in a letter to Kai. She decided against it. *The least amount of contact; the better,* she concluded.

Rosemary also noticed that Alan wasn't quite himself lately. When she asked about his health he simply smiled, stating he'd got a light headache; but, nothing a pill couldn't put right. They both felt, since becoming engaged, they were in a kind of limbo which, in turn, was adding to their stress levels and, therefore, decided to set a date for the wedding, which was to take place in six months' time. Neither felt at ease with their joint decision; both kept their secret feelings to themselves, trying desperately to fight their inner emotions, their fears and anxieties.

Rosemary was not ready for a full-blown commitment; her heart torn between two men who, she knew, neither would, or could, fulfil her desires entirely. *Kai,* she mused, *had been exciting, passionate, interesting, charming but not reliable and he certainly had his flaws. Alan, on the other hand, was reliable, a pillar of the community; he,* she knew, *would never let her down but...* She forced the rivals of her love to the back burners of her mind and started to make initial preparations for the wedding and, while she was busy, preoccupied with the wedding plans, alcohol was not an issue.

Kauai

On the other side of the world, alcohol was very much the issue for Kai. Although he now had a job in a local supermarket, a far cry from his glory days, he lived, dreamed and breathed alcohol and, being surrounded by it on a daily basis, didn't help matters. Residing with Luana and her children did help matters. As much as she loved him, his sister had made it perfectly clear that if he came home drunk, just once, he would find himself homeless and, the mere thought of reliving the life of a beach bum, kept his self-destructive thoughts at bay. But, it was hard, a day to day struggle, and he wasn't sure whether he would win the war that was raging fiercely inside him.

Every day his thoughts would drift to Ocean Tia and to Rosemary. *Why Lokemele?* He asked himself a thousand times and, a thousand times, the answer evaded him. *After all,* he told himself, *he had had many more lovers who were much more exciting; far greater beauties in his bed; he had known wahines with more intellect, who had accomplished much more in their lives; women who had strived for higher goals and ambitions, than to be a mere teacher; a single mother with an illegitimate son. In fact,* he concluded as he was stacking bottles of Mai Tai on a shelf, making sure the labels faced the outward position, *Lokemele was rather plain in comparison, less exciting and a woman who possessed a mountain of issues. But, there was something... something about her he could not fathom and this was, inexplicably, drawing him towards her. Perhaps,* he mused, *it was their mutual search for peace.* His eyes stared starkly at the brown liquid in the glaring bottle in his hand; he could taste the rum blended with Cointreau and lime juice. Hastily he placed the scorching bottle on to the shelf and turned his thoughts to Ocean Tia. He was losing her, he knew. She had grown up into a fine young lady and, while he was in England, he had seen many young men look her way; for, she was indeed a beauty in the eye of the beholder. But one young man played consistently on his mind; Simon Teal.

That evening he decided to put pen to paper and write to the only person, he thought, could give him the answers he needed.

Chapter Sixty-One

Intently she studied the envelope her heart beating rapidly; for, it was not Luana's handwriting she saw. With trembling, excited fingers she ripped the seal and withdrew the contents. Her heart raced faster, as her greedy eyes devoured the words on the page... *and so, if you could tell me anything you know about this Simon...* Her eyes quickly scanned the rest of the words, her heart deflating. She reread the contents and, to her dismay, the words remained the same. She felt herself dying; for, there was no declaration of love. Kai simply wanted to know about Simon Teal and whether, in her point of view, he was the type of guy who was appropriate for Ocean Tia. Folding the letter, she shoved it into a drawer and turned her full attention on to Alan, who had just walked through the door. "I think we should put our hearts and souls into this wedding of ours," she stated, wrapping her arms around his neck and kissing him on the mouth.

As they shared a long, lingering kiss Hanale was writing a letter to his father, which would ultimately affect the course of all of their lives.

Chapter Sixty-Two

Hanale stared at his handsome reflection and failed to see the appeal the girls saw in his twinkling, dark eyes, his golden skin and warm smile. He saw an unfulfilled teenager. Part of him was missing and, he knew, he would never find it here. He had a good home, a caring mother, good friends in Alan and Ocean Tia, a good education and many good friends; but, his roots lay elsewhere. He had hoped that, by now, he would have received a letter back from his father. No letter had arrived, propelling his thoughts to go down a dark path, as doubts began to take root.

On the opposite side of his bedroom wall, Ocean Tia was feeling waves of elation. She had been avidly counting the days to the end of the academic year and especially the dance. A worried frown replaced her smile. *If only her father was here,* she mused. She missed him terribly and, from what she had read in between the lines of his *exciting* words, she wondered whether he was painting over the cracks; whether he was shielding her from the truth. *Was he really doing as well as he had stated?* Forcibly she pinned the smile back on to her worried face. *Tonight she would put all negative thoughts to the back of her mind; tonight was going to be a happy night, a night to remember!*

A hard lump rose to Rosemary's throat, as she watched Hanale and Ocean Tia come down the stairs. *Brother and sister,* she smiled. Her smile faded as her thoughts involuntarily switched to Kai. Quickly, she also forced the smile back on to her lips. *This was Hanale and Ocean Tia's time; she had had her time long ago.* "You both look stunning," she said.

"If only my father was here." Ocean Tia said softly, a faraway look creeping into her sad eyes, as a sharp blade thrust into Rosemary's heart and, simultaneously, pierced through Hanale's heart too. Before tears could fall, Rosemary rushed towards them and the three hugged tightly as Alan knocked on the door, walked in and stared in silent admiration.

Alan wrapped his arms around Rosemary's waist, as both stood in contemplative silence at the window, watching Hanale and Ocean Tia walk happily down the long road, until they disappeared around the corner. "Come on, Rose; let's make our own fun," enthused Alan and, for a few brief seconds, she dared to dream that he was proposing a session of wild lovemaking. Her fast beating heart deflated rapidly as he sat down on the sofa and, from the depths of a carrier bag, produced a wad of pamphlets and booklets. "Wedding venues." He smiled enthusiastically and she smiled back, her heart filling with dread, her ears involuntarily alive to the excitement in his voice, wishing she could just feel a tiny spark of what he was feeling.

Finally they settled on a venue. Alan rose. "And now to celebrate." She watched as he wandered into the kitchen, filled the kettle and grabbed the side of his head. She said nothing, deciding not to burst his happy bubble.

Simon Teal was a respectable, intelligent and caring teenager who, like Ocean Tia and Hanale, had taken the road of higher education. What he was going to do with his life after college, like them, he didn't have a clue; but, one thing he was certain of, he was very much in love with Ocean Tia; the exotic girl who had captured his heart. His love for her was genuine in all aspects of the word; but, he was also a young, hot-blooded male and he yearned to bed her.

Ocean Tia had no such notions. Although worldly in many ways, she was innocent in the art of sex. She was a virgin and aimed to stay one until her wedding night.

Simon put his arm around her slender shoulder and brought her closer to himself and, while in his protective grasp, she felt wrapped in an invisible blanket of security. Placing her head on Simon's shoulder, and interlinking her hand with his, they watched the gyrating dancers on the crowded, heaving dance floor as the loud music continued to pulsate and throb.

From the dance floor, Hanale cast his eyes on the couple and wished things could have been different. *If only she wasn't his half-sister,* he mused as his feet took on various interesting steps, while his mind travelled on a one-way road, bombarding him with many questions. *Why hadn't his father answered his letter? Had he fallen off the wagon? Perhaps he had had second thoughts about their father-son relationship? Maybe he wanted nothing more to do with him?* These and other questions made the young man's guts wrench, his feet feeling like separate entities as a set of new thoughts crashed into his mind. *Should he tell his mother and Ocean Tia about his unrequited letter? Should he write another? Should he phone?* Finally his buzzing head could take no more. Heading for the bar, he ordered himself a double shot of vodka and swilled the liquid down in one go. Within seconds, Ocean Tia was at his side, with Simon following suit. "What are you doing, Hanale?" She asked and, without waiting for his reply, she took the fresh shot he had ordered and gave it to Simon and turned to her half-brother, her concerned eyes firmly fixed on him. "What is it, Hanale?"

The look of her deep concern made him want to throw up. "Go away, Ocean." He snapped as he attempted to order another drink.

"Please don't." She begged, her voice unusually raised so it could be heard above the babble of student voices.

Something made him stop and turn his eyes to her and, in her liquid brown eyes, he saw her anguish; alcohol, the ruin of her father and his mother's silent torturer. Silently he followed her back to the table while Simon's hopes, of a passionate night with the girl he loved, were fading fast.

They sat, drank orange juice and discussed usual student stuff, all three covered with a heavy veil of suppressed tension while two hearts beat with silent resentment, both males craving Ocean Tia for themselves; Hanale wanting her as a half-sister and confidante; Simon wanting her as a girlfriend and lover. Finally Hanale rose, made his excuses and disappeared, leaving Simon and Ocean Tia to head to an all-night party.

While Simon secretly revelled in the fact that he had got Ocean Tia for himself, her thoughts were with Hanale. *He wasn't himself,* she dismally concluded, as she determined to get to the bottom of the matter and to help him in any which way she could.

"Why do you look so sad?" Simon lifted her chin with the tip of his forefinger and gave her a small peck on the cheek. "Come on," he encouraged taking her hand, "let's dance."

She felt his strong arms holding her close and felt his soft breath on her cheek, as he whispered something in her ear and allowed herself to be drawn nearer to his firm, virile body, feeling his male hardness as she felt herself sinking in the mellowness of the moment. He drew her closer to himself as they moved slowly to the beat, their young bodies together as one.

Hanale drank three straight vodkas before exiting the venue, the effects of which stayed with him as he stormed through the door.

Two pairs of bemused eyes abandoned lavish brochures depicting honeymoon destinations and shot to Hanale, lingering on his shirt that was hanging out of his trousers and his black tie, loose and askew around his open necked shirt. "Hanale, we didn't expect you so s…"

He shot to his bedroom and slammed the door hard behind him, making Rosemary's puzzled eyes dart to Alan. She rose, her eyes switching to the empty staircase and froze, as she felt the soft touch of Alan's hand on her arm. "Leave him be, Rose. He is a young man now."

"A young man with a shed load of unresolved issues." She stated sitting back down again, glumly staring at a glossy image of an expensive and very extravagant hotel. Averting her eyes from the opened page a worrying, nagging thought invaded her mind. *Could this new relationship between Kai and Hanale be the beginning of their problems?* Alan answered her silent question.

"You know, Rose, you have to give Hanale and Kai time." He took her cold hands into the comforting, warm clasp of his own. "They may have found each other; but, Hanale needs time to get to grips with his roots."

"I thought he had done, on his vacation in Kauai." Rosemary said in a monotone voice.

"That was only the beginning, my dear; the whole process will take years."

Her heart depleted; she thought it had all been solved and now – Alan's intent eyes observed the thoughtful face and, after squeezing her hands, rose saying, "Cheer up, Rose; we will help Hanale to find his way. Right, I have to go. I have an early start tomorrow. A friend wants me to help him out with some sort of business venture."

She rose not having heard his last words, her thoughts upstairs with a troubled Hanale. As she handed Alan his umbrella, her brow furrowed as he lost his balance. "Are you all right, Alan?" She asked anxiously.

After long seconds, he raised his warm eyes to her, his smile reassuring. "Of course I am, honey."

But, as she watched him walk down the long road a doubt seeped into her mind; a doubt which had firmly taken root in Alan's thoughts.

Chapter Sixty-Three

Hanale felt as if he was in a weird twilight world of swirling emotions; wondering whether cementing the foundation of a father-son relationship was, in fact, a blessing or a curse. Lying on his bed, his stark eyes on the ceiling, he questioned whether it would have been better to have left things as they were; to have lived in a bubble of knowing he had a father somewhere out there and to formulate his own notions and fantasies about him; for, while fantasising, his father could be a knight in shining armour, a brave soldier, a heart surgeon, a marathon runner; anything he wanted him to be. Now he was the Hawaiian, Kai, who had, apparently, once been very successful and was now trying to shrug away the reputation of a beach bum. Now, he was a real man with real thoughts, dreams, disappointments and yearnings and Hanale wanted to know everything about this man, his father; but, for one reason or another, Kai had stopped all forms of communication.

Rosemary and Ocean Tia had noticed a change in Hanale. He had become quiet and moody and everybody wanted the cheerful, happy-go-lucky teenager back.

Their prayers were answered, when the rattle of the letter box sent Hanale flying from the kitchen table to the door. Two pairs of eyes watched as his excited eyes hungrily identified the handwritten address, as a trembling forefinger thrust into the corner of the sealed envelope and roughly tore it open, his greedy eyes devouring the words on the paper, his lips breaking out into an incontrollable wide grin. After reading the contents twice, he thrust the letter into his mother's hands, making her heart race rapidly and then turn to stone. She turned her silent, steady eyes on to her son where she saw in him a renewed hope.

Ocean Tia took the letter from Rosemary, her unmovable lips gradually transforming into a wide beaming smile. Rushing over to Hanale she hugged him tightly exclaiming, "I think this is a great idea!" Turning her happy twinkling eyes to Rosemary, she saw ultimate sadness and her smile died. Rosemary's words cut deep and the teenagers felt her pain.

"How could you both go behind my back in this way?"

Ocean Tia's smooth forehead furrowed in puzzlement as she said, "I didn't know anything about this, Lokemele."

Rosemary's silent eyes darted to Hanale demanding an explanation.

Slowly he turned his eyes to her. "I. I didn't know what you would say, Mum."

"You didn't trust me with your idea, Son." She rose and left the kitchen, leaving the teenagers to stare after her and then at each other.

Ocean Tia picked up the letter once more and turned her eyes to her half-brother. "I think you should go, Hanale. I think a year in Kauai, before you start university, would be great for you and it will also give our father a purpose in life too."

"But; what about Mum?"

"Leave her to me." Ocean Tia winked reassuringly.

On hearing her words, his heart felt a thousand times lighter; for, he knew, in Ocean Tia's hands, it would all conclude happily. *It would,* he thought, *take time and patience, just like the old Hawaiian motto, which never seemed to fail.* He smiled.

Rosemary sat motionless on her dressing table stool and stared unblinkingly at her pale reflection. *It had been a shock; but, it had been her son's secret betrayal which had made it a hundred times more painful.* She stared into her own stark, unblinking eyes of despair… *Kai had planned this whole idea with their son behind her back; the son she, alone, had reared and now… Kai seemed to be taking over, making lifestyle decisions which would affect Hanale's life forever and, all this, without her having the slightest inkling.* She felt her insides seethe, writhe, twist and turn mercilessly… *How could they do this to her? How could father and son go behind her back, plot and plan and leave her out of the entire equation, like an abandoned sock which was no longer useful or needed? Didn't she have any say in anything anymore? Wasn't her opinion worth anything? Was she now just in the way of their cosy father-son relationship?* She asked herself these questions and more as a deep, inexplicable hatred surged through her fast pulsating veins; hatred of Kai, the father of Hanale, her once lover and the man, she thought, she still had feelings for… *When all this time,* she glumly concluded, *he wanted to take Hanale away from her; to lure him thousands of kilometres away from her; to leave her without her beloved son.* She felt herself drowning in the grim set face before her.

The soft click of the bedroom door echoed loudly in Rosemary's ears and she felt Ocean Tia's slim body against hers, as the young woman perched down beside her; her rich, brown eyes sinking into Rosemary's sad reflection. She chose her words carefully. "I think, Lokemele, you need to set Hanale free." She watched intensely as the older woman inhaled deeply, silently scrutinising her clamped lips, her eyes staring starkly into the stark eyes of her dear friend's reflection, where she saw only emptiness; then, witnessing a minute waver in Rosemary's eyes as her words seemed to hit home, Ocean Tia boldly proceeded. "Like my father who set me free. I feel Hanale should be given a chance to spread his wings."

"They betrayed me." Rosemary's words were blunt, stark and icy cold.

The following candid words skewered mercilessly through Rosemary's pained heart. "And, did you feel you had betrayed Hanale and Kai all those years ago, Lokemele?" Ocean Tia took Rosemary's clenched hands into her own. "No, you didn't betray them, just like they are not betraying you. They need to build their father-son relationship and, to do that, they must spend more time together. And... well, the charity work they want to embark on together is a very worthy cause, Lokemele."

"What type of charity work are they considering?"

Ocean Tia beamed with uncontrollable pride. "They want to help the unfortunates, who are suffering from alcohol abuse."

"What!" Rosemary stared aghast at the younger woman, whose eyes were covered with a veil of incredulity. *For Lokemele of all people,* thought Ocean Tia, *should be impressed by her son's interest and concern regarding this worthy venture.*

Inwardly Rosemary felt as if she had died and gone to Hell, where all alcoholics were forced to drown in their quantity of past alcohol intake. *So that was it; her son was punishing her. She had brought all this on to herself. Without her problems with alcohol, there would be no worthy scheme.* "It's because of me." Rosemary's words escaped her mouth before she could stop them.

"It's in spite of you, Lokemele. Don't you see? Hanale has seen and lived through the effects of alcoholism; he has seen it in you; he has known about his father's abuse; he feels drawn towards helping people who have the problem. You should see this as a good, admirable thing that Hanale wants to do." Ocean

Tia rose and left the room leaving Rosemary to brood; the recent image of her son crashing into the house, looking the worse for wear, clearly in her mind. Slowly her thoughts began to change... *Maybe... maybe this may not be such a bad idea; if only to save Hanale from following in his parents footsteps...*

Hanale was delighted that his mother had succumbed to his request. *For,* he reflected, *to deflect his attention on to others he would, hopefully, subdue his own rising temptations.* And just recently, he had been worried about his own lure towards alcohol.

Chapter Sixty-Four

Rosemary hugged her son tightly and watched him walk away from her; her heart tight and heavy, her unblinking eyes glistening with tears as she stared after him, until he disappeared into the bowels of the departures area. He was gone and he took with him a part of her heart. She felt Alan's comforting arm around her waist. "He will be back with us in a year." He soothed; but, it was Ocean Tia's wise words which brought her comfort.

"He shall be doing so much good, helping so many unfortunate people. I am so proud of my half-brother. You must be proud of your son, Lokemele."

Rosemary turned her shining eyes on to the young woman, tears streaking her face. "Yes… yes, I am proud of Hanale."

The days following Hanale's departure were long and torturously quiet. Concentration at work and home was difficult to attain and maintain, as Rosemary's thoughts drifted to her beloved island, only to be ruthlessly snatched back into the here and now as Alan, who had rarely complained about anything, began to mention the odd headache and she sensed he was not confessing to the severity of the pain he was experiencing; for, she had surreptitiously caught him clutching his head with both hands and had heard him vomit, when he thought no one was about the place. When she tackled him with her concerns, he dismissed them changing subjects often on to their wedding preparations, which she secretly wished to avoid.

Ocean Tia's growing relationship with Simon Teal added to Rosemary's concerns; for, while the young woman was under her roof, she was responsible for her and she knew, only too well, how easy it was to be swept away by passion and, now, Hanale was thousands of kilometres away and could not keep an eye on his half-sister and report back. *And, Hanale,* she concluded, *was on the other side of the world under the care of his father, a man he barely knew.* Her only consolation was Luana, who regularly sent detailed reports. *It was all so very messy,* grimaced Rosemary as she brought her cold mug of coffee up to her lips.

Her thoughts reluctantly strayed to her engagement and her eyes closed. *If only she could turn back the clock...* She didn't hear him come in; didn't see him standing in the doorway, smiling down on her. "A penny for them, Rose."

Her eyes shot up. "Alan!" A fixed smile set on her mouth. "You are going to make me a rich woman with all of these pennies thrown at my thoughts."

He sat on the opposite side of the table, his concerned eyes seeking silent answers. Taking her hands into his own hands he asked softly, "Would you like to share your thoughts?" He knew her answer before she opened her mouth; for, he felt that these days they were often poles apart and this gravely concerned him. He felt the gentle withdrawal of her hands and his answer was confirmed; but, he knew something was wrong; something was troubling Rosemary and something was troubling him. He knew deep inside that his severe headache attacks, blurred vision and nausea were symptoms of something more sinister; he also knew this thing could have a devastating effect on their future. He decided to sweep the issue aside, for the time being, and, uncharacteristically, bury his head in the sand.

Ocean Tia felt an undercurrent of silent ruptures in Alan and Rosemary's relationship and secretly worried that, although together, they were drifting apart. Privately she apportioned the blame between her father and Rosemary; for, she could not stop thinking that Kai had feelings for Lokemele and Lokemele was secretly in love with Kai.

Chapter Sixty-Five

Ocean Tia and Simon were inseparable soul-mates and the envy of their fellow students. They were an elegant couple; she the tropical beauty tall with dark, sleek hair to the tip of her waist, swept into a side parting and always sporting a plumeria above her left ear, her eyes brown and sparkling, a warm smile on her luscious lips; he tall, also with dark hair and brown eyes although he adopted a more serious, studious look; both were very popular and well liked; both looking forward to the future.

It was at this time that a seed of anxiety began to take root in Simon's mind. It weaved itself into a tangled mass of doubts and frustration and was seeping through into the very depths of the foundation of their relationship. Finally, he decided there was only one thing to do and that was to confront Ocean Tia. The perfect opportunity landed on his doorstep, when they both signed up for a cultural weekend in Paris.

Ocean Tia, however, decided that the time for a confrontation was now. Joining Rosemary as she washed the dishes at the kitchen sink, Ocean stared out the window at the array of spectacular autumnal foliage, scattered on the ground in a rich interweaving carpet of reds, browns, yellows, purples and greens; the likes of which she had never seen before. Her eyes watched intently as an orange-brown leaf floated gently down and, drifted aimlessly for a few seconds, before joining it's compatriots on their autumnal deathbed. "What is it that troubles you, Lokemele?" She asked softly.

Rosemary placed the soapy plate on to the draining rack and stared ahead, her lips firmly clamped, her heart heaving, wondering what to say. *For how,* she asked herself, *could she burden this young woman with her own worst fears?* She forced a smile and turned to Ocean Tia, her heart breaking. "Nothing, my dear; all is well."

Ocean Tia took Rosemary's wet hands into her own. "But, all is not well, is it?"

And, as older eyes confronted younger eyes, Rosemary knew there was no escape, as a floodgate of emotions crashed open and she slumped down on to a nearby chair and, with heart wrenching sobs, poured out her heart and soul.

For long minutes Ocean Tia let her be; allowed it all to pour out, every last tiny grain of emotion until Rosemary felt bereft of all emotions, feelings, worries, fears, doubts and anxieties and she was an empty vessel. Slowly, cautiously Ocean Tia began to work her magic. Once more she took Rosemary's hands into her own and urged softly, "Tell me how you feel, Lokemele. Let me help you, like you once helped me."

The words poured out as Ocean Tia listened intently to Rosemary's anxieties regarding Alan's health and her worries concerning Hanale. But, the young woman knew there was something deeper that needed uprooting, if Lokemele was to find any peace at all and she plunged in. "And; what about your feelings for my father, Lokemele?" Her searching eyes drilled into Rosemary's soul forcing the older woman's eyes to shoot to Ocean, instantly realising her feelings had been exposed and there was nowhere left to hide. "Do you love him?" Ocean Tia probed further, as eyes stared into eyes and two hearts raced. Rosemary's eyes dropped to the table, as she felt her hands being squeezed as Ocean Tia's words echoed loudly in her head. "Do you love my father, Lokemele?" Rosemary closed her eyes and nodded her head.

Abruptly her hands were abandoned and she felt loving arms around her in a tight embrace, as an icy awareness struck her. *There was no going back now; the truth was out.*

Woman looked at woman; older eyes stared into younger eyes as hearts were linked by one bond. Ocean Tia asked softly, "What are you going to do, Lokemele?"

Rosemary rose, swilled her cold coffee into the sink and stated starkly, "I am going to marry Alan."

Ocean Tia's eyes shot to Rosemary's back and, swiftly, she was standing by her side, hugging her once more, turning her to face her and, as Rosemary searched Ocean's eyes, she finally found the right words. "Alan is ill. He needs me. I have to marry him."

Ocean Tia's soft words wavered. "But you love my father."

"I am marrying Alan." Abruptly Rosemary turned away, not bearing to look at the daughter of the man she loved, as Ocean Tia watched Rosemary hurry up the stairs and heard the soft click of her closing door. Sitting down Ocean buried her head into her long fingers allowing her long, silky hair to fall around her like a cascading veil, as a multitude of disturbing thoughts and scenarios crashed into her puzzled head. Thoughts of… *Lokemele walking down the aisle with Alan, while her heart was yearning for Kai; Alan thinking Lokemele's heart was full of love for him, while Kai was on the other side of the world, ignorant of the fact that Lokemele Longsdale was in love with him. Should she write and inform her father of the fact?* A little voice in her head said… *No; it was not her place to tell her father. And, yet, how could Lokemele go ahead with marrying a man purely out of pity?* She shook her head from side to side. *This was all wrong; so very, very wrong. But, what could she do?*

The Paris trip was fast approaching; Ocean Tia's initial excitement was now replaced by an inner apprehension. *How could she leave Lokemele now? How could she enjoy herself in Paris, a city she had always yearned to visit, when Lokemele was caught up in a whirlpool of emotions and decisions, which could potentially ruin lives?* And, as she was throwing her last items into her small suitcase, Ocean Tia made her decision.

Chapter Sixty-Six

Deflated and dejected, Simon stared unblinkingly at the girl he loved. "What do you mean you are not going, Ocean?"

She raised her soft eyes to his. "I mean I cannot go to Paris, Simon."

His incredulous eyes continued to stare at the girl, who was snatching his hopes and dreams away from him. "You mean," he said curtly, "you have fallen out of love with me." His stomach twisted mercilessly, feeling as if it had been brutally punched.

"No; no." She instantly objected. "Please, believe m—"

He cut in, "You have found someone else; someone who is more exciting; perhaps, more intelligent. I get it, Ocean."

"No Simon," she repeated attempting to reach out for his hands, which he swiftly wrenched away from her grasp, before he could allow himself to feel her soft touch and his skin should burn with the intensity of his love for her. He turned to go. "Simon," she called after him; but, he was gone. For a long time, she sat at the table, with only her conflicting thoughts for company; then, taking the receiver off the cradle she dialled. Click… click… She took a deep breath.

Chapter Sixty-Seven

She stood outside his door, her composed posture belying the rush of whirling anxieties, doubts and fears making her feel weak inside. Now she was here, she wondered what on earth she was going to say; her thoughts and unspoken words spinning round and round in a chaotic whirling mass.

Sitting down on the soft leather upholstered sofa, looking down at her nervously clutched fingers, she tried desperately to formulate the appropriate words. They remained elusive; for what she had planned to say and rehearsed in every conceivable way, she could not now force out of her dry mouth. *How, she asked herself, could she bring herself to tell this wonderful man, that the woman he loved did not love him? How could she tell him that Lokemele loved Kai? How could she so ruthlessly break this kind man's heart?* The words that came out were not the words she had rehearsed so diligently. "I thought you looked a bit under the weather, Alan. I was just passing so I thought I'd just pop in and see you."

His shrewd eyes told her he knew she was partly lying. His brain told him that if she was lying, there would be a very good reason. "I am fine." He lied, his gentle eyes not leaving her questioning eyes.

"Great... great, then I shall be on my way." She smiled though her smile betrayed a thousand anxieties; her swift visit telling Alan there was more to it than met the eye, as a tiny seed of worry rooted itself in his aching head and, with it, came a barrage of questions; for, he had always secretly prided himself on being a good interpreter of body language and Ocean Tia's appearance told him that she had hastily aborted a mission of some sort. What it was he couldn't work out though, he felt, it had something to do with Rosemary.

In the following days, this thought became a constant nagging query which was reflected in his more than usual quiet demeanour that, in turn, gave Rosemary food for thought and Ocean Tia a heart full of regret.

Both women couldn't help but notice Alan's loss of appetite; his frequent visits to the bathroom, from where emitted subdued sounds of wrenching. They noticed Alan's early exits home and both women worried in their own private world of silence, while Alan was formulating a secret plan of his own.

Guilt lay dark and heavy in Rosemary's soul and heart; her sad eyes remaining still and fixed on Ocean Tia, as she hung on each word spoken.

"I have decided that I am not going to go to Paris, Lokemele."

"Why?" Rosemary's eyebrow shot up in question.

Quickly Ocean Tia rummaged for words that could not be opposed. "Because... because I do not love Simon anymore and to spend a weekend in his..."

"What?" Rosemary stared aghast, as a contradictory chuckle escaped her mouth, her head shaking slowly from side to side. "I am sorry, Ocean, but I do not believe what you are telling me." Her stubbornly, questioning eyes remained on the younger woman, demanding a different explanation; an honest answer.

Unable to meet Rosemary's probing eyes Ocean's eyes dropped to her fingers, which were playing nervously with the fringes of the tablecloth, thinking how frazzled her own thoughts were at this moment in time. "I don't love him." She repeated unconvincingly while, at the same time, her heart raced at the mere memory of his image.

"Since when?" Rosemary's eyes locked with Ocean Tia's eyes.

The younger eyes pulled away and dropped back to the enticing fringes of the linen tablecloth. "Oh, for quite some time." She said her voice monotone. She rose and left the table.

Rosemary sat perfectly still, only her eyes followed Ocean Tia as she swiftly ran up the stairs. *None of this,* she thought her eyes staring at the empty staircase, *makes any sense at all. No sense at all,* she repeated to the white, twisted, unresponsive spindles as Alan crashed into her mind.

What she saw broke her heart, as her eyes looked at a dishevelled man in his dressing gown, hair askew, both his hands clutching the sides of his head, as if it was about to detach itself from his neck and roll away. "Alan, what on earth is the matter?" she gasped.

Grabbing a nearby chair he slumped down, still holding the side of his head with one hand whilst, being the gentleman he was, signalling Rosemary to sit down with his free hand. Sitting in close proximity, her eyes scrutinising his every move and involuntary facial grimace, her heart went out to him; for, she knew, something very serious was occurring. Delicately she tried to prise out of him the source of the problem. He played the whole thing down claiming he'd had too much to drink; last evening with an old friend, and now was the worse for wear and paying for the consequences. "I have learned my lesson." He smiled faintly as he avoided her unbelieving eyes.

That night Rosemary lay in her lonely bed, unconvinced and troubled. *Everything in her life seemed to be falling out of sync. Her son was thousands of kilometres away with his father, the man she had always loved; Ocean Tia's life seemed to be falling apart too; but, most disconcerting of all, were Alan's lies.* She knew, without a doubt, that he was lying to protect her and Ocean Tia. *To protect them from what; what was this kind, honest, caring man hiding? What was it that he could not share with the woman, he claimed, he loved; the woman he intended to marry? Whatever it was,* there was no doubt in her mind, *it was serious and mere talking would not entice him to part with his fears. She would need to employ a different tactic,* she concluded. And one quickly came to mind. *But,* she asked herself, *could she betray him in this way? Would he ever trust her again? Would it answer her questions?* Swiftly she swept her doubts aside. *She had to help Alan.*

The grim faced consultant told Alan what he had been expecting to hear. The tumour in his brain was inoperable; it was just a matter of time. Alan shook the hand of the medic, thanked him and walked out the consulting room, his heart lighter than it had been for weeks. Now he knew exactly what he was dealing with, how much time he had and set his plan to work accordingly. *He would,* he mused thoughtfully, *lay his cards on the table and by doing so,* he knew, *he would lighten his burden and give the woman he loved, her freedom.*

Chapter Sixty-Eight

Rosemary's twinkling eyes dropped from Alan's silvery-grey hair; swept down his pristine black suit and travelled down to his polished black shoes. *He still cuts a dashing figure of a man.* She thought as she licked her upper lip provocatively as a sharp, invisible blade stabbed cruelly at her heart. *He is ill,* a voice in her head said; *very ill.*

He looked adoringly at the woman he loved, his fiancée; the woman he could never truly have and pinned a warm smile on his lips. "You look absolutely beautiful, Rose." He said in a low, sexy voice; his eyes sweeping over her blonde hair, swept tightly into a neat bun, and lowered down to her emerald green crepe crepe de chine dress, which went up considerably higher than her knees; his appreciative eyes dropped further down to her dark stilettoes, which framed her shapely ankles.

"You look quite a handsome figure yourself, Alan," she smiled. *Handsome; but ill,* the persistent voice hammered.

In the lavish restaurant, he picked disconsolately at his steak, jabbed his fork unenthusiastically into his mixed peas and carrots; but, his conversation was interesting, absorbing, lively and full of humour. Rosemary listened to, and savoured, each precious word as her plan whirled frantically around her head. *So far,* she told herself, *it was going well.*

Alan thought his scheme was going well too. *Rosemary was in a good, relaxed mood and, hopefully, she would* take his proposition well.

After the meal and a play, performed by the local theatre group, Rosemary threw off her stilettoes, nudged nearer to Alan on the sofa, entwined her fingers with his, as they both listened to a CD playing the lulling sounds of Hawaiian guitars, which Alan had specifically chosen. Surreptitiously she looked up at his set face. *It belies his relaxed body,* she thought. Her sad eyes lingered on his lips, formed into a thin line, and absorbed his pale complexion, his tensed facial muscles and his eyes staring into the faraway distance. *What did they see?* She wondered. *Was he staring at his own mortality?*

Alan was staring at an imaginary scene which often haunted his thoughts… *his rival, Kai, and Rosemary together, bonded in everlasting happiness…* More and more this scene was losing its disturbing touch; more and more it brought him an inner comfort, knowing that when his time came, he would not leave Rosemary to face the world alone; more and more he thought Rosemary's place was with her son, with Ocean Tia and with Kai, her former lover and the father of her child; the man, Alan knew without a doubt, Rosemary still loved. The words he had planned to say and rehearsed a hundred times, changed, polished and re-rehearsed now stuck firmly in his dry throat; stubbornly refusing to be released, as he sat with his mouth partly opened. The kiss on his cheek brought him back to the immediate present, his startled eyes on the woman he loved; the woman he wanted, needed and craved; the woman, he knew in his heart of hearts, he could never have. "What was that for?" His grim set lips turned into a warm smile.

"I love you," she blurted out.

"I love you too." He said robotically, instantly wishing he'd put the feelings he felt into his monotone words.

"Then kiss me." She demanded and he obeyed taking her into his arms, his mouth on her mouth possessive and passionate, as she felt herself being drawn into a sea, she did not willingly want to be drawn into. *But if her plan was to work…* She succumbed to his hard lips on hers, felt his tongue deliciously probing hers, his long fingers stroking the stray wisps of hair which had escaped the confines of her bun, softly tracing the contours of her jaw and along the smooth line of her neck, touching softly the outline of her breasts through the cool fabric of her silky dress.

Tentatively, his fingers found the zip and pulled it down, allowing her to wriggle out of the dress and leaving her exposed in her satin bra and panties, while her fingers frantically tore open the buttons of his shirt, her mind dancing. *So far,* she smiled secretly; *it was going according to plan.* The bra was off exposing her breasts to his greedy eyes. Cupping them in his hands he bent his head and sucked each areola in turn deep and hard, sending tremulous, delicious shivers and sparks up and down her spine, setting her whole body on fire; for this is what she had wanted. *If only they'd done it sooner…*

A disturbing thought crashed into her mind, fighting furiously with her weakening body beneath his sensual fingers. *Now it was going to be an uphill struggle to extract any snippet of medical information from him. Soon,* she rapidly concluded, *she would not be able to think at all.* Half-heartedly she attempted to release herself from his intoxicating touches and caresses, his probing tongue and roaming fingers as they delved further down, tantalisingly caressing the soft forest of dark hair, sending her on an upward spiral to the highest pinnacle of heaven and to the… deepest pit of hell as his lips and fingers abruptly withdrew, followed swiftly by his whole body.

Fire turned to ice as her body froze in shock and fear, her lust-glazed eyes turning into cold pools of anxiety, as she looked down at his opened white shirt, his head in his hands and his eyes buried where she could not see them. "What is it, Alan?" Her voice trembled with concern as she feared the worst.

He raised his head, his eyes on her bare breasts. "Please put on your clothes, Rosemary."

Insult, intermingled heavily with disappointment and rejection, surged violently through every vein in her fast pulsating body, her eyes of incredulity on the man she would have given her whole self to in order to help him, as a new wave of surging fury overtook her and, without thinking, she blared, "What the hell is the matter with you, Alan?" Her angry eyes avoiding him, as she snatched her bra and panties and put them on. She sat down a silent statue staring dispassionately at his still, grim face, her thoughts running wild… *Was she really such a vile person that he couldn't manage a session of pure, undiluted sex?* Hate seeped its negative tentacles into her heart and soul, spreading into the root of her thoughts, where they made a home and gave her no peace. His next words shook her to the very core of her being.

"I am dying, Rosemary."

She sat perfectly still, staring at the delicately flowered wallpaper on the opposite wall, her eyes following the contours of the petal of a poppy of the deepest red and taking in the tiny buds on its long green stem. She wondered what kind of person had designed this delightful image, as the heavy silence in the room deafened them both. His words sliced through the overbearing stillness like a sharp blade. "I have a brain tumour… inoperable." The red poppies seemed to have a life of their own, in her minds eyes, as they danced and intertwined their dainty heads. How she wished she was an inane poppy, instead of having to digest, and respond to, the saddest words she had ever heard, from the kindest man she had ever known. Furiously and erratically an array of disjointed, nonsensical words spun maddeningly in her confused head. *Surely she had just imagined him saying that he was dying; that he had an inoperable brain tumour?* Forcing her body to turn towards him, her eyes to look at the forlorn figure sat rigidly at her side she felt her whole body solidify; her stark, still eyes staring at… *an open coffin where Alan lay; dead.* She snapped her eyes shut, her ears attune to the disturbing silence engulfing them with its deathlike stillness. After long, heavy minutes she summoned up every grain of inner strength and, about to force the stubborn words out of her mouth, she heard the strong, comforting words emitting from her dying fiancé. "I don't want you to be sad; or, take pity on me, Rose. I want you to live."

Anger, incredulity and hurt fatally collided, causing her thoughts to change tact and spew out uncontrollably throwing sadness, pity and empathy into obscurity as she raged, "How dare you come here, take me on a journey to the point of ecstasy and tell me you are dying?" She darted her glassy eyes of undiluted fury on to him. "What kind of man are you, Alan?"

Their eyes clashed and locked.

"I hope, a caring man." He answered softly.

Her eyes of unrefined fury changed into eyes of pure incredulity, as she stared wide-eyed at the man sitting beside her. Rising, she took slow steps towards the window and looked out on to the small desolate garden, displaying a wonderful carpet of multi-coloured leaves of the richest red and deepest brown, illuminated by the discreetly situated outdoor lighting. She shook her head slowly from side to side, trying desperately to take it all in. "I don't know you at all, Alan." She stated almost inaudibly as she continued to stare at the perfectly still lifeless leaves as, gradually, stark realisation began to take over… *He was dying and she was laying into him; he had months to live, maybe just weeks, and here she was giving him a rough time. He needed her now, just like she had needed him and he had always been there for her…* Reluctantly she turned away from the window, her heart heavy laden, and sat down beside him. Cautiously she took his clasped fingers into her own and squeezed them gently. "I shall always be here for you, Alan." She smiled sadly.

She felt him withdraw his hands from her warm clasp and felt them on her shoulders, as he turned her to face him; to silently beg her to look him in the eyes and to face what he had to say. Her heart pounded mercilessly. "I need you to do something for me, Rosemary."

"Anything."

He looked deeply into her still, sad eyes. "Do you mean that; do you honestly mean that you would do anything for me, Rosemary?"

She nodded silently.

"Even, if you don't want to do it?"

Curiosity started to weave its puzzling web around her straying thoughts, as she focussed her eyes on him. "Yes, Alan anything; even if I don't want to do it." Secretly she braced herself for whatever challenge he was about to throw at her.

Her eyes opened like two saucers, as his incredulous request hammered torturously in her head; wishing she could turn back the clock and retract her acceptance to comply with his will. Turning her solemn eyes to his unwavering eyes, she said her words clearly and concisely. "Let me get this straight, Alan. You are dying and you are telling me to leave you for a man thousands of kilometres away who, incidentally, is not a patch on you. Is that what you are telling me to do?"

"Yes." He stated bluntly.

"Then you are more seriously sick in the head than I thought." She snapped, immediately bitterly regretting every word which had spewed out of her venomous mouth.

Uncharacteristically Alan turned on the woman he loved. "I may be sick in the head, Rosemary, but I am not blind."

She opened her mouth and immediately closed it again, her guts twisting and churning without pity.

He continued with his mission. "Anyone could see Kai loves you and, I know, you love him, Rose."

She turned her pained eyes on him. "How do you know; how the hell do you know anything, Alan, when I can't even prove my love to you because you deny me the right?" Her searching eyes demanded an answer.

"You belong to another. Who am I to steal you from him?"

"Oh; my God." She said over and over again, as she lowered her aching head into her hands, shaking it from side to side; wondering how on earth it had all gone so wrong, when she had meticulously planned it all. She stood up, her glaring eyes staring down at her fiancé. "I think you should go, Alan."

"The marriage is off." He stated firmly, rose and disappeared out the door.

Chapter Sixty-Nine

The night was the longest and torturous Rosemary had ever experienced. Added to her erratic and fragmented thoughts was a heavy blanket of excruciating sadness. In the midst of her overwhelming inner despair, her thoughts involuntarily drifted to the tropical island she had loved; the island she had classed as her second home and now hated. One memory, however, she sought comfort in; the memory of Keoki and his wise words… *Then to live you must find the problem, tackle it and learn to be happy again. As they say, life is too short… Wise words,* she mused. *But, how on earth could she tackle the problem when she didn't know what to pinpoint?… You belong to another…* Alan's haunting words, intermingled with Keoki's words, rang loudly and persistently in her ears, making her wonder if his illness was causing him to have distorted views. Her thoughts switched to Kai, the father of her child… *He'd certainly voiced his feelings on a few occasions; but, was that really love; or, was he still in mourning for the things he had lost?* She closed her eyes.

"What is it, Lokemele?" Ocean Tia searched the older woman's eyes, feeling her sadness.

"Alan is dying." She blurted out, as her overwhelming sadness broke the confines of its secret sanctuary and poured out in uncontrollable sobs; impelling Ocean Tia to take Rosemary into her comforting arms and rock her to and fro – to and fro, her own heart fragmented in pieces; for, she dearly loved Alan. Her respectful silence spoke volumes, prompting Rosemary to break free from her grasp, her glacial eyes turning on the younger woman. "You… you knew?" She sobbed, her hot ears spilling over as one sobbing gasp replaced another.

"No… yes… I knew something was wrong, Lokemele. I suspected Alan had an illness of some sort and that it was quite serious." Ocean Tia stated truthfully as she replaced her arms around her friend.

"But you didn't say anything, Ocean." Rosemary said with a tinge of accusation in her voice, her sobs becoming less intensive.

"I didn't want to worry you unduly, Lokemele."

Rosemary turned her glazed eyes on Ocean Tia demanding the truth. "Is that why you let Simon go; to look after me?"

Ocean Tia stared unblinkingly into watery eyes and felt she was drowning in their miserable pools; her silence told Rosemary what she needed to know.

"The marriage is off." Rosemary stated blandly, the chilling finality of her words hitting Ocean Tia like a thunderbolt; but, before she could utter a word of objection, Rosemary sharply cut in. "Alan thinks I am in love with Kai; he thinks your father is in love with me. He wants me to go out there and… and… I don't know what he wants; but, I do know that his dying wish is to leave him be."

"Alan thinks you and my father should be together?" Ocean Tia's astounded words escaped her mouth before she could check them.

"Yes, that's what he thinks. Alan thinks we are pining for each other."

"My father is still pining for my mother." Immediately Ocean Tia wished she could have cut her tongue out as her dark, remorseful eyes flashed to Rosemary; but, she was thousands of kilometres away.

The two women sat surrounded by a heavy veil of oppressive silence, as their scattered thoughts whirled in different directions. And, while Ocean Tia thought it unbelievable that her father should have strong feelings of real love for Rosemary; Rosemary thought it incredulous that Alan had cast her away like an old sock; while, thousands of kilometres away, Kai was finding out more and more about Rosemary through their son, Hanale and both Kai and Hanale were beginning to think that there was a possibility of a future union; if only it wasn't for Alan.

Chapter Seventy

The autumnal days were dark, gloomy and depressing. As Rosemary sat in her small kitchen marking a pile of books, her attention wandered and her eyes followed suit. Dropping her pen on to her discarded marking she rose, filled the kettle and, as she waited for it to boil, looked out the window at the twirling leaves, as they performed their last dance, before joining their comrades on the damp, colourful carpeted ground. "Everything is dying," she said aloud her mind switching to Alan. "And soon, my love, you will be dead too." Pouring the boiling water into her coffee cup a sudden, nagging urgency clawed forcibly at her heart. Grabbing her coat, hat, scarf, gloves and keys she headed out the door.

Her eyes stared at the shadow of the man standing before her; the man who was to have been her husband and her heart crushed. *This,* she thought, *is not a man but a mere skeleton dressed in a man's clothes.* Her eyes rose from his pristine white shirt, hanging loosely over his baggy black trousers, and settled on his pale, excruciatingly thin face and her pained heart bled. Wrapping her arms around his neck, she pulled him towards her in a tight embrace, feeling his ribcage beneath his flimsy shirt. She didn't wait to be welcomed inside; storming into the hallway without preamble, leaving him to gently close the door behind her. He sighed resignedly, knowing full well that she had come to his home on a mission and, being the gentleman he was, he was aware that it was his honourable duty to hear what his ex-fiancée had to say. He braced himself.

Now that she was here, sitting directly in front of him on the opposite side of the kitchen table, she wondered what had possessed her to come here as all thoughts, accusations, questions, denials and words of any sort had swiftly vacated her mind, leaving a vacuum in her head.

Seconds turned to minutes and, laboriously, the minutes ticked away as invisible walls built around them; his wall was Kai; her wall was Alan's impending death. Finally, he spoke. "Have you thought about what I told you,

Rosemary?" His still, shrewd eyes, sunken into their sockets, seemed to bore into her very soul as his words grated roughly in her head.

"I have thought, Alan. Your ludicrous idea is nil and void." She answered coldly and without reserve.

"Then you should think about it again, Rose; before it is too late."

His words cut painfully and deep; their undercurrent telling her that Alan was cutting all ties with her; he was releasing her; he was urging her to go; he was setting her free, while her resolve to stay by his side was growing by the second. Taking a deep, ragged breath she forced her words out. "I do not love Kai. I love you, Alan; if you no longer want to marry me that's okay; but, I am not going to abandon you and, certainly, not in your time of need."

His raw eyes stared at the woman he loved. "I do not need you, Rosemary. Your place is not with me. I want you to go. I want to die in peace. I never, ever want to see you again."

She sat staring unblinkingly at his composed body, his determined eyes, the firm resolve in his stern-set mouth. Silently she rose and left.

In the privacy of their own space, their unrestrained tears poured.

Chapter Seventy-One
Kauai

Kai felt happy, tired and relieved the long day was over. It had been a good day, in which he and Hanale had worked effortlessly at the homeless shelter they had founded; their joy and inner peace at bringing a homeless unfortunate to the safety of their sanctuary, where he could be adequately fed and clothed, was unquenchable. Father and son loved working together as a team and, in so doing, were building a stronger bond between them.

"Aloha." Luana beamed and hugging them handed them both a foreign stamped envelope; both immediately identifying the handwriting on their hibiscus decorated envelopes. Hanale tore open the seal and greedily devoured the words inside, his happy eyes changing to eyes of incredulity. He reread the letter at a slower pace; but, the words remained the same and, as his eyes shot to his father, he noticed that the smile had vanished from Kai's lips. "What do you think, Dad?" He asked cautiously.

"I think, Hanale, that Alan is making a grave mistake; a grave mistake indeed."

Hanale's raging thoughts were torn in two; for, while he respected and appreciated Alan for everything he had done for them; Kai was his biological father, his flesh and blood and – *a union between his mother and father would be the icing on the cake.* "I thought you loved, Mum." He said after moments of reflective thought, his puzzled eyes not leaving his father's façade.

"She does not belong to me and Alan is a very ill man."

"But, I don't understand…" Hanale did not finish his sentence; his father had already vacated the room.

Five people wandered about with conflicting thoughts racing wildly in their heads. Kai and Hanale's thoughts ping-ponged from Rosemary to Alan to Kai himself; with Rosemary always in the centre of the threesome. Alan's thoughts were purely based on Rosemary; the one and only woman he ever truly loved; the woman he was, reluctantly, giving up for the sake of her future happiness. Rosemary's thoughts travelled between Kai, the man she loved, and Alan the man, she felt, she could not abandon. Ocean Tia's thoughts were focussed on the four people she loved most in the world; one more thought crept stealthily into her mind and that was Simon Teal, the boy she loved. All five people resided secretly in their own private hell.

England

One bleak morning, as the rain was lashing down in straight sheets outside the window, Ocean Tia placed her pen down on to the essay she was writing, her mind drifting off to her beloved island, where the sun always shone. In her heart, like outside, a black cloud had descended, surrounded and threatened her inner peace and, until there was a change, it would remain covering her under the umbrella of its bleakness.

Within the home, the atmosphere had changed dramatically. Instead of constant chatter, laughing, planning wedding menus and displays of wedding flora, the rooms were devoid of laughter, preparations and excitement. *It felt,* she thought, *as if she had preceded Alan into the tomb.* The thought of coming home of an evening made her inwardly cringe, filling her with dread; but, she still came home. She could not let Rosemary down; yet, when she was there they barely spoke to each other. Rosemary had clamped up, her conflicting thoughts entrapping her in her own made prison of silence, regret, humiliation, denial and rejection.

Earlier than most evenings, Ocean Tia slipped into the house. The sound of metal against glass made her stop abruptly, her heart racing furiously as, surreptitiously, she peered around the open door and gasped, quickly bringing her hand up to her mouth, lest she should be heard. The stark image of Rosemary, unscrewing the top of a vodka bottle, made her guts churn violently. She peered closer, her eyes watching intently as, for long minutes, Rosemary stared longingly at the bottle in front of her, then quickly replaced the top and buried the bottle into the depths of the kitchen cupboard. Ocean Tia let out a long breath. "Aloha!" She called out cheerfully, opening and shutting the outside door. Inside her heart filled with a new dread; knowing that whatever it was that was gnawing at Rosemary, it had to be dealt with, before it was too late.

Again she rapped at the door and, again, Alan's eyes lit up; for, the woman he saw was like a burst of sunshine after a brutal storm. "Ocean Tia; what brings you here?"

"Aloha Alan." She bestowed him a soft kiss on his hollow cheek, gave him a warm smile and breezed in. Already he felt better; however, this feeling soon abandoned him as he listened gravely to what she had to say, his eyes turning sorrowful. "So you see, Alan; Lokemele needs you."

He raised his sad, questioning eyes to her. "And, she told you that?"

"Well no; no, she didn't; but, without you, she will crumble." He was just about to step in with words of denial when she continued. "Lokemele needs you just like you need her, Alan, and you are both too stubborn to see what's going on. Do something, Alan, before it is too late and two lives are ruined." With these stark words ringing in his ears she left; her words haunting his thoughts throughout the long night. By dawn, he had drawn up a bullet-proof plan.

"Alan!" Her heart thumped as Rosemary extended the door to him, wondering what had propelled this unexpected visit.

She listened attentively to his words and liked them; but, they brought with them a fresh set of anxieties and unanswered questions. Looking directly into his eyes she felt their warmth. "Alan, you told me the last time I saw you that my place is not with you; you told me that you wanted me to leave you to die in peace."

He smiled. "You have to make some exceptions for the ramblings of a dying man, Rosemary."

She returned his smile. "So, let me get this straight. You want me to come and live with you and to take care of you."

"Yes... yes." He nodded his head. "But," he winked mischievously, "I'd rather come and live with you; your place is much cosier."

Her heart leaped as did she, to her feet and towards her dearest, treasured friend, planting an array of soft kisses on his forehead and cheeks, as he brought her closer to himself. She did not feel his bony shoulders, or his skinny body, next to hers; she felt only his warm mouth on hers, kissing her long and tenderly.

Chapter Seventy-Two

Alan's secret plan was slowly maturing into fruition. *And,* he thought smiling to himself, *if he knew Rosemary at all than she would not disappoint him.* He also knew he had to act quickly; his spasms, spells of confusion and increasing headaches telling him there was no time to lose; he had to get to work before it was too late.

He walked into the solicitors a happy man; an hour later he walked out a happier man. Everything was set in place and had been finalised. He would die in peace.

Rosemary and Ocean Tia proclaimed themselves as Alan's personal *guardian angels.* With outwardly happy faces and heavy laden hearts full of pain, they attended to his *every* need, whenever he dropped his guard and allowed them, as he had always been a fiercely independent man and held on to his self-reliance with every gram of strength he had; but, he knew, the progression of his illness was making him weaker by the day; his vision, blurred at times, forced him to stop driving and, with this loss of independence, came the first signs of depression. Uncharacteristically, he would be found sitting in his armchair staring into space, his face motionless; the warmth in his eyes gone. Increasingly this scene became a regular occurrence. Whenever this happened, Rosemary and Ocean Tia would bring him out of his dark well of misery. During times of lucidity they would attempt evenings out at the theatre or a light meal at a favourite restaurant; but, invariably Alan's lack of concentration, lack of appetite or nausea would prompt an early exit. It was during one of his lucid evenings that Alan placed his knife and fork on his plate of uneaten food, turned his eyes on Rosemary and made a statement, his steady eyes watching as Rosemary's face transformed into a vision of radiance. Her eyes questioning as they remained firmly fixed on him. "A Hawaiian evening; you want us to have a Hawaiian evening?" she exclaimed.

"Well, I have always wanted to visit the islands some—"

She cut in. "You shall have a taste of Hawaii, Alan." She pecked him on the cheek, inwardly flinching as she felt his protruding cheekbone, wondering for whose benefit would this be all for. Abruptly she forced her queries away. *This, she told herself sternly, was the request of a dying man. She had to put her own feelings aside.*

Alan's intensions were three-fold. In requesting the Hawaiian evening, he wanted to put a smile back on to Ocean Tia's face. *A touch of Hawaii,* he mused, *would cheer the young woman up;* as for Rosemary, he knew, she was giving so much of herself for the sake of his every need. *She,* he concluded, *deserved some sunshine in her life;* and he himself had always dreamed of visiting Hawaii. This would be a chance of experiencing its magic with the two people he loved most in the world.

Ocean Tia was the powerful force behind it all. She knew the Hawaiian traditions like no one else did. Avidly she poured through her own Hawaiian recipe books; phoned her father, Luana and grandparents to gather further ideas for the luau so that, by the time she was finished, she was armed with a barrage of traditional recipes, Hawaiian music, a supply of Hawaiian printed shirts, colourful Mother Hubbards and an ample set of Hawaiian phrasebooks, given to guests, well before the evening, so that they could familiarise themselves with the language. The leis, Ocean Tia decided, would be made by Alan, on days he wasn't too steady on his feet. *It would, s*he prudently thought, *take his mind off the illness.* And it was while he was stringing white silky plumeria together that he brought up a mutual concern shared by himself and Rosemary and, switching his sunken eyes to her he said, "Beneath the façade, I fear, Ocean Tia is carrying a secret sorrow."

Rosemary nodded. "It's Simon. Ocean Tia won't say anything; but, I know, she misses him terribly."

He dropped the lei he was working on to the table beneath and grabbed Rosemary's hands. "Then, I think, we must do something to help."

Rosemary looked deep into the eyes of the man she cared for; the man who had done so much for her and Ocean Tia. *And yet,* she thought, *in the shadow of death he is still thinking of others.* A small optimistic smile broke on to her lips. "Yes but what?"

Without hesitation he answered. "We must invite Simon to our Hawaiian evening."

Rosemary's optimistic smile turned to one of despondency, as she shook her head slowly from side to side. "Ocean Tia will not allow it; I know that for a fact, Alan."

"Then we will invite him secretly."

Rosemary's eyes grew wide with childish excitement as her smile returned. "Can we?"

He winked conspiratorially as his smile matched hers. "We can and we will."

Chapter Seventy-Three

The guests came from far and wide; for, they all loved Alan deeply and nothing would stop them honouring his last wish. Ocean Tia stood at the lounge window, an image of exotic beauty with an air of tropical mystery. Her silky dark hair lay down her back like a black satin sheet, a silky yellow hibiscus in her hair, matching her yellow printed dress. She wore no make-up; she was a natural beauty. Her feet were bare. Her dark, silent eyes watched the happy guests arriving and her young heart cut in two for the absence of her father. Turning away from the window she disappeared into the kitchen, where she knew her involuntary tears would not be seen.

From his armchair, Alan looked on the happy proceedings, knowing in his heart of hearts this was a farewell evening, as well as an evening to cheer up Ocean Tia. He knew that this would be the last time he would see all his friends gathered together, his sorrowful heart laden. As the first Hawaiian attired guests arrived, he packed away his self-pity, pinned on a smile and made a secret promise to enjoy the evening no matter what pain he suffered.

Rosemary also forced a smile determining sternly. *This was not the time for self-absorption.*

Soon the evening was in full swing. To make Alan's evening special, guests had eagerly researched traditional Hawaiian protocol, learned Hawaiian phrases off by heart; practised their hulas and now all their efforts were coming out in the wash, while Ocean Tia stood at the door as chief lei presenter, smiled warmly and felt truly at *home.* And as she watched the guests, and their somewhat unconventional Hawaiian moves to the soft lilt of Hawaiian guitars, her mind drifted faraway to Kauai. About to move from her post, her heart stopped and turned to ice as a gaily dressed figure, in a blue printed shirt, black trousers and a lei already hanging around his neck, approached.

"Aloha Ocean," he smiled.

Her heart restarted racing wildly, feeling as if it was about to jump out of her tight chest. "Aloha… Simon." She said almost in a whisper feeling the room, and all the happy *Hawaiians* in it, spinning out of control; feeling her young blood bubble and surge through every fast pulsating vein in her body, as she stood perfectly still like an elegant, exotic statue and yearned for the out-of-control roundabout to stop, so that she could get off. She got off, smiled and set Simon Teal's blood on fire. He smiled back, bestowed his lei around her neck and kissed her softly on both cheeks. Two hearts burned.

He took a step back and cast his admiring eyes on Ocean Tia's twinkling eyes, her mouth so inviting. "Thank you for inviting me, Ocean." He somehow managed to say.

Her heart started its rapid descent. *She had not invited him.*

"Hey, no frowns." He touched her bare arm with the tips of his fingers, sending immediate sparks throughout her entire body and making her feel weak at the knees as she grabbed the door and silently urged her good manners to prevail. *After all,* she concluded, *he was here and nobody had forced him to come.* As they walked together into the throng of revellers he turned to her. "Ocean, I hope you don't mind; but I have invited a friend to come along. Is that all right?"

She squeezed his arm gently and smiled congenially. "Of course; the more, the merrier as you English say." *Besides,* she silently conceded, *any friend of Simon's was probably already one of her friends.* Her smile extended. *This was going to be a fun night!*

Surrounded by friends with Rosemary by his side, Alan smiled to himself. *Everything was going according to plan. Ocean Tia and Simon were getting back on track; Rosemary had become the carer she had wanted to be, without losing her freedom and the wheels were set in motion at the solicitors.* He took Rosemary's hand and squeezed it gently. *Everything was falling into place.*

Rosemary's eyes turned to Alan and she smiled; but it was a bitter-sweet smile of unrequited love; for, she had never loved him the way he had loved her and deep – deep down, in the bowels of her heart, lurked heavy guilt, intermingled with deep regret; *for wasn't she secretly thankful of his illness, which had propelled him to cancel their wedding and had provided her with a get-out card; her freedom from – him?* She closed her eyes and squeezed them tightly, obliterating her secret act of betrayal and feeling blessed relief as the soft

Hawaiian guitars took her to another place… another time far, far away in Keoki and Luana's humble home… *She didn't like what she saw an over confident, handsome guy who clearly, she sensed, craved to be the centre of attention… Kai, she thought, liked the sound of his own voice though his smile could mend any broken heart; but, at what cost?…* Her thoughts darted back to the present and she asked herself. *At what cost?*

"Hey." She felt Alan's bony fingers around her hand, her heart slicing in two, as she forced a smile. "Why do you look so sad, Lokemele; I thought this evening would make you happy… bring back some memories?"

"It does… it does." She kissed him gently on the mouth. "It does." She reaffirmed as she wrapped her arms around his scrawny shoulders and hugged him tightly. "Thank you so very much, Alan." She enthused, inwardly cursing herself for being so selfish; so self-centred, when the dying man standing next to her was only too willing to give her the world on a golden platter. *Why,* she silently admonished herself, *couldn't she be grateful for all her blessings instead of reaching out for something or… someone she could never have?*

Ocean Tia felt she was in a blissful heaven. The sound of soft Hawaiian guitars took her back to the evenings spent on the beaches of Kauai listening to slack-key guitars; the revellers sporting their Hawaiian shirts, dresses and artificial leis reminded her of friends and family back home; the roasted pork, salmon, shrimps and, of course, the traditional Haupia cake, she had so diligently created, and the fresh fruits bringing the taste of Kauai into her mouth and heart and, in turn, taking her back to the Hawaiian luaus. Her shining eyes wandered to the artificial foliage, with skilfully created home-made plumeria and hibiscus tastefully placed on window sills, sideboards and wall units, taking her back to the luscious tropical foliage, which grew naturally along the roadsides and lanes of Kauai and she smiled. There was always a place in her heart for her father, Hanale, her family and friends; but, with Simon standing by her side her world, she felt, was almost complete; almost but not quite; for, she felt an inexplicable detachment between herself and Simon. *It would take time,* she told herself as they slipped in and out of snippets of casual conversation. Her heart leaped as his mouth broke into a spontaneous happy grin, his hand shooting into the air. "My friend has arrived!" He exclaimed excitedly. And, at last, Ocean Tia began to relax, hoping to God this mutual friend of theirs would break the ice.

The young woman's heart died a thousand deaths and plummeted rapidly to the depths of deepest Hell, as her eyes refused to take in what they undoubtedly saw, in the midst of a dark nightmare growing into fruition before her shocked eyes.

Chapter Seventy-Four

Her blissful heaven spun wildly until it fragmented and scattered into a mass of cluttered emotional debris and, still she stared as Simon took off his lei, she had given him, and bestowed it around the slender neck of a tall, slim blonde beauty, dressed in a figure hugging, black satin cocktail dress riding high above her knees. Ocean Tia's heart raced to a sudden stop where it became a silent, freezing block of solid ice as her dark, still eyes continued to stare and, for the first time in her entire life, she felt completely betrayed. For long minutes, she stood and stared, while happy guests danced the hula, laughed at each other's attempts at speaking the traditional Hawaiian lingo and enjoyed the endless flow of home-made Mai Tais and, while her eyes were helplessly stuck on Simon and his new girl, Alan's shrewd eyes flitted to Simon and his guest and darted to Ocean Tia, where they remained. And in these brief few seconds he knew exactly how she felt; for, his love was also drawn to another. He took in Ocean Tia's graceful poise. *So stoic,* he mused reflectively, *even in the lap of defeat* and he closed his tired eyes; for, he had not expected this outcome of events.

Neither did Rosemary. *But how could she condemn young Simon,* she asked herself, *when she, herself, was the queen of betrayal?*

Guts turned and twisted in Ocean Tia's young, innocent body; her heart clenched tightly by a band of merciless rejection; her thoughts splayed erratically in a thousand directions, as she stood graceful and majestic like a Hawaiian princess; aloof and mysterious, yet warm and exotic; her eyes on the couple as Simon led the way on to the makeshift dance floor and twirled his new girl about, paying no heed to the gentle rhythm of the music; or, Ocean Tia's feelings, while the sharp iced blade plunged deeper into her iced heart. Abruptly she turned as she felt a light touch on her arm. "May I have the pleasure?" Her eyes rested on Joel, an old friend of Hanale's, and her pained eyes lost a tiny fragment of sadness as she smiled and nodded. "He is a fool." Joel's comment was met with silence.

It pained Alan to witness Simon's blatant rejection of Ocean Tia. *And to flaunt this girl in Ocean's face,* he thought, *was totally unnecessary and a most hurtful thing to do.* And, while Simon Teal rapidly spiralled downwards in Alan's estimation; Ocean Tia rapidly rose. *For here,* he concluded, *was a young woman of intelligence, poise, integrity, beauty, kindness and impeccable manners. Simon's loss would be a rare, precious jewel in a lucky man's crown.*

As Simon and Natasha Parks cavorted around, he inadvertently caught sight of Ocean Tia clasped in Joel's strong, protective arms and a bitter lump rose immediately to his dry throat. He looked away bringing his eyes back to Natasha; but, the image he saw was firmly planted in his head and, he knew, it would haunt him.

Natasha stood out in a crowd; that was always her intention. When the spotlight was not focussed in her direction, when she did not solely claim the limelight, she quickly remedied the situation, whatever it took. Tonight she found the spotlight did not shine on her. She looked for the cause and found it in Ocean Tia, the mysterious girl who seemed to have a secret hold on Simon. Her hatred for the Hawaiian matured quickly. Dancing in close proximity to Simon, she surreptitiously watched beneath hooded eyes, trying to fathom what it was that was drawing the guys towards Ocean Tia. *It was not,* she thought, *her looks; for,* in her estimation, *she herself was far superior in that department. It was not the fact she was an easy lay, as Simon had told her they had not slept together. It was not her family's wealth; apparently they were all penniless.* Like a thunderbolt it hit her. *It was the mystery that comes with an islander who ventures on to English shores; someone different who appealed to the curiosity and fascination of others and that was,* she concluded, *what drew them towards her.* A plan crashed into her head. *She had to act fast if it was to work successfully,* she told herself firmly. *There was no time to lose.* She turned her devious eyes on Simon. "It looks as if the Hawaiians are ignorantly stuck in the dark ages." She giggled, her laughter laced with a heavy measure of spitefulness.

Simon withdrew himself from Natasha's tight hold, his eyes glaring coldly as he stated, "Hawaiians are not ignorant, Natasha."

She drew back her hands held up in mock defence, her long red fingernails standing to attention like obedient sentinels. "Wow! I think I've hit a nerve."

He ignored her and continued to dance; inwardly his guts churned bitterly and his heart went out to Ocean Tia. *How could anyone even consider labelling Ocean Tia as ignorant?* He pondered disconsolately, a seed of doubt beginning to grow about the girl he had decided to call his girlfriend; while Natasha was secretly planning her next move.

All stopped dancing, talking, laughing as they heard the sound of a clinking glass and turned their attention to Alan, who silently prayed his wobbly feet would not let him down as he addressed his friends. "Aloha."

"Aloha!" They all replied in cheerful unison as they raised their Mai Tai glasses.

"I hope you are all enjoying our Hawaiian evening." He smiled and looked from guest to guest as if he was saying his last, silent farewells. "And now it is time for our traditional Hawaiian luau. But, before we tuck into the mouth-watering delights, Ocean Tia will say a few words." He sat back on his chair, completely exhausted, as Ocean Tia stepped to the forefront and, taking a deep breath, she began.

"Aloha." She beamed as her lustrous eyes scanned the multi-coloured crowd, avoiding Simon and his girl. "A luau is a traditional Hawaiian feast. Before eighteen nineteen, all males sat separately from the women and children. In the year eighteen nineteen our King, Kamehameha the Second, decided it would be a good thing to eat with the wahines; sorry, the women, and children and, as a consequence, many hundreds of years of taboo were broken."

"What is taboo?" Someone from the back called.

"Taboo is a religious; or, indeed a social tradition stopping, or limiting, a particular action; or, preventing contact with a place, person or object. It was King Kamehameha the Second who gave us the term luau for these large meal feasts. Nowadays, in Hawaii, we celebrate birthdays, weddings and even the passing of life with luaus."

"How enchanting," sneered Natasha into Simon's ear.

His icy eyes darted to his girlfriend for a few brief seconds and returned to Ocean Tia where they remained as she continued.

"In olden days, only the chiefs would taste certain foods like pork or bananas. Most of the revellers were allowed certain types of fish, sweet potatoes and, of course, poi. By the way, I hope you have all tasted a sample of poi and enjoyed its delightful taste." She smiled mischievously, knowing it was not to everyone's taste. Her eyes darted to Alan and she smiled warmly; then rested briefly on Rosemary who was thousands of kilometres away. She focussed her eyes back on to her attentive listeners. "Today we celebrate with mouth-watering dishes like kalua pork, sweet potatoes, aki poke and shayu chicken with various salads, finishing off with a variety of cakes and always including our traditional Haupia cake. So, I hope you will now all enjoy our Hawaiian luau. Aloha."

"Aloha!" They all cheered rapturously and, after applauding loudly, they all followed the young woman to the trestles laden full of Hawaiian delights.

It was to be everyone's misfortune that Natasha made a beeline for the head table and parked herself in-between Alan and Simon leaving the two men, Rosemary and Ocean Tia with a deep inner foreboding and, while all around eagerly tucked into their delicious fare, two people picked at their food and ate nothing; one person unable to eat anything for fear of it being vomited up; the other disallowing anything Hawaiian to enter her body temple, her icy eyes stuck vehemently on the Hawaiian beauty sitting directly opposite, wishing she was dead like the pork on her plate.

Rosemary forced herself to smile politely. "Perhaps you would like some English food, Natasha?"

A barrage of giggles escaped Natasha's red lip-stick mouth. "Yes please, anything than this Hawaiian trash."

Blood boiling to a dangerous level; clamping her mouth tightly, lest words she could not retract escaped her mouth, Rosemary escaped to the safety of the kitchen.

Simon turned his ice-cold eyes on Natasha. "Apologise," he stated.

Raucous laughter emitted from her mouth. "For what; speaking the truth; or, are Hawaiians so primitive they censor free speech?"

All eyes focussed on Natasha and she revelled in their attention because, while it was on her, it was diverted from Ocean Tia, the girl she despised with all of her heart. The limelight finally on her she stood up, threw her lipstick stained napkin on to her uneaten food and turned her attention on to Alan. "It's no wonder you look like a skeleton, mate; eat more of this Hawaiian rubbish and you'll disappear completely." She turned her eyes on Simon. "Come on, Si, we're going."

He turned his scathing eyes on the object of his scorn and stated in as equally determined tone, "I am going nowhere, Natasha."

She stood arms akimbo all eyes glaring at her, while her eyes looked down at Simon with the look of total disdain. Turning abruptly, throwing silent daggers at Ocean Tia, with head held high, she strode boldly to the door, turned and laughed scornfully and shouted out, "Aloha!"

In the wake of her departure, the air was heavy with silent, and not so silent, recriminations; but none came from the lips of Alan, Rosemary, Simon or Ocean Tia. They sat together, united in their silent disappointment, digesting and assessing the situation. Alan finally broke their reflective silence. "Right, Lokemele, I think it's about time you taught me the hula."

Rosemary's heart gnawed mercilessly, as Alan led her to the makeshift dancing area; for, while she desperately wanted to dance with Alan, she knew, this would be their last dance together; their farewell dance. Her heart tightened as body came closer to body and she could feel the structure of his ribcage beneath his flimsy shirt; she could feel his bony hand clasped protectively around her hand, as they abandoned the hula and clung together in a slow smooch. *It won't be long,* she dismally concluded. *It won't be long.*

Simon took his cue, knowing full well mere words in the form of an apology would not cut it. *He had betrayed his true love and he may still have to pay the heavy price. But,* he sighed deeply, *there was hope, even though it was a minute speck.*

She smiled as he sat by her side and felt his taut body next to her own though, she felt, they were poles apart. Prised apart, she thought, by her own stubbornness and his betrayal. He opened his mouth and immediately closed it; reached out for her hand and rapidly withdrew it. Finally, summoning up all his courage he turned to face her, his heart breaking as he gazed at her finely chiselled cheekbones, her dark alluring eyes, her warm mouth closed but inviting. *Had he lost his rare jewel?* He asked himself. *Had his pride in her rejection of him ruined everything between them? Were they on a road of no-return?* He closed his eyes tight and hoped to God that, somehow, things would be resolved; *But; how?* The nagging question niggled him as he searched his fuddled mind and heard the echo of her soft voice, like the soft whisper of the breeze on a distant shore. "Simon, I forgive you." He turned his glassy eyes on her, his heart thumping maddeningly, his words almost inaudible. "But, I don't forgive myself, Ocean Tia." He felt the warmth of her flesh as she took his hands into her own, sending a thousand minute electric shocks through his entire body.

"You must forgive yourself, Simon; without doing so we have no future together."

Incredulity replaced the glassiness in his eyes. *A future together; it was beyond his wildest dreams!*

"I was wrong too, Simon." She said softly.

He turned to face her, withdrew his hands and protectively placed them over her hands and said, "Then let's plan our future, Ocean."

"Yes, let us do that." She agreed. "But, before we do, we must both agree never to mention this dark time again."

"Never" He gently pulled her away from the chair and led her to the dance area.

Rosemary and Alan looked on and smiled.

Chapter Seventy-Five

The success of the Hawaiian luau was evident in the abundance of thank you messages, phone calls and bouquets of flowers. Alan and Rosemary warmly accepted the appreciation, knowing that Alan was growing weaker by the day and the memory of the evening had to be kept very much alive for the dark days to come.

The following days were bitter-sweet. Determined to live his life to the full to the very end, Alan put on a brave face and adopted an ironclad spirit of bravery and courage; but his dilapidating and progressive illness found him in bed and more and more asleep. When he was awake, prolonged confusion and deteriorating vision became regular and annoying companions. On his good days, Alan knew he had to act quickly; time was of the essence and he had two very important jobs to do. On a morning, when Rosemary had popped out to the chemist, he took out his fountain pen and writing pad and applied himself to the arduous task of writing his farewell letter to Rosemary.

Task one accomplished he embarked on his second task. His secret meeting with Ocean Tia took place when Rosemary had gone to school to finalise her leave of absence. And, as his weak eyes gazed on the young woman's calm, still eyes he knew, without a doubt, he could rely on her to fulfil his last wishes.

Underneath her cool façade Ocean Tia's heart was breaking into a thousand iced fragments and each tiny particle was tipped with excruciating pain for this man who had been her rock; a second father when her own father was going through a hell of his own. She smiled and took Alan's hand squeezing it gently, giving him all the reassurance she could. He smiled back.

"Ocean, I need you to do something for me." Silently she nodded her head and he continued. "When I have died, I would like you to pass on this letter to Rosemary. In it are my final wishes. I am also going to ask you to support her."

She gazed down at the envelope in his trembling hand and asked softly, "Don't you think you should give her the letter?"

A regretful smile slid on to his parched lips. Taking a sip of cool water, his eyes firmly fixed on Ocean Tia, he said, "She is not a strong woman, my dear."

She took the envelope from his hand. "Then I shall make sure that she will get it."

"And…" His intent eyes seemed to bore into her very soul. "You will make sure everything shall come to pass?"

She patted his hand softly, the warm smile sliding back on to her lips. "I shall make sure everything you ask, Alan, shall come to pass; I promise."

He closed his eyes. "Then I think we shall celebrate, Ocean; crack open the pineapple juice carton."

And, in true Hawaiian style, they enjoyed their tropical cordial.

Events rapidly took a turn for the worse. Severe headaches were eased with painkillers; sleep became a regular feature and breathing became a concern. Together; or, in turn, Rosemary and Ocean Tia sat at Alan's bedside, attentive to his every need; managing his catheter, adjusting various sources of soft lights to meet his fading visual requirements, seeing to his medication as and when required; but always at his bedside; always speaking in soft subdued voices and often about the far distant Island of Kauai; an island he found to be fascinating; but one that had remained elusively out of his reach.

During the last stages of his life, his breathing became shallow and rapid and stopped. Ocean Tia bent down to see if Alan was all right. He gasped, making her step back, her eyes wide with alarm. A sigh of relief escaped her open mouth when she heard him breathe rapidly, until his breathing pattern returned to its rapid and shallow pace once more. This went on for days.

In the quiet of the evening, with the sound of soft Hawaiian guitars playing in the background, Alan slipped away. The two women wept profusely.

Chapter Seventy-Six

Rosemary stared at the envelope, immediately recognising the neat copperplate handwriting, her eyes flitting to Ocean Tia.

"Alan asked me to give this letter to you, Lokemele." She smiled and disappeared out of the room, leaving Rosemary with the letter and her thoughts.

The ticking of the clock on the wall seemed to be getting louder and louder by the second, as her eyes stared at the name, *Lokemele,* and a faint smile danced on her lips. *Alan,* she mused, *had always been partly Hawaiian in spirit.* Letting out a deep sigh she reached for the letter knife, eased the seal apart and took out the contents. She placed the paper on to the table, closed her eyes and sat perfectly still; her ears finely attune to the increasingly loud ticking of the clock, which seemed to match the pounding of her fast beating heart. Heaving another deep sigh, she picked up the paper and began to read. *Aloha.* She smiled. *My dearest, Lokemele. And so, the time has come to pass. I shower you with a thousand mahaloes for bringing happiness and peace to my life. I take the memories with me. I have a special request which, if carried out, will ensure, as true friends, we shall never be apart; for, I know, there is a special place that links us all together; Kauai.* She stopped for a moment, took a deep breath and continued only to stop, her heart beating wildly. *Surely,* she told herself, *she must have misread.* Composing herself she continued once more… *And so my dying wish is that you, Lokemele, scatter my ashes on the shores of Kauai; to be washed away in the clear, blue waters of the Pacific, where I shall find my eternal rest. This is my last request…* Like a hot potato she threw the letter on to the table and closed her eyes against the impossible request, shaking her head from side to side in total incredulity. *So, this is what he was up to,* she quietly surmised; *a cunning plan to get her back to Kauai; to get her back with… Kai. This is what he had been planning all along; for he had always known, deep down within his heart that his Lokemele had always belonged to another and he had to set her free.* She stared unblinkingly at his neat handwriting. "And who could deny the last wish of a dying man?" She hadn't realised that she was speaking aloud; neither had she realised that there was a figure standing at the door.

Ocean Tia sat opposite Rosemary and took her hands into her own warm, strong clasp. "I am here for you, Lokemele."

Rosemary handed her the letter and, after reading Alan's words, Ocean Tia smiled.

Chapter Seventy-Seven
Kauai

As the warm breeze swept off the ocean it stirred the palms, as nearby a small group stood on the shores of Kauai; gazing at the majestic sun as it sank lower and lower, lighting the mighty waters with its golden splendour like ripples of liquid gold. Fingers interlocked with fingers as Rosemary, Ocean Tia, Hanale and Kai gazed at the hypnotic brilliance and in their centre stood Alan's urn; inside the ashes of the man who had made all this possible. They stood in solemn silence honouring the memory of a good, kind man who had come to his final resting place; for, in spirit, wasn't he a true Hawaiian?

Each comforted by the fact that they had been truly privileged to have known him, now bestowed to him their silent thanksgivings. Hanale thanked him for being a shining example; Ocean Tia thanked him for giving her a future when all seemed futile; Kai thanked him for setting Lokemele free and Rosemary thanked him for enabling her to, finally, understand the essence of peace.

Part Two
Ocean Tia

Chapter Seventy-Eight
Kauai

A lone figure stood motionless, as the long surge of sun-tipped surf rolled in and the gentle splash of water lazily covered her bare feet, before the cool liquid was recaptured by its master, the mighty Pacific; her ears finely attune to the thundering roar of the moving beast as her observant eyes watched the majestic sun throw its wondrous golden splendour upon the island, she called home, before sinking into the ocean.

She stood statuesque and mysterious, devoid of thoughts and feelings; like an ancient Hawaiian goddess elegantly poised, cold and aloof, as the darkening waves in the distance wrestled in their own private battles, while her fast beating heart fought a secret war of its own; a war she declined to play a part in, preferring numbness to any form of emotion.

She knew not how long she stood in the pearly moonlight while, somewhere in the distance, soft strings strummed indolently on battered ukuleles and the dark, sinister waves rolled on and on, each replacing the last for a moments glory, as had been done for millions and millions of years; their ominous roar enhanced by the surrounding darkness; the ruffled waves matching her tortured soul. But, it had not always been like this. Life for Ocean Tia had once been so very, very different.

Unblinkingly she stared into the comforting dark, thrashing, roaring silhouetted swell in the far distance; the sweet lure of its sinister and mysterious attraction propelling one foot, then another to wander in making her inhale sharply a deep, jagged, salty breath; for, she had not anticipated the sheer coldness of the dark water. One cautious step followed another, her feet quickly adapting to the temperature, her stark eyes firmly fixed on the silver-tipped surf ahead as she waded in further, her whole body conforming to the rhythmic motion of the mighty ocean. One foot in front of the other she boldly ventured further, as the cold, dark water enveloped the lower part of her body; her ears and mind bombarded from every side by the constant roar infiltrating and saturating her senses. On and on, she trudged; boldly, determinedly with one solitary goal in mind. One goal which could bring her the ultimate peace she so desperately craved.

Chapter Seventy-Nine

Eyelids flickered and laboriously opened, only to snap shut; muffled sounds she failed to obliterate and was unable to ignore. They were just there. Thoughts, emotions, feelings stealthily attempting to creep into her consciousness, she crushed dead before they had chance to surface and thrive; for, she was dead to thoughts; dead to emotions; dead to all feelings. DEAD! But for the stubborn beating of her heart which refused to die.

"Ocean!"

From somewhere in the depths of her consciousness, she heard the faint, distant echo of her name; the name she now despised for it was her namesake, the ocean, who had refused to claim her for its own, tossing her back into the world like a soggy piece of seaweed; it was the ocean who refused to grant her the eternal peace she yearned.

"Ocean." The soft echo reverberated loudly in her ears, pounding mercilessly in her head like the mighty waves in the far distance.

Squeezing her eyes tightly she turned her head away, refusing to acknowledge the intruder's presence, only for her mind to be invaded by other intruders as one by one, like a mighty army, they marched into her consciousness and congregated together to form a close-knit pact, haunting her every waking moment, attacking her, looming as large and clear as life; each demanding to be acknowledged, before each vanished back into obscurity, promising to resurface at a future date clearer, larger, stronger. Her father, Kai, and mother, Leialoha, Auntie Luana, Uncle Keoki; Lokemele, Alan and Simon. All except one were ghosts of a previous life; gone now and envied for they had found their peace. Only one ghost had evaded the grave whispering softly... *Ocean... Ocean... Please wake up. I... love... you...* his words transforming her heart into a block of ice. If only, she willed, it would stop beating.

Each long day followed the last excruciatingly torturous day in exactly the same sequence until, one day, the echo of her name remained dormant and her eyes opened wide.

Recovery was a long, slow, laborious process but with good medical help, and the constant encouragement of many friends, Ocean Tia began her physical and mental recovery, the latter taking substantially longer; for, while Ocean was an excellent listener, who had helped many in their mental struggles, she herself was an intrinsically private person and one was indeed privileged to be allowed any access at all into her private world.

Makamae was the privileged one and, as he sat opposite the young woman, his wise eyes closely observing her every move, he was well aware of the mountain they both had to climb. But, he consoled himself, she had allowed him a small glimpse into her world and that was an encouraging first step of their journey. The second positive step came when he saw Ocean Tia's eyes dance, for the first time in a very long time. This happened when he had taken her out into the hospital garden. Holding her hand he guided her out of the confines of her room, along the long corridor and out into warm, bright day. Seeing her eyes shine made his middle-aged heart somersault with irrepressible joy.

Sitting in complete silence the young woman inhaled the sweet, heady tropical fragrances, her eyes alive as they flitted from cream coloured frangipanis, to the yellow hibiscus, to the clusters of white, pink and purple plumerias propelling a ghost of a melancholy smile to slide on to her lips, her numbed heart thawing to the stirrings of life around her. After ten minutes, he walked her back to her room, smiling to himself. The process of recovery had begun. For the first time, since her hospital admission, Ocean Tia slept peacefully and awoke the next morning to the first rays of the sun filtering through the delicate curtains.

She was alive!

Chapter Eighty

Merciless clutches squeezed tightly her heart, her eyes shooting from the page of text before her to the source of her anxiety; her dry mouth opening and closing unable to utter his name, her feet itching to escape but unable to move them a centimetre.

"Aloha Ocean." He smiled but in his smile she saw only deceit, lies and betrayal; her body tensing, like her heart, feeling like a trapped animal with no means of an escape, in dread of what was to come.

Her eyes followed the figure as he grabbed a wicker chair and sat down and she swiftly diverted her eyes and attempted to draw comfort from the luscious abundance of tropical foliage; but, the scent of the sweet smelling blooms and their beauty did not quell the anguish twisting her insides. The natural pulchritude, she thought, looked artificial, like the man sitting opposite her; the man she once loved more than life itself; the man that was her husband. Eyes, unable to meet his gaze, dropped and rigidly remained on her tightly clasped hands resting on her lap.

"Ocean, we must talk."

His words though innocent enough, she mused, were like dripping poison *dripping... dripping... dripping...* venomously into her consciousness. Perfectly still she sat; her whole body perfectly still as her mind prepared for a line of defence.

Reaching out his hand to her, he withdrew it swiftly as she squeezed her hands tighter together until she could squeeze them no more, protecting them from his invasion, while her clenched heart of stone regained a spurt of life and commenced its rapid beating, feeling as if it would jump out of her chest.

"Ocean, we must talk." He repeated his soft, determined tone unchanged hoping for clemency.

Unwilling eyes flitted to him and, for a brief moment, he saw hope; quickly it was dashed to the ground. "Please don't come here or try to contact me again,

Simon." She stated firmly and rising she took one last look at the man she once loved, turned and walked away, while inside her racing heart cried buckets.

He watched her go just as once she let him go, his glassy eyes not leaving her until she vanished into the sanctuary of the hospital. His eyes darted back to the chair she had occupied now empty as a new, raw emptiness enveloped around and seeped into Simon Teal's regretful heart, as he silently and secretly cried for what he had lost. Never again, he told himself, would he ever find a rare jewel like Ocean Tia.

Chapter Eighty-One

Simon's visit had opened raw, painful wounds; his subsequent absence brought with it a balm to Ocean Tia's soul and slowly, with Makamae's invaluable help and support, she began to repair once more. Gradually she opened up her heart and soul to him and slowly he began to formulate a picture of his charge and further slow steps of recovery were made. However, one thing was puzzling Makamae. He had noticed that although Ocean was starting to talk about Kai, Leialoha, Luana, Keoki, Lokemele and Alan; her half-brother, Hanale, and her husband, Simon, were never mentioned. He wondered why.

He listened attentively as Ocean spoke fondly and frankly about her late father; about his wandering eye until he found his Leialoha and his desperation when he lost his love. She spoke about his subsequent love for Lokemele and their son, Hanale, and her praise was unfailing when she spoke of her Uncle Keoki and Auntie Luana, her rock and anchor. Recounting Lokemele's hopes, dreams and fears brought a nostalgic smile to her lips and tears of melancholy to her eyes; for, Lokemele had been a troubled woman but, in the end, she had been lucky enough to have found peace in her soul. Alan, she told Makamae, was their fortress; strong, dependable, a sanctuary in a storm; if it had not been for Alan…

Makamae was a good listener giving Ocean Tia as much time as she needed, knowing that the ghosts of the past played an important role in the present world; for, as far as he was concerned, they were the key to unlock the past, interlink it with the present and take into the future.

Her mind drifted as… *her heart raced wildly in complete contrast to her steady, controlled footsteps as she walked serenely into the interior of the bustling airport, causing men of all ages to stop what they were doing and stare, whilst their wives cast disapproving eyes at the object of their scorn secretly, greedily envying her natural, exotic beauty. Her dark, mysterious eyes flitted around the vast array of rushing people, her ears bombarded with alien sounds coming from a variety of sources; already she missed the soft, lilting sounds of*

Kauai, the roar of the thundering waves with their white-tipped surf, the soft swishing whispers of the palms soothingly stirring in the gentle breeze; the warm sunshine on her face and arms and, above all, the calm and serenity of her beloved island home... Hanale moved from foot to foot, his excitement growing with every passing second, his expectant eyes peering this way and that, in search of the exotic creature resembling the image he held in his tremulous hand. He spotted her from afar, waving furiously trying to catch her eye. It was Lokemele she recognised and it was on Rosemary she bestowed her first lei. Hugging Alan she turned her eyes to Hanale and her heart tugged. "Aloha Hanale." She smiled. "A-Aloha," He stammered, his hypnotised eyes staring unblinkingly at the natural beauty before him taking in her grace, poise, confidence; her evident level of maturity. She saw his smile die on his lips; she didn't feel his guts wrench with dread or see him shrivel up inside and slip into his self-conscious shell. She saw his eyes drop to the floor. Alan was quick to notice the despondency in the young lad's face and leaped to his rescue saying, "Let's get you home, Ocean Tia... Home... home... home..."

The solitary word echoed in her head and pounded in her heart. Where was home? She asked herself. A faint smile rose and danced on her lips, her long fingers playing with the plumeria in her hair. Kauai is my home, she silently whispered. Makamae watched intently as a dark shadow crossed her face and she closed her eyes. *If only I had not followed my dreams and abandoned the Islands.* She squeezed her eyes tightly. *If only I had not gone to England—If only I had not met Simon—If only...* She did not feel or see the crushed petals escaping from her fingers and fall to the floor.

Chapter Eighty-Two

Simon Teal had made one grave mistake in his life; a mistake which had been irreversible; detrimental casting a black, heavy veil of mistrust which was to influence both his and Ocean Tia's lives. He had swerved off course. For that mistake, he would have to pay a heavy price. As he threw his socks into his suitcase and snapped it shut, his mind wandered hither and thither and finally settled on one particular scenario.

England A Year Earlier

Stepping out the plane he felt an alien surge of loneliness sweep through him and envelop him like a heavy, prickly, uncomfortable blanket. Without Ocean Tia, his beloved wife, by his side he felt hollow, alone, incomplete, lonely; without Ocean Tia he did not want to be here at all. Yet, here he was, walking briskly towards the arrivals area with one thing on his mind; to get the job done as quickly and satisfactorily as possible and to get back to his woman, his other half; the love of his life. He pressed the button on his mobile. It was the eleventh time he had contacted her since departing Kauai and he was missing her like crazy. Her soft words always brought a smile to his face; just hearing her dulcet tones made his heart dance. They had been married for two years and twenty-three days and, still, his love for her was as fresh and unsullied as on the day he had promised to be hers until the end of time. Oh, how he wished she'd joined him on this trip; but, she had insisted she had to stay in Kauai; the homeless and the unfortunates needed her help. He had begged, cajoled and done everything in his power to persuade her into changing her mind. She would not abandon the needy. And so, here he was counting the hours to their reunion.

"Si!"

He snapped out of his reverie, forcing Ocean Tia's exotic image firmly out of his head, as he turned and waved to his old friend and Ocean's half-brother.

Hanale threw a cursory glance at his passenger before returning his eyes to the road ahead; the words coming out of his mouth cold, stark, detached. "Why didn't she come, Simon?"

A compilation of excuses whirled around Simon's head. He chose his words carefully, avoiding any eye contact with his brother-in-law. "You know Ocean, Hanale. Where there is a need, she will not abandon her post."

"It's my wedding, Si." Hanale's voice sounded hollow, dead. Simon closed his eyes and opened his mouth to dry words. His ears were not closed. "She's my half-sister. I. I thought she'd make the effort."

The accusing blade thrust sharply through Simon's conscience; for, he was thinking along the same line. Wrong words jumped out of his mouth. "Well I'm here, mate. What more could you want?"

The two friends lapsed into raw silence, immersed in their own private wells of disappointment. Both had wished for a different outcome, knowing full well that Ocean Tia would always put the needs of the needy before herself and her own family; carrying on her late father's work, to the exclusion of all else, was of paramount importance and her priority.

As the bride walked slowly, solemnly down the aisle Simon saw only Ocean Tia, by his side, on the beach as they exchanged their vows. As Maria spoke he heard only Ocean saying softly, *I do*. As Maria turned and kissed Hanale, Simon felt his wife's lips on his own, so soft and inviting it hurt. He opened his eyes to Ocean and saw a mass of multi-attired people, an altar with a beaming priest and the happy couple, united in marriage, proceeding to walk up the aisle. As his eyes lingered on the newly-weds, he caught sight of her and, for a split second, their eyes locked. Abruptly he looked away.

Eyes clashed a second time. The seed of confusion, planted in Simon's head in the church, had now matured into a black mass of bubbling anger, fermenting his twisted guts and making them mercilessly twist and wrench, as he stared at the female in total incredulity. What the fuck was she doing here? And who the hell had the audacity to invite this… this… fiend? The answer to his first question was self-explanatory. Her flowing, powder-blue dress, her attendance in close proximity to the bride during the ceremony, told him she was the chief bridesmaid. The second puzzle was easy to solve too. But, there was a third outstanding question. Had Hanale a part to play in the invitation and, if so, where did his loyalties lie? Simon's questioning eyes darted to his brother-in-law, standing close to his new wife, totally oblivious to his friend's plight. His eyes flitted back to the object of his scorn; feeling the deep-seated anger, which had remained dormant for so long, rise like sickly bile. His eyes snapped shut as he tried to obliterate the memory which stubbornly grew and grew, making him shake his head from side to side with sheer incredulity, as he asked himself the question he had asked himself many times. *Why had he so unashamedly paraded this woman in Ocean Tia's face?*

Once more she caught his eye and he felt the sudden stab of the sharp-edged knife of betrayal slice through his heart, washing his body with a wave of inexplicable weakness. He looked away.

Replenishing her drink she made a beeline for him. "Simon." She smiled seductively, her hungry eyes scanning him from head to toe and back again resting on his wary eyes, as his guts tightened with the force of a mighty vice, his feet itching to run yet wanting to stay as he eyed her cautiously, his heart racing. She watched his eyes drop to his glass but not before she saw the flicker of hesitancy in their withdrawal. "Si; how wonderful to see you; all alone?" Her eyes scanned the immediate periphery before returning to him. "Not to worry; I'll keep you company." She linked her free arm with his. "Let's dance, for old time's sake."

The touch of her hand on his made his skin crawl and tingle simultaneously. He thrust it roughly away; his eyes of disgust shooting to her and wishing desperately they hadn't; for, her undeniable beauty had not diminished in the slightest. If anything, he concluded, it was enhanced; his eyes involuntary appreciating the tall, slim blonde beauty with eyes of crystal blue and whose luscious, inviting mouth was so very, very tempting. Hypnotised eyes lingered there, as haunting words from years gone by came crashing into his consciousness... *It looks like Hawaiians are ignorantly stuck in the dark ages...* Her damning laugh and disparaging remarks rang loud and clear to this very day.

"I do not wish to dance, Natasha." He stated coldly.

Quickly she claimed his hand and just as swiftly she released it when she saw the ice-cold chips in his unforgiving eyes.

"I said, no, Natasha. Don't you understand English?" The second he'd snapped the words he regretted the harshness in his tone. But, he shook his head, as he watched her storm off without a backward glance. *This woman was unbelievable!*

239

From his vantage point, he watched her as he sipped his neat brandy and what he saw confirmed his opinion of the woman, he had used in the past to make Ocean Tia jealous. Nothing had changed. Natasha Parks still stood out in a crowd and, when the spotlight was not directly focussed on her; when she did not solely claim the limelight, she quickly remedied the situation as she did now grabbing the sporran of an infuriating, raucous guest who was showing off to the amusement of all around. Natasha Parks could not, and would not, take rejection without a fight. *She was,* Simon grimly thought, *a dangerous enemy.*

From his vantage point, Hanale had seen it all...

Kauai

Simon snapped out of his reverie. Reopening the suitcase, he grabbed the shirt he had overlooked and haphazardly threw it in, snapped the lid closed and gave it a final click. He was set to leave the house, the island he had grown to love and the love of his life. Everything that had needed to be said was said; all avenues of persuasion were exploited and deemed unfit for any possible U-turns. There was no going back. It was over.

Chapter Eighty-Three

Fixing himself a Mai Tai he walked on to the balcony, drew up a wicker chair and sat down, his head devoid of all thoughts; they had been chewed, digested and fully exhausted. By this time tomorrow, Ocean Tia and Kauai would be his past.

His observant eyes narrowed as he caught sight of two figures turning into the garden; watching intently as they walked side by side in deep conversation, seemingly oblivious to his presence, a surge of pure envy surged furiously through his heart. She would, he dismally concluded, rather be in the company of another native than her own husband. Swallowing a bitter, hard lump, his eyes peeled on the duo and bringing his glass up to his lips he took a generous gulp of the potent rum, feeling a wave of her betrayal sweeping over him. And, yet, wasn't it he who had betrayed and deceived his beloved wife; wasn't it he who had strayed from the marital bed and jumped into the bed of Ocean's nemesis? Ocean had done nothing wrong. She was innocent. She was the victim. Pouring the remnant of the golden-brown substance down his throat he dragged his eyes away, unable to look upon the tropical beauty he had lost; his jewel.

Her eyes had witnessed his presence; her heart pained with the familiar thrust of the jagged blade of loss, as it seared mercilessly through every ventricle. She was losing the only man she had ever loved; her first love and, she vowed silently, *her last.* She willed her eyes to focus on the colourful, scented blooms around. Magically they had always brought a unique solace to her soul; but, not this time. This time comfort eluded her; her soul fragmented in a hundred thousand pieces and each solitary piece mourned for the loss of her husband; for the love they once shared and the future they were never destined to share.

Pouring himself another drink he resumed his position on the balcony; the garden now devoid of her presence. *If only,* he cursed himself, *I hadn't been so damned stupid. If only...* But, Miss Natasha Parks was a woman of the world; a cunning vixen, who knew only too well how to play a man like a fiddle, once he had fallen hook, line and sinker into her trap. For that mistake, he had no one to blame except his cock; for, when Natasha was in the vicinity, it was always on fire.

With a heavy laden heart, Ocean Tia poured herself and Makamae a large glass of freshly squeezed pineapple juice and sat opposite her friend avoiding his eyes; unable to hide her sorrow from her confidante and honorary uncle; the only man she trusted.

He saw the deep-rooted sorrow in her eyes, knowing only too well that it would take time for Ocean to open up and time was one thing they had on the Island of Kauai.

Uncharacteristically she broke the solemn silence; simultaneously, he raised his wise eyes to her. She looked unwaveringly into them and stated, "I will never love another man again, Makamae." As if to prevent a contradiction, abruptly she rose and walked to the door, leaving a solitary Makamae to sit and silently contradict his friend's words; for, he mused, *a woman of Ocean Tia's unique character, who was as beautiful within as she undoubtedly was on the outside, could no longer not love than not breathe. Love was an intrinsic part of her; it was in her DNA. Only time would determine when her love would blossom again; but, blossom,* Makamae knew without a doubt, *it certainly would.*

On the morning of Simon's departure, Ocean Tia was alone in her secluded sanctuary; the only place in the world where she could always find comfort and peace.

As Simon placed one reluctant foot in front of the other towards the waiting plane, he glanced back in one last vain attempt at snatching back a grain of hope. He closed his heavy eyes. *She was not coming.*

Ocean placed a lei of fragrant frangipanis on to a grave; after which she carefully positioned two leis on either side of the first grave. She sat on an old wooden bench, opposite the three well-maintained graves, her eyes flitting from resting place to resting place before resting on the central mound; focussing on the gold inscription on the black marble headstone. "Leialoha and Kai; sleeping in eternal peace. Aloha." She read out aloud, her eyes drifting lazily to the left where, beneath the earth, lay a portion of Alan's ashes; together with Lokemele's body. "Together; forever" Her eyes darted to the third headstone, her lips breaking out into a melancholy smile. "Dear, dear Uncle Keoki," she whispered softly, as if not to wake him from his peaceful slumber; as she remembered his cheery smile, his dark twinkling eyes and, above all, his unquenchable zest for life. She closed her eyes, the smile still on her lips, as she remembered her Auntie Luana; always reliable; dependable and now gone – all gone. And now, Simon was gone too. "Dead!" She stated out loud puncturing the still, quiet air.

She did not hear the sound of soft approaching footsteps; feeling only a presence, making her snap out of her reverie, her eyes encountering her intruder. "Liliana!" She exclaimed; disbelief and joy simultaneously making her heart dance. "Where did you spring from? I-I thought you were on the Big Island. I thought you'd said you'd never…"

Liliana cut her cousin's words, placing a colourful lei around Ocean's slender neck and giving her a tight hug. "Never say, never; that's a lesson I shall take to my grave." She stated her eyes dropping and lingering on her parents' grave, before she placed three identical leis on three separate graves.

"But what made you change your mind, Liliana?" Ocean was both excited and bewildered by the unexpected visit.

"Oh, it's just a flying visit but, anyway, now that I'm here I'm inviting you to a luau." Immediately she dismissed her cousin's defiance. "You're coming and that's that, Ocean; besides, Akamu can't wait to see you." Liliana caught her cousin's wistful smile and knew she'd won.

Tossing and turning amidst an assortment of distorted and fragmented images of Simon, Akamu, Liliana, Natasha, Keoki, Alan, Lokemele, Luana, Leialoha and Kai, Ocean roughly thrust her light cover to one side and strode to the balcony, where everything below and around was still as the grave. Only her racing heart beat wildly, admonishing her for the unwilling decision she had made. Closing her eyes against the twinkling canopy shining down on the silhouetted palms and shrubs, she said aloud into the stark, eerie stillness, "I am not ready to party at any luau. I am not ready! I am NOT ready!" Like a mantra, she repeated the same words again and again and again. The stark, dark silence refused to respond. "I am not ready." She whispered softly, as if to lull the unresponsive stillness into a response. *I am not ready.* The four words reverberated loudly in her head and heart.

In the coming days, Makamae continued to visit Ocean noticing that she had, once again, become a closed book; had withdrawn into her shell and forbade any questioning regarding her feelings and so he had to make do with a cool glass of fruit juice and banal snippets of conversation.

Thoughts of Simon, though uninvited and far from welcome, wandered into Ocean Tia's mind. Randomly they drifted in when she took her early morning

243

swim in the cool, refreshing waves; his image clawing into her mind when she was handing out a meal to a homeless unfortunate; or, when she was gathering the ingredients for the Haupia. Always her meandering contemplations ended up with the same final scenario; Simon and Natasha having sex. Always; Ocean vowed to never again allow thoughts of her husband to gate-crash her consciousness; always they crashed mercilessly through her determined resolve.

She wondered how Liliana's preparations for her forthcoming luau were coming along, knowing that she had made the right decision to abstain from the party. Joy and laughter were her distant friends. Someday, maybe, they would be reacquainted. A dark shadow crossed her thoughts. Why hadn't Akamu got in touch? It wasn't like him.

Liliana's plan was coming into fruition. All invitations had been accepted, the food was almost all prepared, the music chosen, tropical attire ready and secret manoeuvres formalised. It was a shame Ocean Tia had decided to decline the invitation but…

From afar she heard the faint lilting sounds of Hawaiian guitars thrusting a sharp, bitter blade into her heart. These days the familiar sounds brought no joy, no comfort, no solace; only the dull pain of loss. With every passing second, the soft sounds became a little louder, a little clearer, a little nearer and with them the sounds of excited chatter and laughter. There must be a luau in the neighbourhood, Ocean Tia concluded; though, it was strange that she had not been invited.

Stepping out on to the balcony, her eyes scanned the periphery of her beautiful garden. Nothing stirred except for the gentle swish of palm leaves, moved by the occasional breeze. The garden remained desolate except… She took a couple of steps forward, peering ahead into the density of the shrubbery where, for an instant, she thought she had seen something move. *A cat*; she smiled turning back. She froze; her ears pricking to the undeniable joyous sound of approaching laughter and the soft strumming of guitars and ukuleles. Turning she retraced tentative steps. Standing at the edge of the balcony, her eyes stretched wide as saucers, her heart beat wildly like a native drum, as she stared incredulously at the scene unravelling before her very eyes.

With hearty cheer, laughter and enthusiastic waves they swarmed the garden, with further bands of revellers bringing up the rear. Immediately on arrival they eagerly assembled trestles, on which they placed an abundance of assorted traditional Hawaiian fare; then commenced to dance to the lively rhythm of the music.

"Aloha Ocean!"

Her whole body jumped before she turned; her heart stopping for a moment before restarting its excited beat. "Akamu!"

Taking eager steps towards his cousin he placed his fragrant, colourful lei around her neck and hugged her so tightly. She'd thought he'd squeeze the very life out of her; immediately feeling the tenderness and love pouring out of Akamu's heart and infiltrating her own, making her unable to stifle a smile which spontaneously broke out on her lips. "Akamu." She repeated over and over again; for, she had missed him dearly.

Their brief spell of genuine mutual admiration of each other was shattered as Liliana entered stating excitedly, "Well, if all else fails, the mountain must go to..." Ocean Tia didn't hear the rest, her excitement evaporating any remnants of stubborn resistance, as she hugged tightly both cousins and allowed them to take over the proceedings, realising any further resistance was futile where these two were concerned and, after all, she mused, *this was Liliana and Akamu's night.*

For a brief interval, Simon was forgotten but not dead; buried in her box of memories. She knew he would resurface with a vengeance. For the time being, she allowed herself to be immersed in the age-old tradition of the Hawaiian luau.

In the distance, the haunting sound of the conch shell called them all, to what had been until this moment, a secret location, where a couple of young natives dug out the kalua pig, which had been buried and roasted in the earth overnight, to the sounds of rapturous clapping and cheering, after which all dispersed to the various trestles to partake of the mouth-watering traditional fare.

Surreptitiously, from a distance, Makamae watched as he tucked into his sweet potatoes, mixed salad and succulent roast pig. What he witnessed was heavily contradicted by what he felt. Beneath her smile, he knew, lay sorrow hiding a deep, dark, icy-cold hole in her heart created by her husband's adultery. Ocean Tia was putting on a brave front. Makamae's eyes stayed fixedly on the subject of his concern.

Akamu also saw deep into Ocean's heart; his own heart identifying and feeling her sadness. He had suffered his own loss. Abruptly snapping out of his melancholy reflections, he grabbed his cousin by the hand, dragged her over to the nearest trestle, burdened heavily with an assortment of food, and encouraged,

"Come on, Ocean; let's grab ourselves generous slices of Haupia and worry about our figures tomorrow."

She smiled at him, thinking how strikingly Akamu resembled his late father: the chubby figure and the brown, twinkling, happy eyes; the dark curly hair, the carefree attitude to life and always the right words to say at the right time. Oh, how she missed Uncle Keoki. Bringing the portion of coconut cake to her lips she froze, her eyes darting, trying to fix on something, or someone, rustling amongst the tropical foliage. The rustling stopped, her eyes seeing nothing of a conspicuous nature and so she turned her attention back to the cake, taking a delicious bite of its soft moistness and savouring the fulfilled promise of its delight. Her eyes wide she shifted her gaze back to the undergrowth, unable to identify what she had fleetingly witnessed; a figure? Inquisitive, surreptitious eyes flitted to the still bundle and back to Akamu, who was scanning the crowd trying to locate his sister; while Ocean's senses were alerted to the plight of a mysterious intruder.

Liliana emerged from the motley gathering; swiftly Ocean's hand secretly placed her plate of Haupia beneath the trestle, bordering the edge of the lawn.

The luau continued throughout the evening and well into the early hours of the morning and, sporadically, throughout the evening, Ocean's mind was interspersed with questioning thoughts about the identity of the uninvited guest and, as the last jovial guests bade their farewell Alohas and Akamu and Liliana hugged, kissed, promised their cousin a date on the beach the following day and departed, Ocean Tia made her way to a specific trestle and, dropping her eyes, noticed that the plate with the Haupia had disappeared. In its place, she left a plate laden with kalua pig and all the trimmings. Her eyes swept around the desolate, still garden. In her heart of hearts, she knew he was there, somewhere. The poor unfortunate, she silently vowed, would not go hungry on her watch. She would help him in any which way she could; for, wasn't her own father, Kai, in the same unenviable position once?

Exhausted she lay in her bed, her body refusing to succumb to sleep, her mind whirling uncontrollably. One thought prevailed stronger and clearer above the rest. While thinking of the unfortunate being in her garden, not once did she think of Simon. She closed her eyes tightly and vowed silently. *I will seek the poor guy out and I will help him to walk through the portals of survival. This shall be my challenge.*

Chapter Eighty-Four
England

Three loud knocks on the door propelled bloodshot eyes to shoot in its direction. *The caller would go if the door remained unanswered,* the dishevelled blonde told herself, her ears bombarded by a barrage of further determined knocks.

"Simon! What the fuck do you want?" Her red incredulous eyes looked him up and down, settling on his bulging holdall resting on the doorstep. "What the heck are you doing here?"

Forcing a smile, simultaneously curbing the urge to run, he stood perfectly still, staring at the woman he secretly blamed for destroying his marriage though, deep down in his recriminating conscience, he recognised the real culprit. "Hi." His involuntary greeting came out grated, strangled as if forced out of his parched mouth, his incredulous eyes taking in the uncharacteristically untidy figure before him, dropping to her long fingers sporting chipped and broken red painted nails as they brought her red, see-through negligee closer to her skinny body. "It's okay, Natasha," he said drily, "I've seen it all before." He'd seen it and was bored with it. So, he asked himself derisively, why was he standing on her doorstep, silently begging an entrance? The rhetorical question had a simple answer. He had nowhere else to go.

"I think you better go." Her eyes shot upwards to the upstairs landing.

"I have nowhere to go, Natasha." His eyes followed hers to the source of the stirrings above.

"Who is it, Tash?" A gruff voice boomed from above.

"No... no one." She began to close the door. It stopped moving against Simon's foot, his inquisitive eyes darting to the half attired bulk descending the stairs; everything becoming perfectly clear in Simon's head.

"Who the hell are you?" Hissed the unfriendly figure; eyes of pure steel focussed directly on Simon.

"A friend; who are you?"

"A punter." The bulk growled and turned his cold eyes on Natasha. "Same time next week," he muttered before turning abruptly on his heel.

As his eyes followed the man down the short drive, a wave of raw realisation wove its tentacles around Simon's mind, his eyes of disbelief switching to Natasha, who was briskly running up the stairs, abandoning her former lover on the doorstep, as he wondered what kind of hell he had wandered into.

For long minutes, he sat motionless on the sofa, trying desperately to make some sense of it all; but, there was no denying what his ears had heard and eyes had witnessed. *A customer—a punter...* the sleazy image swam around and around in his fuzzy head. He closed his tired eyes. *Natasha Parks, his former lover, was a prostitute who sold her body for sex.* Turning, his eyes shot upwards in the direction of the landing. *Is that where she trades? When did it all start? Was she a pro when...* Violently he shook his head, fiercely attempting to shake away an unsavoury image which had crept into his fuddled brain. Abruptly he rose, refusing to play any part in her sordid games.

The loud bang of the door told her that the one decent man she had known had gone. Burying her head in her pillow she sobbed bitterly, uncontrollably.

The long night rolled laboriously on as he opened his eyes, stared starkly at the dark ceiling, and tried to make sense of it all. Sense, however, refused to knit together; instead, distorted images of random clients walked in and out of Natasha's door big, burly men; seedy, spindly specimens; men in expensive suits; tramps. They all took their cue and walked out with a satisfied smile. He shook his head from side to side. This did not make sense at all; Natasha, the beauty; Natasha who craved the limelight and never failed to get it; Natasha, the servicer of good, bad and downright ugly, as long as they had brass in their pockets. He closed his eyes against it all. Tomorrow, he told himself, he would seek answers.

Chapter Eighty-Five

His bulging holdall resting on a different doorstep, he raised his hand to the knocker, his heart pumping wildly. This was the last place he wanted to grace with his presence, knowing full well what the response of one inhabitant behind the door would be.

They stood perfectly still icily eyeballing each other; their grim lips firmly set while a thousand mixed emotions surged through each man's fast pulsating veins. Finally one broke the still, ominous silence. "You're back."

Simon recognised the unforgiving tone well enough to know he was not wanted. It was, he dismally concluded, going to be a high mountain to climb. But, he needed answers. Desperately and hastily he foraged for the appropriate words and found they were stubbornly elusive. Eventually he spoke. "How are you, Hanale?"

The man on the other side of the door took in a deep, ragged breath; his stark eyes impaled on the object of his scorn. "What do you want, Simon?" Hanale's words were steady, direct, to the point and icily cold, detached; demanding an explanation; his tone indicated no hope of clemency.

"May I come in?"

For long seconds, they stood. Slowly the door opened further to one side and Simon walked into familiar territory; haunting images and ghostly voices bringing a nostalgic smile to his mouth, only to die with Hanale's harsh words. "What the fuck are you doing here, Teal?" making Simon draw each word into his sense of reasoning and asking himself the same question, adding another to the mix. *What right did he have to be here?* For, by rights, he should have been banned within a hundred kilometre radius. Again, he grasped for the appropriate words.

"How is Maria?"

"Heavily pregnant," came the stark reply.

A stab of immediate regret surged through Simon's heart. *A child*, he concluded, *could have saved his own marriage.* His lips remained firmly clamped.

"What do you want?" Hanale impatiently demanded.

"Did you know Natasha Parks is selling her body?" He regretted the words the split second they poured out of his mouth; his ears subjected to a bout of incredulous laughter.

"And I thought you were here to tell me news about my sister."

"Half-sister" corrected Simon.

"Oh my God." Hanale furiously scratched his head, his caustic eyes searing deep into his brother-in-law's soul. "This is unbelievable!" His scathing eyes turned utterly savage, his tone followed suit. "Get out!" He roared, his face contorting with anger and rapidly paling as his eyes spotted Maria.

"Simon; what are you doing here?" Her voice was soft, matching her eyes.

"He's going," snapped Hanale.

Simon rose from the sofa.

"Stay; please sit down, Simon." She said, her eyes not leaving his drawn face.

He stood on the spot his eyes roaming from one to the other, wondering what on earth he was to do.

"Sit!" Barked Hanale resigning himself to defeat; for, when it came to Maria, he softened every time.

Simon obeyed, sat back down and awaited his fate.

Within five minutes, all was revealed. Natasha Parks had lost her spot in the limelight to younger, slimmer, more attractive models; got in with a bad crowd, where drugs and alcohol were added to the mix; whereupon she lost her job, her home and, according to Hanale, a good proportion of her sanity, as she strayed over to the darker side of life.

"Now," Hanale's severe eyes locked with his brother-in-law, "more importantly, how is Ocean?"

The question hit Simon like a sponge soaked with iced water; the shock of it numbing his senses. How could he answer what he did not know? He sat like a solidified statue, while depictions of Natasha intermingled with images of Ocean and swam round and round and round in his head, making the whole room swim before him; chairs, the table and wall unit; the cream painted walls, Hanale and Maria going madly round and round. Robotically he rose. A crumpled heap he slumped back down on to the sofa, aware only of a bulge before him and a hand passing him a glass of water, accompanied by gentle words. "You will stay with us tonight, Simon;" followed by Hanale's harsh words, "He's not fucking staying here tonight, Maria."

"He's staying," reiterated Maria.

The next morning brought sunshine through his window and Hanale staring ominously down at him. As Simon forced his eyes to open, Hanale's words hit hard. "Maria is prepared to give you a second chance; I'm not. I want you out of the house. Why not join Miss Parks; after all, you chose her above Ocean. Here," he threw Simon's trousers, shirt and jacket on to the bed, "you have ten minutes." There was no get out clause. Simon roughly threw the duvet to one side and picked up his shirt. "Before you go, Teal; tell me, what possessed you to do it? What made you choose that slut, Natasha Parks, over Ocean?" Simon had been asking himself the same question repeatedly and recurrently he had failed to come up with a logical answer. His lips remained stubbornly clamped.

The loud bang of the door echoed loudly in his head, as he walked down the drive and on to the long road, his heavy feet going forward. Where to? He did not know.

Chapter Eighty-Six
Kauai

Hand in hand with her secret promise came a steadfast resolve. Once Ocean Tia made up her mind to do something nothing in the world, bar death or a physical incapability, would prevent her from achieving her goal. The mysterious gate-crasher at the luau, intermittently weaved in and out of her mind throughout the ensuing days. *Who was this poor unfortunate?* She racked her brain, unable to identify him from the homeless, who happened to stumble in and out of the sanctuary. If only, she told herself, she had had more than a fleeting glance of this elusive character.

Elusive he certainly was. On a nightly basis, food was left out on the edge of the lawn and by morning it had disappeared. The mysterious recipient remained hidden, his behaviour bringing sharply into focus what Auntie Luana had told her of Kai's behaviour. But, one day, just like her father's identity, this recipient's identity would also be revealed. *One day* Ocean Tia told herself, *she would know.*

Despite her determined resolve and utter frustration, Simon flitted in and out of her mind at unsuspected moments, while she was scouring the desolate beaches for men and women who were down on their luck; in the throes of housework; while purchasing groceries he came; his image fainter now; but, still, he came. Although the searing pain in her heart was still sharp, it was not as acute as it had been; it was gradually lessening and, progressively, she began to see it all for what it was, the past. Through her work, and with the passage of time, she was very slowly starting to heal.

Eyes dropped to the white envelope on the highly polished wooden floor, her interest immediately enhanced by the sight of foreign stamps. As she picked it up her heart raced and immediately plummeted, turning to a block of ice as her eyes identified the sender; the man who had betrayed her. Abruptly she thrust the item into a drawer and almost ran into the solace of the garden. She was not ready.

A fleeting movement in the distance caught her attention, her thoughts rapidly switching from the past to the present, as her feet moved slowly and stealthily to the source of the movement. The last thing she wanted was to frighten the intruder away. Seconds later her eyes darted to another part of the garden, where they followed a grubby hand reaching out for a fallen coconut, before making a quick retreat but not before, for a split second, she saw the intruder's face. She did not see or feel a second presence; his greeting made her jump.

"So deep in thought, Ocean." He smiled warmly, reminding her of her beloved uncle.

She returned his smile. "Aloha Makamae." Graciously she accepted his frangipani lei, linking her arm in his as they walked together into the coolness of her home.

His keen eyes were quick to notice the ill hidden turbulence in her eyes. His lips remained closed on the matter; his wise eyes followed her as she sat, rose, walked over to a drawer, where she withdrew a white envelope and dropped it unceremoniously on to his lap, sat back down and fixed her eyes on the ominous article now in her friend's hands, while his ears captured the heavy sigh which had escaped her lips.

"It's from Hanale." Her words, though quietly spoken, were undeniable icy and seemed to ricochet around the room, while her eyes levelled with the eyes of her confidante.

He knew from the brief comments she had chosen to share, the siblings had fallen out. Why? He did not know. But, whatever the reason, Makamae knew it was serious. Ocean Tia was not known to bear grudges.

Gingerly he turned the firmly sealed envelope over in his hands, his puzzled eyes darting to Ocean, where he found an empty chair and a multitude of unanswered questions. His curious eyes wandered over to the kitchen area, where she stood her back ramrod straight, her stubborn face turned away from his questioning gaze. Rising he thrust the envelope into her hands. "Open it," he said softly; her ears finely attuned to his footsteps withdrawing from her presence.

Seconds… minutes… long drawn out minutes… heavy laden and torturous minutes ticked laboriously into the realms of the past and, still, she stood like a frozen princess memories invading her mind, mingling and intermingling; the

253

sealed envelope scorching her fingers. Back in time her thoughts drifted... back... back... back... *as she danced in Simon's arms, as Hanale picked his way through the smooching teenagers, grabbed her forcibly by the hand and unceremoniously dragged her off the crowded dance floor. "We're going, Ocean,"* he snapped. *Like a meek lamb she followed him, her young heart thumping hard, her calm equilibrium ruffled for the first time in her life and, for the first time in her life, she felt a simultaneous mixture of anger and hate invade her soul as they walked home in complete silence, submerged in their own bitter thoughts... What right had he to drag her off?* She closed her eyes tightly. *What right does he have now to creep back into my life?* She asked herself. Her eyes snapped open. It was he, Hanale, who had brought Simon into her life; it was he, Hanale, who had fuelled the fire of betrayal; though inadvertently, she had to confess; it was he, Hanale, who had, unconsciously, lit the first spark of lies and deceit and watched the fire grow and destroy those around him. Her eyes dropped to the envelope tightly clutched in her hands, staring starkly at the handwritten address, until her eyes glassed over, everything became blurred and she could see no more. Long, slender fingers squeezed in between the seal and roughly thrust the envelope open. Withdrawing the page she unfolded it and read the contents.

England

Hanale sat rocking his new-born son in his arms his joy incomplete; for, while the birth brought him untold happiness, a part of his heart was seared with a pain and emptiness his first-born could not fill; an inexplicable loneliness Maria and his son could not quell; a guilt no amount of confessions could wash away. Unwittingly he had been the perpetrator and now he was paying the heavy price.

She would, he mused, *have received it by now;* imagining his half-sister reading and rereading every word, taking it all in; assessing every single word and phrase. *It was,* he concluded, *all in the laps of the gods.* His faraway eyes dropped to the sleeping infant in his arms.

Chapter Eighty-Seven
Kauai

One word stood out starkly; to this word her eyes were drawn and on this solitary word they remained, until her eyes closed and her mind opened to a tumult of scenarios; in each she played the starring role.

Godmother; an innocent word; an honourable word, some would say. A word loaded with potential associations and possible outcomes, according to Ocean Tia; for, she was silently asked to forget the past; let bygones be bygones and to take up the honourable gauntlet and be godmother to Hanale and Maria's first-born.

She reread Hanale's words three times. There was no mention of Simon; no word, regarding Hanale's secret role in Simon's illicit affair; just a few general words about how things were in England and the gracious invitation; an invitation that would be very difficult to reject. But, she stared into space, rejection was an option; for, how could she drop everything and fly thousands of kilometres away to a country she no longer held dear? How could she face Hanale again after his ultimate betrayal? How could she face Simon Teal, her husband? No, she shook her head vehemently from side to side, she would not go. They would understand. They would have to understand.

Work was a healer; adhering to the needs of others was a sobering dispeller of personal thoughts; but, when the day's work was done, conflicting thoughts rose to the surface and thickly skimmed over her firm resolve covering it with doubts, questions and a niggling sense of duty.

The solace of the graveyard gave her no peace, only further turbulence to her conflicting thoughts; her beloved departed no longer silently assured her that all would be well. Finally, to Makamae's relief, she brought her woes to his door.

He read the words once; once was enough for him to make his assessment of the situation. Raising his eyes to her eyes, he hammered the last nail into her coffin of hopeful reprieve and stated, "In my opinion, Ocean, let whatever has passed between you be the past. Mend bridges; rebuild walls; cease the day for tomorrow you may not have the choice."

Her despondent eyes dropped to the floor, her heart followed suit. Why, she asked herself, did he have to be so infuriatingly Hawaiian? This was not the answer she had hoped to receive. She watched him go as he walked down the winding garden path and out of sight, taking with him her hope of alliance.

To go or not to go, the question nagged, cajoled, niggled, tortured and taunted her mercilessly throughout the long night. The dawn brought with it her final decision.

Getting up earlier than usual, thrusting all thoughts of England out of her mind, Ocean Tia renewed her efforts into finding her mysterious nightly visitor. Like Kai, each night he took the food and drink laid out for him on the edge of the lawn; still he remained elusive until, one evening, her ears attune to a sudden coughing attack she reached the source and found him.

Chapter Eighty-Eight

"Aloha." She said softly into the veil of stillness. "Aloha; is anyone there?" Her eyes stared into the gathering dusk, her heart racing wildly; for, who knew what this stranger was capable of doing? She took her chances and advanced further. "Aloha."

"Aloha!" came the faintest of greetings sending her heart racing once more.

"Please come out. I am your friend." Ocean encouraged.

Something in her softly spoken voice dispelled any fear the stranger had. Cautiously he stepped out of the sanctuary of his hiding place and was greeted with a warm, friendly smile.

"I am Ocean Tia." Her eyes took in his thin bearded face; his eyes stark, big and bewildered; his thin body attired in torn, dishevelled clothes sporting patches of unsavoury looking stains on his grubby Aloha shirt. Her eyes dropped to his ripped black shorts; his spindly legs were dirty and scarred with congealed blood. She saw not a tramp but her own bereaved father and, immediately, her heart went out to this unfortunate man. Offering her hand he took it, averting his bloodshot eyes from her concerned gaze. "What is your name?" she asked.

"Solomao; my name is Solomao, Ma'am."

"Solomao; a man of peace," she said. "I have a good friend called Solomao; he once told me the meaning of his name." She smiled; her smile dying as she focussed on the man before her thinking, *If only this man's soul was not so tortured.* She had seen the signs before.

She left Solomao in the sanctuary, promising to see him the following day; relieved that he had at last secured food, shelter and safety. His parting words to her reverberated loudly in her ears, as her feet walked away from him in the direction of the beach.

As she stood on the border of motionless sand and rolling water Solomao's words, intermingled with the sounds of the heaving waves and the echo of Makamae's advice crashed loudly in her head and echoed repeatedly... *if only I*

hadn't burned my bridges… cease the day… if only I hadn't burned my bridges…
Tomorrow you may not have a chance…

By the time her feet had changed direction, her decision had changed course.

Chapter Eighty-Nine

One among many she sat in the body of the plane, her ears attune to the babel of voices around her, her eyes glued absent-mindedly on the moving screen, as the plane commenced its approach to its final destination. Normally at this stage of the journey her excited heart would be racing. Not this time. This time it was pounding heavily with dread. This time she did not thrust a comb through her long, silky hair and adjust a white plumeria above her ear; neither did she smooth down her tropical printed dress, before elegantly stepping out into the aisle. This time her attire of faded jeans and a smart white blouse suggested nothing Hawaiian; her natural beauty gave the game away and attracted eyes to look enviously in her direction. She ignored them all. Vanity had never claimed this beauty for its own.

With one foot in front of the other, she made her way to the international arrivals her long, sleek ponytail swinging in time to her movements, her heart still pumping dread, while her senses silently and violently admonished her for not sticking with her original decision.

So much had passed since she had last stepped on English soil. A marriage had been soiled; immersed in a sea of deceit, lies and bitter betrayal. Her feet stopped; her eyes closed as she tried desperately to summon up her inner courage; silently asking her God to grant her the grace of forgiveness, patience and understanding. Taking a deep breath, she took a firmer hold of her suitcase, and walked on; her heart suddenly freezing as she heard his voice.

"Ocean!"

Ocean... Ocean... Ocean... It echoed loudly in her head. She turned. "Hanale." She said almost in a whisper, her soft eyes fixed warily on her half-brother. This time there were no colourful leis to be exchanged. "Hanale." She repeated as he brought her to himself in a tight hug, as an empty void grew ever deeper in her heart where, once, love had reigned. Like a meek lamb she followed him out of the busy airport, wishing she was back on her sunny island, as a sudden gust of cold air hit her.

Like two strangers travelling on a forced journey, they touched on snippets of general conversation: their well-being, Maria, the baby, the weather; the real nitty-gritty was avoided at all costs, both knowing that it was only a matter of time before words of truth were laid on the table and, with them, stark feelings would inevitably be laid bare.

Maria and the new-born brought Ocean Tia and Hanale a welcome respite. It was while she watched her half-sibling rock his son to sleep she felt the iced blade thrust deep into her own heart, as an innocent question was asked by Maria. "Did you ever think of starting a family of your own, Ocean?" Two pairs of eyes shot up as Ocean Tia rose abruptly, ran out the room and up the stairs, before Hanale shot his wife a rare, recriminating look.

In the solace of her room, Ocean fell on to her bed and buried her head deep into her pillow, silently begging the whole world to go away. The gentle knock on the door thundered loudly in her ears, making her long fingers clench tightly the tear-stained pillow, which she had pulled over her head. Louder knocking penetrated deeper and deeper into her consciousness; seconds later she felt the unwanted presence sink on to her bed; the soft voice melting her stubborn resolve. *After all,* she asked herself, *wasn't she the intruder in this happy family unit?* Her tightly clenched fingers began to relax, the tear-stained pillow was lifted and she turned to face a concerned looking sister-in-law.

"I am so very, very sorry, Ocean. I should never have…"

"Stop." Ocean stopped Maria's flow of words. "I am the one that should be apologising." She averted her eyes from the anxious face, unable to meet eye with eye. I am sorry for coming here… I am sorry for awakening old wounds… I am sorry for ever setting foot in this country… *I am sorry! Sorry! SORRY!* She wanted to scream at the top of her voice; instead, her long fingers played nervously with the pink tassels of the bedspread, her lips firmly clamped.

"Come; let us have some tea." Maria extended her hand and Ocean Tia accepted it.

The incident was not mentioned again though Maria, Ocean and Hanale were conscious of a deep underlying significance, which had suffused Ocean's outburst and that warned Hanale to refrain from mentioning Simon; for, apart from the fact that his brother-in-law had failed in his role to provide his wife with a much wanted child, there was a rumour Hanale had heard third hand and if the rumour ever came to Ocean's ears it would, he knew, break her heart.

Although she had only just arrived in England, Ocean Tia was counting the days to her departure. Between Hanale and herself she had felt a deep wedge, created by an equally deep wall of silence where Simon Teal, her husband, was silently banned from being mentioned, this preventing any semblance of truth seeping out and seeing the light of day and preventing progress in healing old wounds. Deep inside her conscious mind, Ocean knew there were things Hanale was not telling her and she knew it had everything to do with one person, her nemesis, Natasha Parks; her old rival and her subsequent victor; for, she had won the grand prize, the heart of Simon Teal.

As her eyes stared out on to the bare garden, bereft of colour and beauty, her mind drifted… *Throwing down her knife and fork with a clash on to her plate, she ran out the door into the cold, white floating whirl of snowflakes. Rosemary, Hanale and Kai followed and watched as she danced in the garden; catching swirling thick flakes and holding them up in her hands before they disintegrated into nothing*... "Disintegrated into nothing," she said aloud, "just like my marriage to Simon." She walked away from the window. *Memories,* she silently concluded, *are for yesteryear.*

But Rosemary's image would not disintegrate. With every passing second, she became clearer, more alive. *What would Lokemele say about all this?* Ocean wondered. *What would she advise?* With a clunk she placed an empty glass into the sink and walked away.

Chapter Ninety

There was only one route this disgraced and dejected human being could take. On reaching his destination, his feet tapped... tapped... tapped impatiently on the doorstep while his heart pounded uncontrollably, his intelligent mind admonishing himself for his absolute stupidity; asking him loudly and clearly, *What the fuck are you doing here, standing at this slut's door waiting, like a beggar, for a grain of mercy?* The door opened sharply before he could answer his own question. "Natasha." His eyes shot up to her dishevelled hair; the tell-tale look of recent consensual sex in her eyes and he felt himself going hard. "Natasha." His dry mouth attempted a lopsided grin.

"What?" She snapped impatiently looking down on him contemptuously, as one would glare at a despicable snake; making him inwardly squirm at his own weakness. Time was she wanted him; time was she spared him the time of day and a slice of her attention. Now, she had far bigger fish to fry; or, cocks to satisfy. "Well?" She raised an eyebrow which had lost its finely defined shape.

"We need to talk." He said in as calm a voice as he could muster, bracing himself for a barrage of unsavoury curses to spew out of her heavily, red lipstick mouth and the door to slam hard in his face. His eyes widened with incredulity as he heard her calm words.

"Yes, I agree, Simon; we most certainly need to talk."

There was hope of the proverbial light at the end of the tunnel; he silently sighed with inner relief. There was a chance he would have somewhere to lay his head, preferably on the pillow on her bed.

He followed her inside and sat down, his weary eyes watching as she wrapped her flimsy negligee around her torso and sat down facing him; silence, heavy and ominous, shrouding them; each waiting for the other to start proceedings, while the clock on the wall continued to tick away the heavy laden seconds. Finally, he could not bear the stifling tension a second longer. "Natasha." His eyes shot to the upturned face, locking with her unwavering stare, as he felt himself disintegrating under her crystal-blue, icy scrutiny. Forcing himself out of their alluring wells he blurted, "I need somewhere to stay."

Suffocating silence prevailed once more. The clock ticked. His heart pounded. *Had she heard?* He asked himself as his eyes remained on her inscrutable mask, lowering to her tightly clamped red mouth, as her body sat still as a statue. Opening his mouth he closed it, feeling his whole body shrivel with her sudden announcement. "I am pregnant, Simon." The following words made his shrunken guts, his heart, mind, soul and blood freeze. "The baby is yours; you are the baby's father, Simon." The clock ticked laboriously on as if it had taken on the weight of her revelation, and his potential predicament, into its intricate mechanism.

Had he heard those words; or, was he in the midst of some kind of weird twilight zone, where nothing made any sense? Her next words solved his query. "Simon, I am pregnant; you are the father of the baby; what are you going to do about it?"

Her stark, clear words drilled deep into his consciousness; his eyes dropped to his lap, unable and unwilling to meet her uncharacteristically serious gaze. He closed his eyelids, allowing her damning words to sink in, before he abruptly rose and let out a loud, raucous laugh; his eyes of utter contempt fixed on the object of his scorn. "If you think you're going to pin that one on me, Natasha; you've got another thing coming." He turned and without a second glance strode to the door; desperate to get out, to breathe, to get away from this lunatic of a bitch.

The fresh air brought him no solace and no means of disentangling himself from the clutches of her accusations tightening around him, suffocating the vestiges of life out of him, until he felt he could breathe no more. The echo of her parting words bombarded his ears as his feet raced along the long, desolate road.... *If you don't acknowledge your part in this matter and take responsibility, Teal; the whole world shall know...* Eleven minutes later he could still here her haunting words.

Chapter Ninety-One

Aimlessly he roamed the streets. Where was there to go? Natasha Parks had been his last hope and instead... instead... Her words torturously and mercilessly hammering in his head, he strode into the off-license and came out two minutes later with a litre bottle of brandy.

Eyes flickered open, closed and laboriously opened on to a stark white ceiling. He snapped them shut, his ears involuntarily attune to the alien sounds around him: a trolley being wheeled away, subdued voices, the clink of porcelain against porcelain and hurried, soft padded footsteps. *Where the hell am I?* He wondered. Like his eyes he closed his mind. He did not want to know.

Sometime later he heard a softly spoken voice. "Mister Teal." In and out he breathed eyes closed to the world, denying intruders the right to enter into his world, a world he did not want to inhabit himself.

"Mister Teal; I am Doctor Dale."

Involuntarily Simon opened his eyes staring blankly at a thin face, his eyes lowering to a long white coat. Slowly reality began to seep in. He had been to Natasha's, the off-license and sat on the park bench; gradually it was all starting to formulate a picture. His eyes remained focussed on the kind face looking down on him, wishing the woman would go away and leave him in peace. Seconds later the doctor left his bedside. Peace was elusive; instead surged an ocean of turmoil and unrest; a myriad of unanswered questions and on top of these questions more questions, interspersed with dark thoughts shrouded with a veil of utter despair.

Amidst the dark, desolate despair was a tiny, very minute speck of hope. He would return to Kauai; seek her out and explain everything to her until he was blue in the face; he would make her see sense, begging her forgiveness and doing everything in his power to resurrect his marriage; for, Ocean Tia, his wife, was the only precious jewel in the world worth the fight.

Chapter Ninety-Two
A Week Earlier

Seconds turned into a full minute and, simultaneously, a new minute began as the old one slipped into the oblivion of time, as a wave of undiluted shock drew all colour from Hanale's face and suffused his pale façade with a veil of raw incredulity.

Minutes ago he and his mate, Johnny, had been toasting the safe arrival of Hanale's first child; now, both men stood numb, their dewy beer glasses abandoned on mats, as all around glasses clinked and mouths drank, laughed, gossiped and cursed making Hanale feel as if he was standing in a surreal world. Desperately he tried to digest what he had just heard; turning his serious eyes on his friend he asked, "How do you know all this, Johnny?"

Taking a gulp of his beer Johnny stated equally seriously, "Natasha Parks is telling all and sundry and the news is spreading fast, mate. It may be a rumour but," he switched his concerned eyes on Hanale, "it's a blessing your Ocean is ensconced on her island; at least, out of sight; out of mind."

"She's on her way here, Johnny." Hanale stated, a hard lump lodging in the pit of his heart.

"Can't you stop her, Hal?"

"I'm picking her up from the airport in an hour's time."

"Oh God!" Johnny drained his glass. "Do you want an orange juice, mate?"

Hanale didn't answer; his thoughts were elsewhere; faraway. Could, he asked himself, Natasha be lying, after all she wasn't to be trusted at the best of times? Had Johnny got hold of the wrong end of the stick? This could not be – this simply could not be, he reiterated over and over again; but, the niggling voice of contradiction stated, *This could be. With Natasha Parks on the scene anything could, and often did happen.* His thoughts turned to Ocean Tia. He had, he dismally concluded, been an absolute brute to her covering up Simon's misdemeanours, turning a blind eye, making all the excuses under the sun for his brother-in-law and former friend. Why, he was as much to blame for this mess as the perpetrators themselves, if not more. What had stopped him from picking up the phone and telling Ocean everything? Was it the potential pain he may have caused her by his revelation; the betrayal of his friend; or, was it the fact that he had once strayed from the marital bed himself and never been caught out? Whatever it was, it was now raining down on him like a ton of bricks and he felt himself suffocating under their sheer weight.

Present Time

And now he was sat opposite her at the dining table, consciously aware of his act of betrayal. Her words shook him out of his black reverie only to throw him into a deeper, darker, flaming pit of self-reproach.

"How is Simon?" The words had escaped Ocean's mouth before she could put the brakes on them; for, she had not been consciously thinking about her husband and yet the words were out.

Two pairs of eyes shot in her direction, making her insides tighten and shrivel and her mind wonder at the incredibility of her lapse of self-control; wishing she was the enviable snail, who could, when it felt like it, retreat into its shell. Feeling the descending ominous silence she rose and strode to the sink, her eyes staring blankly out the window. *Please don't answer that question,* she silently urged her kin; *I really don't want to know.*

Two pairs of eyes watched her intently; eyes that knew she was hurting and hurting bad. And, as Ocean Tia continued to stare out on to the desolate garden, Hanale made up his mind. He would never, ever share Natasha and Simon's secret with his beloved Ocean. Never!

Chapter Ninety-Three

Ocean lay on her bed thoughts crashing in and out of her mind. Tomorrow at this time she would be a godmother to Hanale and Maria's son, her nephew. "A godmother," she whispered, "but never a mother." She squeezed her eyes tightly trying to prevent the hot, prickly tears from escaping, as they seeped beneath her closed lids and slithered unevenly down her cheeks *Never a mother... never a mother... never a mother...* The disturbing, haunting words weaved torturously in and out of her mind; a fresh surge of tears falling, leaving a salty trail on her face. Eventually she slid into a restless sleep with images of her giving birth and, instead of Simon, stood a faceless figure. Flitting in and out of this scenario she plunged into another, where she saw herself standing on a virginal white beach, a toddler at her side; but, when she looked down to bestow him a warm smile, she looked into the eyes of a treacherous looking dog, his ghastly teeth glaring, menacing and threatening making her jump out of her nightmare.

Tossing her duvet to one side, she slipped out the bed, down the stairs and into the kitchen. "Maria!" She gasped as her eyes shot to a huddled silhouette sitting in the corner. Switching on the light she cautiously approached her sister-in-law, concern lacing her eyes. Drawing up a chair she sat down.

"It's Hanale," stated Maria in between sobs. "I. I think he's having an affair."

Like lightning striking twice, Ocean Tia felt the full effect of Maria's sorrow, intermingled with a wave of pure incredulity washing over her, threatening to sweep her back under the secret world of bitter betrayal, deceit, lies and adultery where now she felt perfectly at home. Cautiously she placed a gentle hand on Maria's goose-pimpled arm. "Are you sure, Maria; are you absolutely sure?"

"Yes." She answered after several long seconds of heavy silence. "I heard him call her name in his sleep."

"What name?"

"Natasha; I only know one Natasha. I. I don't think…"

Ocean didn't hear the rest, Maria's announcement feeling like an iced blade which had cruelly thrust through her own fractured heart; her hand tightly clutching Maria's arm and her eyes fixed on her sister-in-law's bowed head. *Natasha... Natasha... Natasha...* The synonymous name weaved its black tentacles around her senses, unleashing a silent venomous poison which surged through her entire body, making her chest feel tight; tighter and tighter with every breath she took. *Natasha, her nemesis; Natasha, the woman who had taken her love away; Natasha, the vixen who had pounced on Maria's man and threatened to destroy the foundations of a happy family...*

Memories invaded and like ghosts lingered where they were not wanted, taking her to another time but stubbornly remaining in the same place, in this very house... *It was, when all was said and done, Alan's farewell to the world; the man who had given her a means of obtaining a higher education in England; Alan who was dying, determined in his last days to make everyone around him happy by throwing a Hawaiian luau. And as she watched the guests, and their somewhat unconventional moves, to the soft lilt of Hawaiian rhythms, her mind drifted far away to Kauai. About to move from her welcoming post at the door her heart stopped, restarted and raced as the happy-go-lucky figure attired in a blue printed Aloha shirt, black shorts and a lei hanging around his neck approached. "Aloha Ocean." Her estranged boyfriend, and unexpected guest, smiled. Restarting its furious race, her heart felt as if it was about to jump out of her tight chest. "Aloha Simon." She said in a whisper feeling the room, and all its happy revellers, spinning madly out of control; feeling her young blood bubble, boil and surge through every fast pulsating vein in her body, as she stood perfectly still like an elegant, exotic statue and yearned for the out-of-control roundabout to stop so that she could get off. She got off; her heart dying a thousand deaths as it plummeted to the very depths of deepest hell, as her eyes refused to take in what they undoubtedly saw, as they continued to stare and her darkest nightmare was growing into fruition; her blissful heaven spinning wildly until it fragmented and scattered into a confused mass of cluttered emotional debris. She stared unblinkingly at Simon as he took off the lei she had given him and bestowed it around the neck of a tall, slender, blonde beauty attired in a tight-fitting, black cocktail dress riding high above her knees. Her heart raced to a sudden stop and rapidly turned to a block of impenetrable ice as her dark, still eyes continued to stare at Simon and Natasha Parks and, for the first time in her life, she felt completely betrayed...*

Two pairs of eyes shot up and towards an approaching sound and fixed on Hanale; two minds feeling Natasha Park's poisonous venom killing their minds, hearts and souls; numbing their hearts.

His puzzled eyes switched from his wife, to Ocean and darted back to Maria; feeling himself being intensely scrutinised beneath their mutual, unwavering glares. Finally, he broke the ominous ice that stretched between them. "Last minute christening arrangements?" he quizzed; a lightness lacing his tone, as an alien sense of apprehension seeped through into his being, making his eyes dart between the two women. Deriving no answers he turned, approached the sink and poured himself a glass of water. Like a blast of ice the words hit him with a vengeance, his fingers tightening visibly around the tumbler, which was now moving uncontrollably in his trembling hand; his feet feeling like two blocks of lead, unable to move a mere centimetre this way or that, firmly glued to the spot, while his pounding heart raced on like an frenzied drum. The carefully articulated repeated words told him he had not been hearing things; they demanded an immediate response. They were met with stunned silence.

"Are you having an affair with Natasha Parks?" The interrogator was not his wife; it was Ocean and with this interrogator came a fresh sense of obligation. Closing his eyes tight he willed his thoughts to quickly come to his aid and formulate into appropriate words; *words of truth or words of dishonesty?* He could not immediately decide; the first would bring hurt and pain to his beloved wife; the second would break his half-sister's heart.

"You are cheating on me." Maria softly stated; her words almost inaudible and, rising from her chair, she exited the kitchen heading for the blissful sanctuary of the nursery, leaving in her wake the aftermath of destruction skilfully woven by Miss Natasha Parks.

The clock on the wall continued to tick ominously. Hanale remained glued to the kitchen sink, searching for some kind of reasoning to enter his whirling head. Ocean Tia sat perfectly still trapped in the sordid world of dishonesty, betrayal and deceit. "Is Natasha Parks in the picture, Hanale?" Her gentle but demanding words asked.

Is Natasha Parks in the picture, Hanale... Is Natasha Parks in the picture, Hanale?... The repetitive words hammered in his head until he could stand it no more. Swiftly turning he approached and sat at the table, thumping his tightly clenched fist so hard on the solid wood the impact sent a vase, with its colourful array of silk roses, off centre. "Yes! Yes! Yes!" He hollered. Momentarily closing his exhausted eyes, he managed to make some sense of his erratic thoughts. Opening his eyes he fixed them on Ocean Tia in a steady gaze. "Yes, Ocean; Natasha Parks is in the picture."

This time her eyes closed, her mind fighting to summon up some kind of coherence to this dastardly revelation. Before it succeeded in its venture, her heart suffered the final blow.

"Natasha Parks is well and truly in the centre of the picture," stated Hanale his eyes fixed on the vase as his fingers brought it back to the centre of the table, as he stalled the truth; delayed the pain he was about to bring into Ocean Tia's heart. Inadvertently he looked up and wished he hadn't as his eyes clashed with her eyes and he knew there was no way out. Taking a deep ragged breath, his eyes still locked with the woman he was about to wound, he began. "I heard..." The sickly bile rising to his throat propelled him to cough. "I. I heard that Simon has crawled back to Natasha. I. I heard... I heard that... that... that... he is the father of her baby." Unable to look at her any longer he rose abruptly, the chair falling unceremoniously with a clash behind him, echoing loudly in his ears as he made his way back to the sink, where he did not have to witness the hurt and pain of betrayal, in the eyes of the one he loved.

Ocean remained perfectly still outwardly looking unaffected; inwardly her whole world crashing mercilessly down and around her; her heart left abandoned amidst the debris of the fallout, as Hanale's words sank in and drifted in and out of her consciousness.... *He is the father of her baby... He is the father of her baby...* He is the father of her baby... Round and round went the words in her swimming head swirling and whirling, until reality clashed with unreality and she sank into its chaotic depths.

Maria rocked the baby in her arms to and fro, to and fro; her world broken into a thousand jagged pieces; her mind on one thing and one thing only. The christening had to proceed as scheduled.

Deed done, Hanale wished he could turn back the clock; trying to console himself that he had been cornered and the only route of escape had been the truth. "Oh God!" He exclaimed. "Maria!" Rushing past Ocean he ran up the stairs two at a time and stepped cautiously into the quietness of the nursery.

Ocean felt herself sinking further and further into the mire of black, devastating despair; Hanale's crushing words reverberating cruelly in her ears, hammering the final nail into the coffin of her marriage and, like the final nail, the seal of truth had established the futility of any form of a reunion with Simon. It was over.

The ultimate pain, however, was not the fact that her marriage to Simon had ended on the rocks. It went far deeper. It was the excruciating fact that she had always yearned for a child and now she had learned that her husband was to be the father of her nemesis's child, without apparently having a second thought for his wife's feelings.

Without warning she was back in the midst of Alan's farewell luau, watching Natasha Parks disallowing any Hawaiian fare to enter her body temple – her icy eyes stuck on her rival sitting directly opposite as her hostess, Rosemary, forced a polite smile. *"Perhaps you would like some English food, Natasha? A barrage of giggles escaped Natasha's red lipstick mouth."*

"Yes, anything is preferable to this Hawaiian trash," she sneered… Simon turned his ice-cold eyes on his plus one. *"Apologise,"* he demanded as instantaneous, raucous laughter shot from her mouth. *"For what; speaking the truth; or, are Hawaiians so primitive they also censor free speech?"* She sneered as all eyes focussed on her and, in turn, she revelled in the attention; because when it was focussed on her it was on no one else.

Standing up she threw her virgin-white napkin on to her uneaten food and turned her full attention on Alan. *"It's no wonder you look like a skeleton, mate; eat more of this Hawaiian rubbish and you will disappear completely."* She turned her eyes on Simon. *"Come on, Si; we're going."* But, Ocean Tia now reflected, *he did not go. He stayed. So,* she closed her eyes tightly, *what had happened? What was it that lured Simon Teal back to Natasha Parks?*

A sudden realisation and, with it, an overwhelming crushing dread overtook Ocean. The christening; she could not, under any conditions, honour her role as godmother.

Chapter Ninety-Four

Seconds transformed into minutes; minutes rolled into hours and the first rays of light filtering into her room brought no solace to Ocean Tia's soul. She had tossed and turned all night; ruminated; rehearsed a series of potential scenarios; formed and discarded speeches but, whichever route she took, she came across a stumbling block she could not cross. Relinquishing her role as godmother, she knew, would bring disappointment and problems to Hanale and Maria's door. And yet... She closed her eyes shaking her head slowly from side to side, unable to force the image of being a godmother into her heart. *How,* she asked herself, *could she possibly agree to the responsibility of fulfilling her duty after Hanale's revelation? How could she consent to being a godmother when she had the insane urge to snatch the baby and run—fly—fly high and away back to Kauai, where the sun shone; where there were rarely any clouds in the sky? How could she take on this important role and look Hanale in the eyes, knowing that he had withheld the truth from her? How could she pretend to be happy when, deep inside, all she wanted to do was fade away from this miserable world and all the people in it?*

Summoning up any scraps of courage she could muster, she found herself standing outside Hanale and Maria's bedroom, the sound of light snoring coming from behind the closed door. Gingerly raising her clenched fingers to the wood they paused mid-air, her heart throbbing wildly; her eyes firmly fixed on the wood in front; her feet abruptly turning, stepping forward and standing at another door. Cautiously opening it she walked inside.

Softly, slowly she padded along and stopped, her eyes dropping; feeling as if her uncontrollable heart was about to jump out of her chest. As she stood silent and motionless, she felt her racing heart decrease its rapid beating. Slowly... slowly it subsided into its normal rhythm, a strange calmness overtaking her as she sat down by the side of the cot, her eyes on the small sleeping bundle.

Moments passed as she sat looking, thinking nothing and feeling nothing but a unique sense of calm; an inexplicable inner peace she had never experienced before. Cautiously she extended her hand, her eyes not leaving the bundle beneath, and drew back the light-blue coverlet to one side. Very carefully, as if dealing with a precious jewel, she picked up the sleeping baby and sat back down, gently securing the infant in the crutch of her arms, and rocked to and fro... to and fro... as she felt all the troubles of the world vanish; all her concerns, worries, anxieties and fears disintegrate into nothing, as she tenderly gazed down at the babe in her arms.

How long she sat rocking she did not know; aware only of the peace and calm exuding from the baby, so close to her beating heart. The sound of soft padded footsteps made her turn. Her eyes saw no one; her ears attune to the gentle click of the door, sharply awakening her senses and, with their awakening, flooded back her fears, anxieties and conflicting questions: *To flee or to stay?* How could she stay a minute longer than she had to after the crushing news she'd heard? How could she abandon her duty and go? How could she hold the baby in her arms and promise to be his guardian, when all she wanted to do was escape and forget about babies; to stop thinking about Simon's baby; ignore the fact that she did not have one of her own? Abruptly she placed the baby back into its bed; getting rid of it as if it was a piece of burning coal; averting her eyes from its sleeping innocence; running out the room to avoid any further contact.

Throwing her suitcase on to the bed, she opened it and haphazardly threw in her belongings; the sleeping baby crashing ruthlessly into her head. Snapping the case shut she slumped down beside it and buried her head in her hands, unable to quell the rush of hot, prickly tears slipping out of her burning eyes and trickling over her fingers; a bout of fresh tears following suit; her whole body trembling as a dull, nagging pain and a sharp stab of guilt attacked every nerve, vein and sinew; sickly bile rising to her constricted throat. Rushing to the en suite bathroom, she stuck her head down the toilet wrenching; wishing her guts, heart, soul, thoughts and emotions would exude from her body, leaving her with nothing. Intermittently wrenching and sobbing, her arid mouth emitted only spits of spittle and still she felt the guilt of going; the guilt of staying; the guilt of not being woman enough to produce a baby of her own.

"Ocean."

She hadn't heard the en suite door open or the approach of soft footsteps, until they were almost upon her; quickly she brushed away the still trickling tears from her face.

"Ocean."

His gentle, soft voice felt like a sharp pointed dagger of betrayal thrusting through her heart. Closing her eyes tightly she willed the intruder to go. He stayed. "Please go away, Hanale." Her trembling words were barely audible.

"We have to talk, Ocean."

Inside she knew his words made sense. Reluctantly she sat up, her back leaning against the unyielding toilet bowl; her eyes dropping to the cream-coloured floor-tiling, unable to look her adversary in the eyes, as Hanale slumped down and sat opposite his half-sister, feeling her excruciating pain as if it was his own; for, hadn't he brought it to her door? Didn't he introduce his friend to Ocean all those years ago? Wasn't it he who had deprived her of the truth? And now, here he was, about to plead with her to fulfil her role, despite any feelings or reservations she may be harbouring. Desperate eyes pinned on her; frantically he searched his head for the appropriate words to say, knowing that whatever words he chose they would not be adequate. Hearing a deep ragged sigh, emerging from somewhere in the depths of her well of emotions, he clamped his mouth shut against the words on the very verge of his mouth.

"I will be a godmother to your son, Hanale."

Her softly spoken words floated into his consciousness, immediately propelling a sigh of relief to exude from his dry mouth. "Thank you." He said no more; there was nothing more to say.

Chapter Ninety-Five

The small church was full of Hanale and Maria's friends, neighbours and work colleagues wanting to share their very important day; the men folk casting surreptitious, appreciative glances at the mysterious beauty standing by the font, while their women folk inwardly writhed with envious contempt.

She felt hot eyes running up, down and ascending back along her blue streamlined dress, rising to the silk artificial plumeria above her left ear and ending on her full, sensual lips, until the sources of admiration felt a sharp nudge in their side and their eyes regretfully averted. Their admiration of her physical beauty meant absolutely nothing to Ocean Tia; unlike the chattels of a human heart, which meant everything.

The solemn promise to the child and to God brought with it a heavy weight. *Had she done the right thing?* She asked herself over and over again and, as she walked away from the font and the gloominess of the church, towards the open door and the brightness of the outside, she answered her rhetorical question. *Yes, she had done the right thing; she had fulfilled her promise to Hanale and Maria.* She smiled. As one foot followed the other she spotted him. Her smile vanished.

He had seen her from afar. His heart did not stop; his smile did not vanish. He closed his eyes in relief. There was hope.

Chapter Ninety-Six

His eyes followed her every move as he sat perfectly still, in the shadows of the bowels of the ancient church, his secretive eyes following her as she walked elegantly past him, seemingly oblivious to his presence; his heart aching for the precious love he had squandered while, simultaneously, his brain admonished him severely for straying away from the marital bed. Involuntarily his mind drifted to the object of his scorn. He just hoped to God Natasha Parks hadn't opened her red lipstick mouth and spewed out the lie to all and sundry; for, once it was out, it was out and no amount of pushing and shoving it back would help, regardless of the truth. Closing his mind to Natasha's image, he willed Ocean Tia's image to infiltrate his senses. *So alluringly beautiful she looked,* he mused.

His image haunted her, giving her ruffled heart no solace as it weaved in and out of her mind. Her observant eyes had spotted him in the shadows of a crumbling pillar; hidden but not hidden was her husband and betrayer, like an obscure snake in the grass, which had already spewed its venom and was waiting, no doubt, to spew out more.

She played her role well posing confidently for the obligatory photographs, mingling with the guests, laughing, joking, talking while all the time the invisible blade thrust ever deeper into her heart and a multitude of questions bombarded her head. *Why had Simon come to the church; surely, he didn't think there was a chance of a reconciliation?* She closed her eyes, desperately trying to dispel the niggling questions which were rolling in, like ancient Hawaiian waves; one replacing another and another and another. She hadn't noticed something drop from the unevenly balanced plate in her hand; her subconscious heard the echo of a cheery voice. Her lips partly open her eyes looked up to a pair of warm, blue eyes.

"They're not that bad, are they?"

Abruptly she snapped out of her reverie, her eyes dropping to the sausage roll in the stranger's hand, which he swiftly discarded into a nearby bin and said,

"You dropped it," his eyes savouring appreciatively the tropical beauty before him, wondering who on earth she was. "My name is George." He extended his broad hand.

"A-Aloha... I. I mean, Hello; my name is Ocean Tia."

"Wow! What a beautiful name." He shook her hand, transmitting a tingle of electricity from his hand to hers. Quickly she withdrew her hand from his warm grasp turning to go, his words stopping her in her tracks. "Please stay. I am on my own here and quite frankly I could do with a companion." He hesitated then continued. "You're not with anyone are you, Ocean Tia?" She shook her head, still feeling the tingling sensation she wished she could erase. The warmth of her smile made his heart dance.

And while thy exchanged casual information about their respective lives, a pair of eyes took everything in; a fast beating heart plummeted rapidly into the depths of despair. Unable to look a second longer, Simon withdrew from his secret niche by the window and ran out the drive.

From the opposite side of the packed room, Maria and Hanale witnessed a new friendship forming; both smiled to themselves.

At the end of the evening, four people went to bed with new hope beating in their hearts. A fifth person made his solitary way to a hostel with no hope in his pained heart.

Chapter Ninety-Seven

Darkness reigned in Ocean Tia's heart and soul, as Simon's silhouetted image hauntingly weaved in and out of her head. Still the niggling questions gnawed at her; still she felt a part of her life was out of sync; still she felt she was part of Simon and he a part of her; still…

Simon breathed though in every other respect he was dead; aware he had lost everything that had been precious to him. He had lost his jewel, Ocean Tia.

He had seen everything with his own eyes; the attentiveness of the stranger towards his Ocean, the stranger's eyes of admiration upon her; the way he touched her waistline as they walked away from his view and the way Ocean responded; for, he had noticed that she did not ignore or dissuade her new admirer's advances. She had walked away with him; away from her husband and his betrayal; away. There was, he dismally concluded, nothing more left for him.

Maria drew hope from what she had seen. Her sister-in-law was finally moving on.

Hanale knew different. He knew it would take more than a casual acquaintance at a christening party for his half-sister to move on but, he fervently hoped, it was a start of her recovery.

Discarding thoughts of Simon, Ocean slipped into her nightie, a spontaneous smile creeping on to her lips as she remembered the tingle she felt at the touch of George's hand, which had reminded her that she was a woman and, with that thought, she climbed into bed and closed her eyes.

Flecks of morning sunlight broke through the crack of the curtain, making her thoughts drift far away to her homeland in the sun, Kauai. Immediately thoughts of Solomao filtered through. How was he coping and, more importantly, was he eating enough? His stark words crashed into her thoughts… *If only I hadn't burned my bridges… seize the day… tomorrow, you may not have the chance…* She closed her eyes against the pale winter sun. They were, she conceded, words of experience; words her Uncle Keoki could well have said;

words of wisdom. They haunted her while she took her early morning shower…
tomorrow you may not have the chance… burned bridges… tomorrow you may not have the chance…

Within half an hour, she was attired in jeans and a pink flower printed blouse, her sleek hair tied back in a dangling ponytail and on her way out of the house. In which direction, she was going she did not yet know. The only thing she did know was that she had to find her husband.

Chapter Ninety-Eight

Exhausted from the onslaught of torturous thoughts and dark, haunting images Simon finally fell asleep and for a brief few minutes was oblivious to the vicious disputes, raucous laughter and pent-up demonstrations of anger emitting from his fellow lodgers. The dark, haunting images soon followed him into slumberland, where they fought with each other for prime position and ultimate attention... *Simon, I am pregnant... You are the father of the baby... What are you going to do about it?* A grotesque mouth snarled; Natasha's words resonating in his subconscious world as another image loomed, stark and clear, a beautiful image of someone he once loved; still loved so very, very much. And as one image replaced the other he slipped into peaceful sleep.

In the morning, he opened his eyes, feeling totally refreshed and hungry for food and answers. Abandoning the hostel, with its mix of unsavoury characters, he entered a local café and ordered a full English breakfast with the last handful of coins he possessed and while he heartily tucked into his eggs, sausage, baked beans and toast a plan began to weave and formulate in his mind, causing a faint smile to curve his lips, dying before it fully matured. First of all one job had to be done and that, he knew without a doubt, was not going to be an easy task to accomplish. Wiping the remnants of tomato sauce and a bit of egg from his lips, he stuffed the last bit of toast into his mouth, swilled it down with coffee and rose, heading out on to the path he had to tread.

The knock on the door brought the inhabitant straight to the door and, as a victorious, smug smile danced on Natasha Park's lips, a heavy stone lodged in the pit of Simon's stomach, rising rapidly to his fast beating heart. The last thing he wanted to do in this world, or the next, was to encounter Natasha Parks; the woman he had slept with and wished to God he hadn't. "We need to talk." He stated icily his equally icy eyes fixed on her inviting blue eyes, reigniting the merciless pounding in his heart.

For laborious seconds heavy, ominous silence shrouded them with its brittle, uncomfortable blanket propelling him to think that she hadn't heard him. Opening his mouth to reinstate his requisition, he closed it rapidly as she spoke her tone slow, steady and clear. "You have come to apologise." She smirked, her long fingers playing seductively with her untidy blonde tresses.

A surge of wild anger intermingled with the ice in his heart; incredulity replacing them both. "Apologise!" He exclaimed, his eyes as wide as saucers. "Apologise for what exactly?"

He watched as her inviting blue eyes turned to eyes of pure, cold steel, her smirk vanishing as she stared at him in total disbelief; her mind telling her that his mere presence showed that he was here to play ball. Speedily she rearranged her thought process and, eyes not leaving her former lover, she stated clearly, "You are the father of our unborn child. You have responsibilities."

"I want proof." He stated equally as clearly.

Pedestrians were casting furtive looks in their direction and Natasha, not normally one for hiding her thoughts and opinions, on this occasion did not want all and sundry to know her business. "You better come inside." She extended the door, standing to one side as he passed reluctantly through.

One pair of eyes saw it all and as the door closed so did any hope of a future reconciliation. Ocean Tia emerged from behind the aged oak tree, which had served as a brief sanctuary of concealment, and turned her feet in the opposite direction, a well of scorching tears threatening to spill; her heart dead. Now there was no hope; her bridges were burned.

Chapter Ninety-Nine
Kauai

Her eyes rested on the familiar airport as it came nearer and nearer into view, bringing a tinge of solace into Ocean Tia's broken heart. This was home. This was, she told herself, where her shattered heart would laboriously begin its healing process; this was the only place in this world where she could hope to find herself.

Removing the fake plumeria from her hair and leaving it on the seat of the plane, she pinned on her smile and boldly walked through into the arrivals area; the sight of her own people in Hawaiian attire, their cheerful smiles and easy manner bringing a warmth to her crushed heart.

"Ocean! Ocean!"

Her eyes darted to the source of the excited voice and her smile widened, her steps quickened and her heart raced as she spotted her friend. "Aloha Makamae." She placed an artificial lei of frangipani around his chubby neck and pecked him on his cheek, feeling the sun-kissed warmth of his skin.

"Welcome home, Ocean." He beamed placing a fragrant lei around her neck and watched her bringing the flowers up to her nose and inhaling deep the intoxicating perfume, savouring the sweet moment. *Yes,* she silently confirmed, *I am truly back home where I belong.*

She threw herself into her work, caring for the unfortunates of the island who had, somehow, lost their way in life. One major anxiety nagged her. Where was Solomao? She had been told that he had simply walked out of the sanctuary one day and not returned. No one had seen him. Local beaches, hospitals and churches were scoured daily, identity posters displayed and, still, there was no news, making Ocean's heart heavy and a deep sense of foreboding haunt her waking hours.

Surreptitiously, Makamae observed Ocean recognising confliction. Positivity seemed to ooze out of every pore yet her rich, brown eyes told him a different story; they were the windows of her soul and they could not lie, as they looked out into the distance and silently told him they held a secret pain. Patiently he waited for the right time when Ocean Tia would share her burden.

One evening as they sat side by side watching the golden, majestic sun dip into the ocean, Makamae tentatively broke his resolve and gently probed his tentacles of enquiry into her private world. Placing his untouched Mai Tai on to the glass-topped bamboo table, he saw again the undeniable pain in her eyes; *so deep,* he thought, *it was almost buried.* "You know, Ocean," he said softly his eyes resting on her motionless face, "you haven't said much about your trip to England."

One word pierced sharply through her cognisance, tearing raggedly through her heart and savagely reopening the wound which had begun its process of slow healing. And yet, she mused, the country itself had no part to blame in the blaming game.

"Ocean." Makamae repeated her name like a gentle echo.

Dark pools shot to him, making him instantly regret the road of questioning he had ventured on. Her faint smile reached his eyes. "It was good; all good, Makamae."

"And what about Hanale and Maria?" His eyes scrutinised hers.

She nodded her head silently clamping her mouth tight; for, to speak she would have to lie while all the while she wanted to scream, *Hanale betrayed me; he is no brother of mine;* her mind involuntarily drifting to Natasha's door... *as Simon walked in and the door closed leaving her on the outside; not able to look in; not wanting to look in for she had seen everything she needed to see; all her questions had been answered. Natasha and Simon were an item. The rumours had been silently confirmed. All her questions had been answered. Simon was the father of Natasha's baby. End of story.*

Still silence reigned once more as two pairs of eyes watched the last rays of the sun disappear. Makamae took his leave with more unanswered questions swirling about in his head and reopened memories clawing and gnawing at Ocean Tia's mind, body, heart and soul.

Grabbing a light jacket she hurried down the narrow, bendy, nightly flower scented lanes and along a long quiet road, bordering the beach on one side and native homes on the other; turning a sharp corner she decreased her speed to steady her feet and her fast beating heart, her fingers opening the low wrought iron gates. She walked through.

Shrouded on all sides by an eerie stillness, she placed one foot in front of the other and, covering her bare shoulders with her jacket, she cast her eyes in one direction and then another as the ghosts of old, but not forgotten, friends and acquaintances accompanied her. She passed old Lanakila's grave and smiled saying softly, "You were the finest ukulele player on the whole island." Her eyes darted a couple of graves further along. "And you, Anani; you made the best Haupia a wahine could make." On and on, she walked until her feet reached their destination and stopped. Sitting down on the old bench, her eyes peeled on the final resting place of her beloved she said in a whisper, as if not to wake them, "Thank you." And, as the ghosts of her past marched through her mind, like soldiers on parade, the memories came flooding in. Her eyes rested on her mother's grave. "If only, Makuahine, you hadn't been taken away from us, things may have turned out so very differently; but..." Eyes flitted to Rosemary's resting place. "... I would not have met you dear, Lokemele; or my dear friend, Alan; my dear, wise kanaka who turned despair into hope." Her mind drifted back to Rosemary, "Yet, if I hadn't have bumped into you, Lokemele, on that desolate beach, I would not know Hanale; I would not be married to Simon..." She felt the hot tears slither down her face and allowed them to dry, as she continued to stare down at the graves through a blurry veil, in which nothing seemed real. *Had it all been some kind of weird dream?* She closed her eyes against a rising wave of fresh tears threatening to spill. Too late; they seeped through beneath her closed lids and trickled down the dry trails. *What was the point of anything if it ended up in the grave? What was the point of studying, worrying, dreaming, loving, hoping, living when the destination was always the same? DEATH.*

Stealthily the dark thoughts spun their deathly cobwebs in her mind – A sound – Her ears pricked. Abruptly she turned her body, her alert eyes scanning the periphery, a sigh of relief exuding her dry mouth. Her imagination was playing tricks. Bringing her eyes back on to the graves she tried to rein in her scattered thoughts. Involuntarily her torso turned, her pulse quickened. This time there was no denying that she had heard something. Her cautious eyes roamed, hoping to spot a bird or some other living creature. Frozen, her heart stopped as a figure rose from behind a grave and ran in the opposite direction. In vain, her eyes tried to follow; the figure was too swift. *Was that lone figure Solomao; had he been following her; was he trying to reach out to her?* Sitting back down on the old bench, her eyes fixed on Kai's resting place she made a solemn promise, her words clear as a bell in the still air, "I will find you, Solomao; I will help you."

Chapter One Hundred

Excited voices brought Ocean Tia to the hallway, a sparkle to her eyes and caused her lips to break out into a joyful smile. "Liliana... Akamu; what a wonderful surprise!" She exclaimed her eyes switching from her cousins to the stranger standing behind them; her happy eyes immediately turning into two dark orbs of curiosity, wondering who this handsome kāne was and, more to the point, what was he doing here while, simultaneously, his dark eyes were firmly fixed on the beauty before him, speculating how long it would take to add her to the numerous notches on his bedpost. Akamu broke the spell. "Ocean, this is a friend of mine, Ekewaka; Ekewaka, my cousin, Ocean Tia."

Without averting his eyes from the vision before him, Ekewaka withdrew his lei from his neck and placed it around Ocean's slender neck. Only then did he withdraw his eyes, to bestow the touch of a kiss on her cheek, sending a spray of tingling electric shocks throughout her entire body, making her abruptly turn her face from him, for fear of him witnessing the flush of colour rising to and burning her cheeks.

In the air-conditioned lounge, dotted with exotic potted palms and tastefully arranged fragrant blooms, they sat refreshing themselves with long, cool drinks of freshly squeezed pineapple juice; Ocean Tia's eyes firmly fixed on her dew-bejewelled glass, for fear of a secondary flushing attack; her mind still trying to solve the purpose of Ekewaka's presence. Her answer came in Liliana's next words.

"We dragged Ekewaka away from the Big Island to sample life on a quieter, more serene island, Ocean." She said casually, as if Ekewaka's presence in Ocean Tia's home was the most natural thing in the world.

Involuntarily Ocean's eyes shot to the object of her inner curiosity, immediately feeling Ekewaka's hypnotic eyes burning her face; causing a myriad of unruly butterflies to flutter erratically, hither and thither in her tummy, as she tried desperately to summon up some casual snippets of conversation to throw into the mix. She opened her dry mouth to none.

Ekewaka felt her reticence, secretly admiring this quality in a woman.

"Akamu and I are work colleagues, Ocean." Akamu broke the ice.

"And, Ekewaka is a first-class surfer, Ocean," Liliana stated giving her cousin an encouraging smile.

Ekewaka's observant eyes noticed the slight lift of Ocean's eyebrows and immediately, silently, thanked Liliana for this fragment of information; *for, clearly,* he surmised, *this wahine has some sort of interest regarding the art of surfing.* And, now he had his hook, he knew, he could slowly reel her in.

She was indeed hooked; for, there was nothing Ocean Tia liked better than to sit on the beach and observe the amazing aptitude of the surfers, skilfully weaving their boards in and out and above the waves, as if they were ice skaters on a colossal, ever-moving rink. Oh, how she envied them; never having mastered the skill of surfing herself.

"I could teach you, Ocean." His words cut through her regrets, like swift skates through ice; sending the familiar butterflies to her tummy. She dared to look at him and smile; but, as he returned her smile she felt an ominous shadow of bitter betrayal cross her heart.

Quickly she unleashed her eyes from his intoxicating spell and rose to her feet. "I am so sorry; I have to go to work."

Within minutes, she was hurriedly walking, then running down the lanes. On and on, she ran not daring to glance back; too pusillanimous to assess her tangled feelings, fearing what she may unravel, as the silent knife of betrayal plunged deeper and deeper into her racing heart.

Work was not an obliging partner, refusing to dispel her erratic thoughts. The more she made an effort with menial tasks; the more Ekewaka clashed with Simon, both vying for her exclusive attention.

Taking a break, she felt, she had not earned, she stepped outside and tried to tame her unruly thoughts, place them into a box and symbolically bury them in the deep recesses of her mind, never to be resurrected. They refused to die; her mind drifting to a faraway country which she had learned to love and now abhorred; for, it was where her trouble started; it was where the truth was hidden and, uncharacteristically, Ocean Tia could no longer bear to face the truth.

She had seen it all with her own eyes. She had witnessed Natasha Parks opening the door and Simon walking in... walking in; he had not been hauled, pushed, dragged in by force. Simon Teal, her husband, had willingly stepped over her nemesis's threshold and walked into the bowels of her home. Her thoughts flashed forward, her eyes closing. No matter how much she had denied, and attempted to obliterate the tiny sparks of electricity surging through her veins, the image of Ekewaka's eyes locking with her own eyes created a battlefield of conflicting feelings deep, deep down in her gut. She squeezed her eyes tighter, failing to wipe out his smiling face. Abruptly turning she walked inside.

Chapter One Hundred and One

Ocean Tia felt trapped in a prison of fluctuating emotions; but that was nothing compared to feeling like a prisoner in her own home and while Akamu, Liliana and their *tag along,* Ekewaka, remained a presence in Ocean's home, she felt imprisoned.

Returning home from a particularly gruelling day at the sanctuary her heart sank, and infuriatingly simultaneously leaped, at the sight she beheld; her hand begrudgingly accepting the cool, welcoming juice held out to her. Involuntarily her eyes shot to his dark, twinkling eyes and slid down to his warm smile immediately sending a surge of hot, tingling sparks through her body. "Aloha Ocean."

"Aloha Ekewaka." She returned his smile, her ingrained good manners prevailing, while her heart hammered uncontrollably, as she wished only to withdraw from his electrifying presence and to gain some control on her wayward emotions.

Akamu and Liliana rushed to and from the kitchen, making final adjustments to the table, before they all sat down for their last meal together. As always, Ocean Tia dreaded her cousin's departure. In complete contrast, she secretly counted the hours when, finally, Ekewaka, his dark eyes and sensual mouth; his softly spoken voice; his golden-brown complexion and lean, athletic body; his alluring presence would vanish; silently willing him to take with him the excruciating guilt he had unconsciously, and unwittingly, planted in her heart and soul; the raw guilt of betraying a husband, if only in thought.

This excruciating guilt took hold of her possessively like a tight-fitting dress, silently killing her with the burden of her own weakness; for, never in her life had she felt so fragile in the presence of a man.

Sitting opposite Ekewaka her eyes fixed firmly on her plate, containing lomi salmon, salad and rice; occasionally raising them to Akamu and Liliana and bypassing the man, whose eyes were upon her, at all costs; for, to meet his eyes head-on would be fatal.

Ocean Tia felt his burning eyes penetrating her, searing into her racing heart as they plunged deeper and deeper into the essence of her being; the echoes of laughter and snippets of trivial conversation filtering in and out of her consciousness, until Simon boldly and unashamedly strode into her mind, overtaking all other thoughts. Throwing her pristine white napkin on to her plate of untouched food, she abandoned the table; three pairs of puzzled eyes following their hostess, as she hurriedly walked out the room and into the sanctuary of the garden where she took a long, deep, heavy breath and exhaled it slowly, feeling the tight tension gradually release its hold on her, while her eyes fixed exclusively on the Rainbow Shower tree. Slowly her breathing resumed its normal regular rhythm, the echoes of voices drifting to her ears. Instantly her heart froze as she felt the feather-light touch of warmth on her bare arm. Turning she faced her intruder, his soft words like melted honey. "Come," he extended his free hand, "let's go and eat." And, like a meek lamb she followed him inside.

He couldn't help but see the surreptitious look she threw his way; a mere flash but from it he derived a million signals and on it he placed his hopes. He had never misjudged a woman's secret glance in his life.

As the evening drew to an end, Ocean felt a deep sense of relief overtake her anxieties. The words that followed brought them all back with a vengeance.

"So, Ocean, are you up for a surfing lesson?" Ekewaka's tone was enquiring though playful in its delivery. "It's my thank you for your gracious hospitality."

"There's no need to thank me for anything and, besides, there's no time for a surfing tutorial; you are leaving tomorrow."

"There's always time." He winked sending her blood pressure into orbit. "First thing tomorrow morning and..." He paused for maximum effect, smiling mischievously to himself as he took in her shocked face. "We'll have the whole ocean to ourselves. Akamu and Liliana have declined the invitation."

"And so do I." Ocean Tia smiled stubbornly avoiding his eyes, unable to avoid the sound of his amused chuckle.

Alone she stood her eyes once again peeled on the majestic Rainbow Tree and its yellow and coral cascading clusters. It offered her no grain of calm as she asked herself over and over again, *Why didn't I say, no?*

Why didn't you say, no? The words reverberated in her fragmented dreams as... *Ekewaka weaved in and out the mighty waves... Why didn't you say, no? The reproachful words drowned out the distant thundering, as his lithe body twisted skilfully this way and that, glistening with the early morning intermingled ocean spray and sun... Why didn't you say, no? The Hawaiian sun tilted in question... Why didn't you say, no? The waves and sun asked in unison, as Ekewaka's muscles rippled in majestic glory... Why didn't you say, no? Simon yelled at the top of his voice...* making her jump out of her slumber and into a fresh nightmare of reality. Closing her eyes tight against the semi-darkness around her she whispered, "Why didn't I say, no?" A harsh accusing voice answered her back. *You didn't say, no, because you didn't want to say, no.*

Sitting upright in her bed her eyes stared into the gloom, her ears pricked to the sound of distant waves. Oh, how she loved the ocean; how she loved it with her body, heart, soul and mind; oh, how she loathed it.

Chapter One Hundred and Two

The light knocks on the door thundered loudly in her head. Leaden feet approached the door.

"Aloha!" The cheerful voice resounded; his greeting grating every sinew, nerve and bone in her body. *If only,* she admonished herself for the hundredth time, *I'd said, no.* Forcing a smile she begrudgingly extended the door wider, her mouth gushing out words he had not been expecting and most certainly did not want to hear, his brow creasing in puzzlement and frustration, his words questioning. "But, I thought, you were looking forward to the experience."

She scrutinised his face, the vanished smile; his eyes steady and fixed. "I would suggest Mister—Mister—"

Desperately, Ekewaka tried to rein in his amusement at her sudden formality. "Brown." He prompted, watching her eyebrows lift. "My father was an Englishman."

"Oh." She managed to squeeze out inwardly shocked by his revelation, while simultaneously trying to curb the image of another Englishman breaking through.

"Is that a problem, Ocean?"

"No problem regarding your lineage; however, there is a problem regarding the surfing arrangements." She stated watching his eyebrow rise. "I am afraid I will not be able to join you for a surfing session this morning." Her eyes dropped to the polished floor, unable to meet his intense gaze.

"You're scared." The second his words were uttered he regretted his foolishness.

"Not scared," she said defiantly, her eyes still glued to the shiny floor, unwilling to provide him with a further explanation, while he stood perfectly still and assessed the natural beauty before him, silently contradicting her words; for, he knew fear when he saw it. Frantically he rummaged his head for Plan B. He found it. "Then," he looked her directly in the eyes, "why not join me in an early morning walk along the beach?" He waited with bated breath, hoping against hope this woman would accept his invitation, as the seconds ticked on taking with them his hope.

"Okay." She said softly. *After all,* she asked herself, *What possible harm could it do? In a few hours he would leave the island and she would probably never see him again.*

Step by step, side by side yet kilometres apart, they walked along the white shore. Inhaling deep the refreshing raw tang of the ocean, she felt an inner tranquillity which the constant rhythm of waves never failed to bring. Step by step, side by side they walked bare-footed the rippling water covering and receding from their feet, as tiny electrical sparks tingled through Ocean Tia, her heart tightly clenching to the sound of unforgiving voices stating her betrayal.

She felt Ekewaka's eyes on her, as she tried to suffuse her mind with the sound of the roaring waves. It worked. She felt his presence no longer. Casting a sideway glance she found he was no longer by her side. She looked back and spotted the lone figure standing at the water's edge, his eyes looking out into the distant horizon. *What did he see?* She wondered. *What did he want to see? What did he yearn to see?* She stood still, poised and silent; her eyes taking in the figure and, for a split second, her heart went out to him. He looked so alone. Her pity was short-lived as his words travelled out to her. "Write to me, Ocean. Let me know how you are doing."

His words hit her like a ferocious hammer. Turning, she walked on, his haunting words mingling with the sound of the ocean accompanying her every step; making her question each solitary word which came out of his mouth. *For here,* she silently concluded, *was a guy who seemingly had the world at his feet, and all the wahines in it; a guy who most obviously wanted to add her name to his score of notches* making all the warning signs flag up in her head. "I am married, Ekewaka." She felt the touch of his hand on her bare arm, sending a thousand currents through every nerve and sinew. Turning she looked directly into his eyes and repeated softly, "I am a married woman, Ekewaka; I cannot honour your request."

He held her steady gaze. "I am not asking for your hand in marriage, Ocean Tia; I am, in effect, asking you to be my pen pal. You know, it gets pretty lonely on the Big Island."

She didn't hear his last sentence. Her conscious mind stuck on two words, pen pal, and the images they aroused brought a warm smile to her face, which Ekewaka mistook to be her consent.

"Great." He smiled grabbing her hand, as with complete horror her eyes dropped on their merged hands, while a host of fluttering butterflies caused complete pandemonium in the pit of her stomach.

They walked on in silence, wrapped up in their own private thoughts, while the thrashing waves crashed and burned around them; Ekewaka secretly rejoicing that this was going to be the start of something beautiful; Ocean Tia swallowing a hard lump of submissive regret, knowing she had allowed memories of a time gone by to interfere in the here and now and that, she knew only too well, would only result in pain.

Chapter One Hundred and Three

Ocean Tia felt relieved when Ekewaka left the Island of Kauai. This relief, however, was ephemeral as an unfamiliar, uneasy sense of loneliness swept into her soul overtaking her, overpowering her senses; threatening to take her as its victim. Whatever she did, wherever she went, it shrouded her with its heavy, clinging blanket and whatever she did, wherever she went, she could not shrug it off, no matter how hard she tried. It followed her into sleep, where it haunted her fragmented dreams. It was the first thing she felt when she opened her eyes and the last thing she felt when she closed them. The empty, inexplicable void had rooted deep in the hidden recesses of her heart; surged through the blood in her veins and wrenched mercilessly at her guts. She could not shake it off; it lambasted her ruthlessly and cruelly.

One evening as she sat alone in the garden, her unopened book on her lap, Ekewaka's words crashed through her meandering thoughts... *You know, it gets pretty lonely on the Big Island...*"It gets pretty lonely here too." The words escaped her mouth and seemed to resound around the garden, uniting with Ekewaka's words as they mingled and intermingled and became one.

Placing the last remnants of a mixed salad into her mouth, she grabbed a pen and writing pad, sat down at the kitchen table and asked herself, *What possible harm can it do?* Opening the pad she stared long and hard at the virginal page. Snapping down the cover, she stuffed the stationery into a drawer and shut it firmly.

The solitary walk on the desolate beach brought her no grain of comfort, only a series of unanswered questions and a vivid memory of walking on this same stretch of white sand with a handsome man; a man she was not tied with by the bonds of marriage. Perching down, her back leaning against the trunk of a mature palm, she gazed out on to the roaring ocean. It was, she reflected, on this same spot that she had met Lokemele, an English wahine who had become her lifelong friend. It was on this stretch of beach that she and Simon had walked hand in hand, planning a future together; it was in this same sacred place that they had united in grief for Alan. But, it was Ekewaka and his words which now clamoured, and won, her ultimate attention and a decision was made.

Retrieving her pen and pad she wrote a hasty note, popped it into an envelope, sealed it, and within minutes dropped it into a letter box and, with her fate firmly sealed, she turned her full attention and her feet in the direction of Hope Sanctuary.

Chapter One Hundred and Four

His heart missing a beat, he picked the white envelope from the floor, his lips curling into a smug smile; for he had known that sooner or later, like all the other wahines, she would succumb. Secretly he revelled in her weakness. He had been quite prepared to strive much harder to achieve his desired goal.

Walking back into the bowels of his sumptuous apartment, overlooking the majestic waves of the mighty Pacific, he eased the seal open with a long finger and unfolded the paper; his smile instantly dying, as his perplexed eyes read and reread the brief contents of the note. A third time he read the blunt words. A fourth time he read the words aloud as if to convince himself of their inevitability. "Aloha Ekewaka, I hope you are well. I am writing to tell you that, unfortunately, I am unable to be your pen pal, due to the overload of work at the sanctuary, which needs my personal assistance. Best wishes for the future. Ocean Tia."

"Rubbish!" He exclaimed; cold realisation of unfamiliar rejection and the raw comprehension of being dumped before anything of real significance had started, seeping into his consciousness and becoming reality. Throwing the note on to the coffee table, he hastily changed his attire and in minutes was running down to the beach, his surfboard firmly gripped in his hand his mouth muttering, "When was work ever an excuse for friendship?"

Expertly weaving in and out of the thundering water his mind was void; empty of the mundane trivialities of everyday life; unburdened of thoughts of Ocean Tia, the wahine he had somehow allowed to have escaped his net; vacant. Living and breathing for the moment; excited by the refreshing and exhilarating, interweaving moves and rhythms of the mighty swell he felt totally at one with his powerful friend which, at all times he was aware, could suddenly transform into a dangerous enemy. Finally he allowed himself to be taken on the long surge, succumbing to its sweet temptations, as Ocean Tia's words crashed into his vacant mind... *I am unable to be your pen pal, due to the overload of work at the sanctuary*... He sank allowing the waves and her voice to cover him.

Chapter One Hundred and Five
England

Every single day thoughts of what he had, and what he had lost, hammered mercilessly in Simon's consciousness. Having shacked up with Natasha, he had subsequently lost all further contact with his old friend and brother-in-law. Simon's infidelity, as far as Hanale was concerned, was the last nail in their friendship coffin.

With the loss of his friend, came the inevitable loss of a future alliance in winning back Ocean Tia and, it was this excruciating realisation, that haunted Simon day and night. In vain, he had knocked on Hanale's door and begged for forgiveness; unsuccessfully he had written countless letters to Ocean, only to scrunch them into tight balls and discard them in the bin. No longer did he attempt to hope. It was a futile exercise.

Falling into Natasha's web, he felt like a trapped fly unable to leave; not wanting to stay. There was, he felt, no way out; for, where was there to go? He was a prisoner of his own stupidity.

Many times he had tried to calculate the date of the baby's conception; incalculable times he had secretly denied he was the father of the unborn child; for he had worked out he was nowhere within Natasha's orbit on, or around, the date she had determinedly stated. To openly confront Natasha with this query he did not; for, he told himself, where was he to find another roof over his head? He'd lost his well-paid job due to drinking on the premises. Oh, he'd been warned but what damned good were warnings when his sole desire was to forget his mammoth mistake. There was no way out. He was trapped.

Natasha, for her part, had long passed the stage of gloating over the prize she had won; for, with the prize, came the suffocating burden of his presence and that, to a great degree, stifled her roving eye. Yet, she kept telling herself, *What other fool would readily believe that he was the father of her bastard child? What other idiot would turn a blind eye to the odd punter, sleeping with his woman in the next room? Soon,* she smiled, *the baby would be born; Simon would be its chief carer and she would be free.*

Hanale and Maria's happiness was tarnished; for, while they lavished their full attention on their new-born Hanale invariably felt a deep loss, coupled with a hollow emptiness, which could not be filled. The loss of Ocean Tia tortured his heart mercilessly. The loss of his friend and brother-in-law weighed heavy in his mind.

Maria saw the undeniable sadness in her husband's eyes; witnessed his distant gaze and often wondered what he was thinking, pained by the fact that neither she, nor their child, could fill his void. She knew only one thing; his misery lay with Ocean Tia.

One evening when Hanale was in his rocking chair, his son cradled in his arms, Maria strode into the room her eyes automatically flitting to the comforting, loving scene she was witnessing; father and son totally oblivious to her presence. For long silent seconds, she watched; turning, she quietly left and entered her bedroom, withdrew a writing pad and pen, sat down on her bed and summoned her thoughts.

In half an hour, the letter was written, sealed and on its way to be posted, while Hanale continued to rock the innocent babe in his arms, as his half-sister flitted in and out of his wandering mind, as it drifted back to a time long ago, when he saw her for the first time as she confidently walked into the arrivals area. A raw wave of excitement surged through his veins as he remembered… *spotting the tropical beauty, with the white plumeria above her right ear…* even now, after his deceitful betrayal, he missed her sparkling presence, her words of wisdom, her warm smile and dark, mysterious, twinkling eyes. His mind wandered further back, to a time he'd rather forget, when seated at the table his mother's crushing words crashed into his consciousness… *There is no easy way to tell you this, Hanale, than to tell you straight. You father, Kai, is Ocean Tia's father too…* The words seared through his heart now, with the same burning ferocity as they had done all those years ago. *Now,* he dismally concluded, *everything had changed. There was a barrier between himself and Ocean.* His thoughts turned to Simon and one word loomed, *why?*

Why... why... why... why... WHY? Why did his best friend, he thought, he knew well, *perform the foulest of deeds and play dirty tricks on his wife, with the likes of Natasha Parks, who couldn't even begin to compare with Ocean? Why?*

For endless days, the question niggled him until, one day, his feet stood outside Natasha Park's house and earnest fingers rattled impatiently at the door.

Eyes widened and froze as the door opened. The last thing they expected was what they beheld.

Chapter One Hundred and Six

Man stood before man. Eyes fixed unwaveringly on eyes as a deluge of shock waves interwoven with amazement, horror, surprise, relief and regret surged through throbbing veins. Simon's relief was abruptly crushed with one word which infiltrated, reverberated and repeatedly continued to echo in his head.

"Why?"

He closed his eyes to the stark, icy eyes staring back at him; wishing he was able to close his ears to the one word still reverberating unceasingly in his head, which had been projected loudly and clearly out of his brother-in-law's accusing mouth. *Why... why... why?* It ceaselessly asked, as he desperately craved to scream out at the top of his voice, *I don't fucking well know why.* Slowly, he opened his eyes to the unfriendly mask before him, as Hanale stared back at Simon in pained disbelief; taking in his baggy trousers, stained shirt, the growth of a day's stubble, the ruffled hair, the body which had lost so much weight; but, it was the eyes that alarmed Hanale the most; sunken, stark and so full of pain. His heart softened.

"Simon, are you all right?" He enquired, his eyes steadily fixed on his brother-in-law's jutting cheekbones. Abruptly his eyes darted to the top of the staircase, where a figure was descending two steps at a time, a satisfied smirk on his chubby face. Inquisitive eyes followed the guy as he roughly brushed past the two men at the door, turned back grinning from ear to ear, his words directed at Hanale, "She's worth every penny, mate." Eyes switched to Simon, as the echoes of the punter's raucous laughter permeated both men's ears.

"What did he mean, Simon?"

Simon stood as if in a trance, his eyes glued to the disappearing figure, his fast beating heart threatening to jump out of his chest. Feeling the rough tug of Hanale's hand on his bony arm, his next words hammered torturously in his head.

"What on earth is going on, Simon?" Hanale stood perfectly still, as if his feet had been fixed in solid concrete, his questioning eyes unflinchingly fixed on

302

Simon's ashen face. He was not expecting the words which spewed out of his brother-in-law's mouth, before the door banged firmly in his face.

Chapter One Hundred and Seven

His own words crushed in on him from above, below, from all sides as he felt the devastating fallout of their heavy debris. He wished he could turn the clock back; yearned to withdraw the fatal words he had spewed out; craved to wipe away the look of total incredulity in his brother-in-law's face, which was obstinately stuck in his mind.

With a heavy laden heart, he walked along streets, roads and lanes, unsavoury images mingling and intermingling in his confused head. Walking through the entrance of the park, he found a bench overlooking the pond, sat and willed his brain to come up with some sort of answers. The chubby man with the satisfied grin saturated his mind; clinging to him; haunting him. Interwoven with this ugly vision was Simon's stark statement... *I shall be filing for a divorce... These words,* Hanale thought, *were perfectly clear, decisive, to the point with no leeway for a U-turn.* His eyes caught sight of a duck and her line of ducklings waddling down to the water's edge and, for a moment, he envied their ignorance. *I shall be filing for a divorce... divorce... divorce...* The last word echoed loudly in his head, as he shook it slowly from left to right; the mother duck and her brood still in his line of vision. *If only it was Ocean filing for divorce; if only it was she who had the guts to stir into motion the wheel of divorce proceedings; to start the proverbial ball rolling. If only she had instigated the matter, instead of leaving the decision to Simon.* His eyes followed the ducklings as they strode into the water a heavy, jagged sigh emitting from the depths of his sorrowful soul, exuding from his mouth. *How would Ocean receive the news? How would she cope?*

As he opened the door to the warmth seeping out and the sound of baby gurgles, his mind was made up. He would do all in his power to help his half-sister; for, wasn't he partly to blame for this unenviable state of affairs?

Chapter One Hundred and Eight
Kauai

The gentle touch on her shoulder made her jump. "Solomao!" She exclaimed her lips curling into a happy smile. "Solomao," she echoed, a surge of overwhelming relief rushing through her entire body, her disbelieving eyes looking at the man she thought she would never see again. She listened to his harrowing story relating his mysterious absence. Long seconds passed after he had stopped talking; the young man reliving his ordeal; Ocean taking everything in, tentatively she asked, "And since your uncle's funeral, Solomao; you have not touched a drop of alcohol?"

"Not a drop." He enthused, tears glistening in his dark eyes.

Her observant eyes scanned Solomao's clean clothes, his shaven face which no longer was haggard and his neatly groomed hair; he felt her pride in him suffusing his heart, making him return her smile though it was short-lived and through her perceptive eyes she watched it fade and die; the twinkle in his eyes replaced by a sheen of despondency. Gently she touched his arm. "What is it, Solomao?" His eyes met her eyes of concern and wavered, making her think he was holding something back. She held his unsteady gaze. "Please tell me what it is." She encouraged softly and something in the gentleness of her voice made him crumble.

"I have no job, Ocean, and…"

"And?" She lightly probed.

"And—and…" He looked away, no longer having the strength to look her in the eyes. "And… I. I desperately crave a drink." Her smiling face made him think she had misheard him. "I want an alcoholic drink, Ocean." He stated coldly, furious with himself for his own weakness and equally furious with Ocean's incapability of readily comprehending his inner anguish.

305

How very wrong he was. She understood well his misery; his struggle; his addiction. She had seen it all before in her own flesh and blood. "Thank you for being honest with me, Solomao." She said her warm, encouraging smile striking a chord in his ruffled soul. "There is help here. You will spend the night at the sanctuary, where you will be safe from temptation and tomorrow, Solomao, will be a good day."

An hour later he watched her go, turn and disappear down the road and out of sight, as a ray of hope brought solace, dispelled his fears and brought a smile to his face. "Ocean Tia is an angel!" He exclaimed, repeating his statement louder for the entire world to hear.

Chapter One Hundred and Nine
England

The moment the door banged in his brother-in-law's face, Simon Teal's heart sank to the very depths of black despair. Watching the retreating figure from behind the net curtain he yearned to run after him and prevent him from leaving, knowing that he was taking with him the last link with Ocean Tia. Through blurry eyes he gazed as Hanale stopped, turned, briefly looked back, turned once more and walked on with increasing speed and accelerated determination. Allowing the curtain to slip from his grasp, Natasha's happy humming permeating his blood and making it curdle, a sudden idea crashed into his head.

She heard the door bang. His feet ran at top speed abruptly coming to a sudden stop, his racing heart deflating with defeat, his eyes glued on the fast disappearing figure ahead, his feet stuck firmly to the terra firma unable to move a centimetre, his eyes watching… staring as Hanale turned a corner and was out of his line of vision. He had let his last link go. He stood a broken man, his eyes staring vacantly at a desolate road, except for a solitary car driving past and two young children kicking a football in someone's garden. Dejectedly he turned his feet, as heavy as clay, in the opposite direction, his heavy heart matching the characteristics of his feet, and walked back to the house he could never call home.

Sleep eluded him that night as a thousand conflicting, disturbing thoughts and scenarios fought a raging war in his swimming head; tormented by crude sounds emitting through the thin wall, wrestling with Ocean's soft image, depriving him of a mere grain of peace, as each inharmonious image vied with the other for his undivided attention. Roughly throwing his bedcovers aside he put on his shoes, threw on his overcoat and walked out the door. Where his feet were taking him he did not know, neither did he care, as long as his ears and mind were no longer afflicted by the sounds he could not bear to hear.

Pulling up his collar against the bitter north-easterly wind, he was solely guided by his feet as, one foot in front of the other, they trudged on in through the tall wrought-iron gates and into the solace of the park, where he was enveloped on both sides by inky silhouettes of various trees, shrubs and flowers, their daytime glamour stolen by the velvety, eerie darkness surrounding them. On and on, he trudged, his thoughts scattered, his brain unable to formulate anything coherent; nothing in the world seeming comprehensible anymore. How long he sat huddled on the bench he did not know, as seconds had merged into minutes and all had blended into the mists of time.

"Problems?"

Aware of an ominous presence, his eyes shot up to the source of his curiosity beholding, from what he could make out in the darkness, a bedraggled figure standing directly in front of him. Desperate to escape, Simon stayed put, his quizzical eyes on the bearded man with scraggly tufts of hair sticking out from under a woollen bobble hat; seeing a reflection of himself in a few weeks' time.

"May I?" The vagabond pointed his long, grubby finger at the bench.

Simon nodded and the man sat down next to him as whiffs of raw alcohol, mingled with the stench of an unwashed body, infiltrated Simon's nostrils making him crave a drop. His silent wish was granted.

"Drink?" The man proffered a quarter filled bottle of some dark substance, Simon could not readily identify.

Before he could accept or decline, to Simon's utter amazement, the tramp rummaged through his rucksack, produced two chipped mugs, and diligently poured out his treasured drink, as an amused smile broke out on Simon's lips. The stranger's mouth broke out in a refined chuckle. "I like to drink in style."

The mug sat cradled in Simon's hands; his urgent need fighting a ferocious war with his reasoning, as it warned him of a slippery road should he make the wrong choice, as his thoughts briefly drifted to Kai... to Lokemele. Alcohol had almost destroyed one and ruined the other. He closed his eyes his craving winning the war. He brought the mug to his parched lips. For another second, he hesitated, before allowing the potent liquid to enter his mouth and slide down his throat. Immediately he felt it's comforting warmth, as the stranger's words crashed into his consciousness. "One is okay, my friend; it may loosen your tangled thoughts. More than one could be fatal." Simon's eyes darted to the man, who was pouring himself another drink his bloodshot, sunken eyes flitting to

Simon. "For me, it is too late." He gulped down the drink in one swallow. "I have already lost everything."

So have I; Simon heard the echo of his own silent reply.

The drunk's glassy eyes took on a serious look as they remained steadily fixed on Simon. "My friend, if there is any hope; any way you can resolve your problem, no matter how difficult, do it."

Simon's eyes followed the hunched figure as he became smaller and smaller; his words becoming louder and clearer repeating over and over in his head, giving him food for thought… *If there is any hope; any hope of resolving your problem, no matter how difficult, do it…* The stark words enveloped him; wrapped themselves around his conflicting thoughts until they became a part of him and he a part of them. *But how to do it when all the doors are closed; when all roads and avenues are barricaded; when all hope leads to failure?*

An idea crashed into his swimming head.

Chapter One Hundred and Ten

The echo of his impatient fingers urgently knocking on the door, reverberated loudly in Simon's ears, his heart hammering, his feet turning to flee and turning back to face the door. The door opened. His heart froze.

Raising his eyes they settled on the figure before him as an overbearing ominous silence, thick enough to cut with a knife, shrouded them both. Mercifully the excruciating stillness was broken only to be replaced by gruff words. "What do you want, Teal?"

He shuffled from foot to foot his eyes flitting here, there and everywhere as he desperately searched for appropriate words to come to his rescue, his eyes finally settling on the grim face before him. "May I... I come in, Hanale?" His weak voice stuttered.

"Who is it, Hanale?" Maria's cheerful voice drifted followed by her bodily presence. "Simon! Come... come in, Simon." She enthused to Simon's immense relief and the grating annoyance of her husband, who gave her a withering look she totally ignored, as she ushered their visitor inside; wondering if his unannounced visit had anything to do with the letter she had written to Ocean.

Hanale stared fixedly at his estranged brother-in-law, unable to believe a word which had spouted out of his mouth while Simon, his guts ruthlessly wrenching and churning, waited for his fate to be sealed.

His ears were subjected to an incredulous laugh, his eyes witnessing utter disbelief in Hanale's astonished face; he switched his eyes to Maria who gave a reassuring smile. Finally Hanale spoke. "You mean to say..." He said slowly, each word loaded with meaning. "You mean to say, that you wish me to fund you a holiday in the sun." His fresh bout of laughter, seemed to Simon, to rebound around the very walls surrounding them, before they penetrated his tired head.

"I want you to help me to salvage my marriage, Hanale." He dropped his eyes, unable to look at the mocking laughter in Hanale's eyes.

Silence reigned once more thick, clinging, oppressive as fate lay in the balance.

"No." Hanale rose from the sofa and walked away.

Simon rose, threw Maria a hint of a smile and strode out the door. His fate was sealed.

Chapter One Hundred and Eleven
Kauai

The sight of another white envelope on the wooden floor, forced a heavy sigh to exude from Ocean Tia's mouth and a tinge of uncharacteristic irritation to stir in her hitherto calm equilibrium. She shook her head slowly from side to side. If only Ekewaka would understand that *no means no.* Picking up the envelope her eyes rested on the foreign stamps. The sender was not Ekewaka. A lump rose and settled in her throat. Her finger hastily ripped through the envelopes seal, a relieved sigh escaping her mouth as her eyes dropped to the signed name.

She read the brief letter, her heart rapidly taking on the weight of a hefty boulder as her eyes stopped on one name... *Simon*... Her eyes read on. *Simon can't live without you, Ocean. He will, I fear, end up in the gutter...* She squeezed her eyes tightly to obliterate the stark written words; unable to stop them seeping through, jumping off the page and into her guilty conscience, where they started their elaborate process of skilfully and determinedly suffusing her heart with blame; cold, raw, stark and, oh, so very real it hurt to the core of her being... *Simon can't live without you, Ocean. He will, I fear, end up in the gutter...* The haunting words weaved in and out of her mind, threatening never to leave her in peace. Like handling a burning piece of coal, she threw Maria's letter on to the kitchen table, hastily changed into a swimsuit, threw a floral kaftan on top and rushed out the door. Within minutes, she was walking the soft sands of the desolate beach, silent words of blame torturously burning in her head.

Discarding her kaftan on the white sand she ran into the cool water, wading deeper and deeper, until the mighty ocean lifted her and she fell into its rhythm, swimming further and further away from the shore, willing the water to wash away the haunting words and the image they portrayed.

For half an hour, she vigorously swam; powerfully, skilfully for she was an accomplished swimmer. With each strong stroke, Maria's words held her less and less in their powerful grip until they vanished and, in their place, a calming peace began to suffuse her whole body, soul and mind, until she felt totally at one with her friend and namesake, the ocean.

She stepped out of the water sometime later feeling totally refreshed; her mind clear and decisive as she said to herself, *I am not responsible for Simon; Simon is responsible for Simon.* Slipping into her kaftan she sat on the warm, white sand and gazed into the distance where ocean met sky. Her mind clear of all thoughts, her eyes caught sight of a lone figure striding confidently towards the mighty waves, his surfboard gripped by his hand, and her mind drifted... *Perhaps she had been too hasty in dismissing Ekewaka out of her life, after all...*

Chapter One Hundred and Twelve
England

She watched and waited until the coast was clear, approached the house and knocked on the door. Her heaving heart was heavy and troubled and in the very act of betrayal, as she raised her fingers and gave the door another few knocks.

The door opened. Sunken eyes rose and what he saw made his heart race uncontrollably. "Maria! What on earth are you doing here? How did you know where to find me? Does Han…"

"Please let me in, Simon." Maria urged for having seen Natasha leave the house, she had no inkling when she would be back.

Bewildered he extended the door and she followed his skinny frame inside; taking no heed of the drab décor and clothes-strewn surroundings, her serious eyes directly focussed on her brother-in-law, one hand in her coat pocket withdrawing a large envelope.

For a split second, he dared to hope she'd brought him correspondence from Ocean Tia, his heart beating like a frenzied drum. His eyes followed her hand, his racing heart deflating at Maria's words. "If Hanale knew I was here, Simon; he would never, ever trust me again." She closed her eyes as if to obliterate the potential scenario, as ominous seconds ticked laboriously on and Simon's fate lay in the balance. Silently she handed him the envelope, after which she stated clearly and concisely, "Go and mend your marriage; do whatever it takes before it is too late, Simon." Turning she walked out the door, leaving him to stare down at the wad of cash in his hands, her words intermingling with the words spoken by the tramp he'd met in the park.

Chapter One Hundred and Thirteen
Kauai

Ekewaka's head was infiltrated with one thought… Ocean Tia; her letter having reignited his resolve to entice her into his web. He had never failed where the seduction of wahines were involved; he most certainly did not intend to fail, whether or not she had given him the green light. Minutes after the plane landed, he gathered his thoughts and stepped confidently into the isle of the plane.

She saw him from afar. Her heart raced, her fingers remained tightly clenched by her sides as she willed her heart to still; it accelerated, the beats becoming faster and faster with each approaching footstep Ekewaka made, until it reversed its fast rhythmic beat, stopped and froze and the only thing she was aware of was the rapping on the door and his cheerful voice drifting to her ears, make her legs turn to jelly. "Aloha! Ocean; Aloha!"

For a second or two, she had the impulse to run out the back door. *Where to?* She did not know where to; anywhere… She stood perfectly still on the spot, her dark eyes fixed on the figure, watching it boldly push the glass door open and walk inside; his mouth curving into a warm smile, his dark eyes twinkling; his presence making her want to shrivel up and die while, simultaneously, yearning to leap to the highest heaven.

"Ocean." He said softly, taking off his colourful lei and placing it around her neck; pecking her cheek and sending a thousand tiny electric sparks throughout her entire body.

"Aloha, Ekewaka." She managed to dredge out the greeting, her mouth bone dry to further words; for, what could she say? *Why have you come here, when I specifically stated in my letter that you shouldn't; but, that I am secretly pleased you're here?* Unconsciously she stared at him; seeing not him but Simon as conflicting thoughts, words, questions circled round and round in her head.

He broke the frosty silence, waking her up from her private reverie. "Ocean, it's so very good to see you."

Aware his eyes were on her she diverted her eyes from him, turned away from him and headed towards the kitchen for no particular purpose, except to get away from his magnetic presence; her ears fully attune to his approaching footsteps, giving her no means of escape. Looking out on to the array of assorted colourful blooms she asked, "Why are you here, Ekewaka? You know I have mounds of wo…"

"Everyone needs a respite from work." He cut into her words. "Even you," he added, making her furiously search for an adequate response to match his sensible statement and found none. Instead, she felt the gentle touch of his broad hand on her arm, making her instantly freeze apart from her heart which, once again, commenced its unruly beating; his next words making the beating stop. "I couldn't get you out of my mind, Ocean, and boy, oh boy, did I try."

She heard his light chuckle and, together with his words, they seared deep into her conscience. "I am a married woman, Ekewaka." She stated coldly her eyes locking with his; but, this time she felt nothing but overwhelming guilt.

"Yes I know, Ocean. And I told you before that I am not asking for your hand in marriage."

"What are you asking for, Ekewaka?"

"I am asking for your friendship, Ocean."

His words seeped deep into the depths of her heart of reasoning and there she found her own shortfall; for, *hadn't she regretted his absence?* "Friendship?" She questioned.

"Friendship; only friendship; now tell me, Ocean; what harm is there in a mere friendship?"

Her lips broke out into an involuntary smile.

"I thought so." He smiled back, secretly notching *Battle One* in his favour.

Chapter One Hundred and Fourteen

Simon stepped off the plane into Kauai's balmy sunshine; bitter regrets cleaving to him and a barrage of lamentable memories crashing into his head, as he severely admonished his weakness in taking Maria's money, abandoning Natasha and *their* unborn baby and heading to the other side of the world. "Ocean Tia." Her name like liquid honey poured out his mouth, making a couple of strangers look his way; her mere name making his heart simultaneously swell and deflate, with equal measures of love and dread; his guts twisting and wrenching with nervous apprehension and his feet itching to turn and run back on to the plane. He walked on; each step feeling heavier than the last as his whirling, fuzzy mind staunchly disallowed him to formulate a coherent strategy, to claw back his first true love.

Nervously his tightly clenched fingers knocked on the glass door, his toes curling and uncurling in the uncomfortable confines of his socks and highly polished shoes, his fingers dropping to his tie and loosening the knot, the beads of sweat making his neck clammy, his anxious eyes staring unflinchingly through the glass door, seeing only a well-polished floor and pristine white walls against which, here and there, were dotted large potted palms and a couple of ornate vases, on highly polished wooden side tables, displaying splendid arrays of exotic blooms. Moving to one side, he peered through the ceiling-to-floor windows at the side of the house, before he moved on and glanced through the kitchen window and finally turned in the opposite direction, where he stood wondering which path to take.

The heat of the mid-morning sun determined his next move and, swiftly taking off his jacket and tie and undoing the top buttons of his shirt he made his way to the one place, he knew, would grant him some respite from the oppressive heat; a place where he would plan his next course of action.

Striding on to the quiet beach, he haphazardly threw his holdall against the trunk of a palm, sat down with his back against its trunk and threw off his restricted footwear, curling his toes into the warm grains of sand as he luxuriated in their comforting texture, as the gentle breeze coming off the ocean began to revive his drooping spirit; his eyes focussing on the distant billows rolling, folding in on themselves and crashing down with long, haunting moans of defeat before they rose once more. His mind drifted to the very first time he had walked on the beach with his sweetheart; the hypnotic image of... *her walking by his side, her long fingers entwined with his, her long silky hair sweeping against his bare arm...* thrust a jagged, painful blade into the centre of his heart, making him immediately rise and, with his hand, consciously swipe the image out of his mind. Picking up his holdall he threw it on to his shoulder, turned right and started walking. Destination... unknown; his plan had not been formulated.

Unwaveringly his eyes fixed on one area of the beach where, in the distance, he saw a figure walking away from the heaving ocean. Surfboard in hand, the figure approached a seated figure and pecked her on the cheek. *It was strange,* Simon thought, *that he had not noticed the couple earlier.* His eyes remained on the duo as they sat side by side, seemingly enjoying each other's company. Turning away, willing the raw pain to leave his heart, he made his solitary way back to Ocean Tia's house; the house that was once his home.

In the shadows and shade of overhanging blooms and tropical foliage, he sat, his heart failing to abate its merciless grinding, his thoughts scattered, his stomach churning. How long he sat in his hiding place he did not know, neither did he care; for, there was nowhere else to go.

Faint echoes of female laughter made his whole body jerk. Eyes darted hither and thither around the beautiful garden; everything was perfectly still, as if the garden was captured in an exotic oil painting; his ears aware that the laughter, sprinkled with snippets of conversation, were becoming clearer, drawing nearer. His heart stopped; froze; reignited and beat furiously, threatening to jump out of his tightly clenched chest, his eyes on two figures; one figure holding a surfboard tightly in his grasp, his eyes focussing on the woman by his side, while his free hand held her hand as they approached the glass door and stepped inside, as Simon's world came crashing down on him from all sides, suffocating him with the debris of the fall making him gasp for air. He closed his eyes against the closed glass door and willed Hell to swallow him up, where he could burn for eternity in his self-imposed misery.

Thirty-three minutes later his eyes were still fixed on the door which was closed to him. Jumbled up erratic thoughts flitted in and out of his head. *Who was this guy on the scene? What association had he with Ocean Tia? How long—when—where—why?* The unanswered questions brought him a strange sense of karma. *Justice was doing its job, wasn't it? For, wasn't it he, Simon Teal, who had strayed from the marital bed? Wasn't it he, Simon Teal, who had brought Natasha Parks into Ocean's life and broken her heart? Wasn't it he, Simon Teal, who had betrayed his beloved wife?*

A desperate rush of urgency invaded every throbbing vein in his body; to get away from this place as fast and far away as possible; to get on the first plane back home and to join Ocean's nemesis, Natasha, in her bed.

Chapter One Hundred and Fifteen

One foot in front of the other he walked, trotted, ran accelerating his speed and increasing the distance between his estranged wife, the woman he once loved; still loved; the woman who was no longer his wahine. Abruptly he stopped as he came face-to-face with a familiar figure, making his heart sink further into the depths of despair.

"Simon!"

His heart beating like the clappers, he raised his eyes to his acquaintance, his heart still racing furiously, while Makamae tried to curb his look of surprise failing miserably. "I. I..." Simon closed his mouth, opened it to dry words and closed it firmly shut, his eyes still fixed on the man before him.

"Simon, my friend." Makamae placed his plump hand on Simon's shoulder and focussed his wise, brown eyes directly on him, his voice soft but serious. "Does Ocean know you are on the island?"

Ocean Ocean – Ocean... Her name infiltrated Simon's mind and soul and burned deep... deep into his heart singeing its roots.

"Simon, does O—"

"I heard you, Makamae." Silently Simon shook his head.

"Then she must know, my friend." Makamae patted Simon's shoulder encouragingly, sending a stark array of icy shivers up and down the younger man's spine. Speech which had temporarily deserted Simon now came forth in torrents.

"No; no, Makamae." He untangled his eyes from Ocean Tia' confidante and took a firmer grip of his holdall dangling by his side. "Ocean must never know I was here; she must never, ever know. Promise me, Makamae; promise me that you will never tell her. Promise me." He said the last words with brute finality, shrugging Makamae's hand away from his shoulder and breaking out in a run leaving a speechless, bemused Hawaiian staring in Simon's direction, as the retreating figure quickly made a good distance between them.

As Makamae proceeded to walk questions suffused his mind and, with these questions, came more questions which all stemmed from one rooted question. *Was it in Ocean Tia's well-being to inform her of her husband's presence on the island?* This question, and all others relating to it, tortured his head and brought conflicting scenarios to the forefront. Any which way he went about it, he firmly concluded, would inevitably betray either Ocean or Simon.

Oblivious to her husband's arrival on Kauai and the scene he had witnessed, and Makamae's secret dilemma, Ocean's friendship with Ekewaka was growing deeper with each passing day. She found, to her surprise, that he was fun to be with and, to her further surprise, he was not after her body. In the five days since his arrival, he had proved to her that he was kind, thoughtful, patient, respectful; a true gentleman and so she was willing to spend more time with her new friend.

Ocean Tia's natural beauty and exuberance of life intoxicated Ekewaka. Taking a sip of his cool pineapple juice he glanced through his morning newspaper, dropping it on the table unable to concentrate. Two things niggled him. One, he knew, he could overcome with time and patience; the other went far deeper and could be hard to accomplish, if not impossible.

He took another sip of juice, gazing distractedly through the ceiling-to-floor window. Bedding Ocean would be a challenge; she didn't seem the type of woman to readily jump into bed with any Tom, Dick or Harry. Why should she? After all she undoubtedly had her pick of men. *He would,* he told himself, *have to play the long game.* And, never having been down that particular route before, he wasn't sure how he was going to play it. He was, however confident that, sooner or later, he would achieve the end result.

The other challenge would be a tougher nut to crack; it was the deep rooted sadness imbedded in her mysterious eyes. It was, he reflected, not only evident in her eyes but in her laugh, her words; her touch and in every single breath she took. The true Ocean Tia, he felt, lay deeply buried beneath the outward façade and only when he got to know the true Ocean Tia would he truly begin to know her; only then would he be able to pick the fruit of his endeavours.

Chapter One Hundred and Sixteen

Work was her solace and her secret graveyard, where she could temporarily bury all unwanted thoughts, anxieties, problems and focus entirely on the work what needed to be done.

Hope Sanctuary currently housed three homeless locals and one young man, of about twenty years of age, who had arrived on Kauai full of expectations, and even wilder dreams; only to end up living the unenviable life of a destitute beach bum until one morning, whilst wobbling about on the beach, trying to shrug off the remnants of a hangover, Makamae found him and brought him to safety, whereupon Solomao took a particular interest in the new arrival, taking him under his wing and, while his attention was focussed on the young destitute, the thought of alcohol was not a thought in the reforming drunk's mind. Ocean Tia took all this in.

But, while everything was running smoothly at the sanctuary and her friendship with Ekewaka continued to grow, the sadness in Ocean's eyes pervaded her soul; a stubborn, selfish sadness which refused to leave, no matter how hard she worked, or what effort she made in trying to stifle it. It stayed rigidly put. It was a part of her and she a part of it.

Like two ghosts, Hanale and Maria floated in and out of her mind, silently thrusting the blade of betrayal into her heart and, hot on the heels of betrayal came Simon and the crushing, overwhelming feeling of failure. She picked up the official looking envelope from her highly polished floor.

Chapter One Hundred and Seventeen

Once more her eyes ran to the first word on the page and reread the contents; hot, biting tears blurring her vision and falling on to the trembling paper in her hands, making two words merge into one grey splodge. Roughly swiping the tears away with the back of her hand, she reread the text one final time, before stuffing the paper and envelope into the depths of a drawer. The tap… tap… tap on the door made her jump, her heart beating furiously. He was the last person she wanted to see.

"Makamae." She said softly trying to conceal the evident tremor in her voice.

He detected it saying nothing on the matter as his eyes took in her anxious countenance. He'd clearly come at a most inconvenient time, he concluded, as he searched for an excuse for his ill-timed visit; for, *to broach her with information about Simon was clearly not the right time.* Before he sat down, he'd heard her heartbroken words, throwing more fuel on his fire of confusion, as he stared at the woman before him.

"Simon wants a divorce." She repeated clearly, concisely her words slicing through Makamae's rampaging thoughts, as he failed to comprehend Simon's request of a divorce, coupled with his recent appearance on the island *unless… unless…* his sole purpose was to assert his request in person and for, whatever reason, he failed to do so. His eyes lifted to Ocean where, beneath her façade, he saw a broken young woman; trying without success to conceal her harrowing pain. His heart went out to her, feeling some of her raw anguish.

"Simon is on the island, Ocean." In the second, he finished his sentence Makamae wished he could cut his tongue out, his eyes witnessing a new torment in her eyes. His mouth opened and closed to non-verbal sympathetic words; heavy silence enveloping them crushing their spirits, as the soft tick-tocking of the wall clock bore the only evidence that time had not died. *Tick—tock—tick—tock—tick—tock…* The sound of time grew louder and louder in Ocean's head, crushing dead the sounds of the distant ocean waves, as the passing of time, intermingled with the heavy stillness, and marched on… and on… and on…

Conflicting thoughts weaved their confusion in Makamae's head his still, unwavering eyes fixed on his friend who sat still as a stone, hands clenched tightly on top of her lap, her eyes staring directly ahead. *What did she see?* He asked himself his heavy beating heart going out to her, as time continued its relentless march.

Simultaneously they both jumped out their depressing reveries to the shrill sound of the phone, joining forces with the clock, reminding them that life goes on. Simultaneously their bodies returned to their immobile states. Makamae's eyes shot to Ocean Tia as she sat impassive to the phones shrill demands; to the never-ending *tick-tocking* of the clock; to the presence of her friend and confidante; seeing only the stark image of her husband.

"Yes?" The phone stopped its monotonous ringing. Makamae extended the receiver to Ocean, whereupon she rose and walked to the glass door, her heart clenching tightly as her friend revealed the identity of the caller.

The second he heard Makamae's voice Ekewaka's spirit deflated, a barrage of questions bombarding his head. *Who was this guy on the other end of the phone? What was he doing in Ocean Tia's home?* And the definitive question, *Why did she refuse to answer his call?* For long minutes he sat and pondered. Finally, a decision was made.

Chapter One Hundred and Eighteen

He sat nursing his Mai Tai, staring into its golden-brown depths and seeing nothing but his own dark misery. He had travelled half way round the world to try and salvage the broken fragments of his marriage; he was about to leave with his marriage crushed on the rocks, without any hope of being rescued. A cord of raw bitterness tightened around his heart and, in the depths of his wretchedness, he saw a haunting image as clear as day… *as the figure strode away from the roaring ocean, surfboard in hand, approached the seated woman and pecked her on the cheek*… This image was quickly replaced by another; more starker and real in its portrayal, as… *hand-in-hand they stepped inside and closed the glass door behind them*… As the images merged into one he brought the glass up to his lips, fervently willing the potency of the alcohol to take over. Grabbing his bulging holdall he walked away from the drained glass.

"Simon."

His head, arms, legs, torso, heart and guts froze as the soft sound of his name reverberated in his head, his expressionless eyes staring vacantly into the realms of oblivion, while his mind asked the gods that prevailed what kind of cruel, perverse, despicable joke they were playing on him. *I am going; I am leaving the island; isn't that enough?* He wanted to scream at them.

"Simon." The cruel echo persisted.

His feet hurried forward, his head refusing to turn and acknowledge his intruder. The feel of a light touch on his arm making him stop and turn. His heart stopped.

Eyes beheld eyes and froze in instant time, as two hearts pounded and all around people bustled about, while husband and wife stared into their united past and into the vast abyss of regrets; betrayal, pure and undiluted, stabbing them in the core of their hearts.

"O-Ocean…" He finally managed to squeeze out of his arid mouth, his fast beating heart burning with unquenchable love.

Her dark eyes did not leave him; her lips curving into the faintest of smiles as she tried to formulate some words; any words to douse the unbearable, underlying tension. "Makamae told me you were on the island, Simon. Wh—"

"Makamae," he cut in icily, feeling the thrust of betrayal in his heavy heart.

"Don't blame him, Simon. I knew he was holding something back I practically forced him to tell me." She lied uncharacteristically.

He smiled to himself; a sad smile, knowing Ocean Tia well enough to know that, often, she placed the unjustifiable burden of blame on her own shoulders. "What are you doing here, Ocean?" His tone was detached, as if his words and voice did not belong to him; belying the raging war of emotions he was so desperately trying to quell.

"I will ask you the same thing." Her tone, like her eyes, was steady and calm.

As his eyes gazed into the eyes he adored, he yearned to scream out, *I came to stop divorce proceedings… I came to beg for your forgiveness—I came to tell you how desperately in love I am with you.*

Averting her eyes from him she dropped them to the floor beneath. "I received the papers, Simon."

And his heart broke in two as he felt his whole world, and with it his last hope, come crashing in on him from all sides. An intercom announcement temporarily shook him out of his black nightmare. "I've got a plane to catch, Ocean." He stated turning away, taking a firmer grip of his luggage, desperate now to get away from her intoxicating presence; unable to stand the excruciating pain a second longer.

"Stay… please."

He felt a tighter hold on his arm while, simultaneously, his feet turned to jelly. Cautiously he raised his incredulous eyes to her and in her eyes he saw a reflection of his own act of betrayal.

"We need to talk, Simon. We cannot end things in this way."

He registered each word she said and, while his hope was raised in her last seven words; it was dashed to the ground with Natasha Park's crashing image. Involuntarily he emitted a deep, long, jagged sigh. The end was still nigh.

Hastily, as much as his fuzzy mind would allow, he weighed up the consequences of his potential actions. *To leave her now, without any explanation from either side, would,* he thought, *be foolhardy but to stay; to pick to shreds the minute details of his contemptible behaviour, was not a prospect he would relish either.*

In the moments of conflicting hesitancy, a sharp image crashed into his mind, obliterating his reservation and, as the final call was announced, he took a firmer hold of his bag and proceeded to walk.

Chapter One Hundred and Nineteen

Her eyes strayed into the distance as the tail-end of the plane was enveloped by the cloud, leaving her heart laden with a new wave of pain and regret. For long minutes, her glazed eyes lingered on the Hawaiian sky, unable to look away; unable to walk away and face the undeniable fact that the wheels of divorce proceedings had moved. *After all, hadn't Simon personally sacrificed his own time and money to confirm that point? It was over.*

He sat rigidly in his seat, his ears attune to the chatty girl sitting next to him; hearing her but not registering her words. A broken man he sat staring into oblivion, bereft of his love and partly because a cursed image had invaded his mind, the green-eyed monster had reared its ugly head and his fate had been determined.

As he had walked away from Ocean Tia he knew, deep in the depths of his sorrowful heart, that he had taken the wrong path; he had been perfectly aware that he could have turned back and begged for her forgiveness. But the flames of burning envy had inflamed his conflicting emotions, propelling him to walk away from the woman he loved, increasing his pace with each departing footstep; willing the image of Ocean, and her new man, to abandon him and leave him to stew in his own desperate fate.

His prayer had been answered. The image had evaporated replaced by a new image stark, real and final as his future unravelled before him. He closed his eyes against Natasha Park's half-dressed body, closing his ears to the torturing sounds of ravenous, consensual sex where he played no part.

Ocean Tia stepped into the garden and found Ekewaka seated on a wicker chair on the veranda. "Aloha." He called out, his cheerful greeting sending waves of dread through her. She approached him her glassy eyes rising to him. "Hey, hey, Ocean; what on earth is the matter?" Lithely he rose and stepped towards her enveloping her in his strong, muscular arms. She did not resist; all grains of energy had been sapped by Simon, transforming her into a desolate shell. Instead she fell readily into Ekewaka's inviting embrace, where they stood locked in each other's presence, while silence cast its soothing veil over them, allowing only the gentle swish of palms, stirred by the warm breeze coming off the ocean. And in the security of his warm embrace, Ocean Tia found temporary solace; a brief gift of serenity, where she could feel nothing but total peace.

It was Ekewaka who slowly pulled away from her, gently positioning her at arm's length, while he looked into her unfathomable eyes. "What is it, Ocean?" He asked concern lacing his steady eyes.

Eyes looked deep into eyes. The only certainty he had was that the wahine standing before him was troubled and this knowledge brought with it an uncertainty of its own. *Was she worth it; or, was she going to be more trouble than she was worth?* He asked himself. An out of control awkward smirk slid on to his face. He had never been in this kind of scenario before and it was certainly the last thing he had expected. He had envisaged nothing but a few fun times' the prelude to an easy lay. No problems; no hassle; no ties. And, while he was contemplating his next move, she made it for him.

Walking away from him she turned and stated coldly, "Whatever this was, Ekewaka, it is well and truly over. I do not wish to see you again."

He stood glued to the spot stunned, his mouth opening and shutting to dry words, his eyes on the beauty walking away from him.

Chapter One Hundred and Twenty
England

He stood at the door and lowered his fingers which had been about to knock, his heart and guts clenching with heavy dread. Abruptly he turned and walked hastily away. On and on, he walked until he arrived at a different door and, this time, his nervous fingers knocked, his restless feet waited. The door opened and eyes locked. The door began to close, only to halt as it came into contact with Simon's stubborn foot. "Please hear me out. Please…" For long torturous seconds Simon waited for the door to bang in his face, his eyes nervously peeled on the figure before him.

"What do you want, Teal?" Hanale hissed.

"I. I want a chance, Hanale." Years later Hanale still couldn't fathom out what made him relent. Man stood opposite man; brother-in-law facing brother-in-law with nothing to say to each other and, simultaneously, a hundred and more things to spew in each other's face. Finally Hanale spoke. "Why are you here, Simon?"

"I need you to believe in me, Hanale;" came the stark reply.

The loud chuckle reverberated in Simon's head and weighed ominous and heavy in his heart; it was a laugh of total incredulity. A look of raw disbelief speared from Hanale's cold eyes. "You want me to believe in you, Simon, after what you have done to my family; after what you have done to Ocean. Are you stark raving mad, man?"

Hope in Simon's heart plummeted but a tiny spark still shone and on this he banked his fate. He laid his cards on the table and having relayed the whole truthful story, from the raw beginning to its biter end, his shameful eyes dropped to the carpet, afraid to catch Hanale's eyes for fear of what they may see there, while his heart pounded harder and harder with each laborious beat, his guts relentlessly twisting and gnawing. He did not see Hanale rise from the sofa. "You better go." He heard the echo of his words.

At the door, Simon turned. "Will you think about what I have told you, Hanale?" After what seemed an eternity, a tiny spark of hope reignited.

"I will think about what you said." Hanale firmly closed the door.

Chapter One Hundred and Twenty-One
Kauai

Ocean Tia threw her whole self into her work, it was her only solace; however, her respite, was short-lived. Late one afternoon, as she was peering out the window, she spotted him. Without a doubt it was Solomao and her heart sank as she watched his staggering frame; her eyes taking in his untidy clothes and the half empty bottle waving precariously in his swaying hand. In seconds, she was standing in the same spot he had vacated, her eyes scanning the immediate area. He'd gone; simply vanished and she could not fathom out which direction he had taken.

She took the long way back home, along the boundary of the desolate beach and along narrow winding lanes, the sweet fragrance of flowering blooms failing to quell her rising anxiety.

Pouring herself a large pineapple juice, her eyes flitted to the silent phone, and placing down the glass she picked up the receiver, her finger dialling one number after another. Silence—*click*...

"Hello."

As if holding a burning lump of coal she dropped the receiver.

"Hello... Aloha... Is anyone there?" The distant softly spoken voice asked bringing a sharp, inexplicable pain to Ocean's heart and, with it, the staggering image of Solomao, her racing heart threatening to jump out of her chest. She picked up the receiver. He listened attentively to every word she said and, as she placed the receiver back on to its cradle, her racing heart subsided, the pain vanished, and a tinge of hope emerged.

As the majestic sun began its royal descent to its rendezvous with the ocean, Makamae was rapping on Ocean Tia's door and, without waiting to be invited, casually strode in calling, "Aloha."

His welcome voice drifted to the kitchen and her heart lifted. Makamae, her friend and confidante, had not let her down.

His observant eyes scanned her drawn face. He plunged into the deep. "When we find Solomao, we must persuade him to leave the island."

"Why?" Ocean's eyes shot to Makamae.

"Because, Ocean, he has to disassociate himself from his old haunts; he has to distance himself from any influencing acquaintances and the best way, I feel, is a new start."

"Where?"

Makamae allowed the long seconds to tick away in silence for maximum effect. Finally he stated, "The Big Island." His eyes remained firmly fixed on his friend where they witnessed eyes flinch, giving him the proof he wanted; Ocean Tia's feelings for Ekewaka had not diminished, no matter how much she may object. Again silence reigned as thoughts of Ekewaka invaded Ocean's mind and, with them, a heavy surge of regret.

"No; no... no." She shook her head vehemently from side to side, refusing to raise her eyes to her friend, lest he see in them her false disapproval. "No!" She stated with finality adding, "Even if it was feasible for Solomao to go there, he is in no position to finance the venture."

"I will finance him."

And as Makamae's words crashed into her conscious reasoning, they brought with them a ghost from her past, which rapidly submerged into the present; a ghost of long ago when a kind stranger from overseas helped her.

Makamae rose. "Think about it, Ocean."

She heard the door click behind him. He was gone; his words remained and buried themselves deep into her mind as the ghost of her past re-emerged and words escaped her mouth. "What kind of a future would I have had without your help, Alan?" And now, she mused... *What kind of future would Solomao have if he remained here on this island?* His fate, she knew, lay in the balance; but, if she was to help, as once Alan had come to her rescue, then she would have to overcome one major obstacle.

Chapter One Hundred and Twenty-Two

One stark image permeated Ocean Tia's thoughts; Ekewaka was the key to Solomao's salvation. He was also the last person on the Hawaiian Islands she wished to contact. If only Akamu and Liliana had not gone to Europe, but they had and she knew no other natives on the Big Island she could call on for assistance. Meticulously she worked through one scenario after another, in which Ekewaka did not feature; switching from one fruitless idea to another until all ideas led to Ekewaka where they loomed larger, clearer and more hopeful... *He has to disassociate himself from his old haunts; he has to distance himself from any influencing acquaintances...* Makamae's words rang loud and clear.

Grabbing her sunhat she slipped into her flip-flops and ran out the house, out of the garden and down the narrow, winding lanes and on to the white, warm sand, the roaring ocean suffusing her ears; her sanctuary.

Already the fiery sun was uniting with the ocean in its nightly ritualistic rendezvous, casting an inexplicable sadness in Ocean Tia's heart. This evening the solemn ceremony brought her an extra burden; the dilemma of Solomao's future.

She sat on the cooling sand, her eyes on the last golden-red speck of sun and then it was no more. Gone Would Solomao be prepared to leave his beloved island? She closed her eyes. She had once left the island; her unquenchable heartache giving her no peace until the day she returned. Even if he was willing to abandon Kauai, there was still one major obstacle she had to overcome.

Her namesake and friend, the ocean, did not bring her one iota of peace this evening. Turning her back on the dark, mighty swell, she placed Solomao's fate in the lap of the gods.

Chapter One Hundred and Twenty-Three

Turning the envelope over and over in his hand, a victorious smile dancing on his lips, he eased his finger in and opened the seal. Withdrawing the folded paper, his questioning eyes on the familiar handwriting as, in seconds, his smile withered. This was not what he had been expecting. He reread the short letter, slumped down on a nearby chair, his eyes still glued to the words, seeing only a tropical beauty who had resisted his charms. His rapid heartbeat decreased to a less dangerous level; now becoming laborious and heavy, his eyes hypnotised by the signed name. Yet, despite the evidence on the page, a tiny hope shimmered. She wanted his help. His victorious smile reappeared.

The shrill ringing of the phone brought her sharply out of her reverie, her eyes darting to and staring at the receiver demanding immediate attention. She let it ring, her ears trying to adjust to the silence when it suddenly stopped. Its penetrating ring cut through the eerie stillness once more. "Hello." She barked uncharacteristically.

"Ocean... Aloha."

She froze, the gently spoken greeting slicing through her consciousness. For heavy, suspended seconds time gave her a chance to compose herself, as she desperately urged her words not to shrivel up and die on her lips. "Yes; this is Ocean."

The conversation lasted barely three minutes and left her feeling totally deflated. It left Ekewaka scoring an imaginary point in his favour.

She fixed herself a Mai Tai and sat on the veranda, pondering each word of their brief conversation. *It was,* she thought, *friendly but lacking in Ekewaka's usual exuberance.* Yes, he said he would try and help and, yes, he would get back to her regarding any news regarding the matter; but, there was no personal touch in the communication; no words to indicate that he was missing her, which led to one conclusion. *Whatever feelings he had, had dissipated.*

Inhaling a deep, ragged sigh she took a generous swallow of the amber liquid, swilled the rest down the sink and proceeded to locate Makamae and tell him the news, as she forcibly tried to push Ekewaka firmly out of her mind.

Ekewaka, full of renewed hope, vowed to pull out all the stops to help his friend, and potential lover. He had good connections on the Big Island and knew, without a doubt, he was in a position to help her friend, Solomao. Simultaneously he began to make enquiries and began planning on rebuilding his links with the woman he wanted. The latter, he knew, would be a slow process but, without a doubt, he knew, that sooner or later she would end up in his bed; or, he in hers. *First things first,* he told himself, *he would have to gain her trust and then—*

Chapter One Hundred and Twenty-Four
England

After he had closed the door on Simon, Hanale sat deeply immersed in conflicting, fragmented, jumping scenarios. On the one hand, his brother-in-law seemed determined to change his course in life; on the other hand, flashing scenarios of Ocean Tia walking hand in hand with a handsome surfer, loomed in his confused head, and added to the confusing mix was the stark fact that Simon had freely given his sperm to father Natasha Park's child. As his whirling mind reverted to Ocean and her boyfriend, echoes of a familiar voice infiltrated his scattered thoughts. "Hanale… Hanale…" The echo grew louder, penetrated deeper; his eyes darting to Maria standing before him, holding his sleeping son in her arms. "Hanale, you were away with the fairies; anywhere nice?"

She noticed the grimace on his face as he shook his head. "Nowhere you would like."

"Tell me." She passed him their sleeping child, hovering close by.

"Simon and his murky world," he replied nonchalantly, his eyes dropping to his slumbering son, his ears unable to banish the surprise in his wife's voice. "I don't want to talk about it, Maria." He rose, gave her back the sleeping infant and strode briskly out the room, leaving her to ponder.

In the garden, he wandered aimlessly amongst the red and yellow rose blooms, picking off a dead head now and again, his thoughts far away on the Island of Kauai and his half-sister, Ocean Tia; the beauty who had men at her feet. *But,* he wondered, *who was this surfer? Was he a true contender for her love or just simply a friend? Had Simon, through his own stupidity, lost forever his true love? How was he going to scramble his way back to decency? What part would Natasha Parks, and her bastard baby, play in his brother-in-law's future?* He shook his head from side to side, spotting and picking off another dead bloom. It was not for him to unravel.

Simon's head was full to bursting with one predominant thought. Once and for all, he determined, the baby issue had to be dealt with; only then could he begin to build bridges and start to repair his broken life.

He strode into the unlocked house; *after all,* he asked himself, *didn't he have a right of entrance?* All was quiet on the home front. Unusual Ominous Silent as the grave. "Natasha." He called waiting for a bout of raucous laughter; or, the sound of a squeaking bed to hit his ears. He approached the banister, his eyes rising with his voice. "Natasha." The suffocating heavy stillness and quietness unnerved his every sense. "Natasha!" He hollered, pounding up the stairs two at a time, as an eerie vision of a strangled Natasha laying naked on the bed, filtered through his mind; a ten pound note, next to a half drunken cheap bottle of wine, on the bedside table.

His eyes darted to an empty bottle of pills, laying on its side beside an empty bottle of vodka. His eyes flitted to a half-dressed torso as his scattered, uncontrolled thoughts whirled at two hundred kilometres per second. "Oh my God—Natasha…" The words squeezed out his arid mouth as he stared at her unresponsive face; snatching the phone receiver he dialled three identical numbers.

Hanale arrived as the ambulance, with its flashing blue lights and screeching siren, drove off at top speed and, in its wake, stood a pale-faced, tight-lipped, finger clenching man, his stark eyes fixed on the disappearing vehicle; failing to feel the gentle touch of his brother-in-law's hand on his shoulder, hearing only the echo of the siren in his ears.

Time ticked laboriously on as the two men sat side by side; united and divided as the seconds, minutes and hours ticked on; men and women in white coats rushed in and out of a nearby room. Finally a grave looking man sporting steel-grey hair and steely eyes approached them, his serious eyes silently telling them what his lips had not yet uttered.

As his departing footsteps reverberated in their ears, Hanale turned to Simon and said, "I am sorry, mate." He meant every word.

After heavy, long minutes Simon rose. "I'm not." He stated vehemently and walked out, leaving Hanale in a state of perplexity.

Chapter One Hundred and Twenty-Five
Kauai

The receiver froze in her hand; the ice rapidly spreading to her heart and splaying in a fan of frozen shards and concurrent flames of fire.

"Ocean; are you there?" The voice repeated; ears subjected to a deathly silence on the other end of the receiver. "Oc—"

"Yes... 'em... yes, I am here, Ekewaka," she replied falteringly, her voice cracked and stilted, as her long fingers nervously twizzled the cord round and round.

"Ocean, I am in a position to help you."

Simultaneously her heart leaped and plummeted; his next words hitting her ferociously as her fingers went round and round and round and round the tightly clasped cord, until they could go round no more.

"The guys, who are willing to donate substantial amounts of money into this venture, insist on seeing you in person before the papers are signed and we are given the green light. Will that be okay with you?"

Ominous silence bombarded his ears once more as a tsunami wave of apprehension, mingled with regret, washed over Ocean Tia as she silently condemned the man on the other end of the phone for, unwittingly, stirring up her emotions. *If only,* she closed her eyes, *she could turn back the clock; if only she could dissolve this Casanova's involvement; if only...*

"Ocean; did you hear me? The line seems so ba..."

"I heard you," she cut in, one word echoing loudly in her head... *we... we... we... we... we...*

"Will all that I've related to you be okay with you?" His tone carried with it a tinge of impatience, which she did not detect as she silently screamed, *No! No! No! That will NOT be okay with me; for, when did my venture become our joint project?* As if to answer her silent question, dollar signs loomed into her mind and she slumped down on to the telephone seat, her fingers attempting to unravel themselves from their tight prison, as a wave of cold realisation swept over her. "I'll ring you back later, Ocean. The line is terrible."

Eyes stared unblinkingly into space as... *Solomao staggered on to the beach...* replaced seconds later by an image of a purposeful Solomao coming to the aid of others. *Perhaps,* she pondered, *Makamae was wrong.* Leaving her thoughts to ferment and come to their own conclusions, she rose.

They separated Makamae scouring one end of the beach; Ocean Tia the other. Half an hour later they met up, their faces dismal as both walked on in silence with only the background waves as their roaring companion.

Hours later, the sight that made her eyes dance was a dishevelled, stumbling drunk, staggering towards them; mumbling incoherent words as he gratefully fell into their outstretched arms. Ocean Tia's doubts were firmly laid to rest.

Her heart flickered as the dialling tone ceased and she felt herself jumping into unchartered waters. Seventeen minutes and thirteen seconds later Solomao's fate was sealed and so, she felt, was hers.

Chapter One Hundred and Twenty-Six
England

The news Simon had received at the hospital was the best news he could have possibly hoped to receive. *He was free!*

Yet, as he walked by Hanale's side, out of the confines of the hospital and into the fresh air, he felt his lungs suffused with a heaviness he could not breathe away; his feet felt leaden; his heart a dead weight. "You're coming home with me tonight, Simon." He half-heard his brother-in-law state; his feet plodding on; one foot in front of the other trudging on and on and... on.

In the warmth of Hanale and Maria's cosy home, he sat oblivious to Maria's compassionate words; deaf to his nephew's cries; inattentive to the weatherman announcing tomorrows mild weather; conscious only of his loss; for, despite Natasha, he had had a child in the making, his child, and now it was no more.

In the depths of the dark, moonless night his conflicting thoughts took centre stage and began their ghostly dance, haunting him mercilessly; all jostling for prime position and his undivided attention, as they clambered for the limelight. In one scene, Ocean Tia held a dead baby in her arms, his dead baby; her lips curled in a twisted, victorious smirk; in another scene he was staring down a dark hole, his body struggling to get out and always... always Natasha standing in the background, her red-lipstick mouth howling with raucous laughter. He jumped, his brow laced with beads of cold sweat, his stark eyes staring at nothing; for, all had disintegrated into nothing.

A black veil of despair shrouded his scattered, chaotic thoughts; an emptiness took root in his heart; the invisible mantle of desolation spreading through him like wildfire, burning away any new shoots of hope; a tight knot forming in his congested throat bringing with it an insidious craving, making his eyes dart to and remain on the mahogany cabinet. His feet followed suit, his fingers eagerly reaching and clasping the handle of the door, his ears attune to approaching footsteps as he silently cursed.

"We will have one drink together, Simon," said the intruder, "during which you can tell me everything."

Withdrawing his fingers, as if from a burning hot poker, Simon's eyes continued to glare longingly at the closed door of the drinks cabinet, his craving guts twisting with rage at his brother-in-law's inopportune timing.

"That's the deal, mate."

Hanale's words cut through Simon's want, need, and yearning; his craving becoming stronger with each passing second. Reluctantly he turned away from the soothing *medicine* behind the closed door, shaking his head from side to side. "There's nothing more to tell; I've told you everything." He said; his voice so quiet it was almost inaudible. Abruptly he rose and swept past Hanale. "I'm going."

"Don't go… please."

He heard the plea loud and clear; the click of the door behind him echoing in his ears long after the door had closed; his own words mingling with the reverberation. *There's nothing to tell… There's nothing to tell… There's nothing to tell… And yet,* his feet walked purposefully on, *there was so very much to tell.*

Chapter One Hundred and Twenty-Seven

Again and again he tried. The result was the same. The key would not turn in the lock; the solid wood before his face remained stubbornly closed. For long minutes, he stared at the peeled paint of the scuffed door, a dull shade of green showing beneath the first coat of brown paint which was equally dreary. Moving he peered through the living room window, the front room window, the kitchen window; all empty with no visible sign of life. His eyes rose. The bedroom curtains were closed; he could have sworn they had been opened before their hasty departure to the hospital. Running back to the door he banged ferociously, his eyes rising to the sound of an abrupt swish of a curtain, followed by a window opening. Natasha's head stuck out. "Go away," she hissed. Her appearance, coupled with the fury in her voice, added to his bemusement as he stood in a semi-like daze. "Get the fuck out of here, Teal." She yelled angrily, propelling him to snap out of his jumbled state of reasoning.

"This is my home, Natasha," he yelled back.

"Not anymore."

Her words hit him like a bolt of lightning. Grabbing any straw he could hold on to he pleaded, "We need to talk about the baby; our baby, Natasha."

Her red-lipstick mouth curled into a cruel smirk. "It was never your baby, Teal; now, fuck off to your precious Ocean Tia. If she's still desperate, she just might want what's left of you."

The loud bang of the closing window, and swish of the heavy curtain, went through him like a blunt-edged sword; her haunting words attacking him like uneven shards of broken glass from which, he knew, he would never recover. His exhausted body slumped to the doorstep, her lingering words hammering in his head. *It was never your baby, Teal.* Each thrashing word becoming louder, clearer... *It... was... never... your... baby... Teal... IT WAS NEVER YOUR BABY, TEAL!*... Until he felt his chaotic world fragment around him into minute pieces, shower down on him and suffocate all hope until he felt nothing at all.

How long he remained slumped on the doorstep he did not know; the gathering dusk told him it was a long time. Automatically his eyes strayed to the bedroom window. The curtains were open. A sudden, desperate urge struck him to pound on her door; to demand answers; to demand explanations. Words crashed into his head... *Fuck off to your precious Ocean Tia*... Her image drifted into his head, becoming clearer with each passing second. *Ocean Tia; the only woman he had ever truly loved; still loved; will always love... Ocean Tia...*

Withdrawing his glassy eyes from the window; himself from the doorstep, he walked out of Natasha Park's drive and out of her life.

Chapter One Hundred and Twenty-Eight

The Big Island

On their approach to the runway, Ocean Tia's eyes glanced at the tensed-faced passenger sitting by her side. Taking his unusually cold hand into hers she said softly, "Solomao; this is where you start your life." A reassuring smile followed her encouraging words. She saw the tension in his face lessen a fraction, though his fingers beneath hers tightened.

Solomao did not have exclusive anxiety rights; unbeknown to him he shared them with the woman sitting next to him, though her anxiety was founded on a particular human and not the island they were approaching. *Was she justified in involving Ekewaka? Yes,* the voice in her head replied. *Without Ekewaka's help, Solomao would have little hope.* Reassuringly she squeezed her friend's hand and he, in turn, forced a nervous smile. Her own heart pounded.

She spotted him before he espied his visitors, her racing heart threatening to jump out of her tight chest. If anything, he appeared to be more handsome than she had last seen him. Silently and fervently she prayed for composure.

Her prayer was partly answered as, outwardly, she exuded a cool and calm exterior while, inwardly, she felt her fast throbbing heart about to explode and her jellified feet melt beneath her. Pinning on her sunny smile, instinctively making Ekewaka's heart dance, she proceeded to walk forward.

In the seconds, he placed his fragrant lei around her neck and touched her cheek with a feather-like kiss, her whole body was suffused with currents of tiny, electrifying sparks, her feet about to buckle; thankful he did not notice the colour rising to her cheeks, as he turned to one side and placed a lei around Solomao's neck.

"Aloha; welcome to my island." He smiled at Solomao, fully aware of the colour deepening Ocean's face.

During the short drive along the coast, Ekewaka lavished his undivided attention on Solomao and Ocean Tia sighed a secret sigh of relief; thankful that she was seated comfortably in the back seat of the convertible, away from the seductive nearness of Ekewaka; though, automatically drawn in by the mellowness of his words. She forced her eyes and attention on the passing beaches some desolate, others not; yearning to be in the cool waters of the mighty Pacific, away from Ekewaka's soft voice; away from his intoxicating presence.

Soothed and lulled by soft tunes on the radio, intermingled with the sounds of distant waves her mind drifted to another time; another island far, far away; another man. A frown appeared in her smooth brow. *If only things had been different... If only she had gone to Paris with Simon all those years ago, instead of rushing to Lokemele's aid... If only Simon had not brought Natasha Parks to Alan's farewell luau... If only she could have given Simon a child... If only... If only...*

She had allotted herself one day on the Big Island. One day to make sure that Solomao was settled and then *fly* away from temptation. One day, she had determined, was more than enough; only to be contradicted by her fast beating heart.

It was decided between the three of them that, initially, Solomao would stay with Ekewaka in order to familiarise himself with the island. This also gave Ekewaka and his team time to finalise the finishing touches regarding the new sanctuary. He had argued the point that Ocean Tia should remain on the island to oversee it all; she flatly refused, arguing that Hope Sanctuary needed her more. She won. Begrudgingly he let her go on condition that she would return in one month's time; stay on the island for a week to see how everything was functioning and, of, course, attend the official grand opening.

Both started their secret countdown.

Chapter One Hundred and Twenty-Nine
England

He stood; a beggar pleading for clemency.

Hanale listened and opened the door. Maria listened and opened her heart and, while Hanale's past anger at Simon's behaviour had softened, Maria's prayers were all but answered; she knew that with a sorrowful and regretful heart came hope.

Hanale was not so hopeful. He had condemned his brother-in-law's treatment of Ocean as despicable and though Simon was an old friend and family, he was not entirely ready to forgive and forget; still, he listened.

Simon related all that had happened, warts and all; in his view he had nothing more to lose. Having lost his wife, his job, his home and his self-respect, there was only one way to go and that was up. He'd already been in Hell.

A heavy sigh exuded from Hanale's mouth; he had not been expecting such a raw, frank confession. His steady eyes remained fixed and unwavering on his brother-in-law. Remorse is what he saw and heard. Remorse is not what he had been expecting. It flummoxed him. He did not know which direction he should take with this knowledge; knowing only that Simon seemed truly sorry and hearing his admission that he was still deeply in love with Ocean Tia, his wife.

The first acknowledgement Hanale took on board; the second confession he could not readily digest; for, *how could Simon profess to love Ocean when he had been such a bastard to her? How could he proclaim his love for her when he treated her like shit? How could he possibly hope to win her back when he had thrown her to the lions?* Closing his eyes tightly he took in a deep, ragged breath.

Their eyes clashed and Simon's fate hung in the balance.

Chapter One Hundred and Thirty
Kauai

Makamae looked into eyes of anxiety and knew the source lay on the Big Island. "He'll be all right, you know." He smiled reassuringly.

Ocean Tia snapped out of her reverie, a tinge of guilt pervading her soul as she blatantly nodded. "Oh, I know Solomao will survive." She raised her eyes and her glass to her friend. "It's thanks to you, Makamae." The guilt tugged harder; it was not Solomao she had been thinking about.

For the past week, Ekewaka had invaded her thoughts and dreams; his image haunting her day and night in equal measures. Twenty-one days to go. Twenty-one days until she could see his cheerful face once more. Twenty-one days until she heard his mellow voice and saw his sensual smile. Twenty-one days. Tomorrow it will be twenty.

The thought of Ekewaka brought electrifying sparks making her whole body tingle, her heart to race and her sane mind to tell her this was ludicrous; to remind her that she was still a married woman, be it only in name.

She threw herself into her work only to find him there, staring up from a mound of paperwork; vigorously she tried to swim his image away only for his image to be riding the surf; she read profusely, entertained friends, wrote long letters to Akamu, Liliana and Solomao only for her uninvited intruder to emerge on the page.

Finally, the day arrived.

Chapter One Hundred and Thirty-One
England

Simon listened intently to his brother-in-law's suggestion, digesting every single word. It was going to be a long road; not an easy one to travel but he was willing to take the first step.

Maria was delighted that her persistent effort in subtly encouraging her husband to help Simon was bearing fruit. He listened and, after much deliberation, he offered Simon a place to stay.

Slowly... slowly, like the gradual untying of a strand of cotton from a reel, Simon unveiled his true self; though, the more he revealed, the less he understood about himself. *For how could he, Simon Teal, with the world at his feet and the beautiful Ocean Tia for his wife, have thrown it all away for the sake of a quick fuck?* He closed his eyes feeling the heavy tiredness of life, his ears attune to the running water as Hanale filled the kettle, and he drifted into the nightmare that was the beginning of the end. *If only he had not invited Natasha Parks to Alan's luau...* Of course she had accepted his invitation; she would have accepted a party at Lucifer's establishment if it meant hogging the limelight. *But,* he now wondered, *who was the true culprit; for, wasn't it he, Simon Teal, who had invited Natasha in the first place; knowing exactly how Ocean would feel? Wasn't it he, Simon Teal, who had blatantly and unashamedly cavorted with Natasha on the makeshift dance-floor? Yes,* yelled a loud voice, *it was he, SIMON TEAL, who was the true instigator, who had introduced unhappiness into the marriage.* "Ocean Tia must not be blamed; nor Natasha. Simon Teal was the prime mover; the bulldozer who caused the debris to fall." He shouted aloud for all the world to hear.

"Yes; it was you, Simon!"

Simon's eyes shot to Hanale, who was placing two mugs of steaming coffee on to the glass-topped table beneath.

Eyes clashed. Truth spoke silently making one heart beat heavily with black remorse; making Simon wish it would stop beating all together so that he could escape from his deep, dark well of stark desolation and black inner misery.

"What are you going to do, Simon?"

The words were simple enough to understand, yet they instantly posed a multitude of conflicting scenarios; Simon's eyes stared starkly at the man sitting opposite and saw nothing but a mass of pure and utter confusion. Abruptly he rose and sat back down; there was nowhere for him to go. He had no home, no money and, above all, no self-respect.

After long silent minutes, Hanale inhaled deeply and spoke; words reminiscent of the words his mother had once spoken, "By tomorrow afternoon, Simon, I want you to write down your agenda for life. Then," he emphasised in the strongest of tones, "we can get down to the nitty-gritty and you can start to live again." He left his brother-in-law in the same state he had found him thirty-three minutes ago silent, still, dejected; a mere shadow of the vibrant, energetic, confident, happy guy he once was.

Sixty-seven minutes later Simon picked up the mug of cold, untouched coffee, swilled it down his neck and walked out the house; Hanale's passport for life ringing loudly in his ears... *agenda for life... get down to the nitty-gritty... you can start to live again...* The words echoed louder and louder as his feet walked faster and faster. *Where?* He did not know where; knowing only that he had to create distance between himself and Hanale's words. But, still, they followed him as on and on he walked, faster and faster, until he turned a corner and found himself entering a familiar park. There he found his familiar bench, sat down and slowly began to feel the heavy weight of tension lift; yet, stark words continued to bombard his head; words which had not come from Hanale's mouth; but, like Hanale's words, were wise; spoken by one who bore the scars of regret and Simon listened to them once more... *For me, it is too late... I have lost everything... my friend, if there is any hope; any way of resolving your problem, no matter how difficult, do it...* He remembered the tramp becoming smaller and smaller; his burden of guilt, remorse and regret laying heavily on his shoulders, as he walked away into the distance; his words now intermingling with Hanale's words, growing clearer in Simon's mind ringing, echoing, blasting his mind as flashes of a vodka bottle leapt in and out of his thoughts, trying to disintegrate the words of advice. He rose and headed for the only place, he knew, he could achieve true solace.

Chapter One Hundred and Thirty-Two

The Big Island

From afar, she saw them standing side by side waving vigorously in her direction. The saviour and the saved, she smiled, her eyes resting on a beaming Solomao where they were safe.

With thudding heart, she approached the two men, accepting graciously their leis of plumeria, her nostrils inhaling deep their sweet, heavenly scent as her eyes reluctantly shifted from Solomao to the man standing next to him and her heart raced; her skin feeling the surge of tiny delightful tingles as he placed his broad hand on her arm, guiding the way to his car, while her legs threatened to buckle; her ears oblivious to his words, a wave of regret sweeping over her. *Why had she agreed to come? She could have declined the invitation; she could have sent a replacement. Oh why—why—why?*

"Ocean... Ocean..." Her name echoed through her consciousness, her eyes opened wider staring into the lean, handsome face momentarily glancing back at her, before switching his attention back on to the road ahead.

"I-I'm sorry," she stammered her eyes darting back to the passing scene. "Flying always makes me a little tired."

"Me too." She heard, his light chuckle penetrating deep within her; almost feeling the light touch of his hands on her bare flesh, her eyes dropping to the soft leather of the steering wheel where his hands moved slightly, wishing... Abruptly she jerked out of her illicit reverie as she caught the last word of Ekewaka's sentence. "A speech?" She raised her eyes to him with a look of undiluted horror.

"Oh, it's nothing to worry about; just a few words to cement the opening of the new sanctuary."

They sat down to a light repast of fish, rice and side salad; Ekewaka, with inputs from Solomao, bringing Ocean Tia up to date with the progress of the new sanctuary. Already two young men had found their way through its door; a doctor, nurse and counsellor adhering to their every need. Solomao was, of course, the third official client, although presently he was still residing with Ekewaka. As far as Ocean was concerned, at this moment in time, Solomao was a comforting distraction; as far as Ekewaka was concerned, he was the elephant in the room. Not daring to meet her host's eye her eyes followed her fork, as it played with a slice of tomato.

"Not hungry?" Ekewaka's casual enquiry made inadvertent eyes shoot up to him, wishing to God they hadn't; for, in his dark pools she saw her tiny reflection and felt herself being lured into the very depths of their captivating wells. Abruptly she snapped out of his hypnotic spell and, placing her pristine napkin on to the table beside her plate of untouched food, she rose. "I shall make a start on the speech." She announced to no one in particular.

"You'll be hungry, Ocean; you've not touched a morsel." Ekewaka stated his genuine eyes of concern following the young woman, as she hastily retreated from the table and made a dash upstairs.

Hunger pangs attacked her mercilessly; but, they did not yearn for fish, rice and salad. Writing pad and pen remained untouched in the depths of a cupboard drawer; sleep evaded her exhausted body as her restless mind whirled with thoughts of the man in the next room, mingled and intermingled with fragmented images of a man far away who was still her husband and, as stark reality clashed with blurred fantasy, another unambiguous impression penetrated her head and took centre stage... *Kai her late, beloved father who had once been so alive with hopes, dreams, visions and ambitions; the man who had succeeded and failed; the man who had loved and lost and, in the end, found the true meaning of his life. Kai... Kai... Kai...* His comforting image enveloped all other thoughts and soothed her into sleep.

At six o'clock precisely, the alarm shrilled making her eyes snap open, alerting her body into action. She had much to do; but, one important task had to be accomplished before all others.

With her father's image still firmly planted in the forefront of her mind she sat down, pen poised in her hand and hundreds of words eager to escape the confines of her head and jump on to the virginal page. Within half an hour, the task was accomplished; written; read; reread; done, except for one outstanding matter.

Two sets of thoughtful eyes rested on Ocean Tia.

"Peace and Hope Sanctuary?" Solomao raised his eyes in question.

"Oasis of Inspiration." Volunteered Ekewaka.

"What about Kai's Refuge of Solace?" Ocean asked softly causing two pairs of eyes to, simultaneously, rest on her smiling face.

"Who's Kai?" Solomao's brow furrowed.

"Kai was my father, Solomao." She turned her serious eyes to the puzzled looking young man. "He lost his way and found it. He and his son, my half-brother Hanale, founded Hope Sanctuary on the Island of Kauai. He worked tirelessly for its cause." Her soft voice faded as Ekewaka and Solomao exuded their agreement.

"Yes! Yes!" They exclaimed in unison.

"An ideal name." Ekewaka nodded his head and Solomao stretched his smile of assent from ear to ear; their eyes twinkling as Ocean's heart danced.

After a few words of introduction Ekewaka, turned aside and signalled to Ocean; her heart beating like a wild drum as she rose and approached Ekewaka taking her place on the podium, her eyes sweeping across the sea of influential guests. She smiled and Ekewaka's friends' hearts immediately warmed to her.

"Aloha," she said her warm eyes acquiring a veil of solemnness as she silently prayed her lurking nerves wouldn't get the better of her; Solomao's encouraging smile propelled her on. "Long ago I walked along the shores of Kauai each day. Far away in the distance a lonesome, dishevelled man made his solitary footsteps, each footstep making an imprint in the sand before it was washed away."

I had a dream. The lonesome figure had lost all his dreams. I had hope. He had no hope. I had a home, family, friends; good food to eat and money to spend and, above all, a future to look forward to. He had lost everything. I was in the midst of living. He wanted only to die.

The *I* in the scene is each one of us.

The lonesome figure, ladies and gentlemen, was my father, Kai. It is each unfortunate individual whether it's man or woman, rich or poor, devout or of no faith at all. The lonesome figure represents all who have lost their way.

"Let each of us remember, my friends." She raised her eyes and briefly rested them on her captive audience. "There, but for the grace of God, go I."

Nobody sets out to be a drunkard; to be homeless or to end up a beach bum. A young child will not sit in front of his, or her, school principal and state, Well,

Sir, in a few years' time I'd like to be despised, shunned, stared at, spat upon, kicked, ignored, mentally scarred and tossed by others on to the outer fringes of life.

These people exist. They are in our world; on our islands. They are our brothers and sisters, friends and neighbours. We need only to look. Yes, take a good look for in one of these lost souls we can surely see ourselves.

My father, Kai, was one of the lucky ones. Kind hearts came to his aid and, in time, he found himself; got back his life, his family, his friends and, above all, his self-respect. He also founded the Hope Sanctuary on the Island of Kauai.

We are all here today to witness the official opening of another sanctuary. It gives me a great pleasure to thank each and every one of you for making this possible; a big Mahalo to you all.

"Now, I would like to ask my friend, Solomao, to come forward."

A nervous looking Solomao approached the side of the podium, turned to one side and pulled a dangling cord, allowing a dark blue velvet curtain to open and reveal a shining brass plaque. Clearing his dry throat he read loudly, clearly and proudly, "Kai's Refuge of Solace" and was met with thunderous applause.

Ocean felt her happy heart full to bursting point and about to jump out of her chest. If only makuakāne was here, she smiled whimsically, her happy eyes taking in the enthusiastic, applauding throng. In the very depths of her heart, she knew, he was standing proudly by her side. Her eyes lingered on one man. Like Alan, so long ago, Ekewaka had come to her aid. His eyes crinkled in admiration, smiling back at the enchanting wahine; his heart tightening.

The opening had been a success, with friends and business associates pledging to donate on a regular basis. As the last two guests were walking down the winding drive, Ocean Tia stood at the doorway and watched, inhaling the sweet fragrance of mixed blooms suffusing the air around. She did not detect a figure creeping up behind, her thoughts totally absorbed with memories of her father. Suddenly sensing a presence she turned, unable to prevent hands encircling her waist. Eyes locked with eyes and, for a delicious moment, remained engrossed in each other's world; the gentle squeeze around her waist bringing tiny shards of wild electricity cursing through her fast pulsating veins, while her mouth opened and shut to dry protestations.

"It was a huge success." Ekewaka stated his lips touching her cheek, sending a fresh barrage of sparks through her entire body; her feet stepping away as if they were on fire, like her heart.

"I have to see to our clients." She moved further away from his grasp, the echo of her words penetrating his senses; her coolness towards him making him inwardly shiver. What was it about this wahine that was so damned entrancing; yet, so annoyingly baffling? He closed his eyes and shook his head slowly from side to side, his lips forming a determined line. *Whatever it was,* he told himself, *this rare jewel was definitely worth the wait.*

Stepping out of her bedroom on to the balcony, her eyes gazed out on to the desolate dark garden below, seeing two ghosts of the future, their bodies entwined, their futures sealed. Turning abruptly away she rushed out the door; seconds later standing rigid; fingers raised, clenched, poised; her heart racing and eyes staring unblinkingly at the dark mahogany wood before her; the solid barrier between...

An unruly army of chaotic thoughts and scattered scenarios crashed through her head dancing a merry jig until, slowly, stark reality overtook her throbbing senses. *What on earth was she doing here outside his room?* Turning she ran, unaware the door had quietly opened; oblivious to the pair of eyes following her swift disappearance and a mouth curling into a victorious smile.

Her long night was suffused with bouts of tossing and turning, walking aimlessly around the dark desolate garden, reading text she did not absorb, switching on and off the television and the radio and asking herself the same question again and again. *What was she still doing here?* Although she had been scheduled to stay on the Big Island for an entire week there was, she told herself, no real reason why she should keep to this timetable. After all, Kai's Refuge of Solace was officially opened and running by highly proficient staff and Solomao was adapting to his new way of life. There was, she firmly concluded, no real reason for her to stay. There was, on the other hand, one major reason in favour of her imminent departure and the reason lay behind the solid mahogany door.

Seductively popping a fresh pineapple chunk into his mouth, his dark eyes focussed on her, confirmed Ocean Tia's resolve. Her announcement hit him like a thunderbolt, his empty fork grinding against his bottom teeth as he withdraw it from his mouth, his brow furrowing, his eyes clouding over. It was the last thing he expected or wanted to hear. Adding fuel to his inner being of fire of shock she confirmed, avoiding his eyes, "I shall be phoning the airport to reschedule my flight."

Her determined tone registered loudly in his head, his baffled thoughts hastily forming into a lucid idea. "Well before you go you will, I am sure, honour your promise." His eyes remained firmly fixed on the woman before him as her bewildered eyes shot to his steady gaze, crashed and locked; her brow folding into puzzled creases.

"What do you mean?" Desperately she tried to avert her eyes and found she could not, feeling the familiar frenzied drumming in her heart.

Controlling his lips, which were urging to break out into a mischievous smile, he stated slowly and clearly, in as serious tone as he could summon, "You promised me a date on the surf, Ocean." He paused for maximum effect. "You do not strike me as a wahine who breaks her promises."

A cold wave of recollection, mingled with a heavy mixture of apprehension, washed over her as the memory of her promise came back to haunt her. And before she could assemble a suitable excuse he added, "You do honour your promises don't you, Ocean?" One eyebrow rose in question.

Involuntarily she met his mock questioning eyes and replied, with an icy edge to her words. "Yes, Ekewaka, I do honour my promises but..." She pulled out her trump card. "I can postpone a promise without breaking it." The mere thought of attempting to surf sent cold shards of alarm through her entire body; his contradictory words making her want to scream in utter frustration, creating the immediate desire to squirm and die, as her ears were subjected to the victorious tone in his words.

"Not this time, Ocean; I will not take no for an answer and neither," his eyes twinkled, "will the clients of Kai's Refuge of Solace."

Her world froze and with it all her silent words of protestation; her eyes staring incredulously at the man before her and seeing her utter defeat, swiftly overtaken by a rising inner anger. For, how could this man use others to his advantage? Did he really care one gram for their well-being? And, before she had a chance to condemn him as the most despicable man she'd ever come across, he hammered in the final nail in their coffin of verbal contradictions.

"All the staff at the sanctuary endorse this excellent idea!"

Chapter One Hundred and Thirty-Three
England

As the distance between the tramp grew Hanale's words crashed mercilessly into Simon's head... *agenda for life... getting down to the nitty-gritty... you can start to live again...* With each solitary step he took, the fragmented phrases seemed to take a life of their own; with each step they became clearer, more meaningful and, to Simon's surprise, doable. For a few precious seconds, his steps became lighter, before a heaviness of heart brought a heavy solidity back to his steps. *Without Ocean Tia it would all be worthless. Without Ocean Tia life would not be bearable.* He plodded on his feet feeling like two clods of clay plodding... plodding... plodding—*Where to?* He knew not where and without Ocean Tia he neither cared. Out of nowhere the tramp's words careered into the roots of Simon's despondency... *If there is any hope; any way of resolving your problem, no matter how difficult, do it...* He shook his head slowly from side to side concluding contemptuously, *The tramp did not know what he was talking about; he was too busy burying his own head in the bottle... The bottle...* Its image floated alluringly into the forefront of his mind, dissipating Hanale's words and vanquishing the tramp's advice; temptingly inviting him into the comforting world of escapism. He turned direction; his feet of clay suddenly feeling light, as they almost ran towards his place of promised sanctuary. Placing the last coins he owned on to the scuffed counter, he grabbed the bottle and fled.

Sitting on the bench he brought the bottle out of the depths of his deep overcoat pocket, stood it on his lap and stared hard at the golden substance, before his impatient fingers unscrewed the metal top and the cool lip of the bottle touched his waiting mouth. The bottle tilted. He could almost taste the raw, bitter taste; his heart racing wildly with eager anticipation. At the touch of the liquid, his lips snapped shut, a little of the golden substance overflowing the rim of the bottle, as his trembling fingers screwed the top back on tightly... tighter and tighter until it could not move anymore. He thrust the bottle deep into his pocket. "Out of sight; out of mind." He said aloud, rose and swiftly walked out the park.

But, the raw smell of alcohol had filtered through and penetrated his senses, denying him a grain of peace; taunting him; tempting him; luring him into the soothing world of oblivion. His feet gathered speed. He walked briskly, trotted, ran as fast as his legs would carry him. He stopped.

Thrusting the full bottle into his saviour's hand, tears streaming down his face, he fell into his brother-in-law's arms. "Save me, Hanale. Please… save me."

Chapter One Hundred and Thirty-Four
The Big Island

Excitement was in the air.

Bone-numbing trepidation, mingled with an incomprehensible tinge of animation, coursed through Ocean Tia's veins, as she desperately tried to fight off her inner fears and face her challenge. *After all,* she told herself severely, *the guys at the sanctuary have far bigger mountains to climb.* Her eyes darted to a happy looking Solomao before flitting to Ahe and Konane, two young clients from the sanctuary whose eyes were firmly fixed on their teacher, Ekewaka, who was explaining in great detail the safety aspects of surfing; though being average surfers themselves, they did not really need the in-depth instructions.

The person who would benefit was not listening; her unfocussed mind was full to the brim with anything but the safety rules of good surfing. She was here under duress.

Ekewaka was well aware of her distraction. Her obvious lack of experience on the surfboard, gave him the impetus of offering her private tuition.

Ocean caught the thoughtful look he threw her way, in the midst of answering Ahe's question; feeling a strange excitement tingling at her bones and a rising warmth surging through the whole of her body. Her eyes remained stubbornly fixed on the leaning coconut palm behind Ekewaka.

With surfboards tightly clasped in golden-brown hands, three surfers eagerly withdrew and waded into the refreshing water of the Pacific. Ocean Tia clasping tightly her board followed suit; though what she was going to do with her surfboard, once she was in the throes of the ocean she had no idea whatsoever. The splashing sound of waves and the guys excited laughter drifted to her ears and so did Ekewaka's call, "Ocean; stop!"

On the verge of the border, where the sea meets the white sand, she stood perfectly still, as if frozen in time; the waves lapping around her and her fellow surfers growing smaller and smaller by the second. Oh, how she'd wished she'd listened now.

She felt his presence; her heart thundering like the distant waves, making her close her eyes and wish fervently it was all over and done with. "I will help you, Ocean." His voice was steady, warm, soft; yet, she felt an icy chill entering her racing heart, making it suddenly freeze. With the chill came a slow, rising anger at his sheer audacity of acknowledging her obvious ignorance.

"How hard can it possibly be?" She forced a nervous laugh, avoiding his eyes, as she waded in further. Again she stopped feeling his broad, wet hand on her bare flesh.

"It can be fatal." He stated, clearly defining each word. "If you don't know what you are doing."

"I know." She plunged onwards allowing his hand to slip.

"I think not." He prised the surfboard out of her tight grasp and ordered her on to the dry sand, before lacing both arms around her arms and turning her towards himself, looking directly into her reluctant eyes. "For a start off; you need to do a warm-up."

Tightly clenched lips loosened as she stated defiantly, making him inwardly smile. "Well; I didn't see the guys warming up."

"Well; obviously you were busy daydreaming, Ocean."

Her lips opened, about to contradict, and closed. *Yes; she had been in her own world,* she silently conceded.

"Anyway," he stated authoritatively, "this is not the beach on which you will start your surfing experience." With inner amusement, he watched her eyes widen. *She had,* he mused, *a lot to learn.*

Like a lamb led to slaughter, she followed in his footsteps, abruptly stopping. "I cannot leave without Solomao and the others," she stated.

He stopped, turned to face her and questioned. "Didn't you once tell me, that anyone who enters the refuge does so out of their own free will and is allowed to leave accordingly?"

She nodded her head silently and continued to follow him.

The drive was laden with heavy, silent tension. The beach they approached was more secluded and sheltered; the water calmer and the waves steadier and ideal for beginner surfers. This did not ease Ocean's inner anxiety regarding the whole surfing experience; nor, did the thought of Ekewaka as her personal surfing tutor calm her ruffled nerves.

Once on the white sands, surfboards propped against a sturdy palm, Ekewaka began to demonstrate a stretching exercise. She followed his every move. "You know, Ocean, before you become a good surfer, you need to dedicate effort and time into the subject matter."

"I am honouring a promise; not training for the Olympics, Ekewaka." She stated coldly, her eyes deliberately avoiding his flexing muscles.

He couldn't help but detect the deficiency of *l'amour* for the sport; still, like his pa used to say, *A faint heart never won a maiden.*

Having warmed-up Ocean extended her hand to grab her board, rush into the ocean and get it all over and done with.

"Em... I don't think so."

She turned her eyes dropping to the white sand, where Ekewaka was lying on his belly on top of his surfboard. "You will need to be well acquainted with this position, Ocean." He stated using his arms as if paddling. "Above all, you will need to feel at ease with your board, while you are still on dry land. Come on, grab your board; lay beside me and have a go."

Her eyes gazing unblinkingly at the athletic form beneath her, his innuendos sending secret shivers of delight up and down her spine, she grabbed her board. "This is not my board." He heard her say, his eyes deliberately peeled on the water ahead.

"I think you will find that it is, sweetheart. A soft-top board is ideal for the beginner." He continued to *paddle* while she carefully scrutinised the board she was holding. "It's gentle on your bum and bare feet. You are going to spend a lot of time sitting on your board, rather than standing, at the beginning."

"I plan to do neither." She retorted. "I shall have my session, as promised; then I shall never touch another surfboard as long as I live."

"We'll see." He smiled to himself, his defiant tone making her blood boil as she, begrudgingly, placed her soft-top board next to his and positioned herself on top. "Now paddle." He demanded, witnessing an icy glare thrown his way before she, reluctantly, simulated a paddle technique, feeling an utter fool. "You must work on this skill as..."

She did not hear the rest, concentrating instead on her out-of-control breathing; his proximity causing her heartbeats to fall sharply out of sync.

"Stop!" He shouted and saw her stop abruptly at the water's edge. "Now, what do you see in front of you, Ocean?"

Throwing him a disparaging look she decided to play him at his own game, a mischievous smile dancing on her lips. "A fine bunch of grapes." She dared to look at his disapproving glare. "Water," she retorted staring at the vast, blue undulating blanket and wished she was a fish hidden in the tropical waters; far away from this man's unnerving scrutiny.

"Ocean." He stated giving her a sideway glance. "Before you wade in take a long, hard look at the waves; keenly observe them; study and assess them. Get to know at what point, and in what manner, they break up as well as taking a mental note of other surfers. Do this every single time you are about to surf."

"This is a one-off, Ekewaka." She said nonchalantly her eyes fixed on the rolling waves, as if entranced by them.

"We'll see." He smiled to himself.

His last words made her blood boil; her lips remained tightly clamped. She did not wish to enter into a dispute. She wanted only to go in, have a go and honour her promise and never touch the experience again in this life; or, the next.

He took her hand and guided her in and, to her utter shock, guided her out again.

On the soft dry sand, drops of water dripping on to the white grains and immediately turning their shade darker, he turned and smiled wickedly. "Here endeth the first lesson."

To have said the experience had left her feeling short-changed would have been the understatement of the century. She felt utterly bemused, let down and frustratingly chagrined. And, her pent-up feelings did not start to release their tensed grip on her until her eyes fell on Solomao, Ahe and Konane sitting, chatting away merrily in the foyer of the sanctuary; glasses of freshly squeezed pineapple juice in their hands and exchanging exhilarating surfing experiences with anyone who cared to listen.

"There; I told you our friends would be okay." Ekewaka left her side to join them in their excitement; leaving dry words in Ocean Tia's slightly opened mouth and her whole body wanting more –much more.

Chapter One Hundred and Thirty-Five
England

Physically, spiritually, mentally Simon Teal was a broken man; defeated in love, ambition; crushed by life. There was nowhere for him to go; he had reached rock-bottom. There was only one way out; upwards. In every which way he had sunk into the depths of Hell with the awesome, disjointed facades of the demons of loss, despair, loneliness and fear gnawing and jeering at him unceasingly.

On more than one occasion, he had seriously contemplated on ending it all and cursed his weakness, hoping that tomorrow he would find the courage. Tomorrow never came, leaving him to squirm in his self-made black pit of self-hate and misery; the only speck of hope so remote, he deemed it an impossibility to attain.

The tiny speck of hope was Ocean Tia, his wife; the only woman he had ever truly loved; still loved and had lost. But, hadn't he seen the vivid scene of her walking into her home with a handsome, attentive man. Wasn't this evidence enough? He closed his eyes. *What if he had got it all wrong? What if they were merely friends?* The faintest flicker of a smile edged his dry lips. It was on that flicker of hope, and that alone, that he rested his whole recovery.

Slowly he began to take an interest in others; helping Hanale and Maria with housework, shopping and other menial chores; never once did he offer to help with their baby, always averting his eyes from the infant; the pain of what could have been raw and lacerating.

Gradually he took steps on his road to recovery walking, sometimes stumbling and falling but always getting up and continuing his journey.

The exception came one afternoon when Maria, oblivious to her brother-in-law reading a spy thriller in the corner of the room, came rushing in, an unfolded piece of paper waving in her hand, excitement heavy in her voice. "Hanale, I think your sister is falling in love again."

In that split second, Simon's heart turned to stone; the tiny glimmer of hope extinguished and, in its place, a dark unfathomable hole, beckoning him to slither inside; for, now there was nowhere for him to go. Obediently he skulked in and covered himself with a thick, impenetrable blanket of black remorse, as Maria's ebullient words pierced his ears and sliced his heart in two.

"She's just set up a new refuge with the aid of this Ekewaka guy and, apparently, she's counting the days to going back to the Big Island where Ekewaka, who's an excellent surfer, has promised to teach her the techniques. She says…" Maria's words stuck dead in her mouth; her shocked eyes on Simon, as she witnessed the colour drain from his face; his eyes stark and unbelieving; his hope dead and buried.

The irreparable damage, she knew, was done. No amount of backtracking; no amount of soothing words would heal. In those few seconds, she had taken the spirit of a man.

When her dying words had died on her lips, they sprang alive in Simon's head and, with them, the renewed image of Ocean Tia and the stranger, which had burned so intensely in Simon's mind, came to haunt him once more. Snapping his eyes shut, the opened book falling with a thud to the floor, he tried, in vain, to obliterate the intense image; his heart now in a thousand pieces, each piece a poignant reminder of a mistake he had made; an inappropriate word spoken; a thoughtless action taken; a betrayal… until he felt his world falling off its axis and spinning wildly out of control.

At first, he did not feel the feather-light touch on his arm. It was her softly spoken words that pierced into his dark and dismal reverie of heartache and confusion. "Simon… Simon." His name echoed somewhere in his foggy consciousness; detached; suspended as if it didn't belong to this world. "Simon." The firmer tone thrust him back into the present; a world he no longer wished to inhabit; his closed eyes remaining stubbornly clamped shut against this intruding world and its inhabitants.

The gentle squeeze of his hand sent a surge of inexplicable anger towards this kind woman sitting next to him; the messenger of doom; the angel of dead dreams. Sharply he withdrew his hand, clenching both hands tightly on his lap, as he willed her to go away and leave him in his dark misery. She stayed by his side silent, still, supportive and that's how Hanale found them.

"Has someone died; you two look like a pair of ghosts?"

Maria stood, handed over the damning letter to her husband and walked out.

Hanale scanned the contents, a surge of relief surging through his heart. *At last,* he silently sighed, *there was hope for Ocean.* His eyes dropped to Simon and immediately pity diluted his relief; but did not drown it. *For surely,* he asked himself, *wasn't this the springboard for all concerned to move on?* His heart tugged with guilt. *This,* he told himself, *was not a time to start rejoicing; it was a time to mend.*

Chapter One Hundred and Thirty-Six
Kauai

Try as she did to forcefully lock him out of her thoughts and dreams, Ekewaka became a vivid fixture in her conscious mind and dreams. Going to bed he was the last image in her head; in her dreams and nightmares he played a starring role and in her waking hours he was her constant companion, one she secretly did not want to be without; for, when Ekewaka was in her thoughts, Simon was not.

Gnawing at her Ekewaka infused mind was the heavy weight of deceit and betrayal; something so alien to Ocean she was at a loss what to do. She could not retract what she had written to her sister-in-law; she could not take back the intention with which it was written and, above all, she could not deny what she felt.

Simon's visit to the island had perturbed her. It told her he still had hope where there was no hope. The letter she had written to Maria, relating her friendship with a new man would, she knew, filter through to Simon dashing all his dreams. Now in the cold light of day, the potential consequences of Simon receiving such news haunted her mercilessly and yet... yet it was he, her husband, who had thrown caution to the wind and tossed away their marriage; it was Simon who chose to have Natasha Parks in his bed; it was Simon who had instigated the beginning of the end.

The shrill ring of the phone brought her sharply back to the present and her feet to the phone. The voice on the other end made her feet involuntarily turn to jelly, propelling her to sit down before her legs buckled beneath her; scolding herself severely for feeling such unruly symptoms, more akin to a teenager in the first throes of young love than a mature, married woman.

After relating Solomao's on-going progress of recovery, the general well-being of the seven clients now residing in the refuge and of the sanctuary's smooth, professional and successful running, Ekewaka turned his attention on a different course. "So Ocean; when are you flying over for some more surfing lessons?"

Her well-rehearsed answer remained stubbornly lodged in her dry mouth.

"Ocean?"

"What is Solomao up to?" She grasped on a diverted lifeline of thought, playing for time while she could again rehearse her feeble excuse.

Knowing her tactic well he played accordingly. "Solomao can't wait to see you on the surfboard." He paused for maximum effect before continuing. "And neither can I."

She could not see his mischievous smile curling his sensuous lips, the playful twinkle in his eyes, while his soft words played like a seductive violin. Jellified feet which had turned to clods of clay mollified her sudden urge to run and though, four hundred and ninety kilometres plus apart, she felt entrapped within the solid walls of Ekewaka's prison; her jailer demanding a reply to his question, as Simon invaded her mind and she blurted out any words that came to her mind, before dropping the receiver as if it was a red hot poker, and questioned her sanity.

Ekewaka gently placed his receiver back on to its cradle, his lips curling into a victorious smile; the sound of door chimes sweeping all thoughts of Ocean Tia temporarily out of his head, as he opened the door to his date.

Chapter One Hundred and Thirty-Seven
England

Where a spark of hope had once glimmered there now flared despair gloriously fanned by gloom, despondency and suicidal thoughts.

Ocean Tia, his wife, had found another; the woman he loved was turning her back on him and opening her heart, soul and probably her legs to another man. He closed his eyes tightly, drawing himself into the familiar depths of blackness. If only he could blame another; Natasha, Ocean, Hanale, Maria—anybody and everybody. His aching, exhausted head shook from side to side; the deep, ragged sigh exuding from the inner well of his soul, heavy laden with loathing, self-hate, self-recrimination, remorse and deep regret.

Hanale stood silently in the doorway, his concerned eyes set on the despondent, hunched-up figure. For long seconds, he stared, feeling a tiny fraction of the consuming pain his brother-in-law was harbouring. Heaving a heavy sigh he approached and sat next to the broken body, furiously searching his head for appropriate words to say.

Maria's soft words alerted both men to her presence; both raising their eyes and resting them on her calm face. "You have to fight, Simon." She said softly, firmly.

His glare intensified, as if his eyes were on fire. "I've lost her; you stupid, stupid woman," he hissed.

"Hey… hey, Simon," Hanale's tone was cold, demanding. "Apologise to my wife; now!"

"There is no need." Maria soothed.

"There's every damned need. Apologise; or, you are out of this house."

Suspended silence hung clingingly in the heavy air.

"Damn you, Teal; apologise!"

"I am sorry, Maria." Simon's words seemed detached his stark eyes boring into Maria's eyes seeing only Ocean, and the mysterious man he had seen her with; the man who was to be her potential surfing instructor. *What else was he going to teach, Ocean?* He wondered snapping his eyes shut, only to see Ocean and Ekewaka on surfboards laughing, sneering; jeering at his stupidity.

There was no reprieve. He saw them everywhere in his bowl of cornflakes, on the television screen, in his mirror; everywhere and as he lay, stark eyes set on the ceiling he was counting the hours, the minutes, the seconds to his blessed release – Five hours... four hours and twenty-one minutes... three hours and fifty-seven seconds... two hours... one hour... The last hour crawled laboriously; unbelievably and excruciatingly slowly like a slithering, old snake who had lost his will to live... forty-six minutes... fifty-eight minutes... fifty... forty-six...

Racked with surges of uncontrollable need, mingled with gnawing bouts of impatience and gut twisting, he roughly tossed the duvet aside and bolted out of bed fully clothed; every single nerve on high alert. Eleven minutes to nine. Again, his eyes darted to the digital clock. Ten minutes and fifty-three seconds to go. In his rush to get to the bedroom door, his feet got caught up in one of Hanale's slippers. Kicking it to the wall he cursed, "Shit! Shit! Shit!" The unbearable, raw craving now surging, like wildfire, through every fast pulsating vein in his yearning body, swimming in his head, bulging out of his eyes as he scrambled down the stairs, two at a time, heading for the outside door his racing heart thudding, threatening to jump out of his tight chest, his trembling hand reaching for the door handle, his ears subjected to the voice of doom.

"And where do you think you are going, mate?" Hanale's stark question made Simon's resolve crumble; but, only for a few seconds. Reluctantly, he turned his pale, drawn face to his brother-in-law. "If you go to the off-licence, where I presume you were heading, you will never set foot in this house again, Simon." Simon's dry mouth opened and closed. "If you choose alcohol that's okay but..." Hanale stared intently into his friend's eyes, "but, let this sink into your head, if this is your choice, we as a family and friends are over. There will be no going back. No more chances. No further reprieves." He saw Simon's eyes rise up the stairs as Maria was descending. "Maria is with me on this."

Ocean and a full bottle of vodka lay alluringly on opposite sides of the same pendulum. Two loves. His trembling hand was poised on the door handle. He pressed it down; the air cloyingly laden with a heavy stillness and silence, spreading thickly around the two old friends, as each waited for the other to make the move.

Thoughts of Ocean intermingled and jostled for attention with her present rival, the bottle, and both intermingled with conflicting scenarios of life without the other, making Simon close his eyes against one black, all-too-real image; the debris of his broken marriage. The handle pressed further down. Slowly, very slowly, as his heart thudded furiously, he released the pressure and, reluctantly, turned away from the closed door and all it symbolised.

Empty, lonely and barely clinging to sanity Simon was a dry drunk. Constant thoughts of immersing himself in the comforting solace of alcohol, intermingled with gnawing scenarios of permanent release, were blended with images of his wife, Ocean Tia; alive and kicking; thoughts as clear as day; semblances which stopped him from reaching for the bottle.

Hanale and Maria felt deeply their brother-in-law's plight. Both were privately anxious about his future; both asked themselves the fundamental question, *Does he have the strength and courage to live the rest of his life without Ocean Tia?*

Chapter One Hundred and Thirty-Eight
Kauai

He swung the door of his convertible open, dropped his keys into the pocket of his black shorts and headed straight for the arrivals area, a triumphant smile dancing on his lips. *She had relented. It had been,* as he had predicted, *a matter of time.* His smile widened; his steps unhurried, firm and confident.

The minute the plane had taken off, regret invaded and lay heavy in Ocean Tia's conflicted heart. The sanctuary on the Big Island was running perfectly well without her presence; Solomao was progressing well; surfing lessons she did not need or want and as for Ekewaka... She closed her eyes tight, severely scolding herself. *Why hadn't she thought it all through?* A loud voice crashed through her thoughts... *But you had thought it all through; every single aspect of your impending visit was carefully scrutinised. You wanted to come—needed to come—yearned to come...* Her eyes snapped open. *She was here. There was no going back.* And, to confirm the matter her fluttering heart, as she saw him waving in her direction, swept away her niggling hesitancy.

"So; you're here on the Big Island to brush up on your surfing abilities." He cast her a sideway glance, his broad hands lightly touching the bottom of the steering wheel, as the flashy sports car swiftly swept past palm-fringed beaches.

"I'm here to check that all is well at the refuge."

Inwardly he smiled at her calculated answer, a mischievous twinkle dancing in his eyes. "And... to improve your surfing."

An involuntary ragged sigh escaped her lips, her mind wondering if he could detect her suppressed inner excitement. "Tell me about Solomao's progress." She forced the words out of her arid mouth.

She didn't hear a word.

Solomao's progress was evident. Away from his former haunts, he seemed to have found the happiness that had been so elusive to him; serenity; an inner peace; a purpose in life; all invaluable aspirations that many spend a lifetime trying to acquire, only to fail. She smiled. He had found his niche in life. Her short-lived smile died on her lips, as she watched him energetically sweep the veranda, a few broom scratches still visible between specks of fine dust; Solomao had found serenity while she had lost her peaceful state of mind. Sitting a few metres away from her friend, her eyes following his every move, she brought the glass of freshly squeezed juice to her lips tasting her own misery. *What was she doing here,* she asked herself, *chasing after a guy who could have any wahine at the click of his fingers? And yet—and yet she did not wish to be anywhere else. Why was she lusting over a Casanova, when she had a husband?* Placing her empty glass on to the glass-topped table she rose and ran out of the vicinity; hearing and ignoring the echo of Solomao's call.

She couldn't answer his question. She didn't know where she was going. She didn't want to know. One sandalled foot in front of the other ran… ran far and fast away from the refuge; away from Solomao; away from Ekewaka. She ran and ran to the only place where peace reigned in all its glory.

With each advancing footstep, the sound of the mighty ocean became louder, clearer, nearer; more thunderous and as one foot stepped on to the beach, the vast expanse of rolling water rolled towards her; energy, hope and peace suffused her soul.

For how long she walked along the smooth sand she did not know. Time was of no consequence as the eternal waves pounded and boomed, as they had done for millions of years. Eyes gazed on to the long surf as it advanced, like an army on a mission, as she pondered on the vastness of infinity of the sky and sea, immersed eternally in timelessness.

Like a Jack-in-the-box she jumped at the light touch on her shoulder; a surge of undiluted resentment taking over her as, begrudgingly, she turned to face the intruder, her heart instantly freezing.

"I thought I'd find you here."

"Ekewaka." The echo of his name hovered on her open lips, resting still in the balmy air as she tried to still her racing heart, her eyes dropping as she watched him sitting down on the smooth sand, patting it with his hand. "Sit Ocean." He smiled cheerily making her blood boil; but with infuriation or forbidden secret desire, she could not decide which. Obediently she sat curling her long, slender legs beneath her, her eyes strictly focussed on the energetic ocean, wondering why she hadn't made a quick escape when she had the chance.

Long pounding seconds passed, as they sat wrapped in their own private thoughts. Finally, Ekewaka spoke. "You seem on edge, Ocean. Is something the matter?"

A new wave of resentment bubbled and frothed beneath her calm exterior, her eyes peeled on the waves forming and reforming; tension, like a tight vice, squeezing the last remnants of serenity out of her soul; telling her she had to get away from the close proximity of his body; away from the island and out of Ekewaka's life, before it was too late.

Chapter One Hundred and Thirty-Nine
England

Her fingers froze, as if struck by a sudden attack of paralysis. Nothing moved; not even her eyes, which were starkly stuck on the cream tiles lashed with cascading water. For how long, she stood like a solidified statue, Maria did not know; stirred out of her frozen terror by Hanale's call.

Slowly reality began to seep in... *the shower cubicle—the lashing water—the—the...* With renewed vigour the raw, undiluted fear took a firmer grip of her naked, water-streaked body; her fingers still in the exact area when they had stopped moving; frozen.

"Maria!"

Forcefully snapping out of her trance she stepped out of the cubicle, threw on her pink towelling robe and peered over the banister; the fear of what she had undeniably felt with her fingers swimming in her head.

"Maria... there you are. It's the cosmetics lady at the door. Do you want anything?"

Temporary relief took over her fear as she focussed on her make-up order, knowing the other issue would have to be addressed... urgently.

Hanale and Simon noticed a distinct change of behaviour in Maria. Both men came to their own personal conclusions; both sought to remedy the situation.

Maria was immersed in her own hell of hells. Her fingers had felt the lump in her left breast and, lest she be mistaken, they felt it over and over again with the same devastating outcome; each time she continued to will the verdict to change; to go away. Each time it stubbornly reaffirmed itself with crystal-clear clarity. *The small, hard lump was cancer.* Still, she hoped with all of her heart, that her personal diagnosis was incorrect.

Maria's uncharacteristically quiet, reserved behaviour made Hanale question the part he played in child rearing and, immediately, he stepped up to the mark. Simon came to the conclusion that he was the spare part in the household and resolved to do something about it. His resolve, however, was temporary and soon he slipped back into his melancholy brooding ways, unable to see any problems but his own.

Contrary to the consultant's advice, Maria determined her own fate. She had years ago, though still fresh in her mind, lived through the stages of her mother's cancer and subsequent death; she was not willing, or wanting, to inflict the same emotional pain on others.

After her last consultation, she headed straight for the off-license, bought what she required and, together with her medication, she stashed it away in a secret place, where she would retrieve it when she was ready.

Chapter One Hundred and Forty
Kauai

Shocked eyes shot directly to the man sitting on her opposite side, his question ringing loudly in her ears long after the last syllable was uttered. It was a question she could not answer. She did not know the answer.

"Ocean, why did you go all the way to the Big Island to return a day later?" Makamae repeated his words his steady, wise eyes fixed enquiringly on his friend, while hot fury burned in her eyes.

What right had this man to question her decisions? Her flaming eyes looked into his eyes of concern and she felt her inner anger subsiding. "I wanted to see for myself how Solomao and the other clients were progressing."

"And?"

"They're doing brilliantly."

"And?"

"And?" She wished her infuriating friend would drink his juice and go.

"What other reason?"

"What do you mean; what other reason?" There was an element of touchiness in her voice, she wasn't aware of exuding and which Makamae picked up immediately.

"Ekewaka?" He prompted softly; eyes not moving a millimetre.

Lids closing her eyes to obliterate Makamae's focussed scrutiny, she wondered how her friend had found out about Ekewaka; swiftly coming to the conclusion that her friend always knew everything, before she had the faintest inkling.

Silence heavy and undiluted shrouded the two friends as one waited patiently for an answer; the other not daring to give it. It was broken by the sound of approaching footsteps and two sets of eyes shot up.

"A letter for you, Ocean and it comes all the way from England!" A cheerful young native exclaimed, turning the intriguing envelope over and over in his hand, smiling hopefully. "May I..."

"Of course you may have the stamps, Nahoa." Her warm smile belied her chaotic thoughts, wondering who had sent her the letter, as she held it stiffly in her trembling hands.

"Aren't you going to open it?" Makamae's soft tones thrust her out of her reverie; his silent, inquisitive eyes drilling into her very soul, waiting for her response. Stuffing the envelope into her pocket, she turned and purposefully strode towards the house, Makamae's words echoing loudly in her ears... *It seems to me, Ocean, that just lately, you are running from everything, including yourself...*

For a split second, she hesitated before rushing inside; Makamae's words firmly registered in her head.

... Why did you go to the Big Island, to return a day later... It seems to me, Ocean, that, just lately, you are running away from everything, including yourself... These words performed a riotous dance in her swimming head throughout the long night, propelling her to thrust the light cover off her bed, run to the drinks cabinet and, at eleven minutes past one in the morning, fix herself an uncharacteristically early Mai Tai breaking her golden rule. After her father's and Lokemele's disastrous relationship with alcohol, she had secretly vowed never to allow the strong stuff to medicate her feelings; no matter what kind of black cloud was hovering above her. In the early hours of this new day, she brought the glass of golden-brown-liquid up to her mouth, Kai and Lokemele's image crashing into her head. Seconds later she listened to the stuff gurgling away down the plug hole.

With a heavy, ragged sigh she slid open the glass door and stepped into the hauntingly silent, cool garden, drew up a wicker chair and sat down. For long minutes, her mind was completely blank, devoid of all thoughts; still, like the shadowed, motionless blooms around her. She was at peace...

The faint rustle of some night creature, moving stealthily in the shrubbery, thrust an image into the forefront of her mind... *Solomao was accompanied by another—Ekewaka...* She snapped her eyes shut. *What was she running away from?* The mystifying question slid into her head. *Was she running from Ekewaka or—herself?* Her eyes opened to the dark velvety sky, punctured by the bright lights of faraway galaxies. The answer was not there.

Her mind drifted to a man and his wise words, spoken in times of trouble and uncertainty… *Find the root of the problem, tackle it and then you will be free, Ocean…* A faint whimsical smile hovered on her lips. *Dear, dear Uncle Keoki; he truly was a wise man… And so too is Makamae,* she nodded, but whether she could face her demons or not; that was another question entirely.

Chapter One Hundred and Forty-One
The Big Island

Ekewaka had had his fair share of women, but none as mysterious and frustrating as Ocean Tia. The others had been only too willing to jump into his bed; with Ocean Tia he had not got past the first post.

Her sudden exit from the island had baffled him. No explanation; no reason was given, just the words, "I'm leaving for Kauai on the next available flight, Ekewaka." His questions; his subtle hints of persuasion to stay fell on deaf ears. Her mind was made up. Before he had revved up the convertible to take her to the airport, hoping she'd change her mind en route, she'd jumped into a taxi and departed leaving a stunned Hawaiian wondering, for the first time, where he had failed and the more he wondered, the more perplexed he became about the whole darned scenario.

For the first time, he felt wounded, rejected and dejected; for the first time he started to question his behaviour. Had Ocean Tia seen him for the man he truly was a womaniser; a seeker of sexual gratification, no matter what it cost the woman; had she seen through his twinkling eyes, his sensual mouth, his athletic frame, his charms and found someone she clearly did not want to associate with? The answer, he sadly concluded, was obviously and absolutely; yes!

Kauai

... You are running away from everything... Makamae's words drummed in Ocean Tia's consciousness long after he had left her premises... *You are running away from everything... You are running away from everything...* The unopened envelope burned in the depths of her pocket... *You are running away from everything...* Her fingers dived in, touched the scorching envelope and swiftly withdrew feeling the burn. After seconds of lucid reasoning, her fingers dived back in and extracted the offending object.

Her fingers on fire with excitement she ripped the seal apart and, sitting down comfortably, prepared herself for a few minutes of delightful pleasure as she caught up with Maria's news.

Eyes of joy rapidly transformed into eyes of raw shock; the sparkle instantly disappearing, replaced by a sheen of sorrow; disbelief seeping through her and, with it, a tiny grain of hope.

She reread the sombre words, hoping against hope that she had misread or misinterpreted the neatly handwritten news. A third... fourth time she read the now familiar words and, still, the stubborn words refused to change except for one visible difference a dark, grey splodge where her tears had fallen.

The clock chimed the half hour reminding her she was due at the sanctuary. Stuffing the paper into its envelope and into a drawer she made for the door, resolving to sweep Maria's devastating news out of her mind.

Maria's words, however, had a life of their own, refusing to be stuffed into a drawer and be forgotten; refusing to be dead and buried, even for a short period of time. They danced a haunting reel of their own, making each word weave, mingle and form a clear image of a wizened-faced Maria; her skeletal hands clenching tightly as she gasped, yearned, begged for death to take her for its own. The picture was interwoven with another image. It was so real, it hurt. It was Alan.

Menial tasks became automatic responses as Maria's words and Alan's image swirled and whirled around in Ocean Tia's head, spinning wildly out of control and disappeared to the shrill sound of the ringing phone.

"It's for you, Ocean."

His words were steady and clear, tearing through her like the jagged teeth of a blunt knife; his image dissolving everything and everyone around her, creating a fresh hell in her head; her fingers curling tightly around the cord making her knuckles prominent.

"Ocean?"

"Yes; I'm... I'm here, Ekewaka." Trying desperately to focus, his words made no sense to her at all. *Click* The receiver was back in its cradle.

Once more it rang and rang and rang; each ring ominous and deafening, until she thought her head would explode. "What?" She snapped uncharacteristically.

What she heard made her insides freeze; then dance before she banged down the receiver.

A third time it rang. *Click* His words were rushed, conscious they could be met with the same fate. What he heard made his heart stop.

"Ekewaka; never, ever ring me again. I have found someone else. Leave me alone!"

As the click sounded for the third time regret, sadness and perplexity marched into the hearts of two people; both staring at their silent handsets; Ekewaka wondering what he had done to have warranted such icy behaviour; Ocean Tia enveloped in a thick veil of sadness wishing she was living in another time; another place where things were very different. Both walked away from their respective phones, feeling this was a sad end to a chapter in their lives.

Withdrawing the folded paper from the envelope, she sat and allowed her pained heart to absorb every single word as, simultaneously, the devastating words swam around and around in her head... *breast cancer—six months, maybe a little longer—Hanale is taking this very badly—please come...* Her eyes froze on the last two words as they almost jumped off the page. The appeal stark; silently pleading for her to be at a dying woman's side... *Hanale is taking this very badly—please come...* The silent words hammered and thundered and, before the echo of the last syllable of the last word died, the words began their haunting litany once more; each time becoming louder, clearer, more desperate sending her conscience aflame with all-consuming guilt; words, she knew, Maria would only use if the situation necessitated their usage.

Mental exhaustion finally took over, dissipating words and images as Ocean Tia fell into dreamless slumber.

With the bright Hawaiian dawn came a pivotal decision, bringing with it its own problems.

Chapter One Hundred and Forty-Two

Leaving in its wake the Los Angeles lights the plane merged into the clouds. Ocean Tia's guts clenched and churned with growing apprehension; her heart lacerated with raw pain; failing to quell images of a dying Maria, a broken hearted Hanale and a cheating husband; three images merging together instantly becoming allies against her, refusing to grant her any semblance of peace. Scrambling in her bag, she brought out the sizzling bestseller she had bought at the airport and opened its cover. Ten minutes later the opening page remained staring at her; the promise of sending her into a land of intrigue and sexual delights on hold; not one single word read. Eyes switched to the small screen in front, attempting to follow the plane's flight path; an activity she had never failed to enjoy. Today it irritated her, making her wish the plane would change course and fly into obscurity, where she did not have to face the inevitable.

Trying to focus her mind on happier times; for a brief few moments she succeeded. Curt seconds of tranquillity; taking her back—back—to the days preceding the New Year's celebrations as… *she gazed at her reflection in the full-length mirror and smiled. Her choice of a floral print dress made her feel she was not betraying her Hawaiian roots and, as she picked up her fake frangipani and attached it above her right ear she said, "I am not taken—yet."*… Oh, how she now wished she had been taken and had denied Simon the privilege. Her mind crashed into another scene as… *she refused to take in what she undoubtedly saw; her darkest nightmare maturing into fruition before her very eyes*… If only Simon had not brought Natasha Parks into their lives… As if on cue her nemesis's cruel words exploded in her head, as loud and as clear as the day they were spewed out to a dying Alan… *It's no wonder you look like a skeleton, mate; eat more of this Hawaiian rubbish and you will disappear completely*… What must Alan have felt? Whatever it was, she closed her eyes to the seemingly motionless plane on the screen, it was well hidden. Oh, if only he was sat beside her now; if only he could once again give her his invaluable advice, on how to comfort and bring solace to a dying woman; how to comfort a husband who was already grieving for his wife. She nodded her head slowly, assuredly. *Alan would know what to say; what to do. He had been there himself.* Her mind continued to journey on bumpy terrain. *Where did Simon fit into the grand scale of things? Did he fit in at all?* In all forms of communication he had not been mentioned. *Was he even on the scene; or, had Natasha Parks lured him back into her bed?* An involuntary sigh escaped Ocean Tia's partly opened lips. *Soon she would know.*

Chapter One Hundred and Forty-Three
England

They hugged tightly.

Ocean Tia's heart seared with raw emotion as she felt Maria's skeletal body against her own; thankful her face was averted for fear of what they may see in each other's eyes. For long moments, they clung on to each other; lost, for a few precious moments, in the shrouded mists of happier days; clinging for comfort, aware that hope had abandoned them both. It was Ocean who gently withdrew and Maria who spoke, grateful tears glistening in her eyes. "Thank you." She softly said; two words speaking poignant volumes. Briefly Ocean Tia's attention was diverted, her eyes earnestly scanning the bustling crowds. "He's not here." Maria intercepted her sister-in-law's thoughts and softly added, "He has not been able to come to terms with it all."

Ocean noticed regret lacing Maria's words; a surge of anger sweeping through her. *How could Hanale be so selfish when his wife needed him so?* Tighter she enveloped her sister-in-law and friend as, simultaneously, an image of Lokemele comforting Alan swept into her thoughts. "I am here for you, Maria." She said soothingly. "I am here." Her insides seethed.

The two women, united in grief and Hanale's abandonment, sat in silence; the soft purring of the car engine providing the only background noise; both immersed in their own silent worlds, where Hanale was cast in the starring role; only he refused to perform, leaving the two women bereft of the one solid rock, they thought, they could rely on. Finally Ocean spoke gazing sideways at the pale-faced, sunken-eyed woman beside her staring starkly ahead, her white-knuckled hands firmly clutching the steering wheel, as if it was her only reliable anchor. "What was Hanale's initial reaction to the news, Maria?"

"The second I told him he clamped his mouth against the subject; refusing to discuss any aspect of it and carrying on as if the whole thing is not happening."

Raw anger, which had once been so alien to Ocean Tia and now so familiar, resurfaced bubbling and frothing, ready to spill out in a surge of verbal spew. Another sideway glance made her mouth compress tightly. *Maria had enough to contend with. But,* she told herself firmly, *one way or another this issue had to be resolved; Hanale needed to face up to his responsibilities, no matter how difficult and uncomfortable the challenge.* She was prepared to make him, even if it meant losing him.

Chapter One Hundred and Forty-Four

Standing at the open doorway she stared fondly as father and son watched some engaging cartoon. Her heart tightened. *It would have been such a happy scene if only…*

Hanale turned, aware of a presence. His eyes lit up. "Ocean; you've arrived!"

For a brief moment, she witnessed the undeniable, raw sadness in his eyes; but, only for a moment. *He acted well,* she thought. The tight hug he gave her told her all she needed to know; feeling his inner, silent pain transmitting to and penetrating her heart, soul and senses; pain he had unsuccessfully attempted to hide by pretending everything was okay. Maria hadn't got her devastating diagnosis and subsequent prognosis; she was here alive and well; a mother to her son and a dear, beloved wife. Everything in the garden was rosy. All was well; or, so he tried to prove as he attempted to mask his pain in the daily rituals of the day. *Yes,* Ocean smiled sadly, *he was a good actor but not that good.* The all-consuming ache was burning deep in the depths of his heart and soul and it was stealthily seeping out.

"We need to talk, Hanale." She stated as she withdrew herself from his tight embrace, feeling him instantly shrink.

Swiftly his eyes diverted from her scrutinising eyes and turned to his giggling son, who had just seen an absent-minded cat crash head first down a hole, followed by an eager looking mouse, who stopped abruptly at the mouth of the hole watching his nemesis disappear out of view and laughed raucously. Hanale laughed. Ocean Tia cried silent tears. *This,* she concluded, *was not going to be easy.* Silently she walked away.

Rigidly she sat on the edge of the bed, the chimes of the clock downstairs striking fifteen minutes to midnight. Sleep, she knew, would once again evade her as, one by one, long forgotten memories surfaced and fought for her attention. One memory took centre stage and around it the others circled, like ravenous vultures, to claim their stake in the limelight. Lokemele was the star of the show and what a performance she gave! For unlike her son, Hanale, she had not given up when it mattered. In the paroxysm of Alan's despair, she shone brilliantly; she had opened her eyes to the truth, stared it in the face and acted accordingly. A better, more diligent and devoted carer, Alan could not have hoped for and yet... yet... Ocean sighed inwardly, *her heart must have been broken; broken but not dead, like Hanale's heart seemed to be.* Her thoughts lingered on the half-brother she loved and, as he grew in her mind, so did her resolve to bring peace to a dying Maria; just as Lokemele had made it possible for Alan.

Chapter One Hundred and Forty-Five

Ocean Tia knew that Maria's life was drawing to an end; amongst other symptoms her loss of appetite, nausea and insomnia were only too evident and, still, Hanale carried on as if all was normal.

As the sound of Maria's wrenching travelled from the bathroom to the kitchen, Ocean's concern for both Maria and Hanale deepened; her eyes following Hanale one morning as he flitted from cupboards to table, in the process of preparing breakfast. Abruptly she rose from her chair, hearing it fall behind her with a bang. Ignoring it she approached Hanale placing a firm hand on his arm, an empty bowl held precariously in his hand. "Stop!" She demanded. "Hanale; just stop." For a split second, their eyes locked. "Sit." She indicated a chair with her hand. Obediently, like a small child obeying his mother, he sat his unblinking eyes fixed on the cornflakes box, his ears attune to the deafening stillness.

Pulling up a chair beside him she reached for his hands, enveloped them in her own and looked into his unresponsive eyes. "You and I have to talk, Hanale. You have to face up to the truth." She selected her words carefully and added, "You have to stop being an ostrich; take your head out of the sand and be there for Maria, Hanale." The clock ticked on innocently; excruciatingly loudly in their ears, as if time was forcing its way into their private nightmare... *tick-tock... tick-tock... tick-tock... tick...*

Slowly, very slowly, he raised his expressionless eyes to her concerned eyes, his hands still secure in the warmth of her hands, as the clock continued its ominous whisper... *tick-tock... tick-tock... If only,* he thought, *he could turn the clock back or—forward.*

Ocean Tia broke the monotonous silence, her words soft and compassionate as if belonging to an angel. "Maria is dying, Hanale."

Sharply, as if from a burning flame, he snatched his hands from her delicate touch; quickly she reclaimed them, while her head searched frantically for the appropriate words, while he squeezed his eyes tight in a futile effort to eradicate Maria's diagnosis, the world and everything and everyone in it.

"Maria is dying, Hanale." Ocean Tia reinstated the stark, undeniable truth; each word, each syllable drumming ever louder in his head.

Abruptly he rose, letting her hands slip and drop to the table, and stormed out the kitchen, leaving his bowl of cornflakes untouched and Ocean's ears registering his fading footsteps, mingled with the sounds of Maria's wrenching.

Deep in the depths of his sorrowful heart, Hanale knew his beloved wife's days were numbered and if ever he was tempted to slip into the luxurious world of doubt Ocean's words, like an ancient Hawaiian drum of doom, beat the devastating truth… *Maria… is… dying… Maria… is… dying…* Maria… is… dying… The words of truth, like a sharp-edged blade, thrust repeatedly and mercilessly through his breaking heart, his swimming head, his reeling senses in his waking hours and followed him into the long hours of restless slumber… *Maria… is… dying… d… y… i… n… g… DYING!* Like a Jack-in-the-box he jumped, his stark eyes staring into the impenetrable darkness and darted to his bedside clock. *2-16… 2-17… 2-18…* His eyes glared at the luminous green numbers… *2-19…* And as the numbers changed a disturbing realisation crept stealthily into Hanale's consciousness… *2-37… Time was running away.* Snapping his eyes shut he willed for the impossible. His eyes opened. The impossible was denied. Time marched solidly on. It would not stop for him. It would not stop for Maria.

Each hour, minute, second that passed was never to be reclaimed; lost in the sands of time. Each ticking second was a second less to live until… until the last precious second was reached and Maria would breathe her last and he would not be there… *Maria… is… dying…* Ocean's echoing words reverberated in his head becoming louder and louder, as each passing second dwindled and slipped away into eternity. *And, where was he, the loving husband? Wallowing in his own misery; already grieving for his beloved who had not yet passed away; mourning for a wife, who desperately needed her husband by her side.*

Click. The sound of the opening door vibrated hauntingly in his heavy head. Taking a solitary step inside the room he stood motionless his heart, like his limbs, paralysed; afraid to advance a centimetre further, his eyes adjusting to the semi-darkness. He stood, stuck in no man's land, between life and death; his feet yearning to run in the opposite direction far, far away where death was not the final destination. They remained solidly glued to the carpet beneath, his heart thudding.

"Is… Is that you, Ocean?" A faint voice murmured.

Hanale died a sudden death; struck with the icy stab of awareness that Maria was not expecting him. *Had she given up on him?* He wondered. He wouldn't blame her if she had. Soft footsteps interrupted his dismal thoughts and turning his eyes met those of Ocean Tia.

"Hanale!" The shock of seeing him there was clearly visible in her widened eyes. Her heart danced with renewed hope. "I'll go." She said softly and, before he could stop her, she had disappeared out the door; leaving Hanale in a perplexing state of indecision as the thought of escapism, once again, rushed into his mind. He turned.

"Ocean… Is that y…" The feeble voice trailed off.

… *Tick-tock… tick-tock… tick-tock…* Time was passing.

A light cough escaped his mouth. "It's… It's me, Maria; Hanale." He managed to squeeze the words out of his constricted throat, where a hard lump had lodged refusing to budge; wishing fervently that time would STOP; wishing that he could take his wife's place and jump into her waiting, cold, dark grave; never to rise; the bleak reality of what he had done, and what he had not done, overpowering.

"Hanale…"

Though barely audible Maria's voice boomed in his head, propelling his feet to rush to her bedside, urging his eyes to look down on the wizened bundle beneath, breaking his heart into thousands of pieces which, he knew, would never be made whole again. It would be broken until the end of TIME.

"Hanale… Hanale…" She repeated his name over and over again and he wished she would never stop. Taking her skeletal body to himself, salty tears streaming silently down his cheeks, he rocked her to and fro… to and fro feeling her pain, her abandonment; his bitter regret.

He clung on to her as if she was the most precious jewel, fresh tears sliding down dried trails; never, ever wanting to let her go. "I am sorry, Maria." He sobbed bitterly. "I am so very, very sorry. Forgive me, Maria. Please… please forgive me." He hugged her tighter repeating over and over again, "I am sorry. I am so very, very sorry…"

How long they clung on to each other, time only knew. Both were oblivious to everything but each other; neither wanted to let go and face reality. It was

Maria who spoke as she reluctantly withdrew from his grasp. "W. we have to talk, Hanale."

Her words, laden with meaning, lay heavily in his heart. It was the very last thing he wanted to do.

"Tomorrow." She raised her pale face to him and smiled reassuringly.

His heart breaking afresh, he returned her smile. "Tomorrow," he said softly.

Chapter One Hundred and Forty-Six
The Islands

I have found someone else… Ocean Tia's words were cold, detached and most definitely incredulous, Ekewaka concluded. Not for a split second had he believed her announcement. He had seen the way she had looked into his eyes, however, this fact did not soothe his troubled heart. With a cover up, he wisely surmised, there was usually a reason, no matter how strong or futile it may be. And that was the reason he now found himself on a plane.

Approaching the front garden, his holdall firmly grasped in his broad hand, his brow furrowed at the sight of a man's back.

Feeling a presence behind him the man turned from the lawn mower and, using his chequered handkerchief wiped beads of sweat from his brow, his mouth breaking out into a genial smile. "What brings you here, my friend?"

Ekewaka extended his hand to his acquaintance. "Ocean." Makamae's words making his heart freeze. "What do you mean; gone?"

Undeterred by Ekewaka's intense, lingering gaze Makamae explained as briefly as possible, without giving away a confidence. "England; family affairs, I believe. I'm house-sitting. Do you care for a drink?" He cocked a bushy eyebrow, swiping away a fresh layer of perspiration from his forehead, before heading towards the door.

"I came for a detailed explanation." Ekewaka replied, following Makamae into the cool interior of the house.

But Makamae had been pre-warned and, therefore, he was well armed with a justifiable, brief explanation. First of all he wanted to know why Ekewaka was here.

Ekewaka gave nothing away, saying he merely wanted to catch up with a friend; after which he was given a little more information.

Back on his island her image, as pure and clear as crystal, pervaded through Ekewaka's thoughts, heart and soul making him question his own reasoning and sanity. Never before, in his thirty-three years on this earth, had a female taken hold of his senses in such a ruthless way. Take 'em or leave 'em, that was his motto in life and none had resisted his charms; though, some had fruitlessly tried. None until Ocean Tia had ventured into his life. His mind drifted as... *they stood side by side on the white sand as the thundering, mighty waves rushed towards them...* He snapped his eyes shut against the scene. He had lost his chance; he'd lost Ocean Tia and, as subtle streaks of morning sunlight filtered through the still palm leaves, Ekewaka made a firm decision.

Chapter One Hundred and Forty-Seven
England

Tomorrow never came for Maria. She died peacefully in her sleep. The last words, she so desperately wanted to share with her husband, died with her.

As she lay still, silent and at peace Hanale howled, his cries coming from the depths of Hell; his heart-wrenching sobs penetrating the deathly silence.

His heart-breaking lamentations reached Ocean Tia who was sitting perfectly still, her eyes focussed on the sleeping child who was innocently unaware that his mother had died. Her thoughts jumped erratically in her head, as she leaned over and adjusted the young boy's bedcover. One distorted thought became clearer, more prominent and gradually formed into a coherent picture, precluding all other thoughts. This thought settled stubbornly in the forefront of her mind.

Her fingers darted into her skirt pocket and withdrew an envelope, the tears in her eyes distorting the neatly written name. Taking a deep, ragged breath she tore open the seal and withdrew the folded paper. For long seconds, her obstinate eyes refused to look down, preferring to focus on the light cover as it gently rose and fell with regular rhythm; opting to focus on the living than to focus on the words of a dead woman.

Slowly, reluctantly she dragged her eyes away from the sleeping bundle and fixed them on to the paper in her lightly trembling hand. Unfolding it she read.

Aloha, my dear Ocean,
It is with a grateful heart that I say a special, thank you, to my dearest friend, sister-in-law and confidante for the privilege of having known you; thank you for everything you have done for me.
I have one dying request, Ocean. Please show Hanale and Luke, as only you can, that life goes on; that, after the grief there is happiness to grasp; that after the rain comes the sunshine. Take them back to the Hawaiian Islands with you

and teach them; show them; guide them. In the midst of their raging storm, be their lighthouse; a beam that shines forth hope. Please tell them that I shall never leave them.

It is with a heavy, sad heart that I must say, goodbye.

Thank you for the sunny memories, my dearest friend.

Aloha

Maria x

Unable to restrain the flood of tears they fell on to the page, instantly creating small, irregular patterns of smudged grey, the smeared paper trembling in her hands, as she felt the entire world crashing in on her from all sides; wishing it would crush her into smithereens, so that she no longer had to face the empty world Maria left behind.

She did not know how long she sat immobile, her stiffened body alerting her to the fact that it had been a good while. Reluctantly she stretched, rose and abandoned Luke's room. With heavy slow steps, she approached the closed door; loud, heart-wrenching sobs penetrating the solid wood and infiltrating Ocean's ears. Gingerly her fingers knocked on the door and her disinclined feet walked in.

What her eyes saw her heart grieved; a hunched-up, heaving bundle sobbing for all the world to hear. For a solid moment, she stood perfectly still, her own heart heaving heavily, wondering if she had the right to encroach into Hanale's grieving world. Maria's silent words echoed loudly in her ears... *In the midst of their raging storm, be their lighthouse... Oh, she had made it seem so very easy and yet it was the greatest of challenges... In the midst of their tempest, to be their beacon...* She closed and squeezed her eyes tightly; squeezed them tighter until she could squeeze them no more. *If only Lokemele was here or Uncle Keoki or Alan; her beacons. They would know exactly what to do and they would do it.*

Eyes snapped open, feet stepped boldly forward and gentle arms enveloped a broken man, as two broken hearts fused into one and mourned for a woman they both loved.

They stood at the edge of the open grave, which was silently waiting to take Maria for its own. United in their grief, their ears were attune to retreating footsteps and subdued, fading voices of the many mourners who had gathered to pay their last respects. From the depth of her coat pocket, Ocean Tia retrieved two sealed envelopes and handed them over to Hanale saying softly, "One for you; one for Luke; from Maria." She noticed the faintest of smiles on Hanale's lips.

Declining the chauffeur driven limousine they walked the three kilometre walk home; both immersed in their own thoughts and memories. As they walked into the drive Ocean Tia's heart, in unison with her feet, stopped; her stark eyes staring fixedly at the figure at the door.

Chapter One Hundred and Forty-Eight

Her dry mouth opened to non-existent words, her legs about to buckle as a horrible sickly feeling surged through her entire body, threatening to spew out of her arid mouth; the smile on the visitor's lips, combined with the warmth in his eyes, making her stomach churn. It was Hanale who spoke. "What on earth are you doing here?"

Eyes switched to Ocean and fixed. "I. I heard about Maria."

Three figures stood like perfect statues; the eerie stillness overbearing.

"Simon." Ocean broke the uncanny silence, still not quite believing that her eyes were staring blatantly at her husband.

His smile died as he witnessed the undeniable incredulity in her eyes; his own reaction at seeing his wife mild, having suspected that she would be here for Maria's funeral. After further excruciating seconds of standing, shuffling and staring Simon took the initiative, as he reluctantly unglued his eyes from Ocean and focussed on his brother-in-law. "I am truly sorry for your loss, Hanale."

Hanale closed his eyes and nodded. Silence pervaded once more.

… *Be their lighthouse… lighthouse… LIGHTHOUSE…* Maria's words crashed into Ocean's head, like a mighty sea against rocks and, though inwardly her heart was fragmenting into pieces of conflicting shards, each piece raw and infused with pain, she urged enthusiastically, "Come on; let's go inside."

Meekly the two men followed her into the house and the door closed.

Suspended silence hung over three souls drowning in their own pool of despair; all three aware that this was the epigrammatic calm before the storm. Apart from the pangs of grief and regret, Hanale was dead to the world; Simon's heart was full of Ocean while she was yearning to fly away from the stench of death and from the mourners of lost wives; to fly to Kauai, her homeland, where the sun always shone; to a man who wanted her; to a place where she felt free. Involuntarily her eyes gazed on the two men in turn. *What would Lokemele do?*

What would Alan advise? As if on cue, the answers came flooding into her head; answers she did not want to hear, let alone acknowledge.

He stood outside the door, his eyes taking in the neat semi-detached house and its neatly organised garden. *Neat,* he surmised. *Everything seemed neat; in order; everything in its correct place. Everything seemed cold; it lacked warmth and the charm of randomly growing blooms. It needed the warmth of the Hawaiian sunshine.*

The knock on the door brought three souls out of their selfish reveries. Ocean raised her hitherto immobile eyes. "Are you expecting anyone, Hanale?" He shook his head silently. Striding to the door, feeling Simon's penetrable gaze on her back, she made up her mind to sort things out once the visitor had disappeared.

The door opened.

Chapter One Hundred and Forty-Nine

Eyes locked with eyes. One heart raced wildly; the other clenched mercilessly squeezing... squeezing the very life out of her.

"Ocean."

The resounding echo of his soft voice crashed through her, like a phenomenal tsunami, making her senses numb as she stood wide-eyed and perfectly still, like a solidified statue. He had been the last person in the world she had been expecting. His sensual lips curled up into a smile, making her stir out of her temporary paralysis, her trembling hand grasping the door, her eyes tearing away from the figure, fleetingly darting back to the bowels of the house, her heart beating furiously and uncontrollably.

"Ocean." He repeated, automatically bringing her astounded eyes back to him.

"What are you doing here, Ekewaka?" She pushed the words out of her mouth, her chaotic senses reeling uncontrollably.

"Can we talk, Ocean; please?"

She detected a sense of urgency in his words; saw the eyes of a beggar and felt deeply his selfish need; her eyes fixed on his eyes as she desperately willed her energetic heart to cease its furious march.

His hand reached for her hand which stubbornly, beneath his, clutched tighter the door; a splay of tiny electric currents shooting randomly through her body, making her feel weak and vulnerable under his close scrutiny. "Please, Ocean; I need to talk to you." He reiterated.

"This is not the time, Ekewaka. We are a house in mourning." She stated her words feeling alien, detached, belonging to someone else. She felt the loosening of his hold on her hand.

"Mourning?" He raised a concerned eyebrow.

"Maria; my sister-in-law has died." She averted her gaze from his. She did not want to witness his false sympathy.

She did not feel the sudden joy in his heart; the sheer relief that the woman he loved had not gone back to her husband. There was hope. "I am sorry, Ocean."

"I must go, Ekewaka; Hanale, Luke and… Simon need me."

His short-lived hope came crashing down on him, forcing him to plunge from the pinnacle of Heaven to the very depths of deepest Hell. There was no hope.

On either side of the closed door, two hearts sank in the cold waters of reality. The final nail had been hammered into the coffin of their friendship, determining its death and, as both walked away from the door and each other, *their fate,* both sadly concluded, *had been sealed.*

Chapter One Hundred and Fifty

Loss, deep and crushing, invaded and made its home in Ocean Tia's heart and with it a sense of duty. The sense of duty concerned three people; Hanale, her grieving half-brother; Simon, her husband and Luke, her nephew and godchild. The one who needed her the most, she decided, was Hanale, then Luke and, finally, Simon. The latter was going to be the most challenging, of that she had no doubt; it was this challenge, she knew, she had to overcome if there was to be any hope of them both moving on.

Reading the child a fairy tale, her eyes switched from the text to the boy already captured by sleep, his bedcovers rising and falling gently in tune with his regular breathing rhythm. *So young; so innocent; so alone; abandoned,* she thought, feeling the familiar tight clench in her heart for the child she never had. *There was still time,* a soft voice in her head whispered. She snapped her eyes shut against the potentiality shaking her head vigorously, rose from her chair and wandered over to the window, where she watched the gathering dusk perform its nightly ritual, casting its dark veil over all it surveyed, her mind drifting to an island far away; an island of glorious sunsets; an island of warmth; her home.

Ekewaka gate-crashed her pensive thoughts making her heart tighten as... *the tall, handsome figure skilfully weaved in and out of the majestic waves; the sovereign of the ocean and king of her heart... If only,* she mused, *things were different then maybe—just maybe we could have had it all.*

She watched the huddled figure staring blatantly at the full bowl of untouched cornflakes and felt his pain. It was a pain she had felt so many times following the loss of her father, Kai; her dear Uncle Keoki and Auntie Luana; her beloved friend, Lokemele and of course dear, beloved Alan; the truest friend; and, though her mother had died when Ocean was a young child, she felt her loss deeply. She knew there was only one medicine for this specific pain... TIME.

Her eyes rose from the bowl of soapy water to the sound of knocking. In equal measures, she had been expecting and dreading this visitor. There was no escape route.

He stood on the doorstep, his fingers poised and about to knock once more; his heart clenching treacherously while simultaneously his guts twisted mercilessly. This was his chance.

The door slowly opened. Husband and wife stood eye to eye, body to body, as fate danced a merry dance around them.

"Ocean." Simon said softly, his smile making something stir in the depths of Ocean Tia's heart.

"Simon." She returned his smile, making his heart dance. "Come in."

He followed her slender figure inside, secretly praying she would grant him the chance he craved.

In the quiet room they sat, the familiar clock ticking the minutes away the way it had always done, until each second became a miniscule grain in the forgotten sands of time.

Cautiously she raised unwilling eyes to rest on her husband's eyes, her racing heart threatening to explode as, furiously, she struggled to find the right words; the words she had been rehearsing and had now become elusive. Failing to obey her silent command other words, raw and direct, spewed out of her mouth. "Simon, I want a divorce."

In that split moment of moments, his whole world crashed in, around and down on him; the love of his life disintegrating before his very eyes as, simultaneously, her eyes visibly observed hope disappear from his paling face, replaced by a conspicuous sheen of defeat and hopelessness... *Tick-tock... tick-tock... tick-tock...* Tick... The faithful servant of time whispered... *tick-tock... tick-tock...* Two statues sat while fate hung in the balance... *tick-tock... tick-tock... tick-tock... tick-*

"Simon, I..."

"I heard." He snapped his raw eyes set on the woman he had loved, had cheated on and still loved taking in the golden sheen of her skin, her dark unfathomable eyes, her long hair so dark and silky, aware that she was slowly slipping away from him. *Divorce... divorce... divorce...* The word repeatedly hammered in his head. She wanted a divorce. It was the end of the road. She wanted OUT!

Raw, constrained emotions fought a bitter, raging war. Part of her still loved the young student, she had fallen in love with all those years ago; another segment hated him for the hurt he had caused; the part that loomed larger than the others was her mistrust of him; for, she knew, she would never fully trust him again and, without hundred per cent trust, the foundation of their marriage would inevitable crumble and fall.

... Tick-tock... tick-tock... tick-tock...

"I no longer love you, Simon." She lied, knowing this was the most viable course of action open to her and, as she dropped her eyes to her clasped hands, he was only too aware that the reason for her lie was lost, irretrievable trust. "If only I hadn't have slept with Natasha." He mumbled his glassy eyes focussed on her bowed head.

"If only you hadn't have brought her to Alan's Hawaiian party, Simon." She said so softly her words were barely audible.

In Simon's ears, they thundered loudly and clearly diffusing any lingering hope. "If only—"

They sat motionless enveloped in a heavy pall of eerie silence, lost in their private worlds of regret; the remnants of their marriage suffocating in their cauldron of mistakes.

When she raised her head, his seat was empty and Simon was gone.

Like the marriage the house Ocean, Hanale and Luke occupied was dead; its soul had departed though the illusion of life was evident; meals were prepared and eaten, housework done, Luke was looked after, trivial talk took place. Important issues were buried deep... deep in their dark grave. Maria's dying words haunted Ocean Tia's waking hours, clinging to her conscience; they refused to be buried with their mistress. Silently and fiercely they clamoured to be heard and would not grant their recipient peace, until she had given them justice in the form of a fair hearing.

It was after Luke had gone to bed one evening and Hanale and Ocean sat at the supper table that words were spoken; words that cut through both their hearts and lay heavily suspended in the air, as Hanale's glassy eyes rested fixedly on his half-sister, waiting for her to digest what he had just announced, while she tried desperately to make sense of it all. Intently her eyes penetrated his eyes. "What do you mean you cannot cope, Hanale? You have to cope. You are the child's father. Maria's last wish was—" Ocean's words trailed away her sister-in-law's words boomed in her head, one word clearer than the rest; the beacon of light... *LIGHTHOUSE.*

"... someone else will have to look after Luke; Perhaps a foster parent. Perhaps... perhaps—adoption..."

"Stop!"

Her solitary word froze his remaining words as eyes locked with eyes; one pair seeing only darkness; the other seeing a wonderful light.

Chapter One Hundred and Fifty-One
Kauai

They stepped off the plane into the bright Hawaiian sunshine which eluded two figures; one was too young to appreciate its healing powers; the other visitor too grief-stricken to notice. Ocean Tia breathed a deep sigh of relief.

Makamae was waiting for them, his astute eyes picking up the invisible veil of grief shrouding the approaching figures. He was well prepared to play the role of a compassionate friend.

Ocean Tia hugged her old friend heartily accepting his lei, bringing the colourful blooms up to her nose and inhaling deeply the alluring, sweet fragrance of home.

Makamae felt her inner pain, his eyes straying to the forlorn looking man and child by his side and saw the pain in Hanale's eyes.

The mellow sounds of Hawaiian guitars filtered out the car radio and intermingled with the purring of the car engine and Makamae's soft voice; permeating the journey as Ocean Tia gazed longingly on to the passing mighty blue ocean and her mind drifted and words echoed in her head... *I am a married woman, Ekewaka... a married woman... married... married... married... MARRIED!* The death knell had sounded.

Sharply she withdrew her eyes from the inviting waves and focussed them on Makamae's chubby face. "How are things with you, my friend?" She did not hear his answer; Ekewaka's cheerful image refusing to leave her. Makamae's words a few seconds later chilled her to the bone.

Time stood still. The car moved on; the radio continued with its soothing serenades; Luke jabbered for England with childish exuberance; Hanale simply breathed. Ocean felt as if she'd died inside; her friend's words hanging suspended in the still air and Hanale wishing his tongue hadn't, uncharacteristically, spontaneously run away on its wayward tangent.

The mention of Ekewaka's name, blended with his image, played havoc In Ocean Tia's head. Somehow, in the space of a few seconds, he had become more real; no longer a mere memory but someone who had stamped his presence in her life.

The prevailing silence, combined with Ocean's distant look, told Makamae all he needed to know.

The following days brought wall-to-wall sunshine and a heavy, cold shadow across Hanale's heart. Geography had simply added to his burden of grief because here was sunshine, sea, happy-go-lucky natives; here were bitter-sweet memories of happier times spent with Kai, his father and Lokemele, his mother; here was hope; here was despair. For how could he hope the sunshine would lighten his heart, when it had died and was buried with his beloved Maria? How could he build a sandcastle with his son, when he wanted to bury himself deep… deep… deep in the depths of the white sand? How could he begin to live again, when all he yearned for was the blessing of death?

Ocean saw the deep ingrained sadness in Hanale's eyes and the unwillingness to engage with his son and decided, over breakfast, to approach Makamae with her concerns. "What am I to do, Makamae?"

He raised and focussed his brown eyes on her firm fingers holding a knife, about to slice a fresh pineapple. "Give him time, Ocean. It is our most precious gift."

She closed her eyes, Uncle Keoki springing up like a Jack-in-the-box, and smiled whimsically. The echo of Makamae's next words lingered in her head… *Give yourself time too, Ocean…* Ekewaka leaped into the forefront of her mind.

Days turned into weeks and little progress was made; but, it was made and on that crumb Ocean Tia pinned all her hopes. Her patience was richly rewarded. Hanale began to prepare Luke's meals; taking a stroll with him in the garden; a fifteen-minute jaunt to the shop; a short walk to the beach and back. The half hour outing became an hour until, one afternoon Ocean glanced at the clock and wondered where father and son had got to. A quick scan of the beach found them splashing happily in the oceans waves. It was not a time to intrude. She withdrew. *TIME*; she smiled, was doing its magic. Slowly Patiently Methodically Time marched to its own pace… T… I… M… E… Allowing buried bits of Hanale to shine through; allowing the heavy veil of grief to gradually, bit by bit, lift; allowing the young boy to take first place; allowing Maria to filter into a happy memory and a source to draw upon.

And all this took place with Ocean Tia's subtle encouragement, found in her silent, reassuring smiles, her touching comments and the happy twinkle in her eyes.

Plucking dead blooms from a flowering bush she turned to the sound of approaching footsteps. "Makamae."

Her smile did not fool him as he secretly assessed his friend, feeling her anguish. Unlike Ocean, he knew there was a way out of her dilemma. *If only,* he thought, *she would be brave enough to take it.*

As they sat in the cooling shade of the pink showering tree, Makamae continued to study his charge with his dark, discerning eyes. "Your thoughts lay heavy on your shoulders, Ocean."

"Hanale is starting to live." She smiled, her eyes set on the distant horizon.

"But; you're not."

The stark statement made her heart lurch her eyes steady and fixed, while his eyes took in her tightly clamped mouth, her distant eyes buried in their own pain, as silence reigned once more; though, it was a silence heavily bombarded by unanswered questions. "Ocean." Makamae's voice was laced with softness. "It is time to think about yourself; your future; your life."

She registered each single word. *So wise; so true were his words,* she thought; *they could have come out of Uncle Keoki's mouth. So astute and yet,* she dismally concluded, *so utterly impossible to achieve; for, how could she possibly reach for the stars, when she could not tear her thoughts away from the ruins of her miserable life; her failed marriage; her inability to conceive a child; her incapability to love another man, truly, unreservedly love him despite his faults and failings—If only she could learn to love another—If only—If only...* She closed her eyes squeezing them tightly, trying desperately to obliterate Ekewaka's image, which had stealthily crept into her head becoming clearer, larger and, oh, so very real. Abruptly she rose and just as abruptly she sat back down, as Makamae's words hit her with a sudden, mighty force.

"Ekewaka loves you."

Forcefully she unglued her body from the wicker chair and walked away, Makamae's words ringing louder and louder in her ears... *Ekewaka loves you... Ekewaka loves you... Ekewaka loves you!*

Chapter One Hundred and Fifty-Two
The Big Island

He didn't see the silhouetted figure cross the ceiling-to-floor glass pane; didn't hear the gentle knocks on the door; didn't witness her lips pressed into an ominous line and the apprehension in the depths of her dark eyes, as they stared unblinkingly at the closed door; didn't feel the tight constriction in her throat or the fast pulsating of her racing heart. His full attention was lavished on the beauty beneath him as he drove into her, momentarily paused and collapsed on to her, as Ocean Tia stared through the window.

Her pounding heart stopped abruptly, instantly becoming a frozen chunk of ice; her feet glued to the ground; her stark eyes glaring at the scene before her; the echoes of satisfied voices and light giggles filtering through the transparent partition and suffusing her heart and soul with bitter regret.

Simultaneously as the two figures on the other side of the pane began to unravel from each other, Ocean Tia forced her feet to unglue themselves from the ground below and run… run… run… out of the boundary of the extensive garden and on to the pavement beyond. Where she was going she did not know; did not care as long as it was far, far away from Ekewaka and the spectacle she had just witnessed.

Part of her wish she accomplished. However, the picture of what she had seen remained crystal clear in her mind, refusing to evaporate. Decreasing her pace her fast run changed into a steady jog and, eventually, slowed down to an evenly paced walk. In total contrast to her feet, racing questions bombarded her head… *Who… why… when… what… where?* Single words jumped out at her, making her furiously search her whirling head for answers; stark, restless, erratic, haunting questions burning rigorously and unquenchably in her fuddled brain. *How could he have deceived her in such a treacherous way? Why did he have to lie?* These and other questions became her unwanted, constant companions and her enemy, destroying any grain of feeling she had for Ekewaka.

She headed for the beach. This time it did not grant her solace.

Solomao saw straight through his saviour's smile, as he surreptitiously watched her preparing lunch for the seven residents. The transformation he had witnessed in the space of half an hour, alerted him to the fact that all was not well and desperately he wanted to help the woman he owed his life. Cautiously he approached saying softly, "What is the matter, Ocean?"

Efficiently she set the cutlery on the large table, her ears attune to his repeated question. Turning she forced a smile. "Nothing; nothing at all is the matter. I'm just a little tired, Solomao." She turned back to her task, relieved she did not have to look at his perplexed façade especially his questioning, knowing eyes.

He left the matter gazing after her as she left the dining room, knowing that something had happened during the time of her absence; something which had saddened his special friend. He had seen the undeniable pain in her eyes and heard the sadness in her voice. He knew.

Uninvited, unwanted thoughts of Ekewaka seeped into her mind throughout the torturous, long day. At odd moments, they came when she was helping with the laundry, chatting casually to residents, sitting in on their lectures; Ekewaka jumped into her mind and always accompanied by his latest conquest and, while she tried to blank all thoughts and images, Solomao was vowing to help Ocean; to repay her for the constant kindness she had bestowed on him.

Hurriedly she packed the few items of clothing she had recently unpacked and snapped the case closed. She had only one thing on her mind. *She had to get away from the island and the sooner, the better.*

Chapter One Hundred and Fifty-Three

Eyes focussed on the sullen face before him, his lips extending into a friendly, warm smile. "Solomao, my friend Aloha; what brings you here?"

Solomao's feet shuffled from one to the other, his opened mouth as dry as the Sahara Desert.

"Is everything all right at the sanctuary?" Questioned Ekewaka, still bemused at Solomao's unexpected appearance at his door.

"Y-yes, I-I—" His arid mouth closed; cautious, unwavering eyes peeled on the handsome man before him; feeling inferior and inadequate in his presence, his feet still shuffling.

Seeing and sensing Solomao's unease Ekewaka extended his door. "Come in; come in, Solomao."

The younger man stepped nervously inside, his eyes dropping to the highly polished wooden floor, on which his feet resumed their shuffling, while his mind wandered on everything and nothing, his erratic thoughts broken by Ekewaka's soft cough. "How can I help you, Solomao... a pineapple juice?"

Sitting gingerly on the edge of a very expensive plush sofa, Solomao wondered what on earth had propelled him to make a personal appearance, in favour of a phone call or even a letter.

For long moments, the two men sat in complete silence, their bodies facing each other, their minds poles apart; Ekewaka thinking of his next conquest and Solomao's eyes seeing only Ocean Tia's sad face.

Finally, after speaking sternly with himself, Solomao coughed nervously and focussed his eyes on his host's perplexed face. "It's... It's... It's... Ocean Tia."

The name plunged straight into Ekewaka's heart where he felt it intermingle with the memory of his most recent conquest; twist and pierce savagely. "Ocean Tia." He said softly as if in a trance, his still eyes on Solomao though seeing someone completely different.

"She's on the island, Sir. I. I think she's in a bad way, Sir."

"It's Ekewaka, Solomao; no sirs here. What makes you think she's in a bad way?"

Solomao felt Ekewaka's eyes drill through him with such burning intensity, he started shuffling a new dance in his chair, wishing to God he wasn't sat there betraying *his* Ocean's trust; wishing he was thousands kilometres away from the haunting image of her sad eyes and Ekewaka's enquiring eyes. His eyes darted to the drinks cabinet, craving for the power of alcohol to assuage the bitter feeling of betrayal invading his mind, body and soul.

Ekewaka's eyes swiftly followed Solomao's trail of vision. "Another pineapple juice, Solomao?" He volunteered rising abruptly in an attempt to break the recovering alcoholic's thought process.

Solomao's burning eyes remained firmly fixed on the Mai Tai bottle, his mouth already savouring the familiar rum, laced with lime and orange, flavour; his body luxuriating in the warmth of the potent liquid and senses taking him to—

"Solomao!" Ekewaka called a third time, a glass of cool juice in his hand.

Hearing his name crash loudly into his blissful yet dangerous thoughts, begrudgingly Solomao tore his eyes away from sweet temptation. "Thank you, Sir." He took the glass.

After giving Solomao a few seconds to collect his thoughts, Ekewaka plunged in. "So, my friend; why do you think Ocean Tia is in a bad way?"

Forcibly the younger man rested his eyes on his host. "I know her, Mister Ekewaka. Her heart is breaking. I just do not know why."

"And you tell me that she's on the island, Solomao?"

"Yes Sir." He coughed nervously correcting himself. "Mister Ekewaka."

For a moment, they held each other's gaze, each man secretly drowning in his own well of thoughts. "Right." Ekewaka lithely rose after minutes of silent reflection. "Let's go."

And like a meek lamb Solomao followed his friend not caring where, no longer focussing on why he had come here; craving only for alcohol a curse, he knew, would never leave him.

At top speed, Ekewaka drove his powerful motor down narrow lanes, skilfully navigating hairpin bends, racing along long stretches of road bordered on one side by tropical desolate beaches; making him wish he was riding the surf on the crest of an exhilarating wave, instead of trying to catch an elusive dream.

Too late they arrived at the sanctuary. Too late they wandered on to the beach in search of the woman they had lost. Too late they had arrived at the airport.

Too late, Ekewaka arrived on the Island of Kauai.

Chapter One Hundred and Fifty-Four
England

The long flight from Los Angeles to Heathrow was a soothing balm to Ocean Tia's tortured soul. It was a time during which she took stock of herself and of her life. It was a time in which her mind had drifted in various directions, until she took a tight rein of her scattered thoughts and gathered them into a methodical, sequential order; but, not before she gave her mind the luxury of wandering back in time... *as she wandered up and down the quiet, desolate beach her eyes searching desperately for her father who, in the depths of grief, had lost his way in life. Then, she did not find her makuakāne but she found a lady, Lokemele, who had helped her not only to shape her future, but who had also brought Hanale into her life and he had brought...* Tightly she closed her eyes; too late to prevent Simon's profile crashing into her thoughts; the man she had promised to love, honour and obey for the rest of her natural life. The familiar serrated blade plunged ruthlessly through her heart, her marriage vows echoing in her head while Simon's image became more defined; more real, as did the image of Natasha Parks the tall, slim blonde beauty with eyes of crystal blue, who had brought their marriage to a sudden crash landing leaving debris, heartbreak and two shattered lives in her wake while she moved on to her next victim. She stared blankly at the attractive flight attendant... *and then there was Alan; dear, steadfast, level-headed Alan who always took the good, bad and indifferent in his stride; saw the good in everyone and a way out of every problem...* Her eyes shifted from the busy attendant and stared at the image of a small plane on the screen in front, watching its deceiving slow progress across the ocean, while endless questions infested her head... *From whom or what was she escaping? Where was she escaping; was it into Simon's arms?* The last scenario had not, until now, entered her mind and now it was torridly ravaging her consciousness, like a ferocious wildfire greedily consuming all other thought processes in its path. Closing her eyes firmly she willed her husband's image to disappear. It etched deeper and deeper through the inferno of her mind and became her focal point.

She had left Kauai in a state of confusion and hopelessness, the sting of betrayal and heavy disappointment imbedded deep within her; the image of Ekewaka's naked body entangled with another in the forefront of her mind; their playful giggles echoing tauntingly in Ocean's head. *How could she have been so utterly stupid?* She asked herself over and over again. What on earth made her presume that Ekewaka would be waiting for her with open arms, when she had clearly given him negative signals of her feelings for him? Only a complete fool would have waited on the off chance of her changing her mind and Ekewaka was no fool.

Maria drifted into her thoughts, forcing her thoughts to change course; making her wish that she was Maria dead and buried, devoid of all thoughts and feelings DEAD Inaccessible to betrayal. DEAD!

"Do you require an extra blanket, Ma'am?"

Shaken out of her reverie Ocean Tia's eyes rose, as if in a go-slow setting, to the attractive woman and dropped to the blanket in her hand. "No… no thank you," she replied softly looking away into oblivion. She did not need anything.

The familiar door opened after the second round of knocks.

"Ocean!" Astounded eyes widened and stared unblinkingly, disbelievingly at the Hawaiian beauty standing at the door a small, battered suitcase perched by her feet. "Ocean; I can't believe this!" Hanale explained unable to conceal his excitement, his incredulous eyes firmly stuck on his half-sister as Luke rushed to his side, a wide smile spreading on his young face, his happy eyes twinkling.

For long seconds, the siblings stood at the door taking each other in. Ocean's lips broke into an enquiring smile. "Aren't you going to let me in, Hanale?"

The three words Hanale uttered made her heart stop.

Chapter One Hundred and Fifty-Five

The three innocent words, and yet so heavy laden, crashed mercilessly through her consciousness, as she stood perfectly still, her unmoving eyes focussed on Hanale, her mind racing like an out-of-control Formula One motor.

"Simon is here." Hanale repeated his eyes watching the colour drain from her face.

Once more, like an energised tsunami wave, the three words washed over her awakening her cue to act. "Then... then... I'll go, Hanale. I'll phone." She turned her guts churning mercilessly. The gentle sounding demand hit her like a thunderbolt.

"S... T... A... Y" Each letter of the word separated, blended and formed a solitary word of command; booming in her heart, making it simultaneously dance and weep. She turned slowly, her eyes resting on her husband's eyes.

They stood still as statues eyes locked, hearts racing; unable to move a single muscle, while the echo of a child's urgent request boomed in three pairs of ears. "Daddy; will you, Uncle Simon and Auntie Ocean play Cowboys and Indians with me?"

Ocean's eyes dropped to Luke who was pulling at his father's hand, her head in a state of total confusion.

"Please stay, Ocean." Simon's gentle request sent her nerve ends on fire, her eyes no longer able to meet her husband's eyes.

The light touch of bare flesh on bare flesh sent an electrifying tingle throughout her entire body and, in that moment, Ocean Tia made her decision.

Chapter One Hundred and Fifty-Six

In the solace of her hotel room, Ocean Tia tried in vain to stop an image joining forces with an echoing word in her head; only for them to unite and become more defined. *Simon Teal... husband;* the emphasis of tone changed continually as the persistent echo chanted... *husband... husband... husband... husband!* It screeched, screamed and shouted making her scramble for her coat and rush out of the door and out the confines of the hotel grounds.

Her feet took her in an unfamiliar direction; she did not care where they took her. On and on, she strode, her mind whirling around in a dense mass of conflicting thoughts and scenarios. Round the corner she went and through a broad, opened wrought-iron gate. On and on, she placed one foot in front of the other; on and on until finding a bench she sat down, her eyes captured by a row of pink blossoming cherry trees, where she sought serenity and found more confusion.

In the distance, she spotted the lonely figure. *Was he a tramp; a loner; or, maybe a lone person simply taking a walk?* She wondered, her eyes following the man as he sat, produced a paper bag and withdrew a bottle which he carefully placed beside him, making her heart clench. *Another unfortunate,* she sighed heavily. *The world, it seemed, was full of these poor people.* Her eyes rose to the man sitting rigidly still, his eyes staring ahead. *What did he see?* Instinctively she rose. Perhaps she could talk this guy out of taking a drink? Calmly, slowly she took steps towards the stranger. Abruptly she stopped, her heart instantly turning into an iced block, her eyes staring incredulously at the man before her who had remained oblivious to her presence, immersed in the depths of his black thoughts.

"Simon."

Her gentle tone was like a soothing balm to his tortured soul. His eyes shot up to the woman standing before him, noticing her eyes had refused to meet his eyes. With harrowing anguish, he tore his eyes away from her natural beauty and rested them on the destructive force beside him. "I'm sorry." He murmured in a faint whisper barely audible.

"I'm not." She smiled as she sat on the other side of the brandy bottle. "The bottle is unopened."

Silently he nodded his head his heart thudding, threatening to explode if he didn't hurry up and share his rapturous joy. He could hold it no longer. "You are here, Ocean. You are here!"

Her rich brown eyes absorbing his beaming face speckled with dark stubble, her twinkling eyes and familiar smile did not mirror her inner feelings of foreboding doom; for, she was not to be the bearer of the news he so desperately craved to hear; she was the envoy of bad tidings she did not want to break for fear of the potential consequences.

He watched her smile die and his heart clenched, his own smile fading. "Why… why are you here, Ocean?" He forced the strangled words out of his rapidly drying mouth. The torturous seconds turned into full minutes; the ominous silence broken only by a solitary bird, singing its heart out high in the distant branches.

"It's over, Simon." Her steady gaze remained firmly fixed on her husband, as she drove the final nail into the closed lid of their marriage. "I want a divorce." She sat perfectly still preparing herself for agonising minutes of painful silence; or, an uncomfortable outbreak of surging emotion; anything, but not what she received.

"I'll grant it." He said softly, defeat veiling heavily his words. Rising he picked up his treasure and proceeded to walk away, without a second glance thrown her way, while she sat and tried to digest the whole scenario, her eyes watching him go; slave and master hand-in-hand.

Are you going to let him go and drink himself to death? A voice boomed in her head, her eyes glued on the figure as it became smaller and smaller and… smaller; ghosts from the past simultaneously invading her consciousness and her conscious. *Are you going to watch your husband kill himself?* Alan asked softly. *Help him, Ocean.* Lokemele gently encouraged, as the sound of metal against glass echoed in her head, her heart heavy and troubled, her mind wandering back in time as… *surreptitiously she peered around the open door and gasped, quickly bringing her hand up to her mouth lest she should be heard. The stark image of Lokemele unscrewing the top of the vodka bottle made her guts churn violently. She peered closer, her eyes watching intently as for long minutes her friend*

417

stared longingly at the bottle then, swiftly screwed the metal top back on, hurriedly burying the bottle into the depths of the kitchen cupboard... A wave of relief swept over her now as it had done all those years ago; fervently hoping Simon would see sense and, like Lokemele, turn his back on alcohol and all that came with it.

The door opened; the light touch of her hand on his arm sending wild electric shocks through his entire body, renewed hope surging through his fast pulsating veins as their eyes locked, his heart burning like a raging inferno as he heard her soft words.

"Simon; I have a plan."

Chapter One Hundred and Fifty-Seven
Kauai

They sat side by side, husband and wife, as the wheels of the plane touched the shimmering tarmac; two hearts raced with hope. Ocean Tia's eyes swept to her right. "Are you happy, Si?"

He nodded. "Yes… yes; I am happy. Thank you, Ocean. Thank you for giving me a purpose to live. Thank you for giving me hope." He squeezed her hand gently.

Her sandaled feet ran… ran… ran down the lanes and road, her speed decreasing to a snail's pace as she approached and stepped on to the warm, white sand of her homeland; Kauai. *Oh, how she had missed it!* The desolate beaches; the sound of her friend, the thundering ocean; the swaying palms fringing the beaches; the sound of soft, distant guitars; the blossoming, colourful blooms and happy cheerful faces; her land; her people.

So much had happened. Time had seen to that. And, yet, one thing remained constant; an emptiness; a hollowness deep… deep within her heart.

Standing on the brink, where ocean meets land, she turned and gazed back at her own footprints imprinted in the sand. *Just like,* she thought, *the imprints of her mother, Leialoha; her father, kai; Simon; Uncle Keoki and Auntie Luana, Alan, Maria, Hanale, Makamae, Solomao, Ekewaka… Ekewaka…* Her heart tightened and began its merciless pounding, making her turn away from the majestic ocean and the hollow memory of an elusive dream.

Chapter One Hundred and Fifty-Eight

The throbbing muscles around his constricted heart clenched tight... tighter threatening to strangle the life out of him; his eyes lingering on the couple walking hand in hand, becoming fainter and more obscure with each passing second until they were out of sight. Slumping on to the warm sand, his straight back perched against an aged, hunchbacked palm, his eyes gazed out on to the vast thundering vista before him; *the ocean of despair.*

Less than half an hour ago his heart brimmed with hope; now it fragmented into bitter, ragged pieces of desolation; the seascape before his eyes not portraying the magnificent, mighty Pacific; instead depicting husband and wife walking side by side; reconciled.

Heavy eyes lingered languorously on the heaving, undulating blanket, his laden heart harbouring bitter regret... *He never did teach her how to surf... Still,* a voice in his head stated, *there will be other wahines only too willing to learn. But,* his sorrowful heart replied, *it will not be Ocean Tia.*

Motionless she sat on the top balcony of her home, her eyes gazing far out into the distance where the majestic waves of the Pacific met the blue, cloudless Hawaiian sky. All was still sun, sky, foliage; all, except her heart in unison with the restless ocean... *In the swell of the distant waves she saw him weaving in and out interlacing, intertwining; skilfully threading his way between, on top, beneath, around the frothy tips; uniting with them, mastering them as they succumbed to their master and he became their king...* She closed her eyes. *He never did teach her how to surf, after all. Perhaps, it was never meant to be.*

He'd seen him from afar as he took his evening stroll along the cooling sand; a speck against a bent over tree, both becoming larger and clearer with each footstep until he was almost upon them. "Ekewaka Aloha."

Eyes shot up; tired, sad, defeated, eyes which told Makamae a whole host of things and nothing at all. "Makamae." Ekewaka scantily acknowledged his acquaintance before focussing his eyes back on to the moving water. There was nothing to say.

The older man slid down beside Ekewaka, his mind searching for the appropriate words, to console a man who had lost something precious. They were elusive. And the waves continued to roll one over the other... over the other... over the other... as two Hawaiians sat united by a common thread. Finally Ekewaka rose, his eyes unable to unglue themselves from the hypnotic, rhythmic movement before him. "I shall be leaving Kauai," he said softly, his words barely audible above the thundering waves.

Makamae watched him become smaller and smaller, until he became a blur and then the blur vanished.

She heard his light cough before she saw his silhouetted shadow. How long she had been sitting there she did not know. What she had been thinking she could not recollect. The only certain fact was that it was light when she sat down and now the night had cast its dark mantle around her home and around her sad heart.

Feeling his presence she made no move, silently resenting Makamae's unsolicited visit, wondering what he wanted; knowing whatever brought him here must be important for him to come a calling at this late hour.

"Ocean... Ocean... Ocean Tia..." Mentally she counted her name calls. *One—two—three—four—five...* She drew a deep, ragged breath. *Just go, Makamae.* She silently willed. *Go!* She urgently demanded, her ears picking up the sound of retreating footsteps, her fingers picking up a folded piece of paper from the side table, her eyes read—*Meet me at the cemetery; tomorrow 6pm. We must talk. Makamae.*

Stuffing the paper into a drawer she made her way to her bedroom. Talking was the last thing on her troubled mind, which was full to the brim with conflicting emotions; she had not felt since Simon Teal had first walked into her life all those years ago.

Chapter One Hundred and Fifty-Nine

Once again sleep was elusive. Stark images of Simon and Ekewaka mingled, weaved, interlinked and evaporated only to return with a vengeance; clearer, sharper, more refined. Eyes open wide she stared unblinkingly at the ghostly silhouetted shadows of long fingered palms, as they hauntingly created eerie patterns on her bedroom walls. Never completing a formation; never constant or static *resembling,* she thought, *the ever changing configuration of her life.* People she had loved and lost; hopes and dreams which had dissipated into nothing and left behind a hollowness deep in the depths of her aching heart; an emptiness that could never be filled. Ghosts of her past filtered through... *Kai... Leialoha... Uncle Keoki... Auntie Luana... Alan... and dear, dear Lokemele; a kindred spirit in her quest for inner peace.* Lokemele had not found it an easy mission; though, in the end, she had found what she had been searching for in destiny itself.

Involuntarily she found herself thinking about Ekewaka. Like a growing cancer he matured in her mind, his presence she felt. Like a puff of smoke he vanished, merging with all the other ghosts until they became a massive blur going round and round and round in her head.

During the day the phantoms of her past wrestled with each other, competing for exclusive rights of attention, until she could stand it no longer. At a quarter to six, she walked through the old cemetery gate, her ears immediately attune to the sound of a soft melancholy tune, Makamae was strumming on his old battered ukulele. She smiled. Uncle Keoki had once told her that ukuleles were often referred to as jumping fleas; even now, so many years later, she thought the image amusing. "Makamae." She said softly.

Languidly he raised his eyes, his chubby fingers lingering on the last note and then it died in the still, balmy air and entered into the everlasting mists of time.

They sat silently; Ocean Tia wondering why her friend had summoned her to this special place; Makamae wondering how he was going to broach the subject burning in his mind.

His late friend, Keoki's words came to him in the whisper of a breeze and weaved stealthily through Makamae's thoughts, prompting him to spill them out. "To live, you must first find the problem, tackle it and learn to be happy again… life is too short, my dear Ocean."

Like a soft balm the familiar words touched Ocean Tia's heart and soul, the faintest flicker of a smile hovering on her lips. The flicker died; a bitter lump rising to her throat. She snapped her eyes shut, a surge of unrighteous indignation bubbling to the surface. It was all right for Uncle Keoki to live by these standards, his life was so simple and carefree; he never seemed to have a worry in his head. *Why?* A voice in her head questioned, immediately proffering an answer. *Isn't it because he lived by those words that his life was so happy; so blessed, despite the many responsibilities on his shoulders that came with being a family man and friend to many on the island?* Lokemele's image jumped into her mind; Lokemele who had found her quest for serenity because she had taken on board Keoki's words and tried to live by them. *So why,* Ocean asked herself, *was she so different?* She turned her solemn eyes on her friend. "I don't know what to do, Makamae." She said so quietly her words were barely audible.

Softly spoken words which were loud and clear in Makamae's consciousness made his heart dance. There was hope.

Chapter One Hundred and Sixty

After a heart-to-heart talk with Makamae, Ocean Tia felt as if her heart which had been full to the brim with anxieties, indecisions, negativity and broken dreams had been replaced with a heart of hope. The process of rehabilitation had begun. There was work; hard, unenviable work to be done but with her Uncle Keoki's advice, interwoven with Makamae's words, weaving through her mind she slowly began to see the light.

Up until the graveside talk with Makamae, she had not allowed herself to be fully aligned with her true feelings. Only after her confidante had asked her to picture herself in ten years' time with Simon by her side and ask herself, if she thought her life would be complete, did her heart clench tightly with sudden despair. The task of confronting Simon, she knew, would be hard. Would he be strong enough to accept her decision and move on? Would he regress?

Her anxieties were unfounded. In his eyes of resignation, she saw a tinge of sanguinity for, with her help, he had found a purpose in life and with that purpose, in time, the past would be buried. He had decided to go back to England, retrain and seek a career in social welfare.

Ocean Tia smiled at the news her father, Kai, immediately springing to the forefront of her mind. "It's funny," she said to Makamae as they sat in her garden, as the sun shed its farewell rays upon the Island of Kauai, "everything seems to have come full circle."

She felt the light touch of his hand on her hand, his wise eyes upon her. "Not quite, my dear Ocean." He took a firmer grip of her hand making eyes clash, both feeling the presence of the elephant in the garden; the unspoken truth; the unresolved dream. Laborious seconds of heavy silence were shattered. "Ekewaka."

One word; one name consisting of seven letters speaking volumes, making Ocean Tia's heart clench tightly and a thousand unruly butterflies flutter erratically in her tummy, while it performed one somersault after another;

Ekewaka's image becoming ever more clearer in her head creating fiercer heart clenching, more wild butterflies and energetic somersaults. "You love him?"

It was a straight forward simple question and, yet, to Ocean Tia it was a definite, unendurable statement of fact. Silently meeting Makamae's eyes she nodded her head. She didn't see the happy smile on her friend's lips.

Chapter One Hundred and Sixty-One

Two surfboards were propped against the aged, hunchbacked palm as Ekewaka took Ocean Tia's hand in his own firm grasp, his soft questioning eyes on her. "Ready?"

With Ekewaka by her side, she knew she would always be protected, guarded, defended and, above all, cherished. He was her guardian angel.

Grabbing their surfboards, they ran, tripped, laughed, fell on to the soft white sands of Kauai, their boards carelessly abandoned as he smothered her with kisses, while the surf rolled on and on and on as it had done for millions of years.

And as he claimed her mouth and body for his own, she knew, like Lokemele, she had found her quest for inner peace.